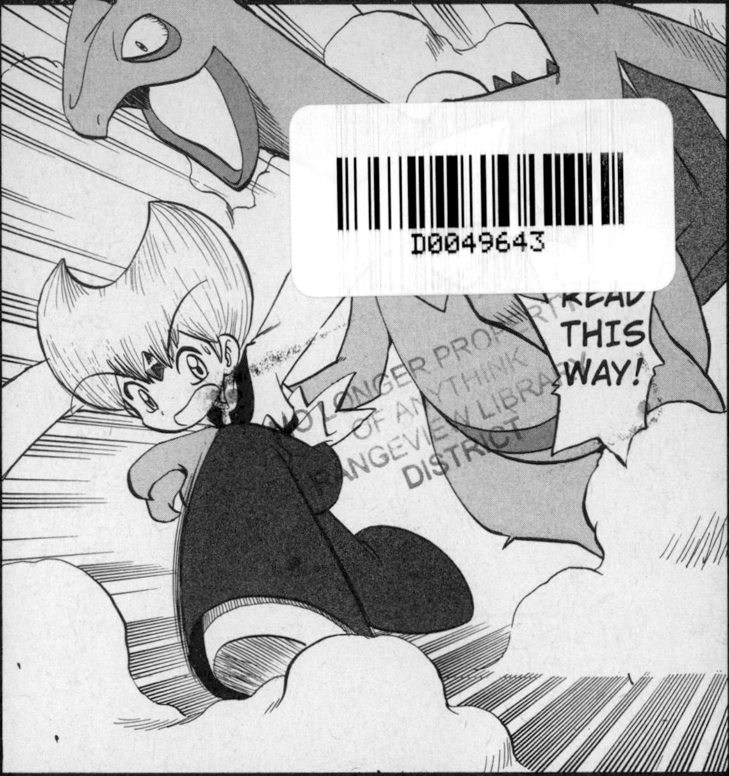
READ THIS WAY!

THIS IS THE END OF THIS GRAPHIC NOVEL!

To properly enjoy this VIZ Media graphic novel, please turn it around and begin reading from right to left.

This book has been printed in the original Japanese format in order to preserve the orientation of the original artwork.

Have fun with it!

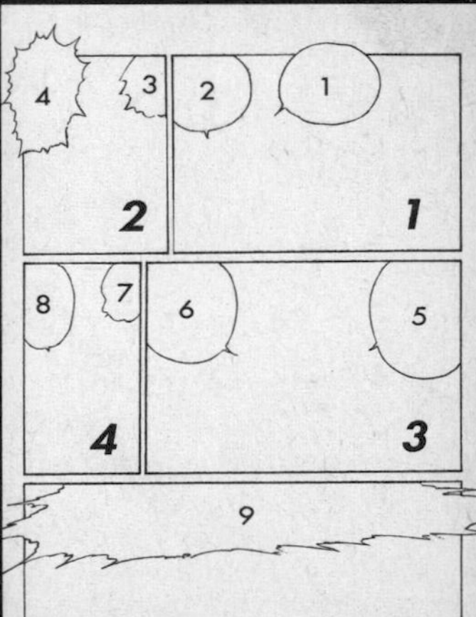
1
2
3
4
5
6
7
8
9
1
2
3
4
5

FOLLOW THE ACTION THIS WAY.

POKÉMON™

ADVENTURES

EMERALD

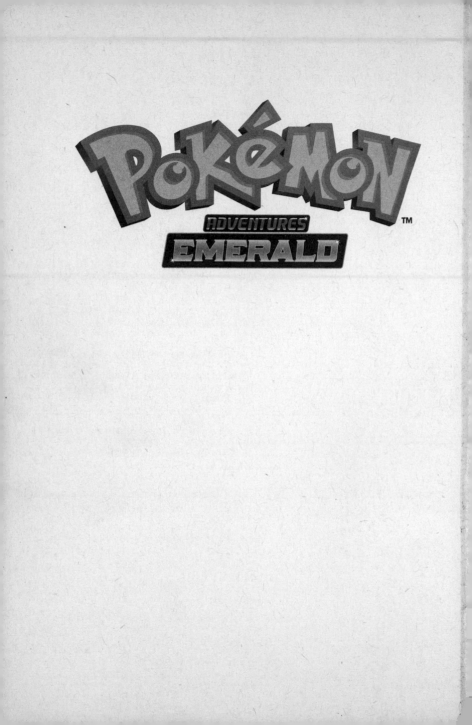

Pokémon ADVENTURES
Emerald
Volume 27
Perfect Square Edition

Story by **HIDENORI KUSAKA**
Art by **SATOSHI YAMAMOTO**

© 2015 Pokémon.
© 1995–2015 Nintendo/Creatures Inc./GAME FREAK inc.
TM, ®, and character names are trademarks of Nintendo.
POCKET MONSTERS SPECIAL Vol. 27
by Hidenori KUSAKA, Satoshi YAMAMOTO
© 1997 Hidenori KUSAKA, Satoshi YAMAMOTO
All rights reserved.
Original Japanese edition published by SHOGAKUKAN.
English translation rights in the United States of America,
Canada, the United Kingdom, Ireland, Australia and
New Zealand arranged with SHOGAKUKAN.

English Adaptation/Bryant Turnage
Translation/Tetsuichiro Miyaki
Touch-up & Lettering/Annaliese Christman
Design/Shawn Carrico
Editor/Annette Roman

Printed in the U.S.A.

Published by VIZ Media, LLC
P.O. Box 77010
San Francisco, CA 94107

10 9 8 7 6 5 4 3 2 1
First printing, March 2015

www.perfectsquare.com   www.viz.com

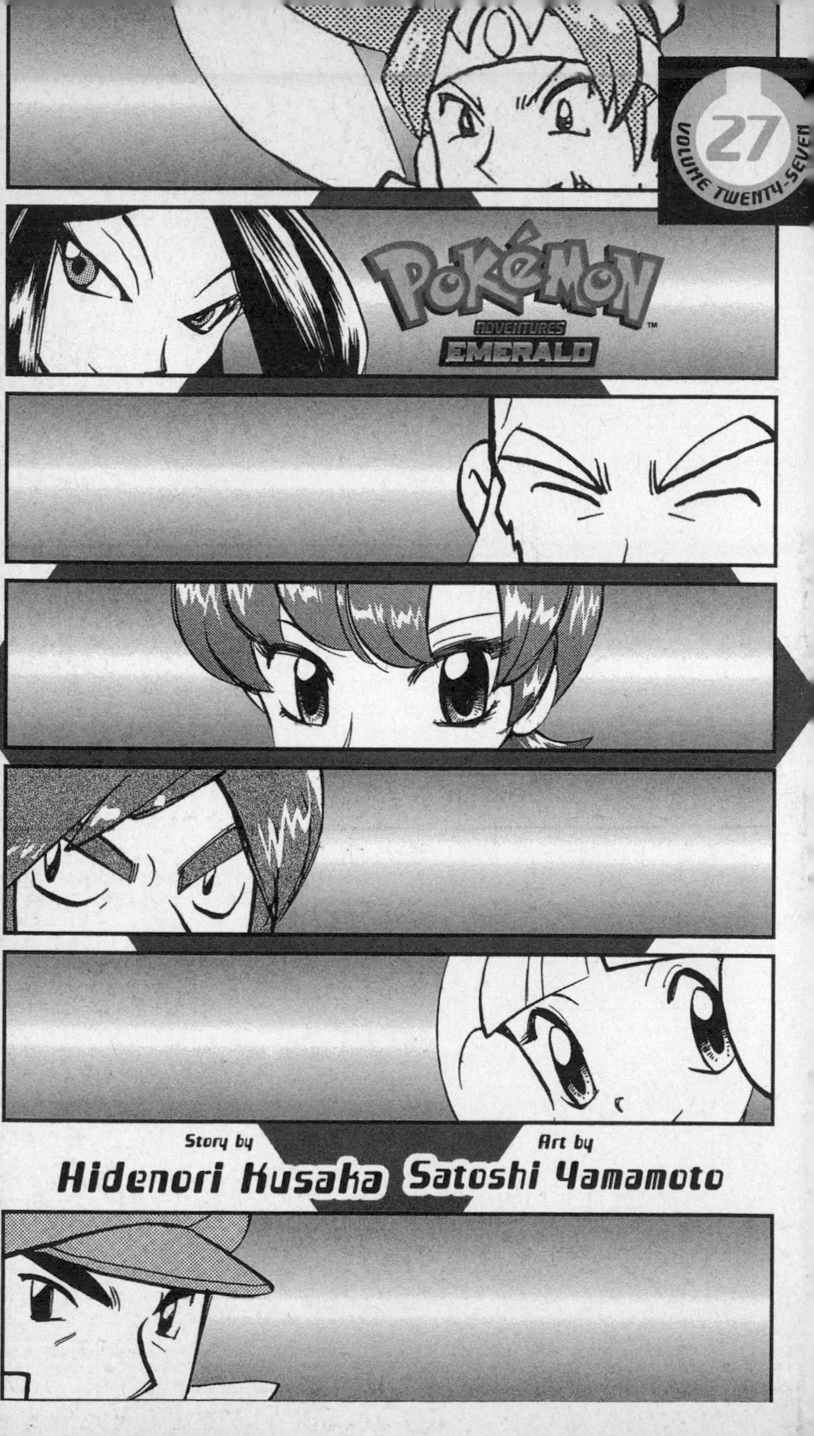
27
VOLUME TWENTY-SEVEN
POKÉMON
ADVENTURES
EMERALD
Story by
Hidenori Kusaka
Art by
Satoshi Yamamoto

SPECIAL OBJECT

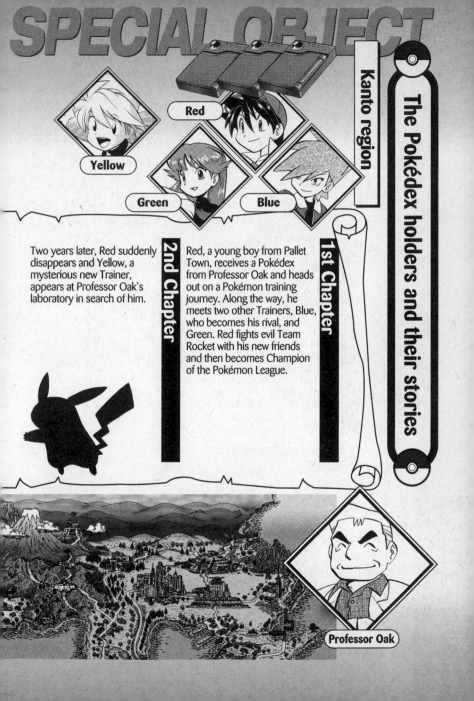

The Pokédex holders and their stories

Kanto region

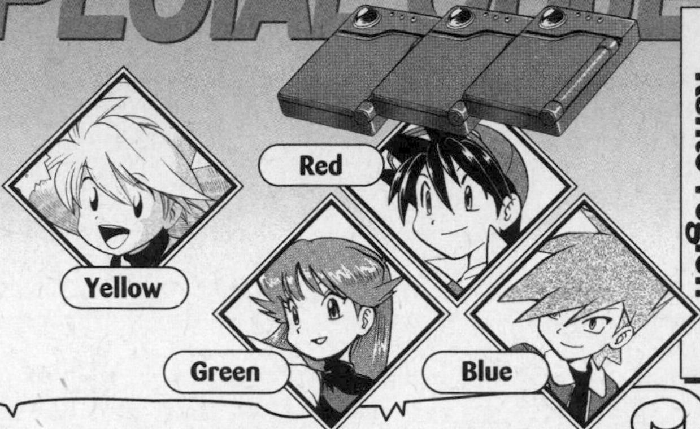
Red
Yellow
Green
Blue

1st Chapter

Red, a young boy from Pallet Town, receives a Pokédex from Professor Oak and heads out on a Pokémon training journey. Along the way, he meets two other Trainers, Blue, who becomes his rival, and Green. Red fights evil Team Rocket with his new friends and then becomes Champion of the Pokémon League.

2nd Chapter

Two years later, Red suddenly disappears and Yellow, a mysterious new Trainer, appears at Professor Oak's laboratory in search of him.

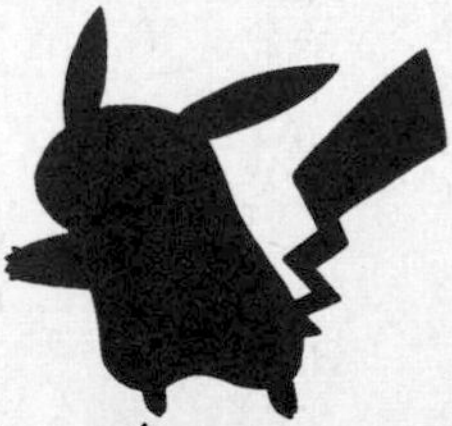

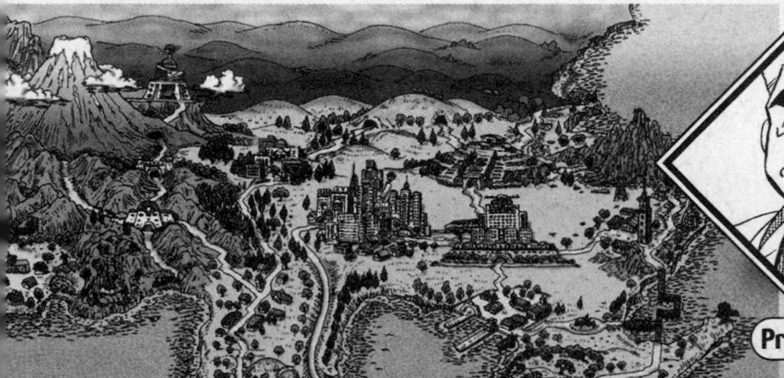

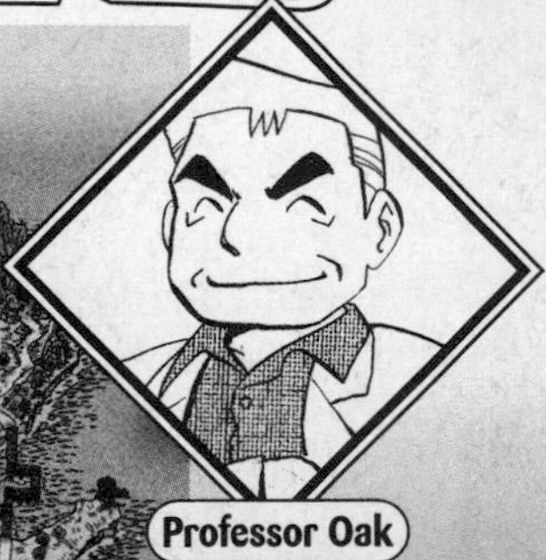
Professor Oak

POKÉMON

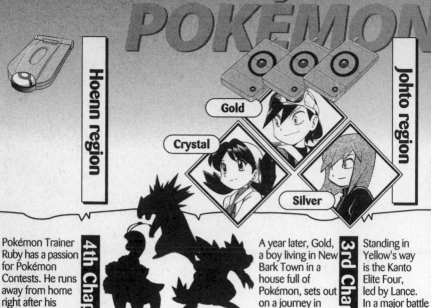

Johto region

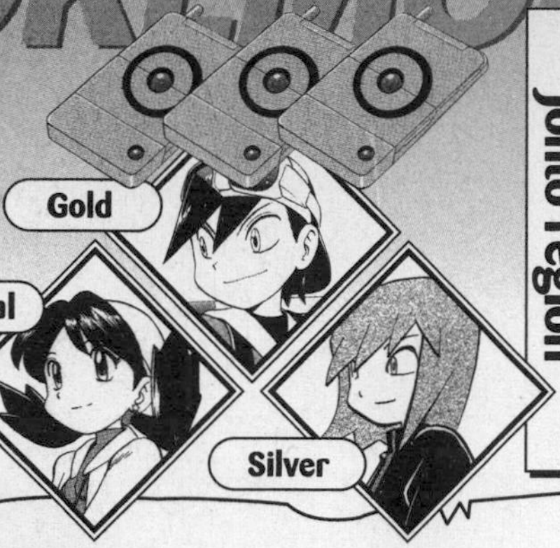
Gold
Crystal
Silver

3rd Chapter

Standing in Yellow's way is the Kanto Elite Four, led by Lance. In a major battle at Cerise Island, Yellow manages to stymie the group's evil ambitions.

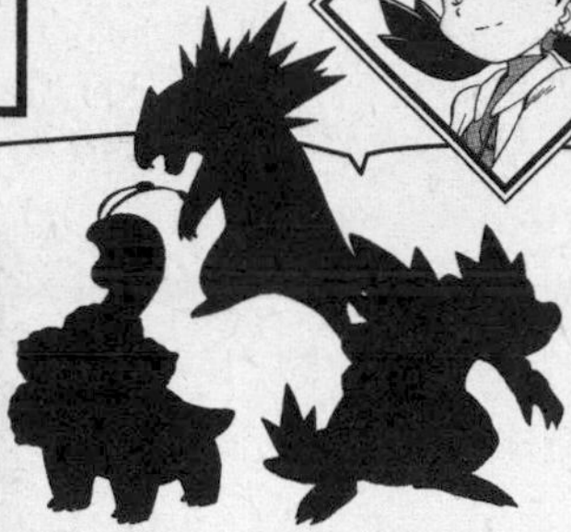

A year later, Gold, a boy living in New Bark Town in a house full of Pokémon, sets out on a journey in pursuit of Silver, a Trainer who stole a Totodile from Professor Elm's laboratory. The two don't get along at first, but eventually they become partners fighting side by side. During their journey, they meet Crystal, the trainer who Professor Elm entrusts with the completion of his Pokédex. Together, the trio succeed to shatter the evil scheme of the Mask of Ice, a villain who leads what remains of Team Rocket.

Hoenn region

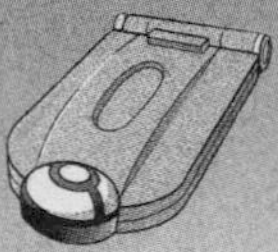

4th Chapter

Pokémon Trainer Ruby has a passion for Pokémon Contests. He runs away from home right after his family moves to Littleroot Town. He meets a wild girl named Sapphire and they pledge to compete with each other in an 80-day challenge to...

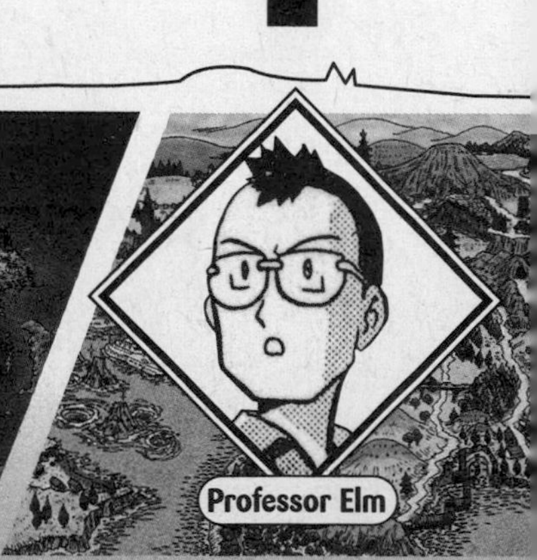
Professor Elm

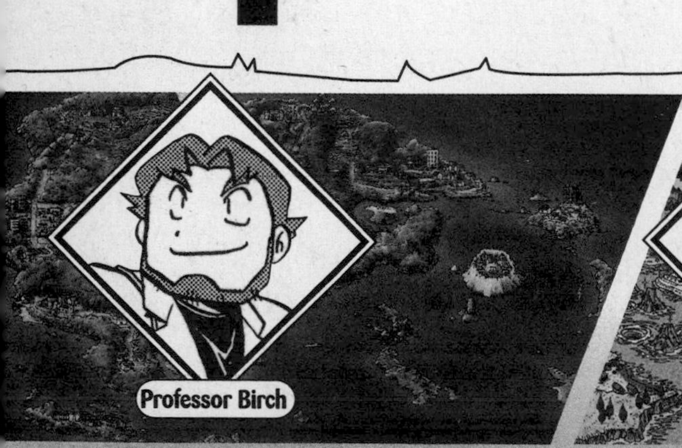
Professor Birch

SPECIAL OBJECT

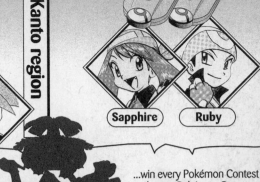

Kanto region

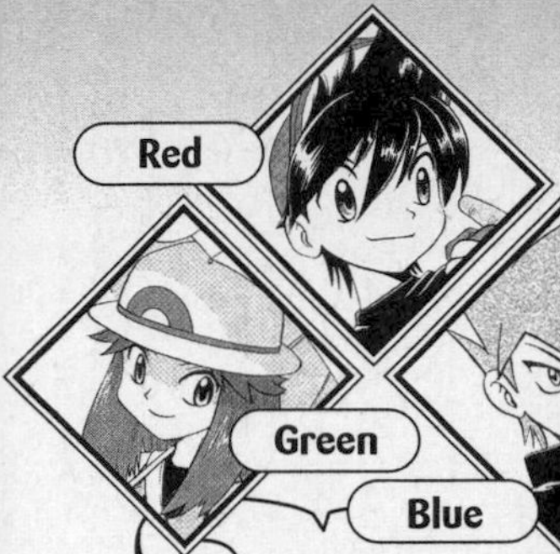

Red
Green
Blue

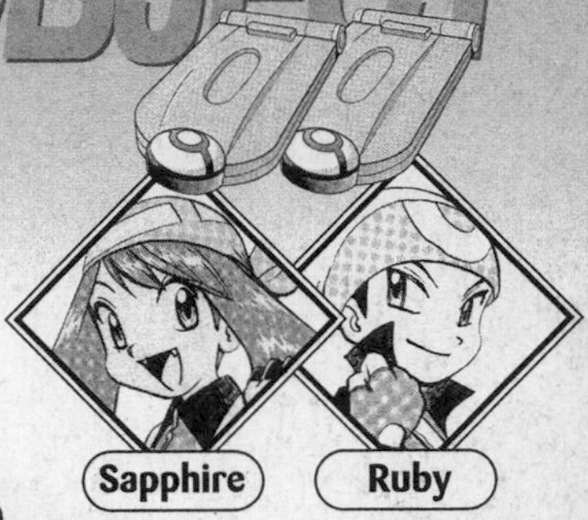

Sapphire
Ruby

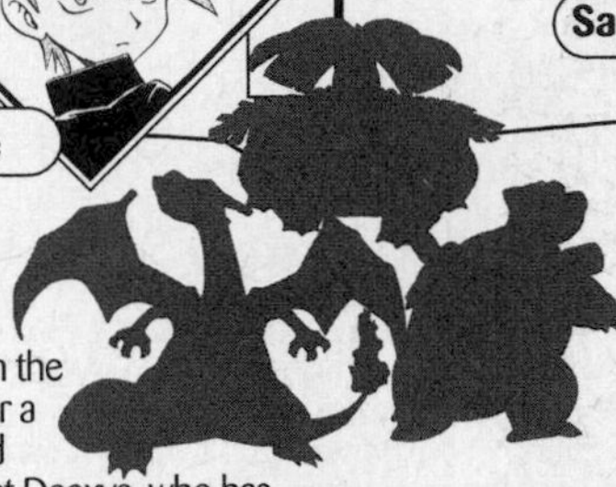

5th Chapter

Six months later, a new adventure unfolds for Red and his friends on the Sevii Islands. After a deadly battle, Red manages to defeat Deoxys, who has fallen into the hands of Giovanni. Silver, in search of his true identity, is faced with the shocking truth that Giovanni is his father. Red and his friends manage to safely land the Team Rocket airship, which was flying out of control thanks to Carr, one of the Three Beasts, who betrayed Team Rocket. But then another of the Three Beasts, Sird, appears, and in a mysterious flash of light the five Pokédex holders—Red, Blue, Green, Yellow and Silver—are petrified. Literally!

...win every Pokémon Contest and every Pokémon Gym Battle, respectively. Meanwhile, in the Hoenn region, Team Aqua and Team Magma set their evil plot in motion. As a result, Legendary Pokémon Groudon and Kyogre are awakened and inflict catastrophic climate changes on Hoenn. In the end, thanks to Ruby and Sapphire's heroic efforts, the two legendary Pokémon go back into hibernation.

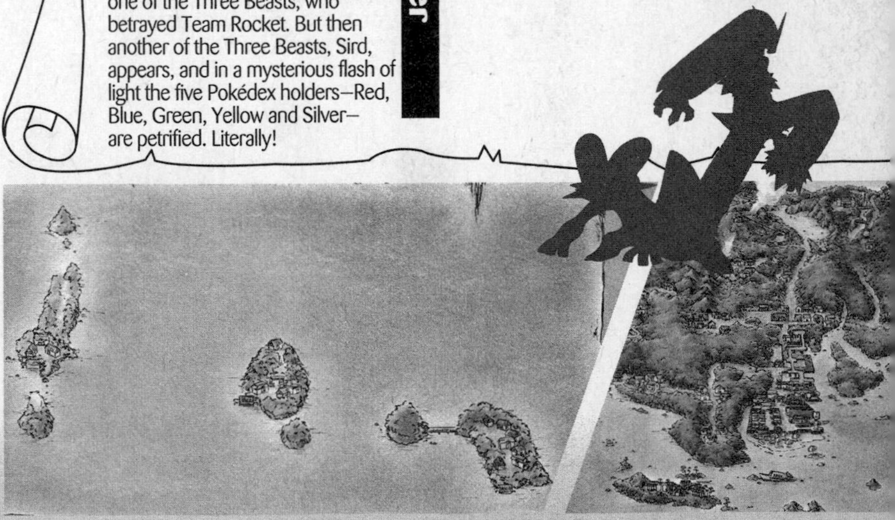

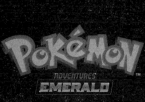

Pokémon Adventures Emerald

Volume Twenty-Seven 27

CONTENTS

POKÉMON

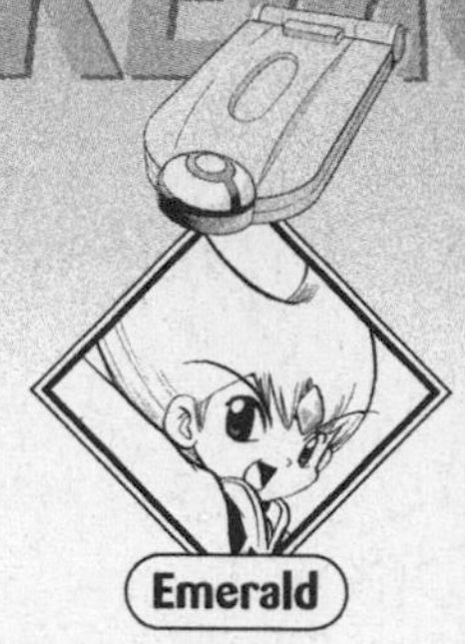
Emerald

Hoenn region

6th Chapter

A few months later, construction is completed on a thrilling new Pokémon Battle facility, the Battle Frontier, located in the Hoenn region. A young Trainer named Emerald crashes the press opening for the media to challenge the facility's Frontier Brains. Now he has just seven days to defeat them all! Thus far, Emerald has won his battle against Factory Head Noland and has moved on to face Pike Queen Lucy... But it seems that Emerald is simultaneously on some sort of top-secret mission! What could it be...?

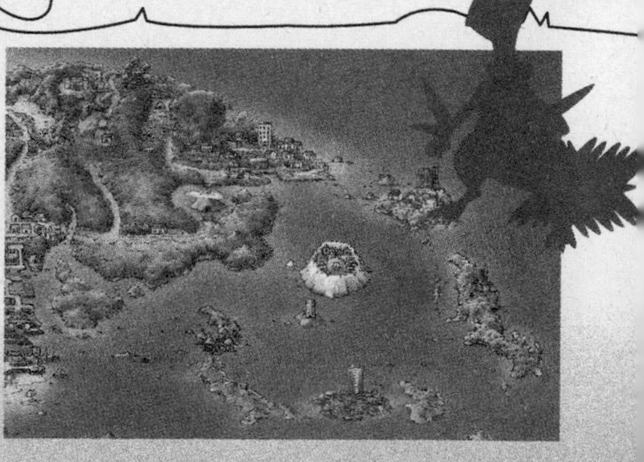

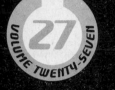

◆ 309 ◆

Moving Past Milotic

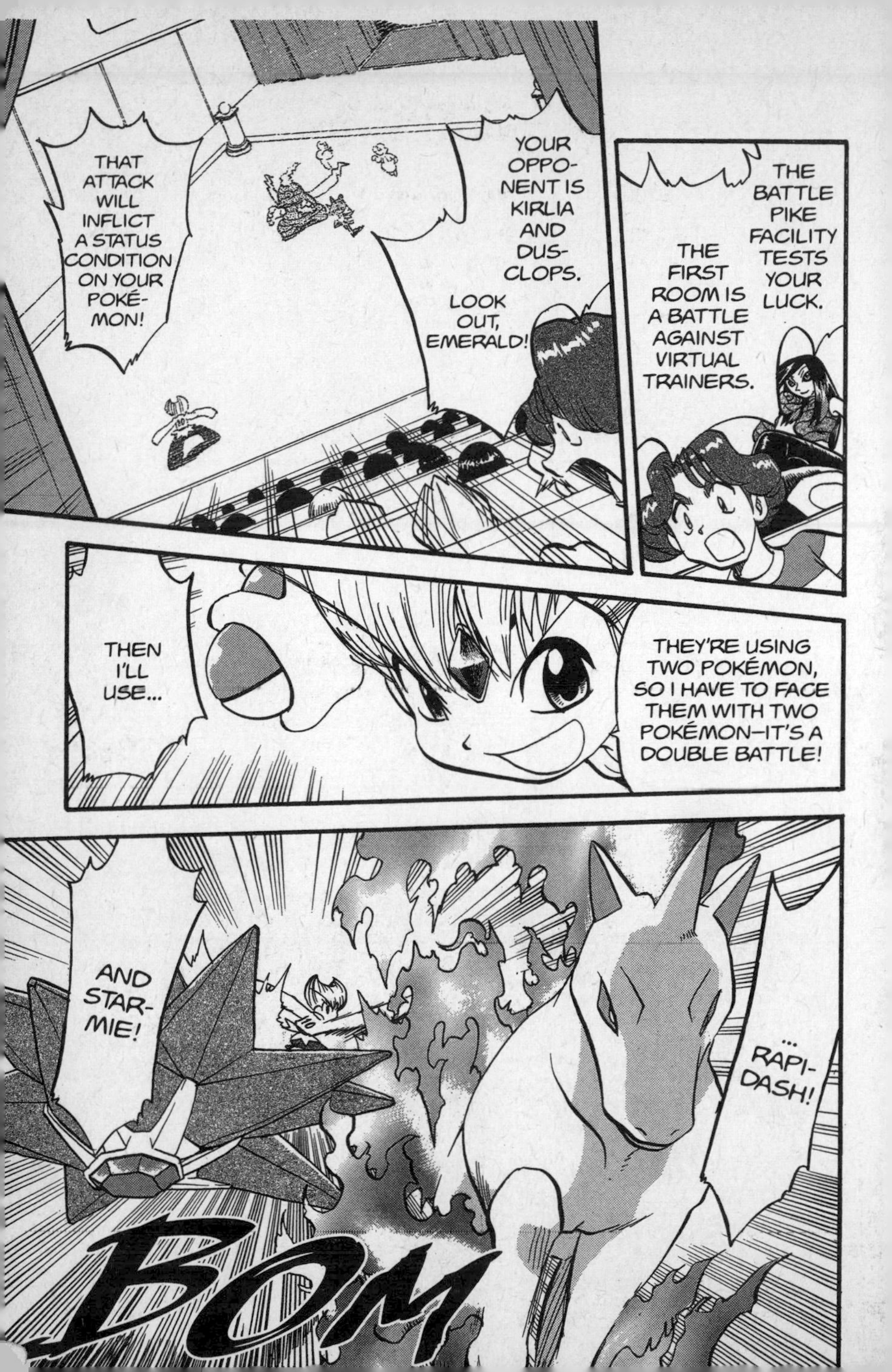
THE BATTLE PIKE FACILITY TESTS YOUR LUCK.
THE FIRST ROOM IS A BATTLE AGAINST VIRTUAL TRAINERS.
YOUR OPPO-NENT IS KIRLIA AND DUS-CLOPS.
THAT ATTACK WILL INFLICT A STATUS CONDITION ON YOUR POKÉ-MON!
LOOK OUT, EMERALD!
THEY'RE USING TWO POKÉMON, SO I HAVE TO FACE THEM WITH TWO POKÉMON—IT'S A DOUBLE BATTLE!
THEN I'LL USE...
... RAPI-DASH!
AND STAR-MIE!
BOM

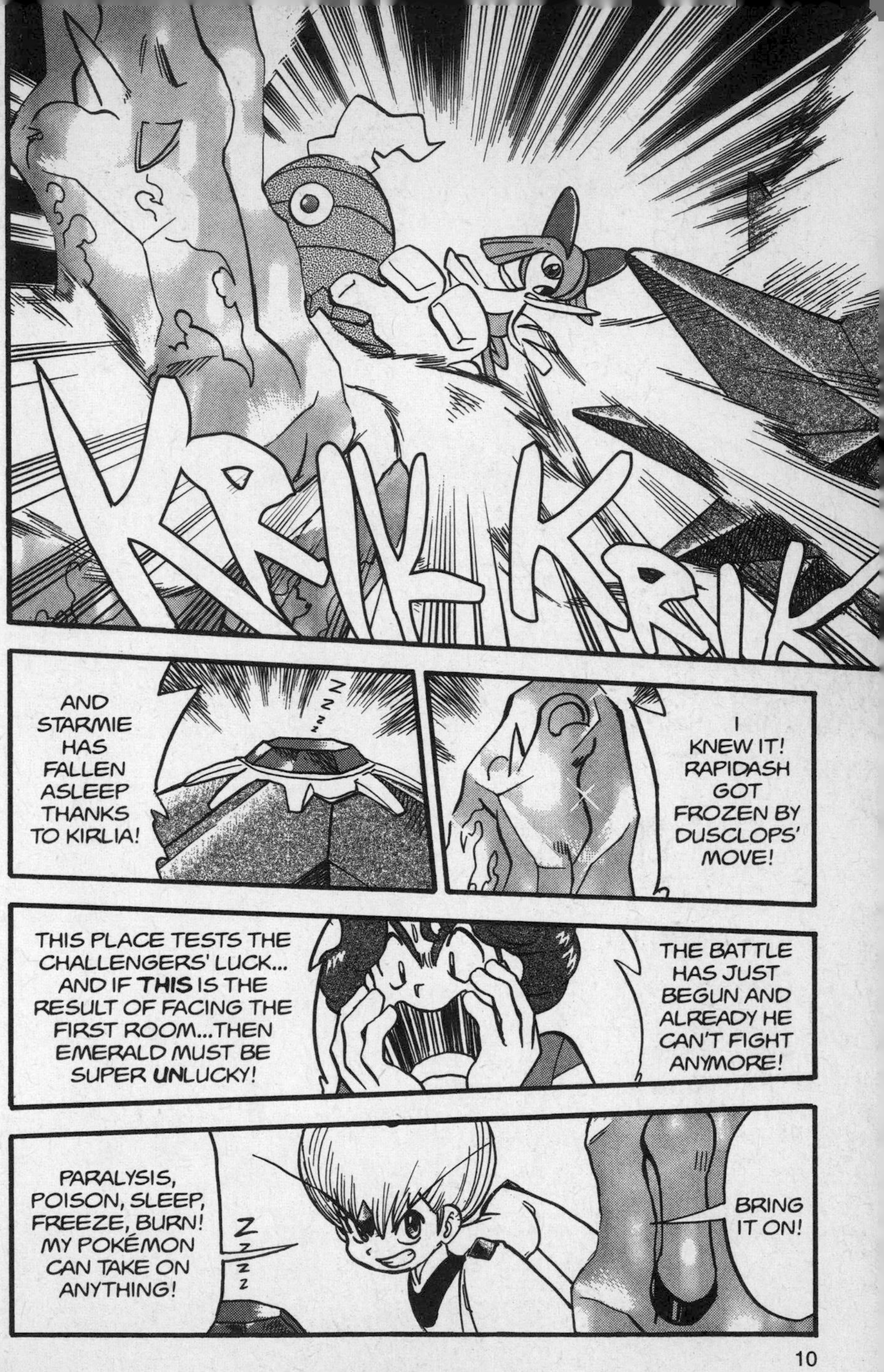
KRIK KRIK
I KNEW IT! RAPIDASH GOT FROZEN BY DUSCLOPS' MOVE!
AND STARMIE HAS FALLEN ASLEEP THANKS TO KIRLIA!
ZZZ
THE BATTLE HAS JUST BEGUN AND ALREADY HE CAN'T FIGHT ANYMORE!
THIS PLACE TESTS THE CHALLENGERS' LUCK... AND IF **THIS** IS THE RESULT OF FACING THE FIRST ROOM...THEN EMERALD MUST BE SUPER **UN**LUCKY!
BRING IT ON!
PARALYSIS, POISON, SLEEP, FREEZE, BURN! MY POKÉMON CAN TAKE ON ANYTHING!
ZZZ

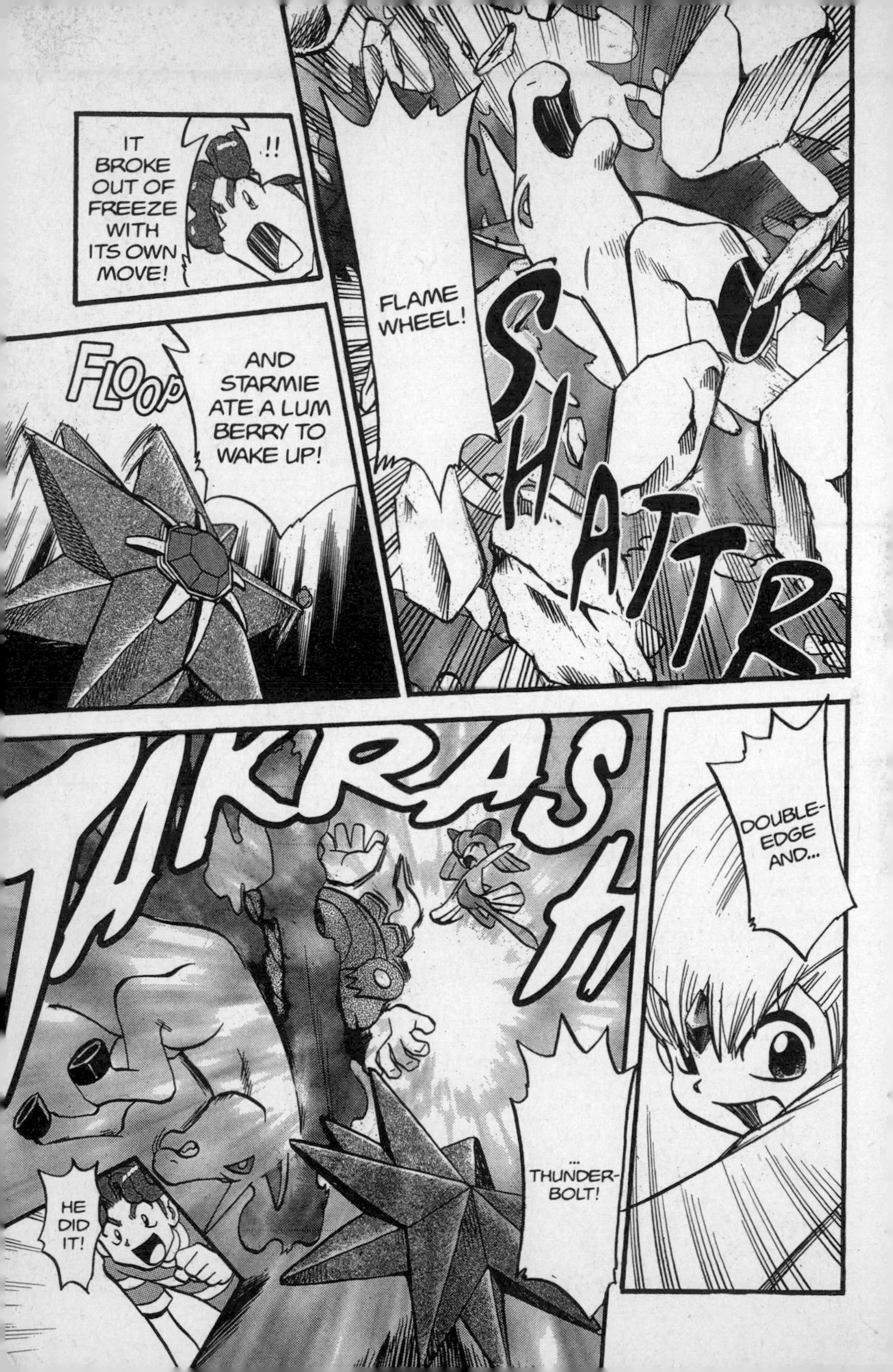

FLAME WHEEL!
SHATTR
!!
IT BROKE OUT OF FREEZE WITH ITS OWN MOVE!
FLOOP
AND STARMIE ATE A LUM BERRY TO WAKE UP!
DOUBLE-EDGE AND...
KRASH
...THUNDER-BOLT!
HE DID IT!

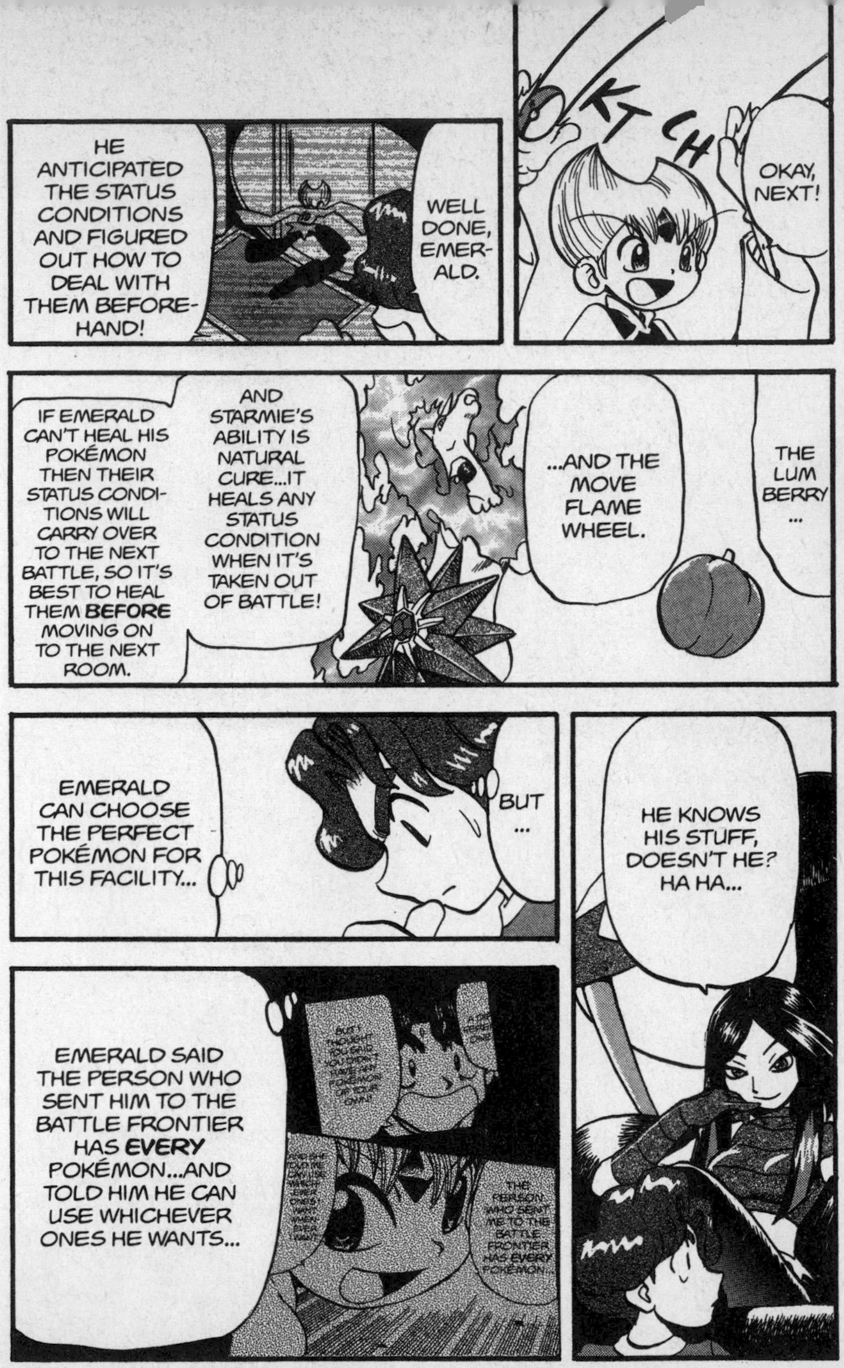
KTCH
OKAY, NEXT!
WELL DONE, EMERALD.
HE ANTICIPATED THE STATUS CONDITIONS AND FIGURED OUT HOW TO DEAL WITH THEM BEFOREHAND!
THE LUM BERRY...
...AND THE MOVE FLAME WHEEL.
AND STARMIE'S ABILITY IS NATURAL CURE...IT HEALS ANY STATUS CONDITION WHEN IT'S TAKEN OUT OF BATTLE!
IF EMERALD CAN'T HEAL HIS POKÉMON THEN THEIR STATUS CONDITIONS WILL CARRY OVER TO THE NEXT BATTLE, SO IT'S BEST TO HEAL THEM **BEFORE** MOVING ON TO THE NEXT ROOM.
HE KNOWS HIS STUFF, DOESN'T HE? HA HA...
BUT...
EMERALD CAN CHOOSE THE PERFECT POKÉMON FOR THIS FACILITY...
BUT I THOUGHT YOU SAID YOU DIDN'T HAVE ANY POKÉMON OF YOUR OWN!
EMERALD SAID THE PERSON WHO SENT HIM TO THE BATTLE FRONTIER HAS **EVERY** POKÉMON...AND TOLD HIM HE CAN USE WHICHEVER ONES HE WANTS...
THE PERSON WHO SENT ME TO THE BATTLE FRONTIER HAS **EVERY** POKÉMON...

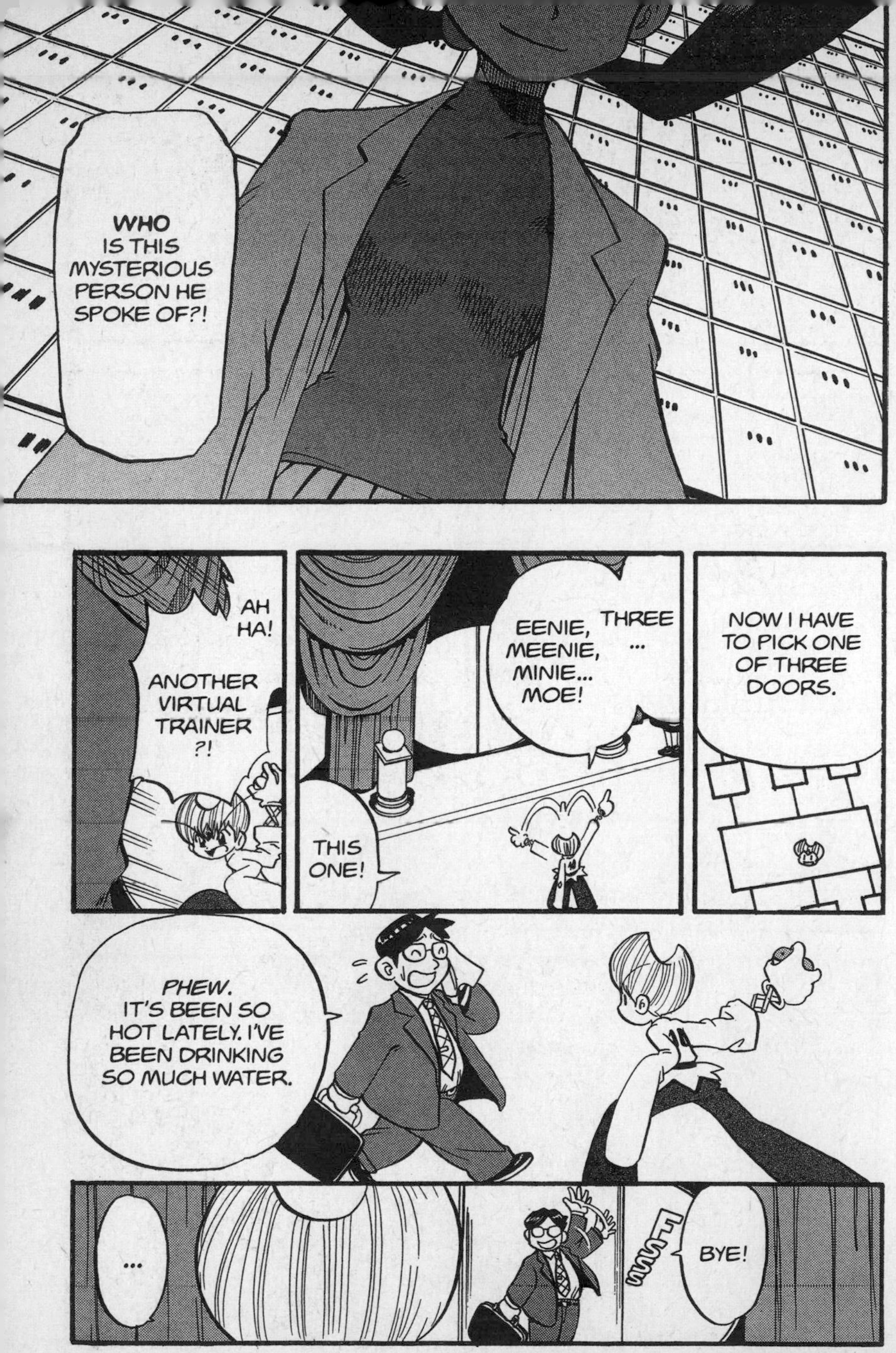
WHO IS THIS MYSTERIOUS PERSON HE SPOKE OF?!
NOW I HAVE TO PICK ONE OF THREE DOORS.
THREE ...
EENIE, MEENIE, MINIE... MOE!
THIS ONE!
AH HA!
ANOTHER VIRTUAL TRAINER ?!
PHEW. IT'S BEEN SO HOT LATELY. I'VE BEEN DRINKING SO MUCH WATER.
BYE!
...

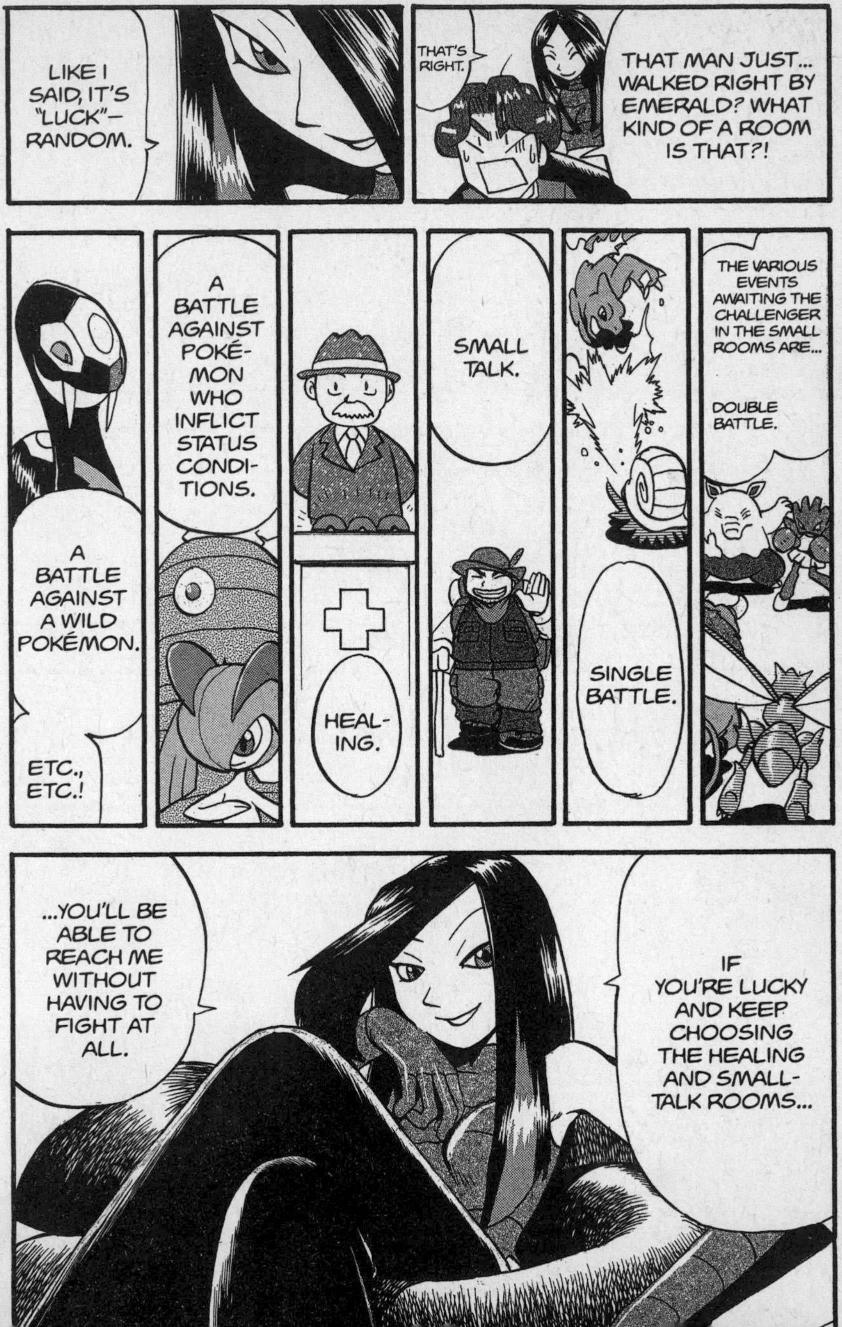
THAT MAN JUST... WALKED RIGHT BY EMERALD? WHAT KIND OF A ROOM IS THAT?!
THAT'S RIGHT.
LIKE I SAID, IT'S "LUCK"— RANDOM.
THE VARIOUS EVENTS AWAITING THE CHALLENGER IN THE SMALL ROOMS ARE...
DOUBLE BATTLE.
SINGLE BATTLE.
SMALL TALK.
HEALING.
A BATTLE AGAINST POKÉMON WHO INFLICT STATUS CONDITIONS.
A BATTLE AGAINST A WILD POKÉMON.
ETC., ETC.!
IF YOU'RE LUCKY AND KEEP CHOOSING THE HEALING AND SMALL-TALK ROOMS...
...YOU'LL BE ABLE TO REACH ME WITHOUT HAVING TO FIGHT AT ALL.

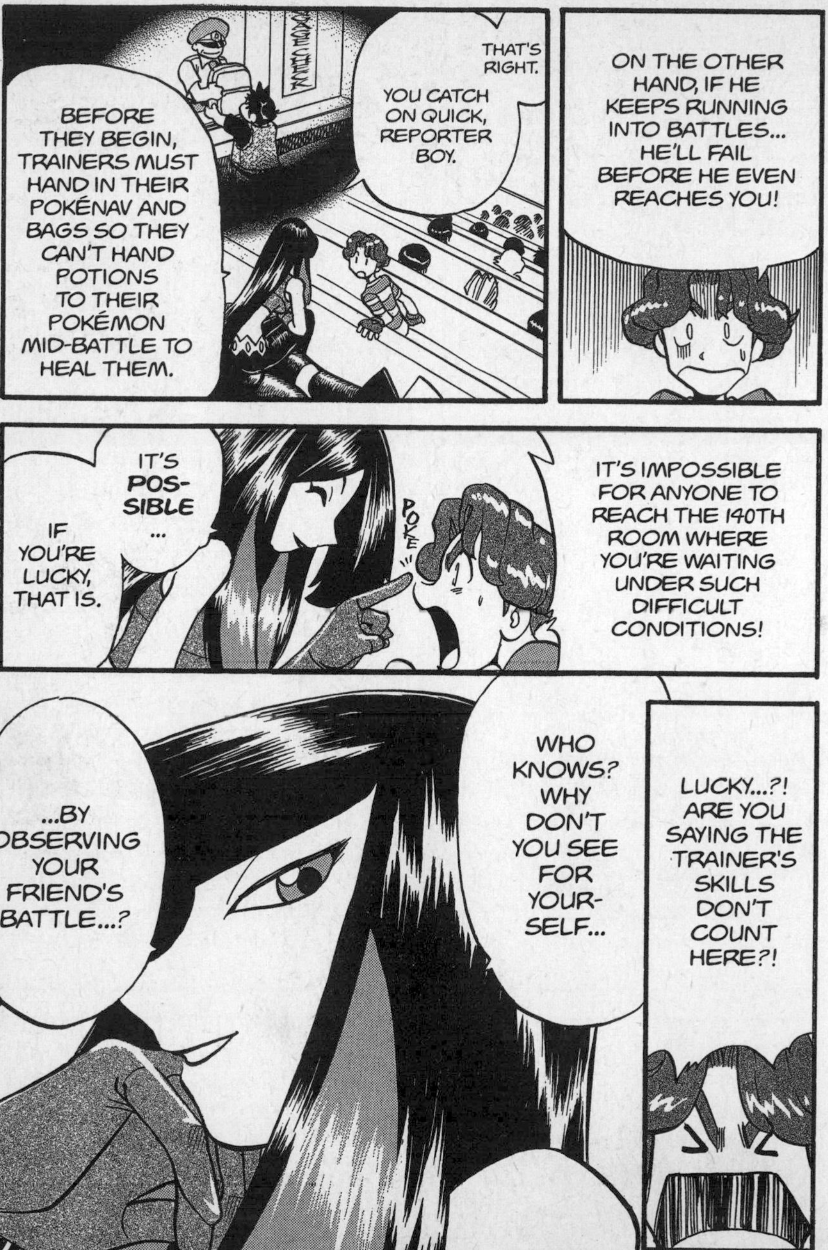
ON THE OTHER HAND, IF HE KEEPS RUNNING INTO BATTLES... HE'LL FAIL BEFORE HE EVEN REACHES YOU!
THAT'S RIGHT.
YOU CATCH ON QUICK, REPORTER BOY.
BEFORE THEY BEGIN, TRAINERS MUST HAND IN THEIR POKÉNAV AND BAGS SO THEY CAN'T HAND POTIONS TO THEIR POKÉMON MID-BATTLE TO HEAL THEM.
IT'S IMPOSSIBLE FOR ANYONE TO REACH THE 140TH ROOM WHERE YOU'RE WAITING UNDER SUCH DIFFICULT CONDITIONS!
POKE
IT'S **POSSIBLE** ...
IF YOU'RE LUCKY, THAT IS.
LUCKY...?! ARE YOU SAYING THE TRAINER'S SKILLS DON'T COUNT HERE?!
WHO KNOWS? WHY DON'T YOU SEE FOR YOURSELF...
...BY OBSERVING YOUR FRIEND'S BATTLE...?

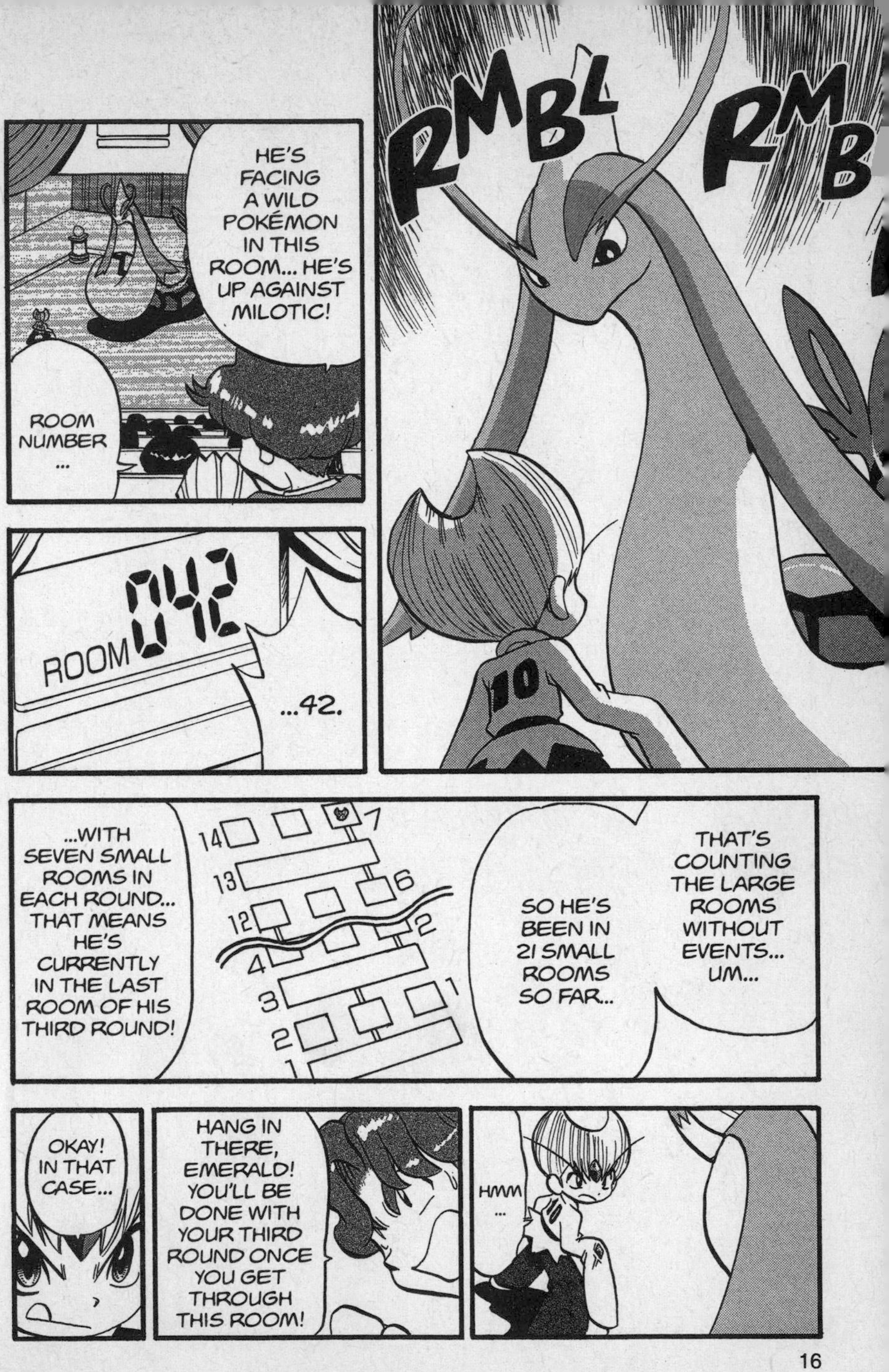
RMBL RMB
HE'S FACING A WILD POKÉMON IN THIS ROOM... HE'S UP AGAINST MILOTIC!
ROOM NUMBER ...
ROOM 042
...42.
THAT'S COUNTING THE LARGE ROOMS WITHOUT EVENTS... UM...
SO HE'S BEEN IN 21 SMALL ROOMS SO FAR...
...WITH SEVEN SMALL ROOMS IN EACH ROUND... THAT MEANS HE'S CURRENTLY IN THE LAST ROOM OF HIS THIRD ROUND!
HMM ...
HANG IN THERE, EMERALD! YOU'LL BE DONE WITH YOUR THIRD ROUND ONCE YOU GET THROUGH THIS ROOM!
OKAY! IN THAT CASE...

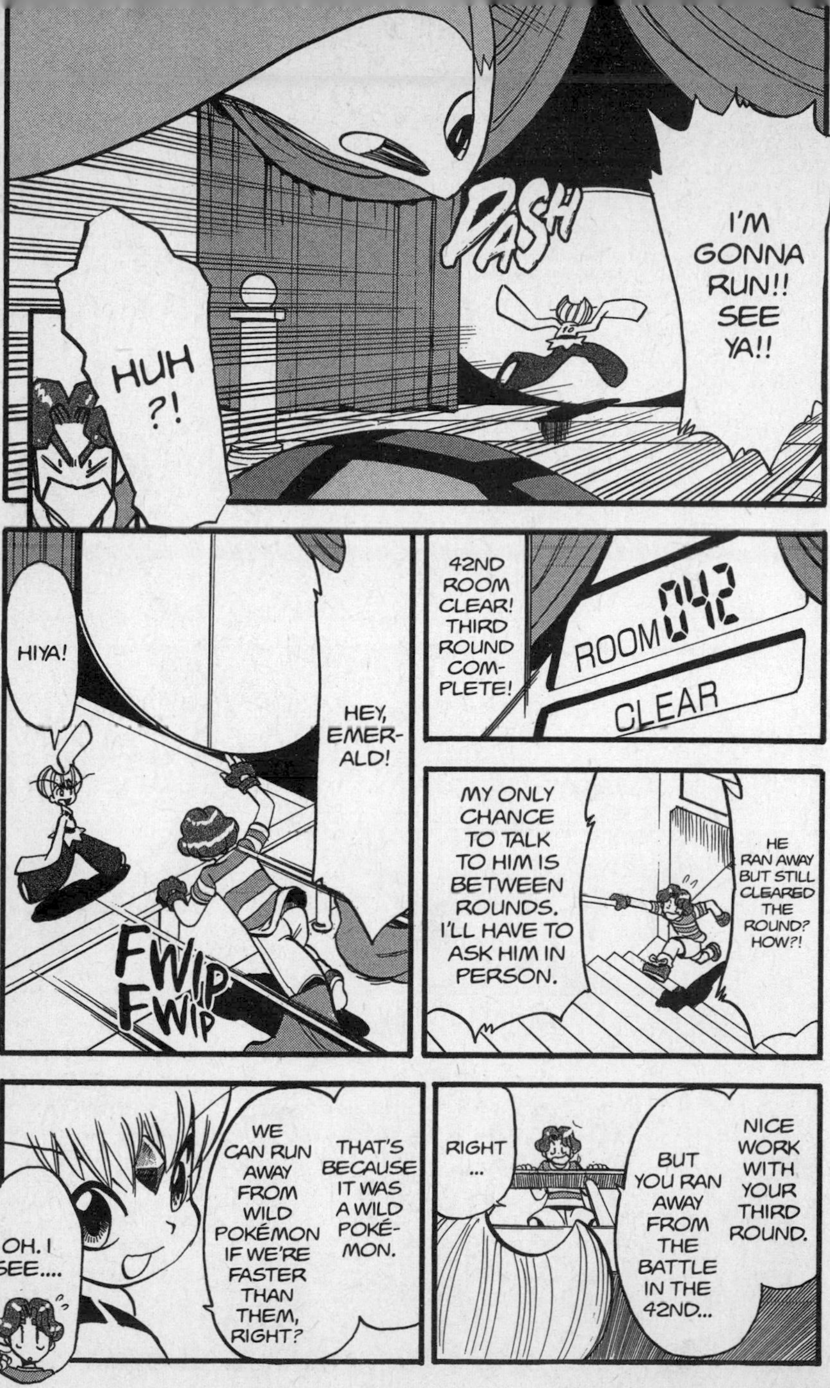
I'M GONNA RUN!! SEE YA!!
DASH
HUH ?!
ROOM 042
CLEAR
42ND ROOM CLEAR! THIRD ROUND COMPLETE!
HE RAN AWAY BUT STILL CLEARED THE ROUND? HOW?!
MY ONLY CHANCE TO TALK TO HIM IS BETWEEN ROUNDS. I'LL HAVE TO ASK HIM IN PERSON.
HEY, EMERALD!
HIYA!
FWIP FWIP
NICE WORK WITH YOUR THIRD ROUND.
BUT YOU RAN AWAY FROM THE BATTLE IN THE 42ND...
RIGHT...
THAT'S BECAUSE IT WAS A WILD POKÉMON.
WE CAN RUN AWAY FROM WILD POKÉMON IF WE'RE FASTER THAN THEM, RIGHT?
OH. I SEE....

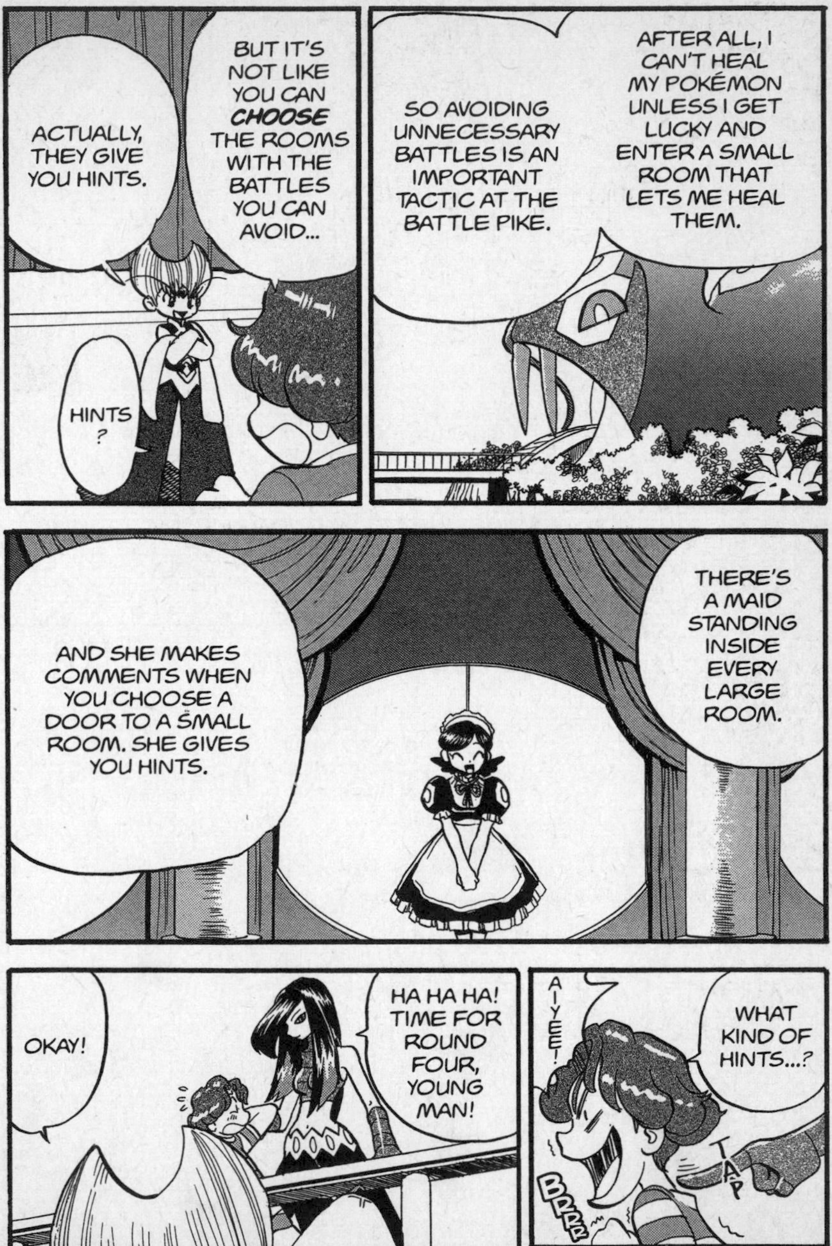
AFTER ALL, I CAN'T HEAL MY POKÉMON UNLESS I GET LUCKY AND ENTER A SMALL ROOM THAT LETS ME HEAL THEM.
SO AVOIDING UNNECESSARY BATTLES IS AN IMPORTANT TACTIC AT THE BATTLE PIKE.
BUT IT'S NOT LIKE YOU CAN *CHOOSE* THE ROOMS WITH THE BATTLES YOU CAN AVOID...
ACTUALLY, THEY GIVE YOU HINTS.
HINTS?
THERE'S A MAID STANDING INSIDE EVERY LARGE ROOM.
AND SHE MAKES COMMENTS WHEN YOU CHOOSE A DOOR TO A SMALL ROOM. SHE GIVES YOU HINTS.
WHAT KIND OF HINTS...?
AIYEEE!
TAP
BRRR
HA HA HA! TIME FOR ROUND FOUR, YOUNG MAN!
OKAY!

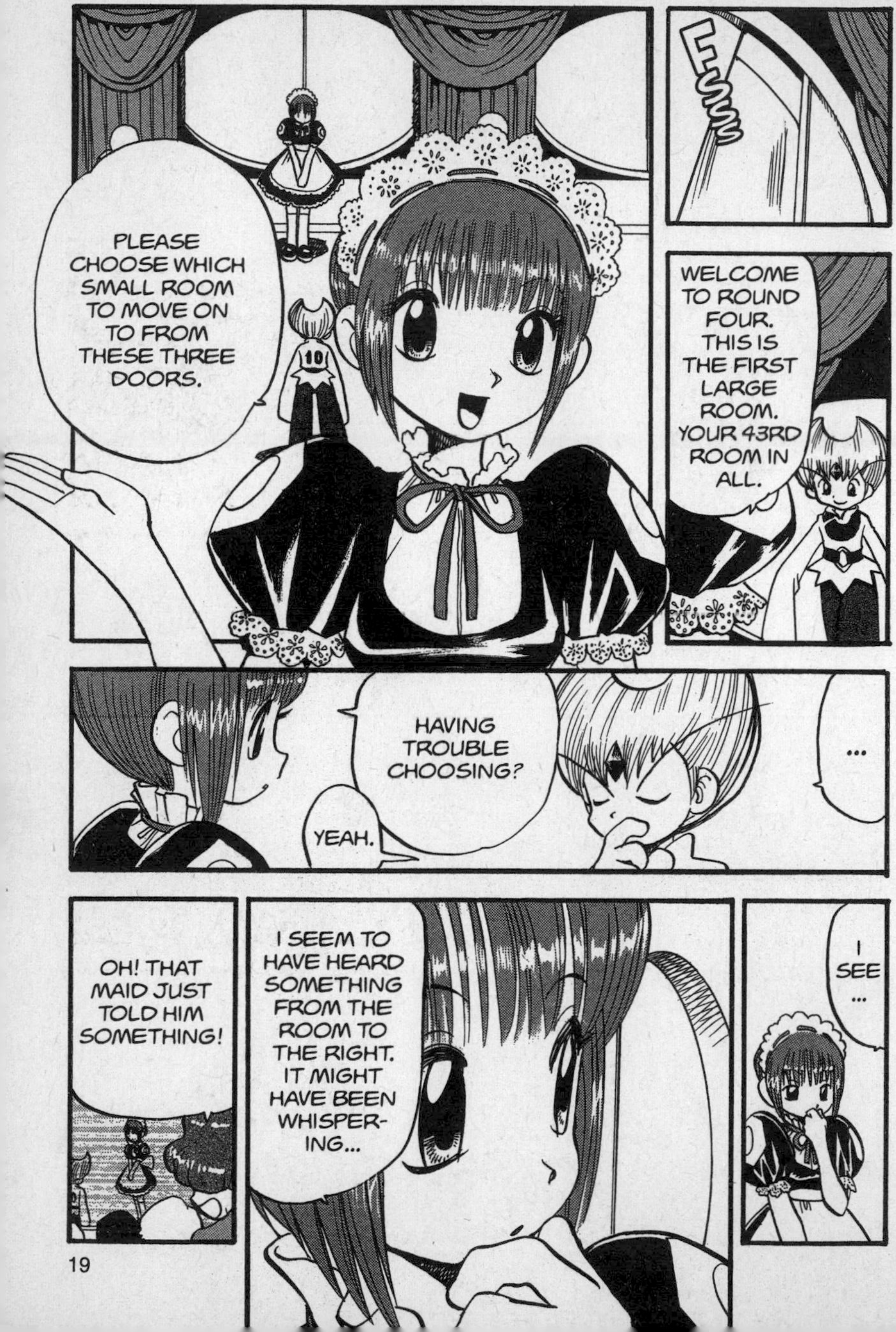
FSSS
WELCOME TO ROUND FOUR. THIS IS THE FIRST LARGE ROOM. YOUR 43RD ROOM IN ALL.
PLEASE CHOOSE WHICH SMALL ROOM TO MOVE ON TO FROM THESE THREE DOORS.
...
HAVING TROUBLE CHOOSING?
YEAH.
I SEE...
I SEEM TO HAVE HEARD SOMETHING FROM THE ROOM TO THE RIGHT. IT MIGHT HAVE BEEN WHISPER-ING...
OH! THAT MAID JUST TOLD HIM SOMETHING!

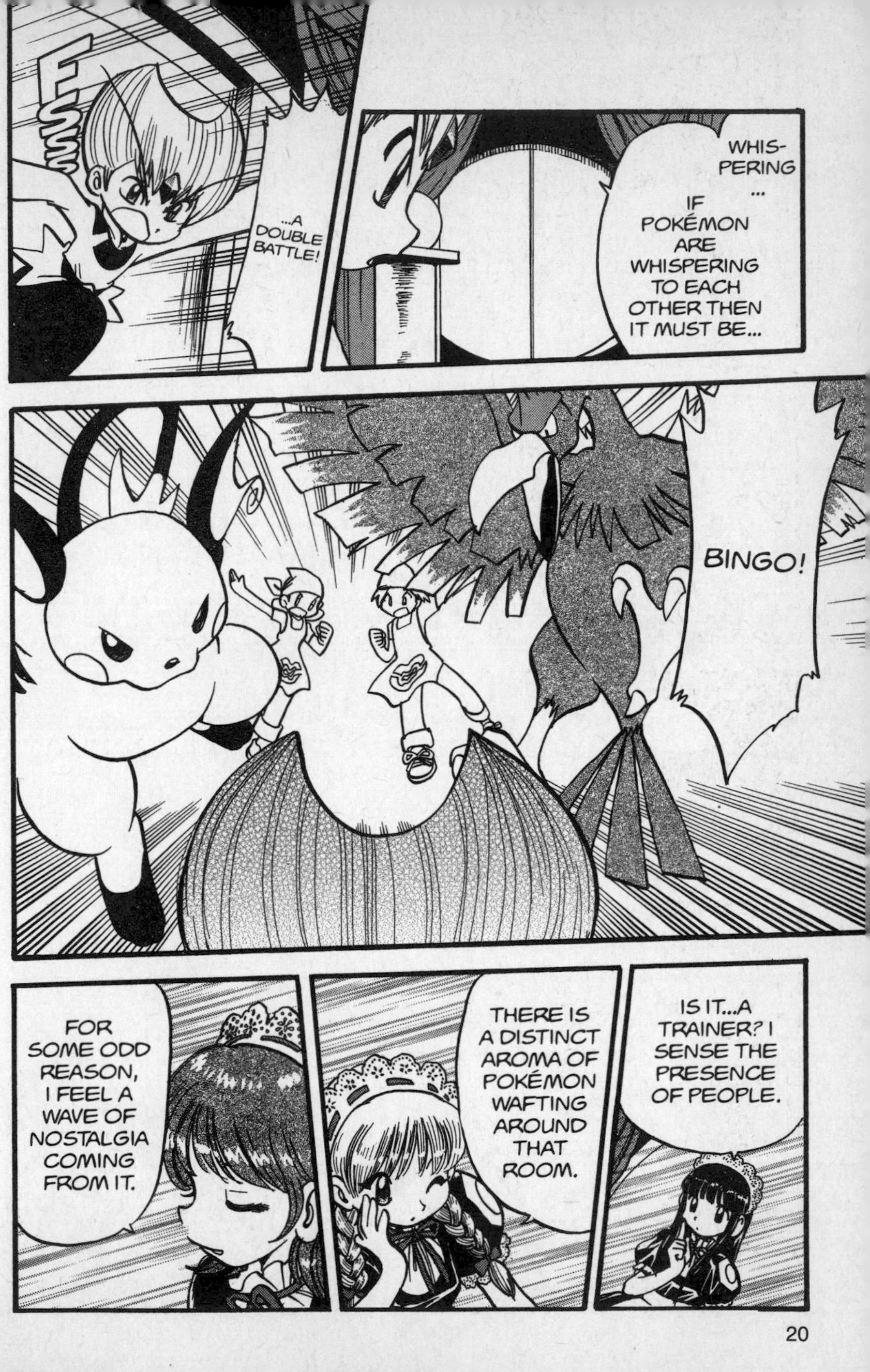
WHISPERING...
IF POKÉMON ARE WHISPERING TO EACH OTHER THEN IT MUST BE...
FSSS
...A DOUBLE BATTLE!
BINGO!
IS IT...A TRAINER? I SENSE THE PRESENCE OF PEOPLE.
THERE IS A DISTINCT AROMA OF POKÉMON WAFTING AROUND THAT ROOM.
FOR SOME ODD REASON, I FEEL A WAVE OF NOSTALGIA COMING FROM IT.

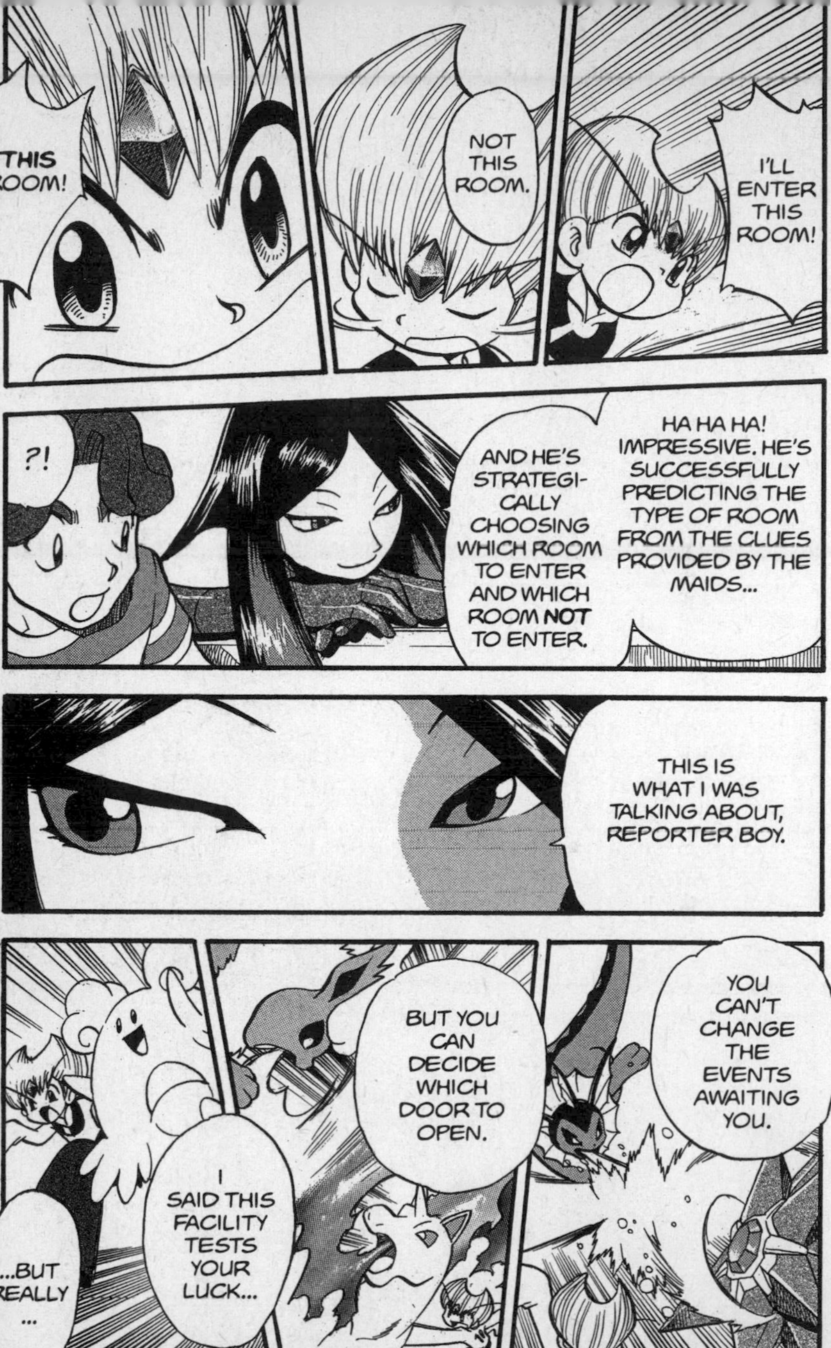
I'LL ENTER THIS ROOM!
NOT THIS ROOM.
THIS ROOM!
HA HA HA! IMPRESSIVE. HE'S SUCCESSFULLY PREDICTING THE TYPE OF ROOM FROM THE CLUES PROVIDED BY THE MAIDS...
AND HE'S STRATEGICALLY CHOOSING WHICH ROOM TO ENTER AND WHICH ROOM **NOT** TO ENTER.
?!
THIS IS WHAT I WAS TALKING ABOUT, REPORTER BOY.
YOU CAN'T CHANGE THE EVENTS AWAITING YOU.
BUT YOU CAN DECIDE WHICH DOOR TO OPEN.
I SAID THIS FACILITY TESTS YOUR LUCK...
...BUT REALLY ...

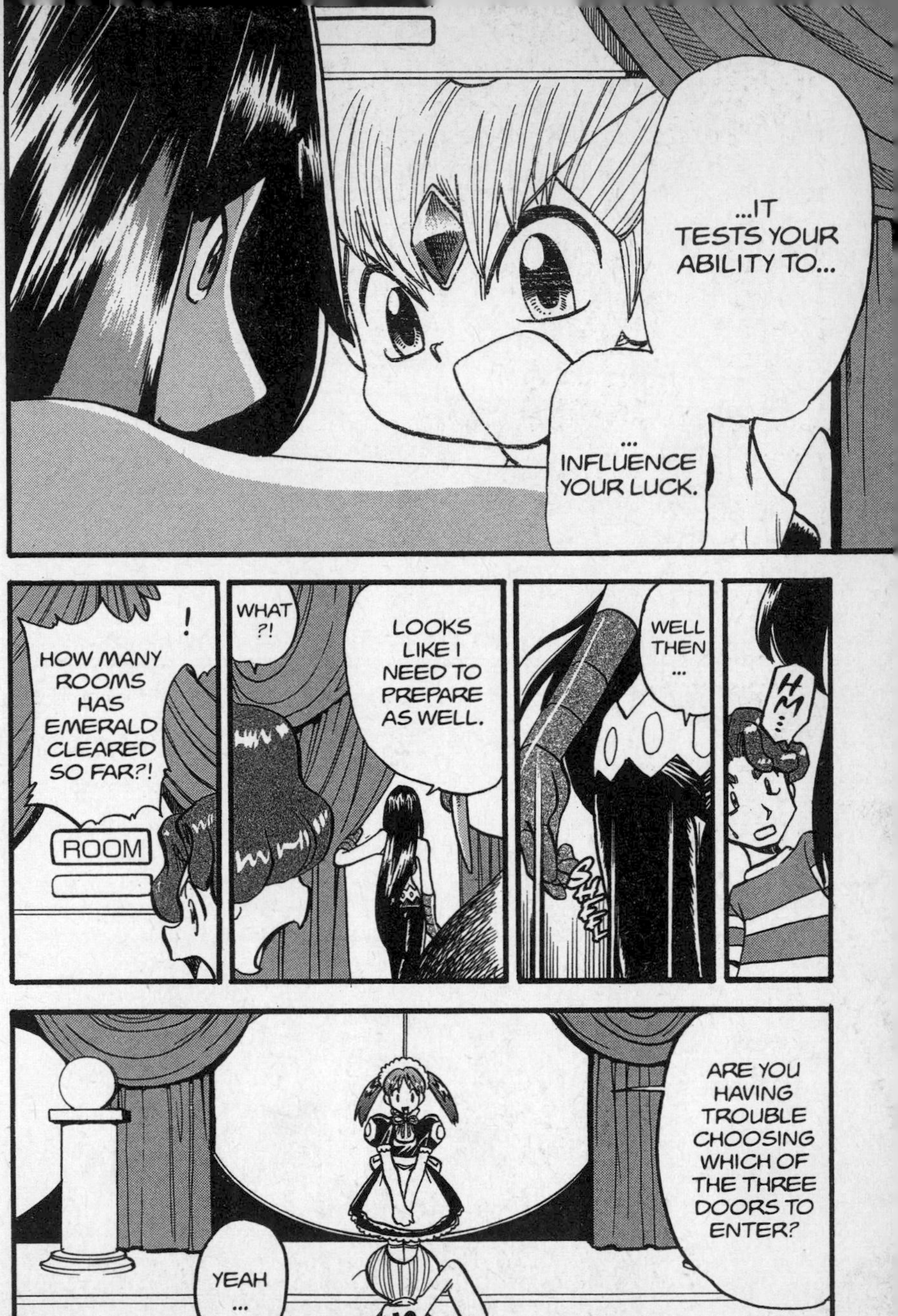
...IT TESTS YOUR ABILITY TO...
... INFLUENCE YOUR LUCK.
HM...
WELL THEN ...
SHFFL
LOOKS LIKE I NEED TO PREPARE AS WELL.
WHAT?!
!
HOW MANY ROOMS HAS EMERALD CLEARED SO FAR?!
ROOM
ARE YOU HAVING TROUBLE CHOOSING WHICH OF THE THREE DOORS TO ENTER?
YEAH ...
10

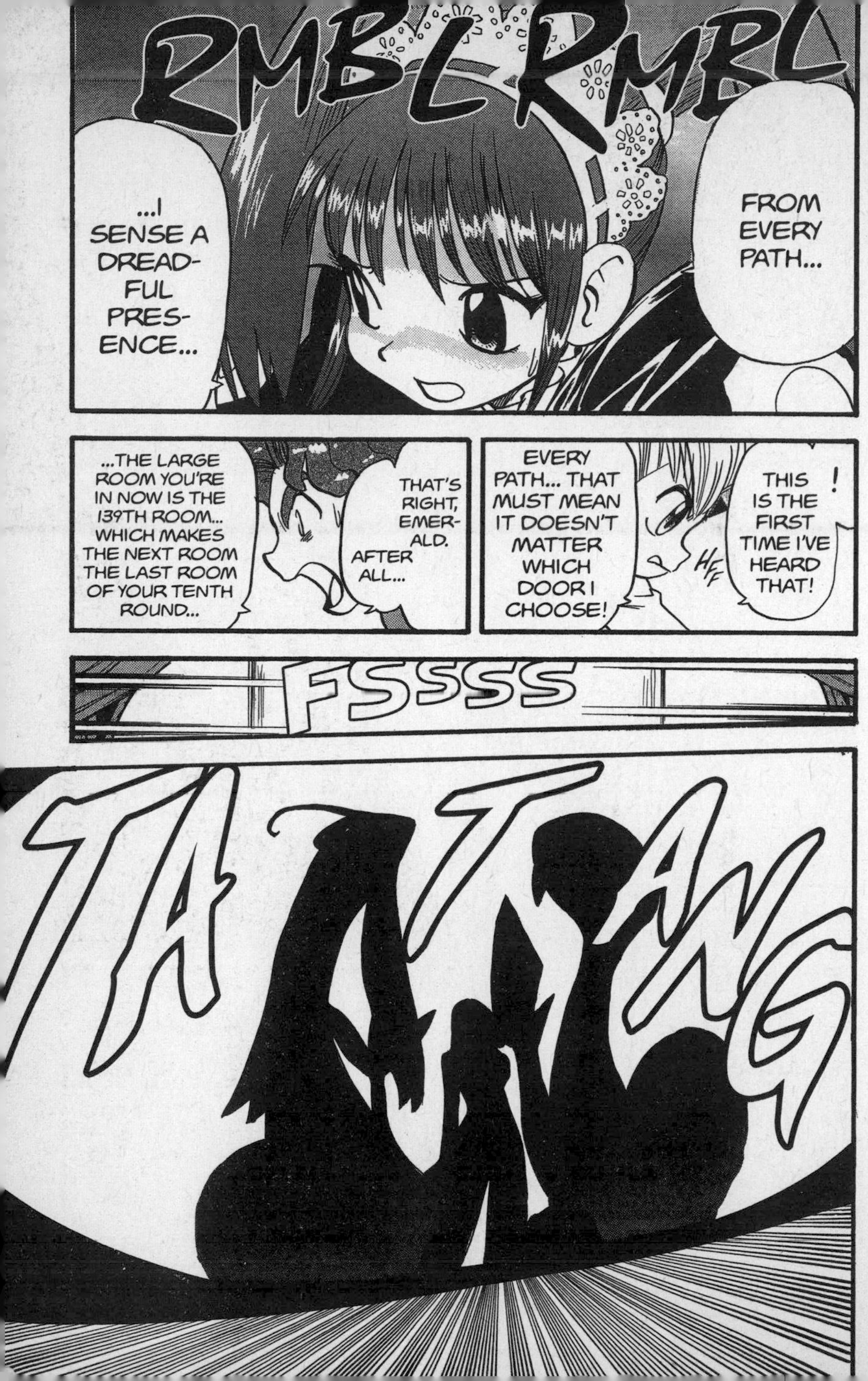
RMBL RMBL
FROM EVERY PATH...
...I SENSE A DREAD-FUL PRES-ENCE...
!
THIS IS THE FIRST TIME I'VE HEARD THAT!
HFF
EVERY PATH... THAT MUST MEAN IT DOESN'T MATTER WHICH DOOR I CHOOSE!
THAT'S RIGHT, EMER-ALD. AFTER ALL...
...THE LARGE ROOM YOU'RE IN NOW IS THE 139TH ROOM... WHICH MAKES THE NEXT ROOM THE LAST ROOM OF YOUR TENTH ROUND...
FSSSS
TA TANG

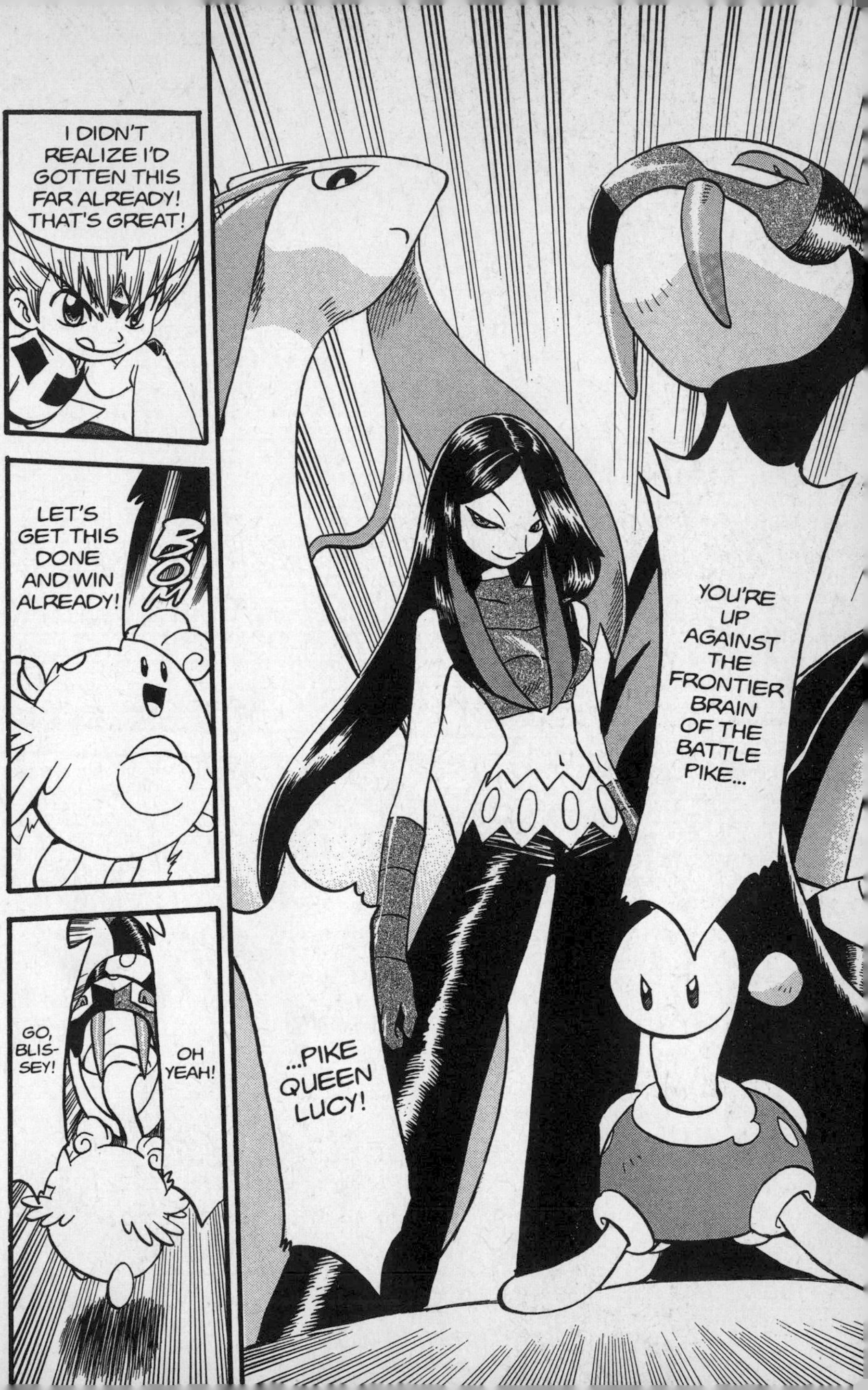
YOU'RE UP AGAINST THE FRONTIER BRAIN OF THE BATTLE PIKE...
...PIKE QUEEN LUCY!
I DIDN'T REALIZE I'D GOTTEN THIS FAR ALREADY! THAT'S GREAT!
LET'S GET THIS DONE AND WIN ALREADY!
BOM
GO, BLIS-SEY!
OH YEAH!

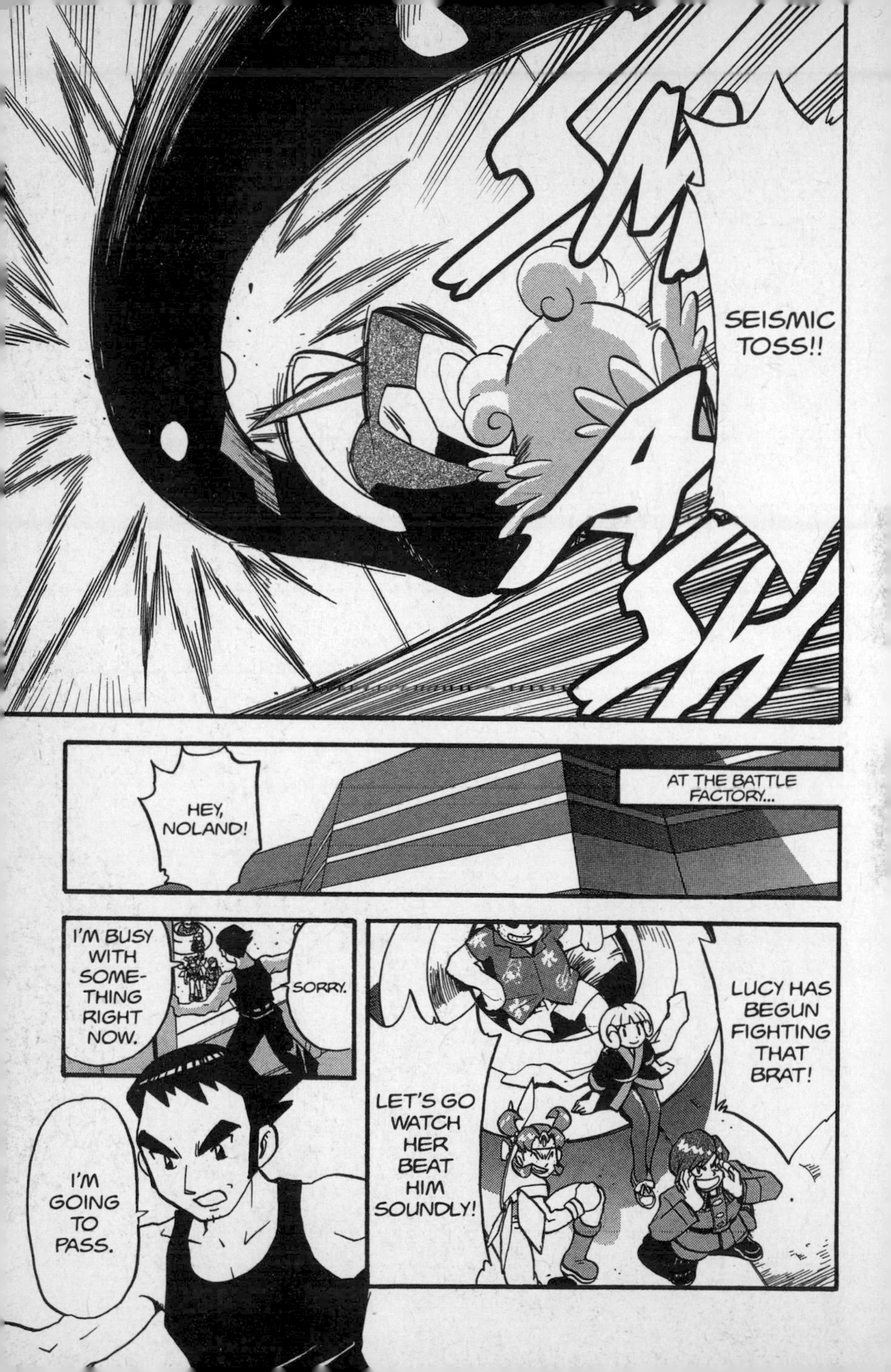
SEISMIC TOSS!!
AT THE BATTLE FACTORY...
HEY, NOLAND!
LUCY HAS BEGUN FIGHTING THAT BRAT!
LET'S GO WATCH HER BEAT HIM SOUNDLY!
SORRY.
I'M BUSY WITH SOME-THING RIGHT NOW.
I'M GOING TO PASS.

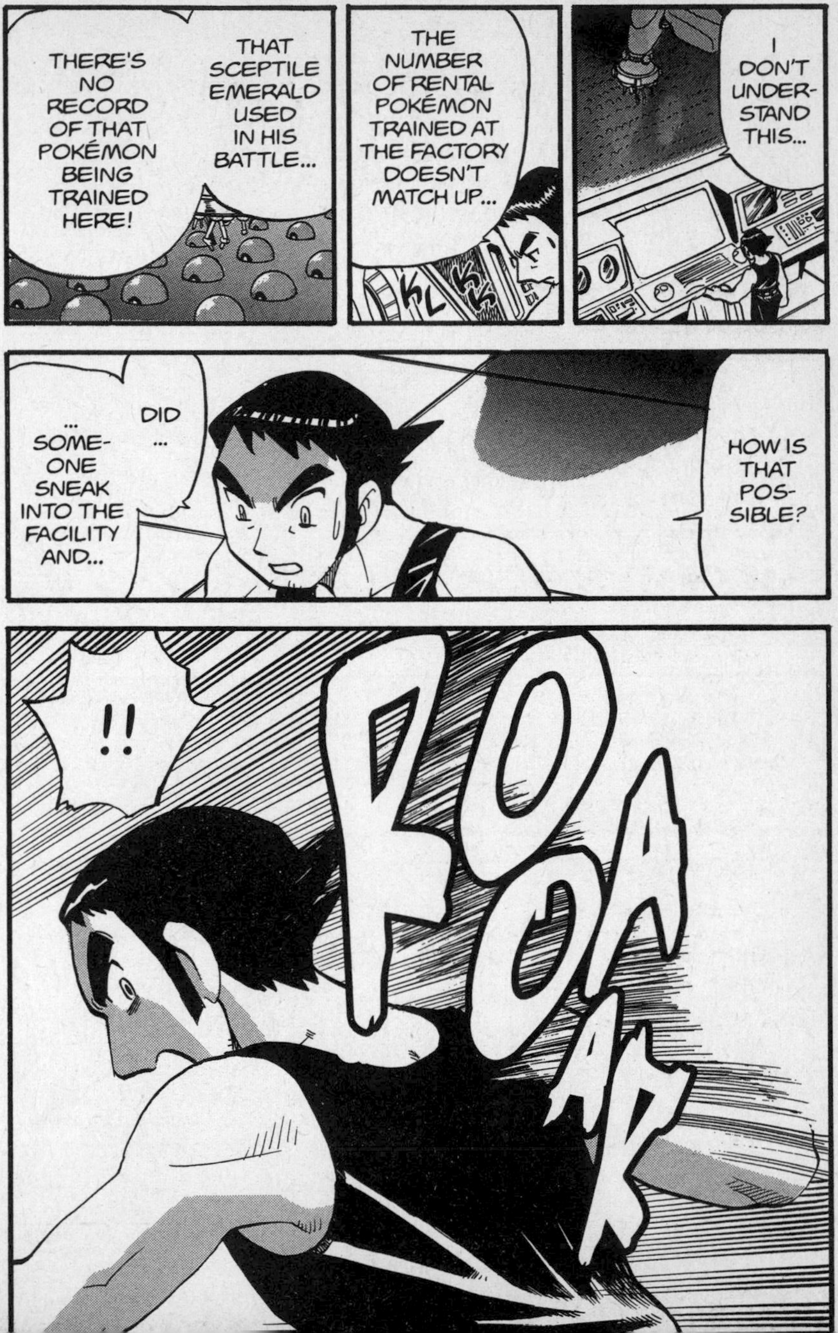
I DON'T UNDER-STAND THIS...
THE NUMBER OF RENTAL POKÉMON TRAINED AT THE FACTORY DOESN'T MATCH UP...
THAT SCEPTILE EMERALD USED IN HIS BATTLE...
THERE'S NO RECORD OF THAT POKÉMON BEING TRAINED HERE!
HOW IS THAT POS-SIBLE?
DID ...
... SOME-ONE SNEAK INTO THE FACILITY AND...
!!
ROOAAR

DEAR MEMBERS OF THE PRESS...

Thank you for visiting the Battle Frontier today. Permit me to continue explaining the rules of this facility...

OWNER: SCOTT

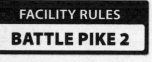

FACILITY RULES

BATTLE PIKE 2

There are eight encounters you may experience inside the small rooms in the Battle Pike. I will describe them here.

■ SMALL ROOM ENCOUNTERS (8 TYPES) ■

① Single Battle Room
A single battle against a Trainer with three Pokémon.

② Double Battle Room
A Double Battle against two Trainers who each have one Pokémon.

③ Tough Opponent Room
A Single Battle against a skilled Trainer with three Pokémon. If you win, your Pokémon will be fully healed.

④ Wild Pokémon Room
You will face wild Pokémon like Seviper, Milotic and Dusclops who have moves that inflict status conditions.

⑤ Status Condition Room
Kirlia or Dusclops will attack your Pokémon with Poison, Paralysis, Sleep, Burn or Freeze.

⑥ Small Talk Room
A Trainer inside this room will make random small talk about topics unrelated to Pokémon Battles. You may ignore the small talk and move on.

⑦ Healing Room (1 to 2 Pokémon)
Someone from our facility will randomly heal one or two of your Pokémon.

⑧ Healing Room (All Pokémon)
Our facility staff will heal all three of your Pokémon.

LARGE ROOM 10
SMALL ROOM
SMALL ROOM
SMALL ROOM
LARGE ROOM 9
SMALL ROOM
SMALL ROOM
SMALL ROOM

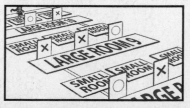

310

Just My Luck... Shuckle

POKÉMON ADVENTURES•THE SIXTH CHAPTER•EMERALD

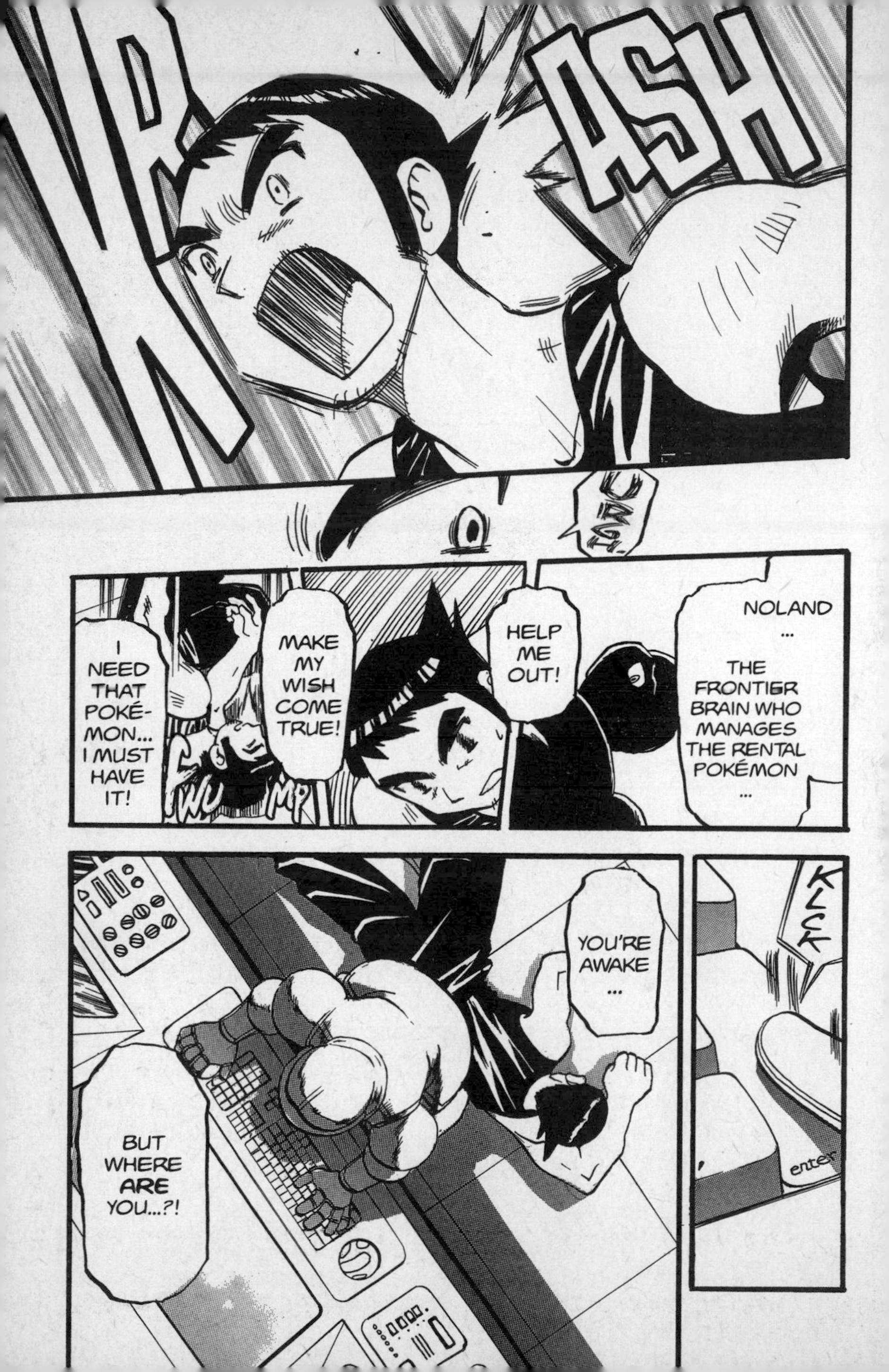

ASH
URGH
NOLAND ... THE FRONTIER BRAIN WHO MANAGES THE RENTAL POKÉMON ...
HELP ME OUT!
MAKE MY WISH COME TRUE!
I NEED THAT POKÉ-MON... I MUST HAVE IT!
FWUMP
KLICK
enter
YOU'RE AWAKE ...
BUT WHERE **ARE** YOU...?!

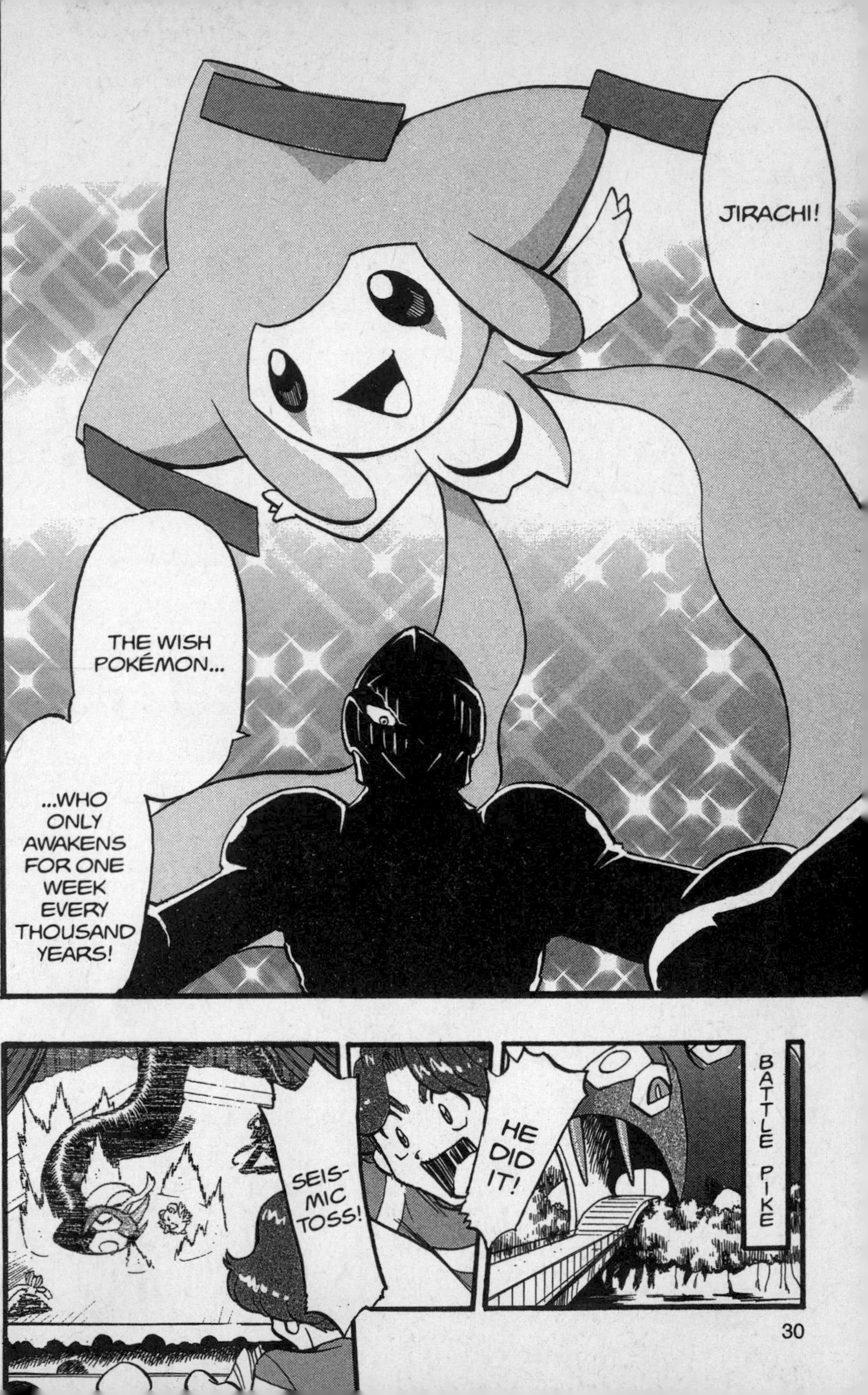
JIRACHI!
THE WISH POKÉMON...
...WHO ONLY AWAKENS FOR ONE WEEK EVERY THOUSAND YEARS!
BATTLE PIKE
HE DID IT!
SEIS-MIC TOSS!

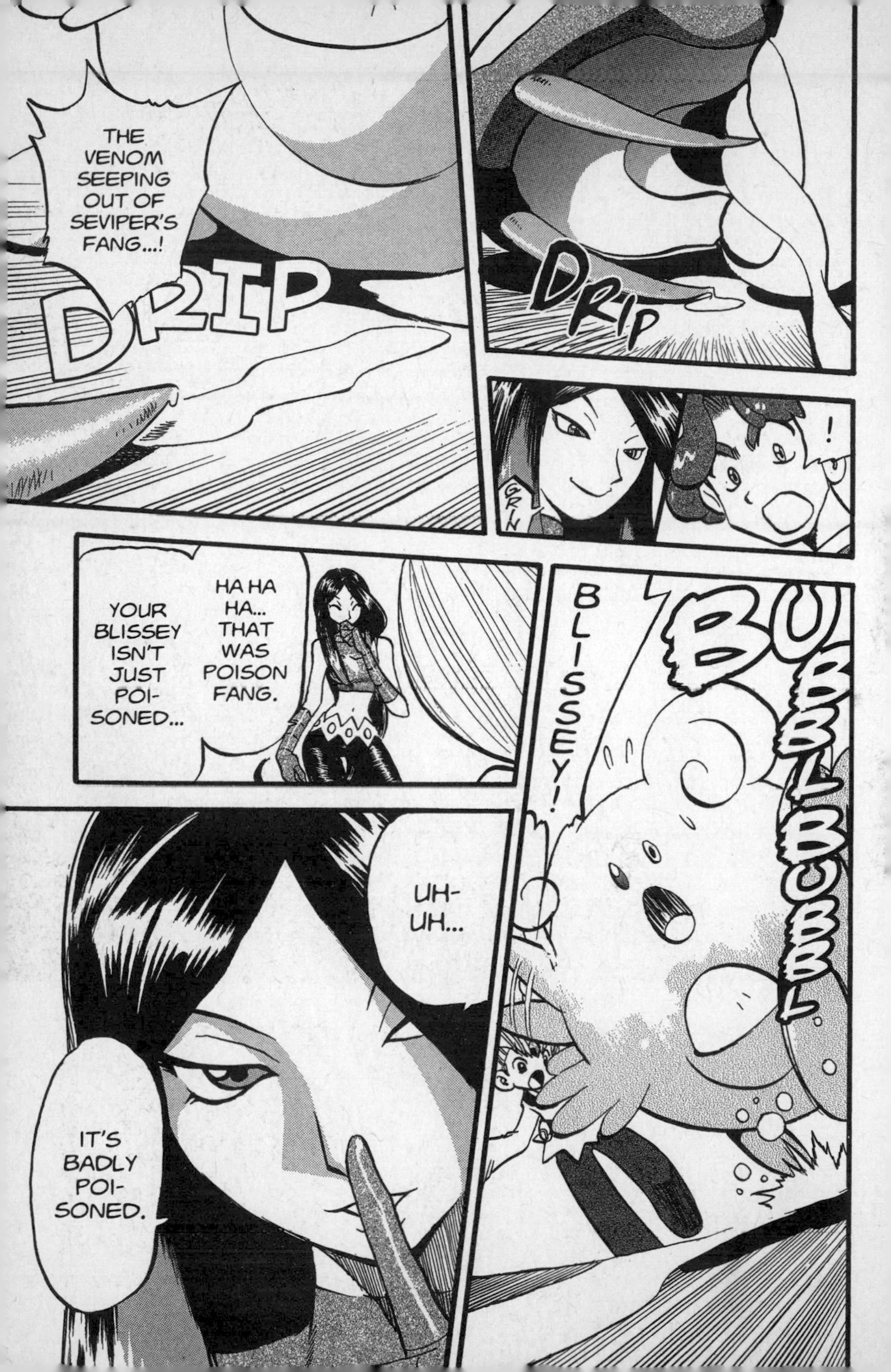
DRIP
GRIN
!
THE VENOM SEEPING OUT OF SEVIPER'S FANG...!
DRIP
BLISSEY!
BUBBLBUBBL
HA HA HA... THAT WAS POISON FANG.
YOUR BLISSEY ISN'T JUST POI-SONED...
UH-UH...
IT'S BADLY POI-SONED.

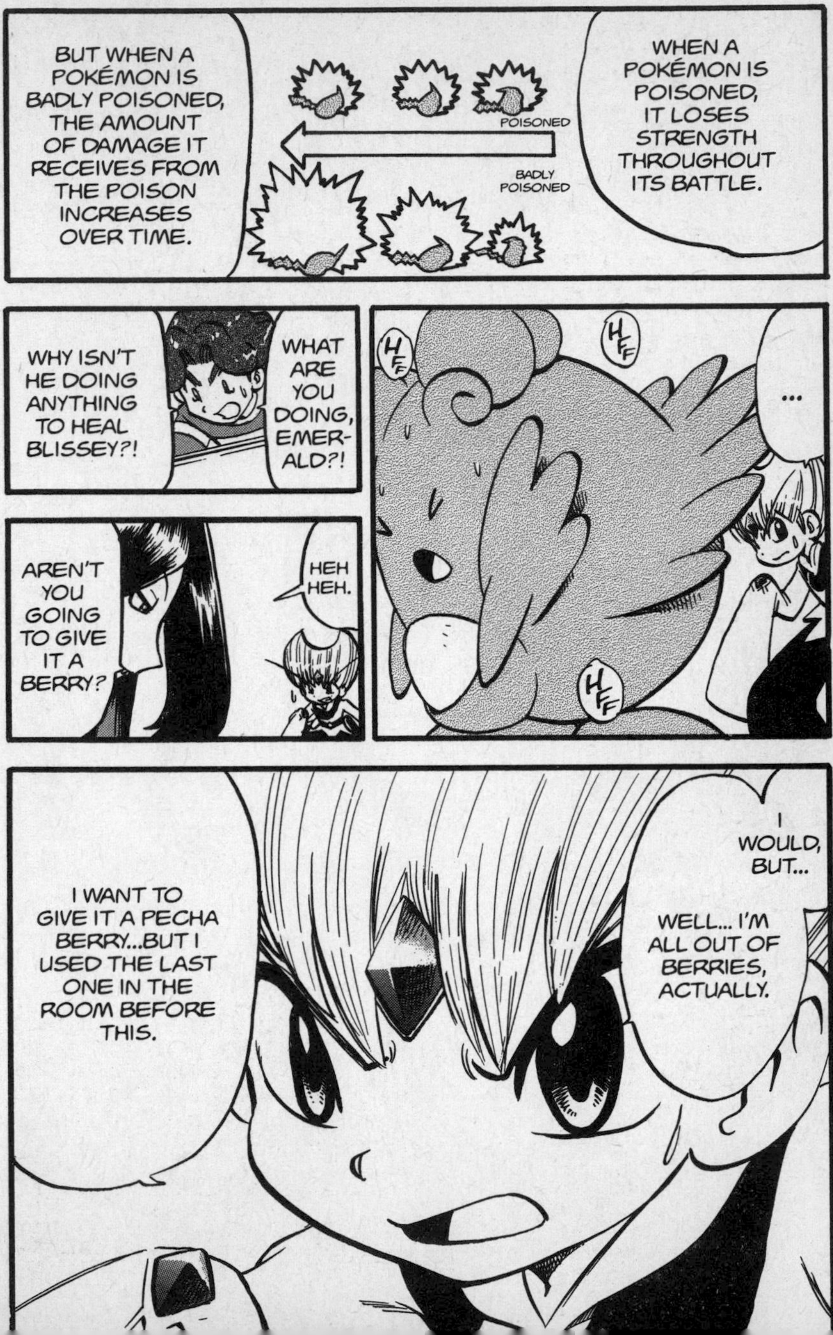
WHEN A POKÉMON IS POISONED, IT LOSES STRENGTH THROUGHOUT ITS BATTLE.
POISONED
BADLY POISONED
BUT WHEN A POKÉMON IS BADLY POISONED, THE AMOUNT OF DAMAGE IT RECEIVES FROM THE POISON INCREASES OVER TIME.
...
HFF
HFF
HFF
WHAT ARE YOU DOING, EMERALD?!
WHY ISN'T HE DOING ANYTHING TO HEAL BLISSEY?!
HEH HEH.
AREN'T YOU GOING TO GIVE IT A BERRY?
I WOULD, BUT...
WELL... I'M ALL OUT OF BERRIES, ACTUALLY.
I WANT TO GIVE IT A PECHA BERRY...BUT I USED THE LAST ONE IN THE ROOM BEFORE THIS.

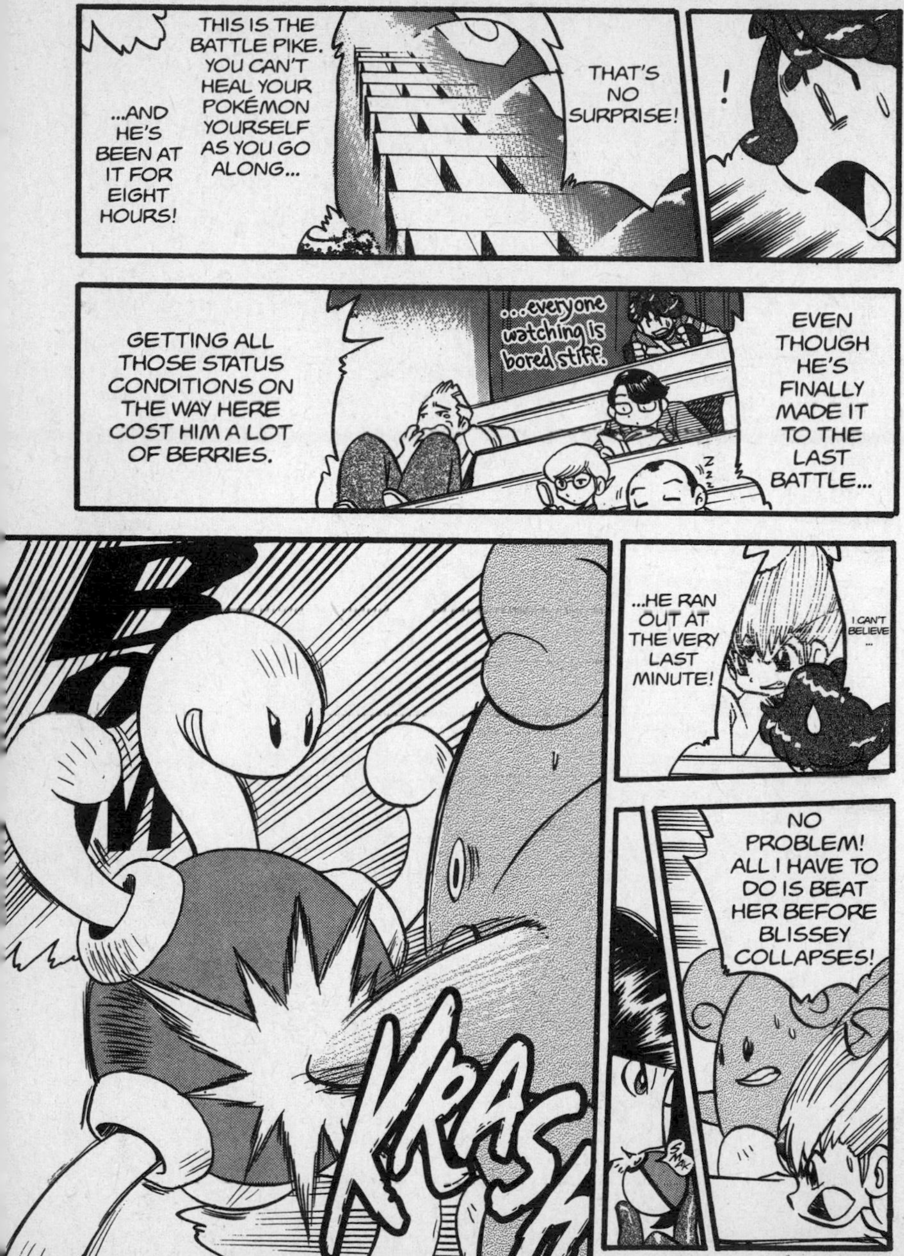
!
THAT'S NO SURPRISE!
THIS IS THE BATTLE PIKE. YOU CAN'T HEAL YOUR POKÉMON YOURSELF AS YOU GO ALONG...
...AND HE'S BEEN AT IT FOR EIGHT HOURS!
EVEN THOUGH HE'S FINALLY MADE IT TO THE LAST BATTLE...
...everyone watching is bored stiff.
ZZZ
GETTING ALL THOSE STATUS CONDITIONS ON THE WAY HERE COST HIM A LOT OF BERRIES.
I CAN'T BELIEVE ...
...HE RAN OUT AT THE VERY LAST MINUTE!
NO PROBLEM! ALL I HAVE TO DO IS BEAT HER BEFORE BLISSEY COLLAPSES!
SMAK
KRASH

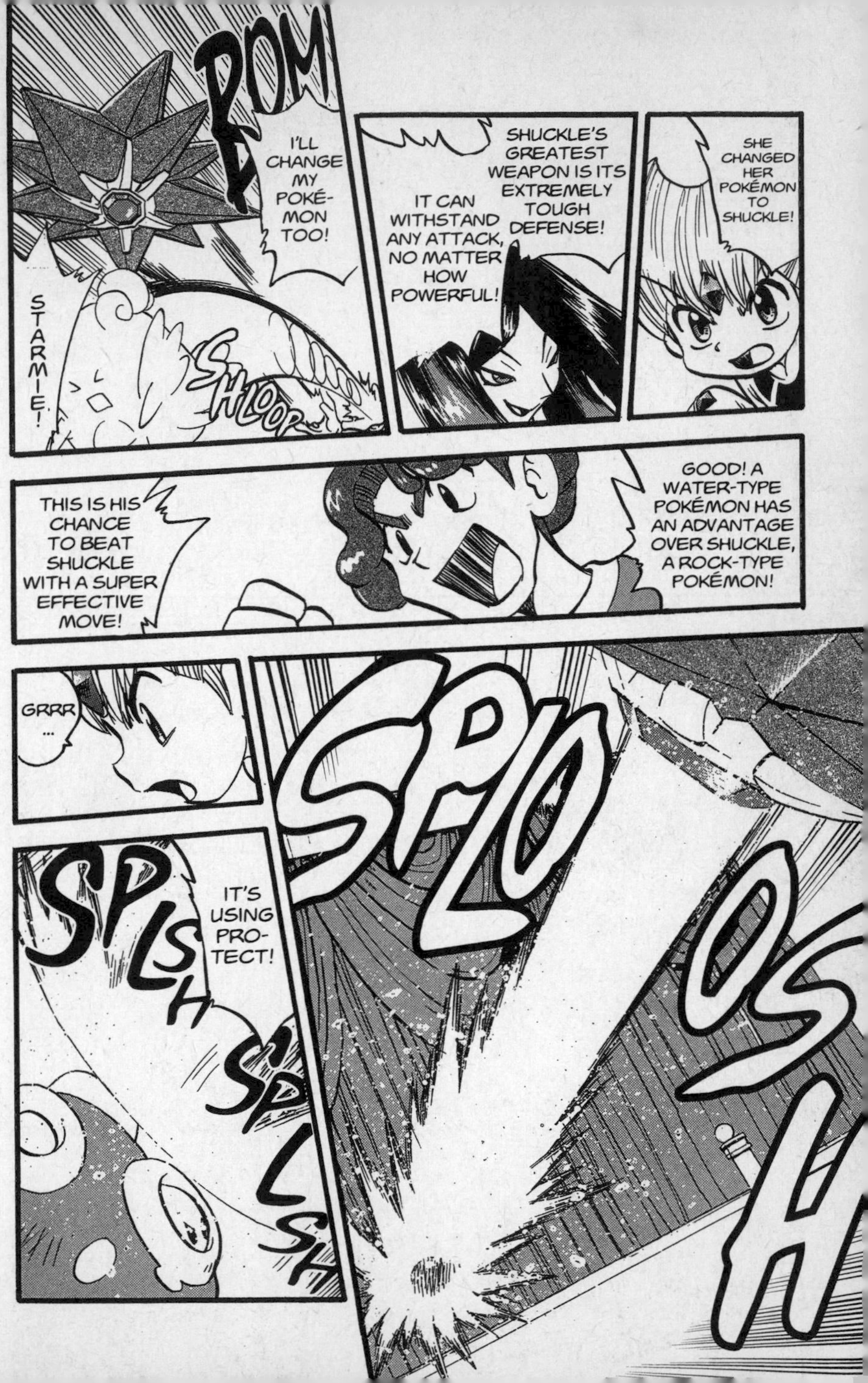

SHE CHANGED HER POKÉMON TO SHUCKLE!
SHUCKLE'S GREATEST WEAPON IS ITS EXTREMELY TOUGH DEFENSE!
IT CAN WITHSTAND ANY ATTACK, NO MATTER HOW POWERFUL!
POM
I'LL CHANGE MY POKÉMON TOO!
SHLOOP
STARMIE!
GOOD! A WATER-TYPE POKÉMON HAS AN ADVANTAGE OVER SHUCKLE, A ROCK-TYPE POKÉMON!
THIS IS HIS CHANCE TO BEAT SHUCKLE WITH A SUPER EFFECTIVE MOVE!
SPLOOSH
GRRR...
IT'S USING PROTECT!
SPLSH
SPLSH

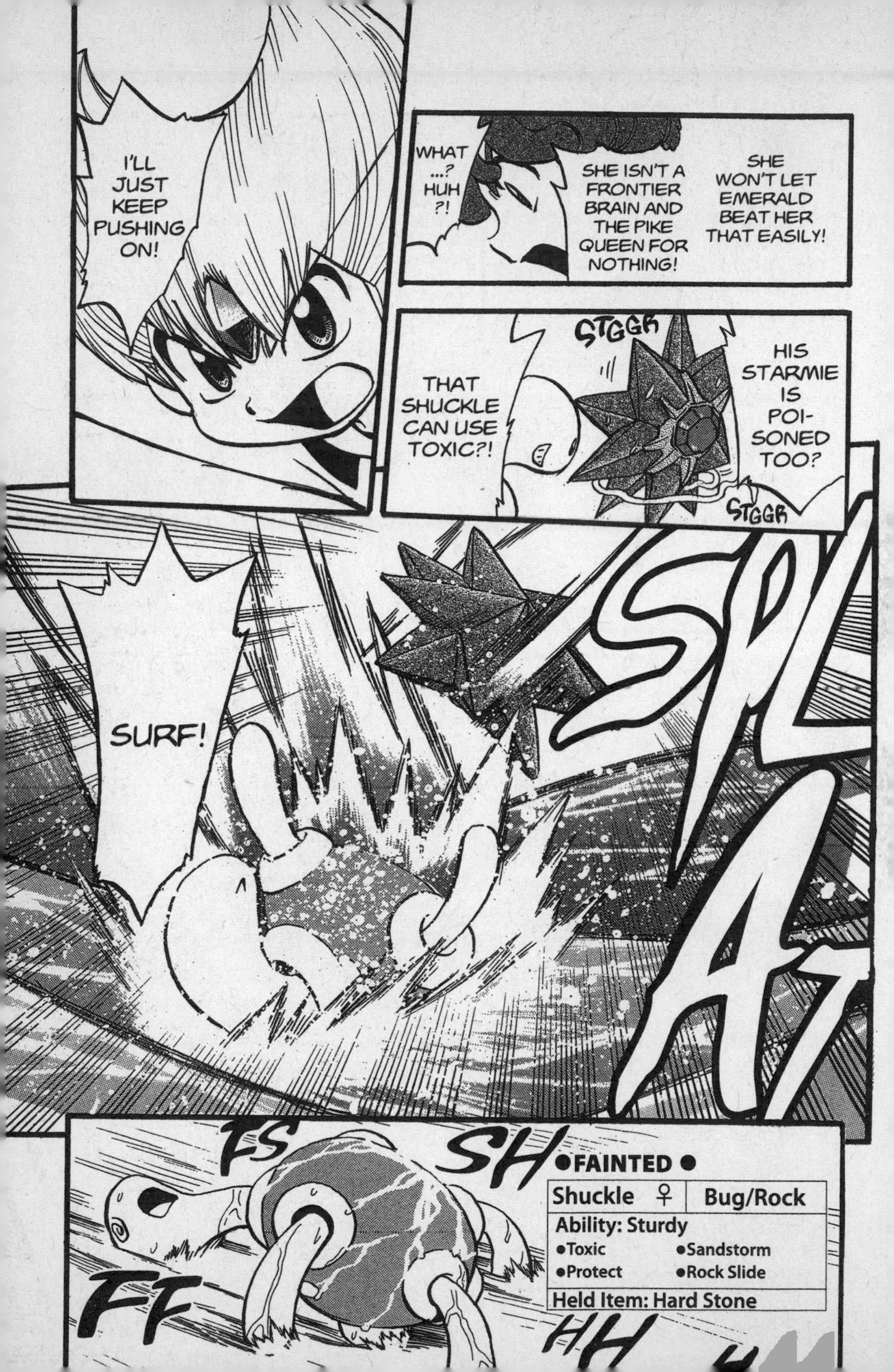
SHE WON'T LET EMERALD BEAT HER THAT EASILY!
SHE ISN'T A FRONTIER BRAIN AND THE PIKE QUEEN FOR NOTHING!
WHAT ...? HUH ?!
HIS STARMIE IS POI-SONED TOO?
STGGR
THAT SHUCKLE CAN USE TOXIC?!
STGGR
I'LL JUST KEEP PUSHING ON!
SPLA
SURF!
SH
FS
●FAINTED●
Shuckle ♀ Bug/Rock
Ability: Sturdy
●Toxic ●Sandstorm
●Protect ●Rock Slide
Held Item: Hard Stone
FF
HH

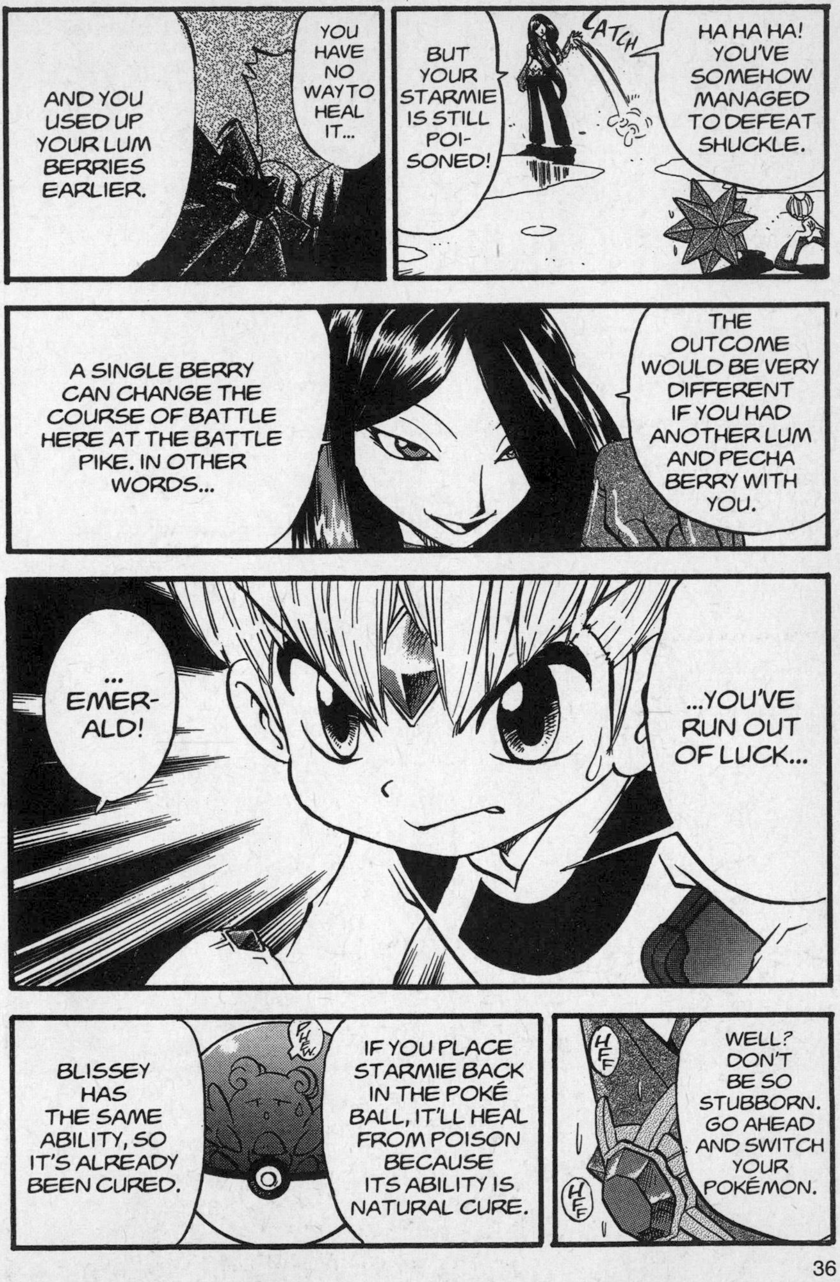
LATCH
HA HA HA! YOU'VE SOMEHOW MANAGED TO DEFEAT SHUCKLE.
BUT YOUR STARMIE IS STILL POI-SONED!
YOU HAVE NO WAY TO HEAL IT...
AND YOU USED UP YOUR LUM BERRIES EARLIER.
THE OUTCOME WOULD BE VERY DIFFERENT IF YOU HAD ANOTHER LUM AND PECHA BERRY WITH YOU.
A SINGLE BERRY CAN CHANGE THE COURSE OF BATTLE HERE AT THE BATTLE PIKE. IN OTHER WORDS...
...YOU'VE RUN OUT OF LUCK...
... EMER-ALD!
HFF
WELL? DON'T BE SO STUBBORN. GO AHEAD AND SWITCH YOUR POKÉMON.
HFF
PHEW
IF YOU PLACE STARMIE BACK IN THE POKÉ BALL, IT'LL HEAL FROM POISON BECAUSE ITS ABILITY IS NATURAL CURE.
BLISSEY HAS THE SAME ABILITY, SO IT'S ALREADY BEEN CURED.

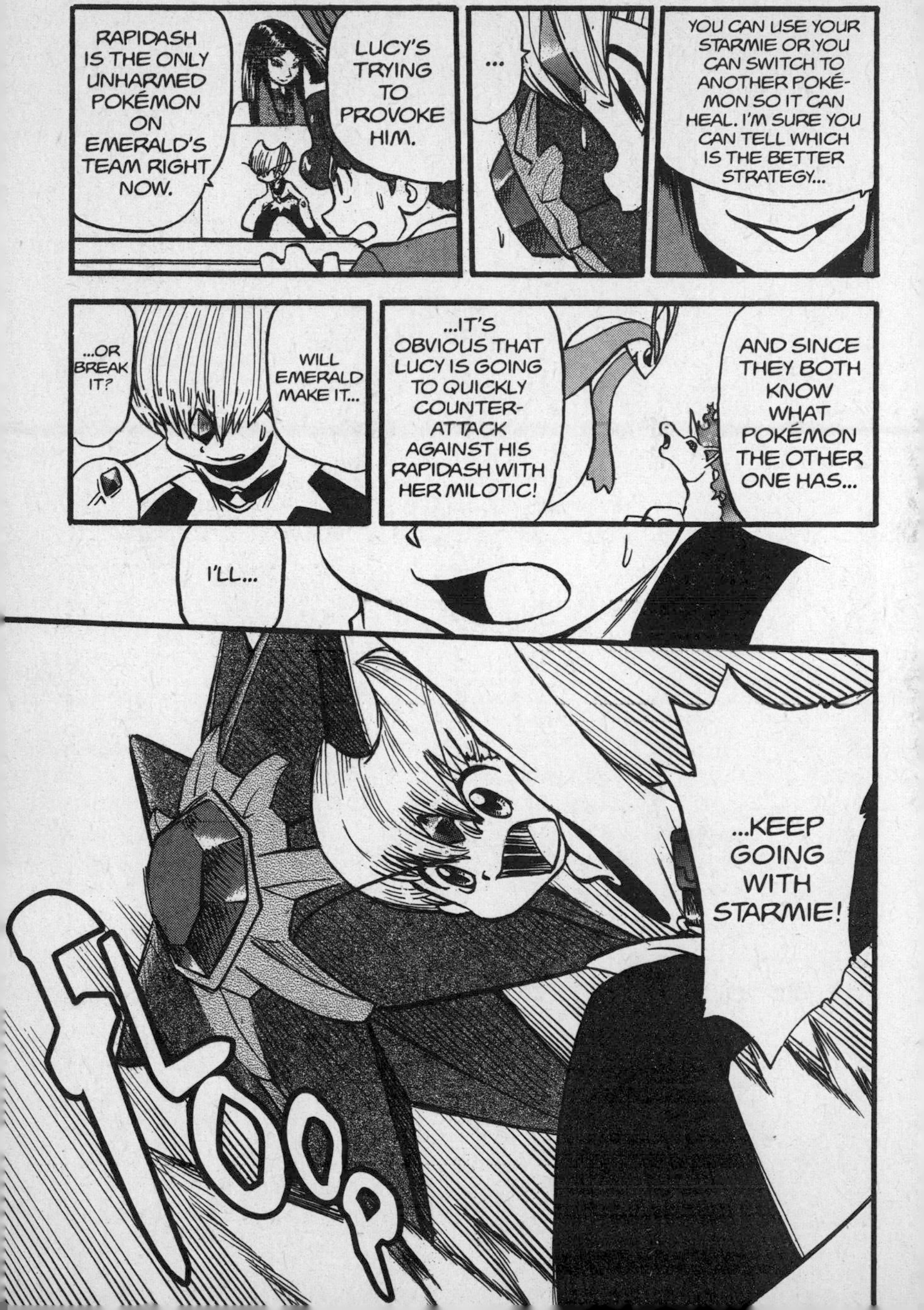

YOU CAN USE YOUR STARMIE OR YOU CAN SWITCH TO ANOTHER POKÉMON SO IT CAN HEAL. I'M SURE YOU CAN TELL WHICH IS THE BETTER STRATEGY...
...
LUCY'S TRYING TO PROVOKE HIM.
RAPIDASH IS THE ONLY UNHARMED POKÉMON ON EMERALD'S TEAM RIGHT NOW.
AND SINCE THEY BOTH KNOW WHAT POKÉMON THE OTHER ONE HAS...
...IT'S OBVIOUS THAT LUCY IS GOING TO QUICKLY COUNTER-ATTACK AGAINST HIS RAPIDASH WITH HER MILOTIC!
WILL EMERALD MAKE IT...
...OR BREAK IT?
I'LL...
...KEEP GOING WITH STARMIE!
FLOOP

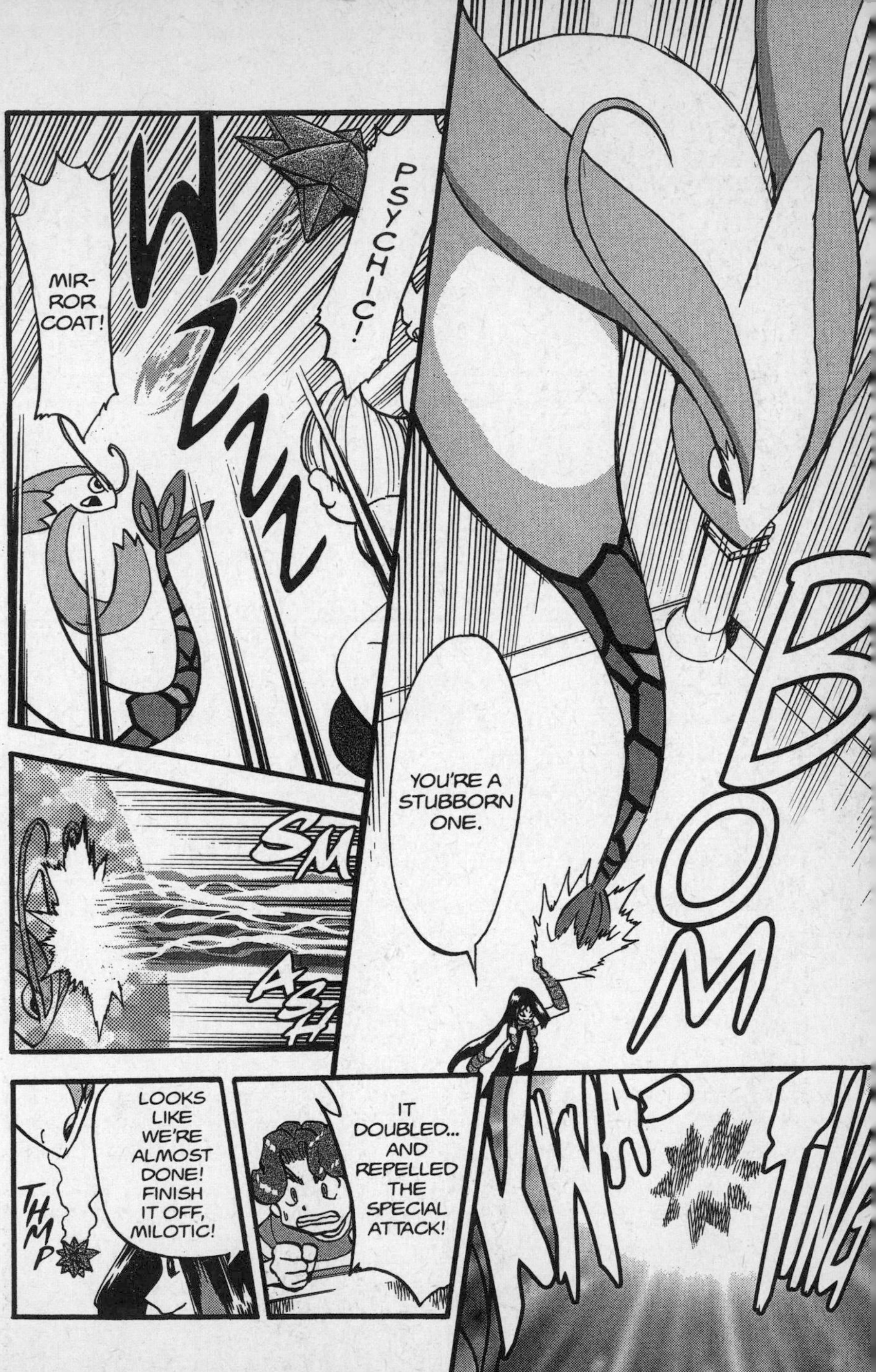
BOOM
YOU'RE A STUBBORN ONE.
PSYCHIC!
MIR-ROR COAT!
THMP
IT DOUBLED... AND REPELLED THE SPECIAL ATTACK!
LOOKS LIKE WE'RE ALMOST DONE! FINISH IT OFF, MILOTIC!
THMP

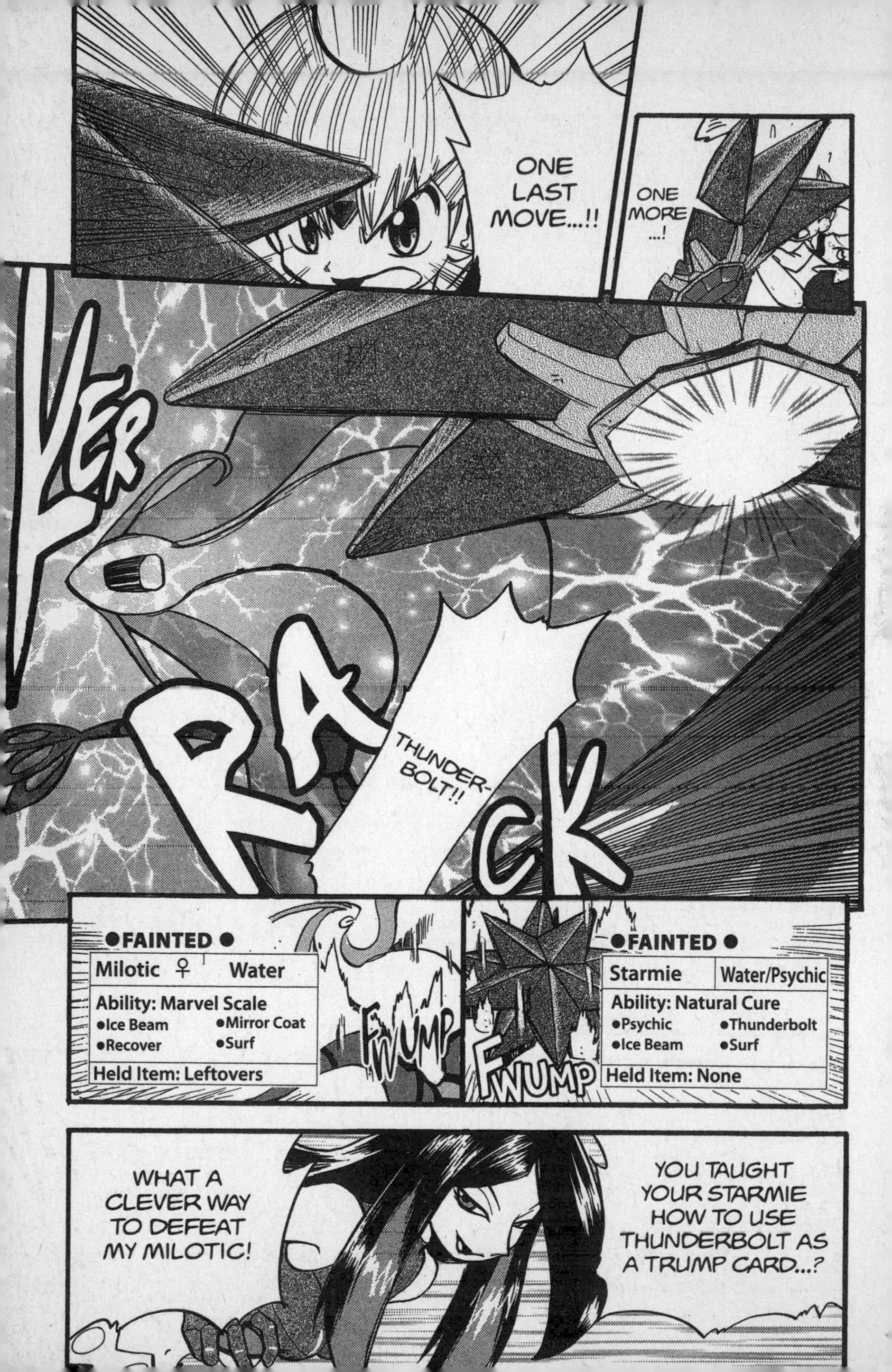
ONE MORE ...!
ONE LAST MOVE...!!
KERRACK
THUNDER-BOLT!!
●FAINTED●
Starmie Water/Psychic
Ability: Natural Cure
●Psychic ●Thunderbolt
●Ice Beam ●Surf
Held Item: None
FWUMP
FWUMP
●FAINTED●
Milotic ♀ Water
Ability: Marvel Scale
●Ice Beam ●Mirror Coat
●Recover ●Surf
Held Item: Leftovers
YOU TAUGHT YOUR STARMIE HOW TO USE THUNDERBOLT AS A TRUMP CARD...?
WHAT A CLEVER WAY TO DEFEAT MY MILOTIC!

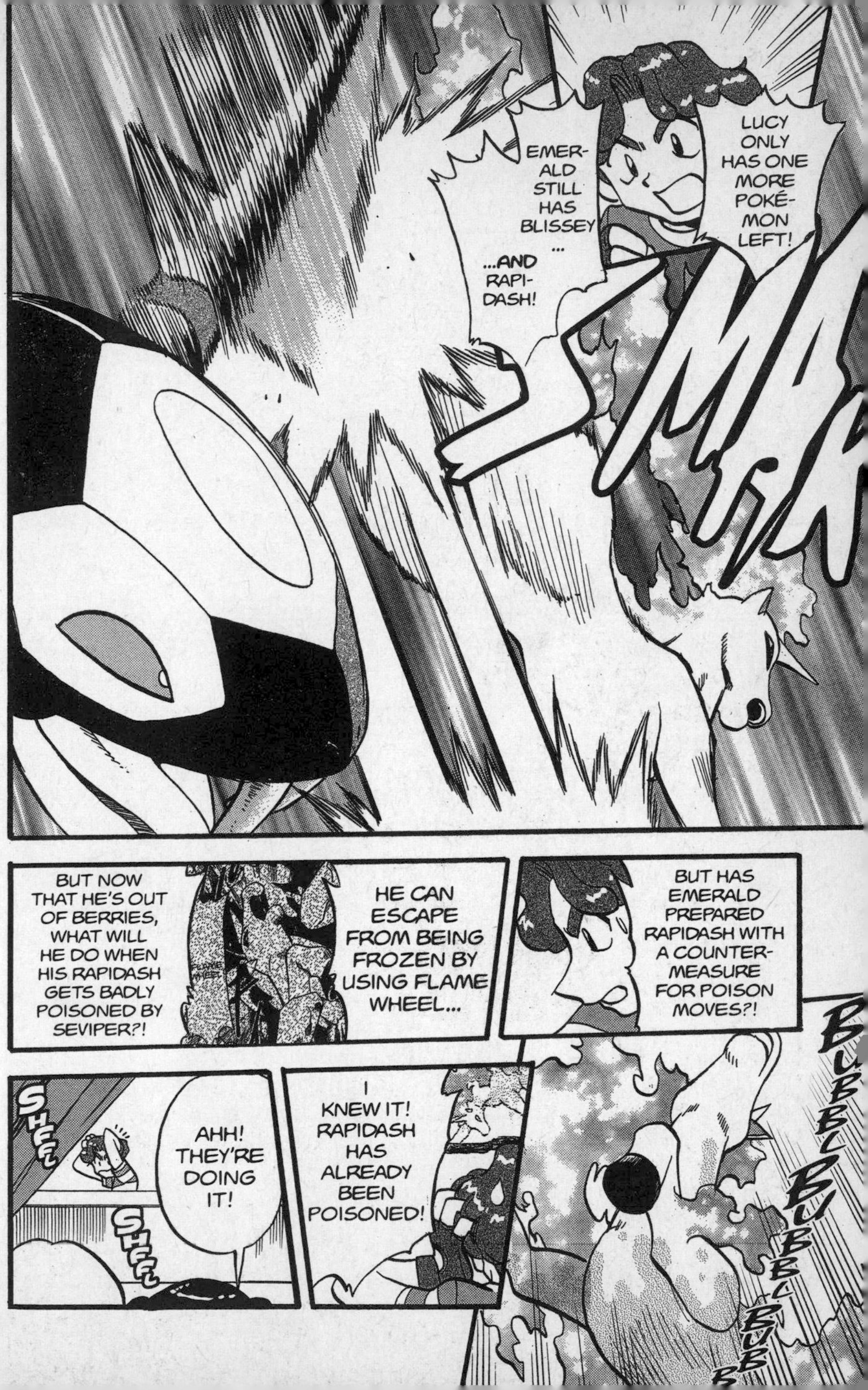
LUCY ONLY HAS ONE MORE POKÉ-MON LEFT!
EMER-ALD STILL HAS BLISSEY ...
...AND RAPI-DASH!
BUT HAS EMERALD PREPARED RAPIDASH WITH A COUNTER-MEASURE FOR POISON MOVES?!
HE CAN ESCAPE FROM BEING FROZEN BY USING FLAME WHEEL...
BUT NOW THAT HE'S OUT OF BERRIES, WHAT WILL HE DO WHEN HIS RAPIDASH GETS BADLY POISONED BY SEVIPER?!
BUBBL BUBBL BUBB
I KNEW IT! RAPIDASH HAS ALREADY BEEN POISONED!
AHH! THEY'RE DOING IT!
SHFFL
SHFFL

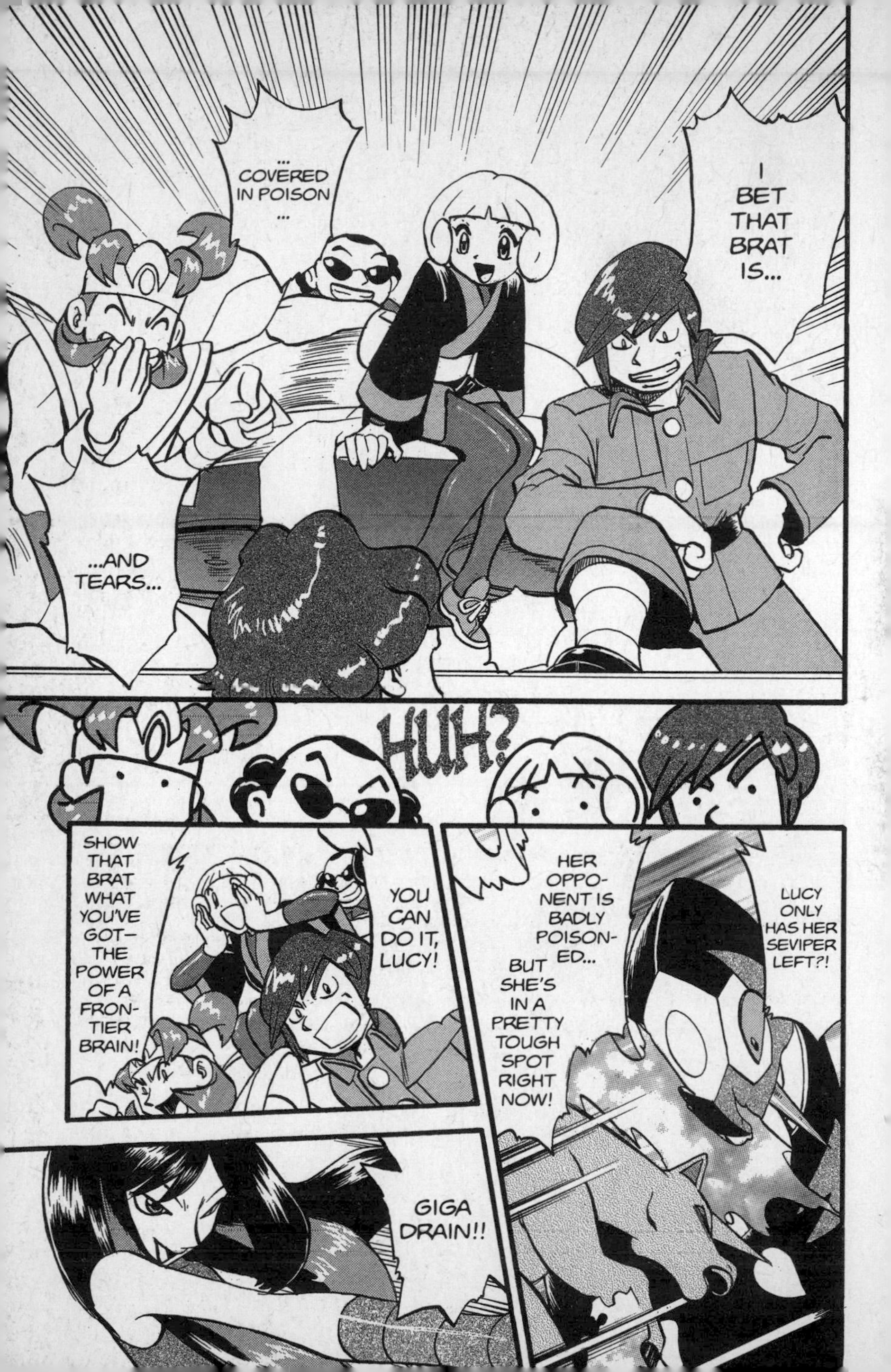
I BET THAT BRAT IS...
...COVERED IN POISON...
...AND TEARS...
HUH?
LUCY ONLY HAS HER SEVIPER LEFT?!
HER OPPONENT IS BADLY POISONED...
BUT SHE'S IN A PRETTY TOUGH SPOT RIGHT NOW!
YOU CAN DO IT, LUCY!
SHOW THAT BRAT WHAT YOU'VE GOT—THE POWER OF A FRONTIER BRAIN!
GIGA DRAIN!!

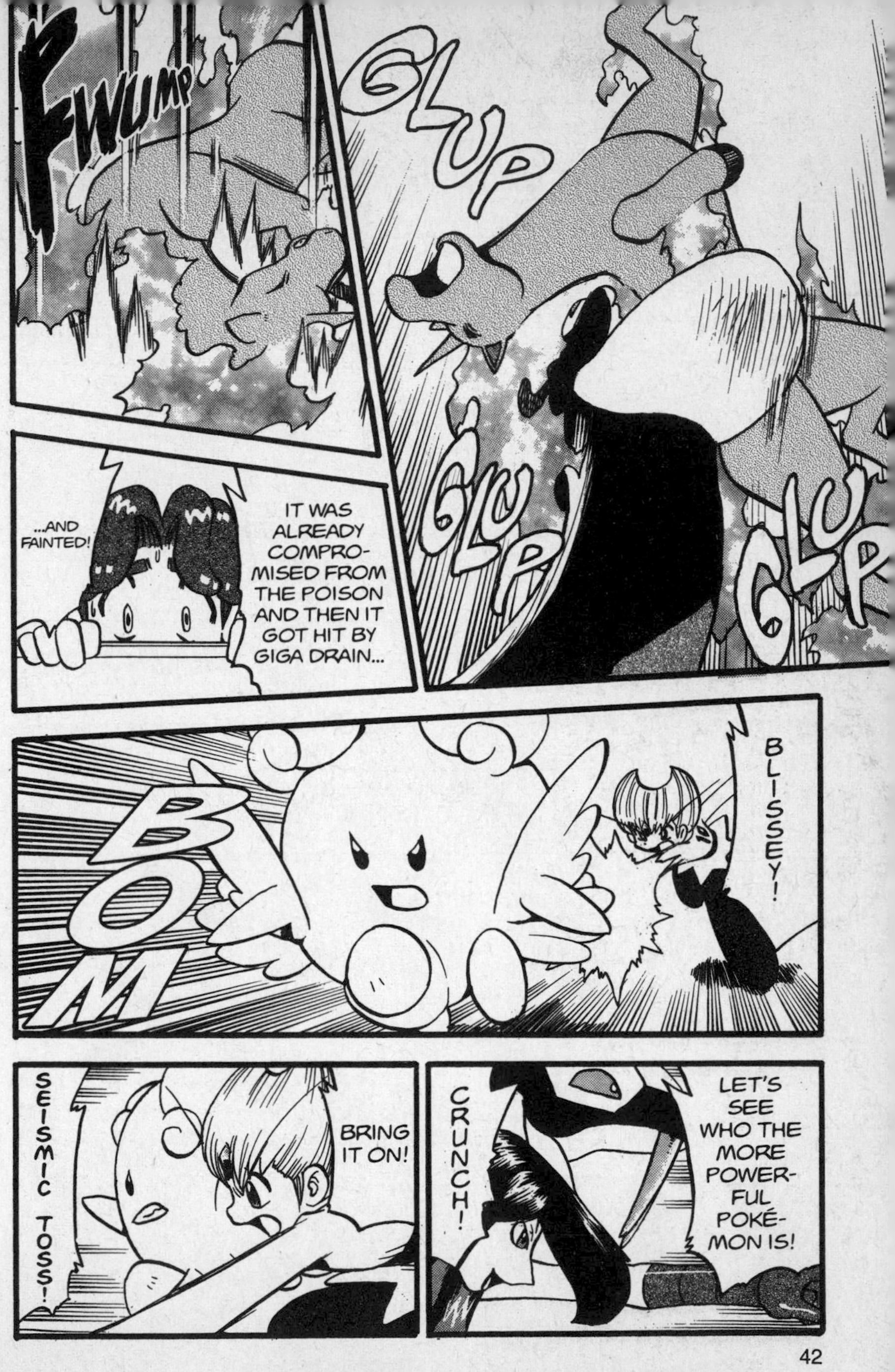
GLUP
GLUP
GLUP
FWUMP
IT WAS ALREADY COMPROMISED FROM THE POISON AND THEN IT GOT HIT BY GIGA DRAIN...
...AND FAINTED!
BLISSEY!
BOOM
LET'S SEE WHO THE MORE POWERFUL POKÉMON IS!
CRUNCH!
BRING IT ON!
SEISMIC TOSS!

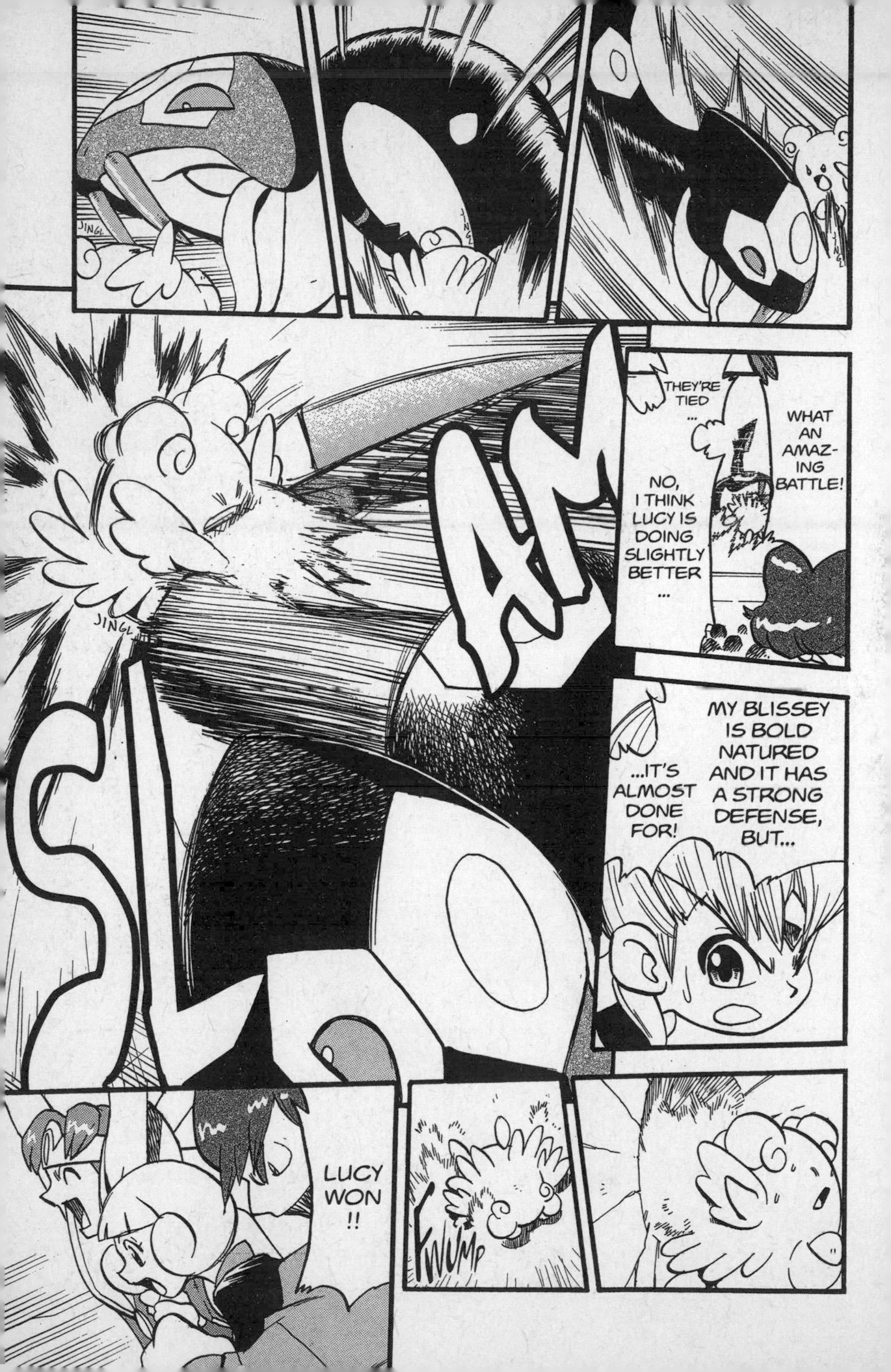
JINGL
JINGL
JINGL
WHAT AN AMAZ-ING BATTLE!
THEY'RE TIED ...
NO, I THINK LUCY IS DOING SLIGHTLY BETTER ...
MY BLISSEY IS BOLD NATURED AND IT HAS A STRONG DEFENSE, BUT...
...IT'S ALMOST DONE FOR!
JINGL
SLAM
FWUMP
LUCY WON !!

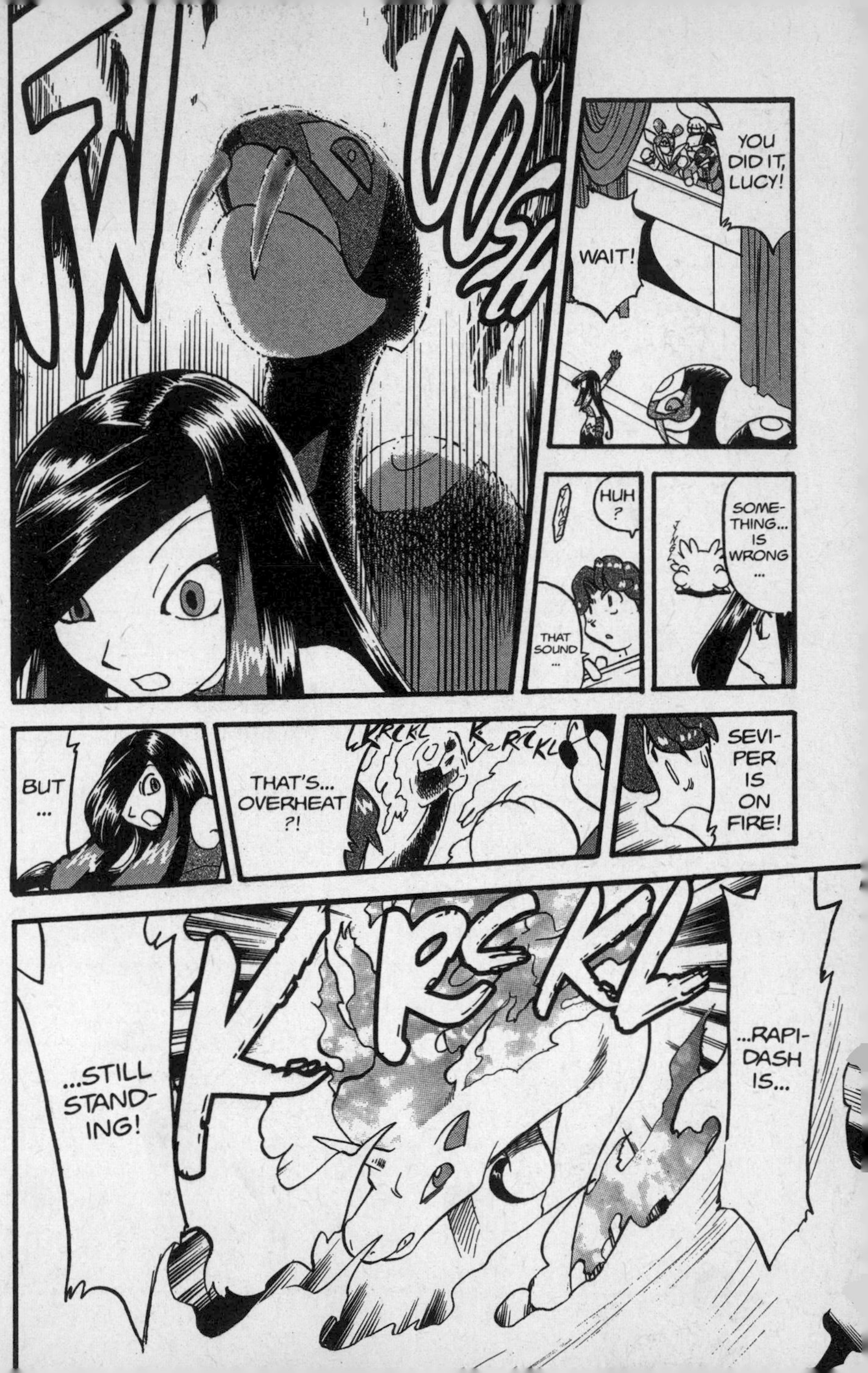
YOU DID IT, LUCY!
WAIT!
SOME-THING... IS WRONG...
HUH?
THAT SOUND...
SWOOSH
SEVI-PER IS ON FIRE!
KRCKL KRCKL
THAT'S... OVERHEAT?!
BUT...
...RAPI-DASH IS...
KRCKL
...STILL STAND-ING!

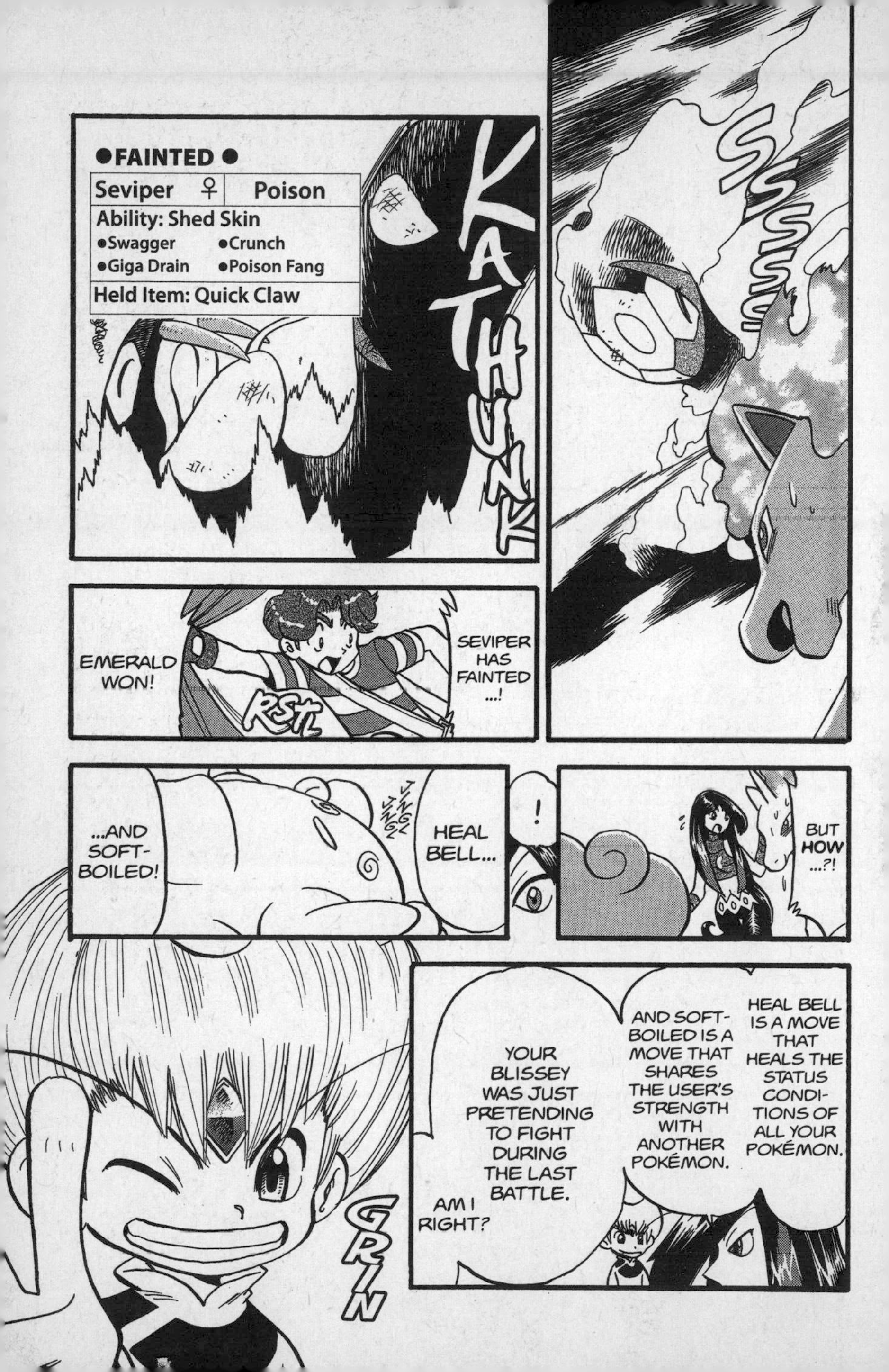
SSSSU
●FAINTED●
Seviper ♀ Poison
Ability: Shed Skin
●Swagger ●Crunch
●Giga Drain ●Poison Fang
Held Item: Quick Claw
KATHUNK
SEVIPER HAS FAINTED ...!
EMERALD WON!
RSTL
BUT HOW ...?!
!
HEAL BELL...
JINGL JINGL
...AND SOFT-BOILED!
HEAL BELL IS A MOVE THAT HEALS THE STATUS CONDITIONS OF ALL YOUR POKÉMON.
AND SOFT-BOILED IS A MOVE THAT SHARES THE USER'S STRENGTH WITH ANOTHER POKÉMON.
YOUR BLISSEY WAS JUST PRETENDING TO FIGHT DURING THE LAST BATTLE.
AM I RIGHT?
GRIN

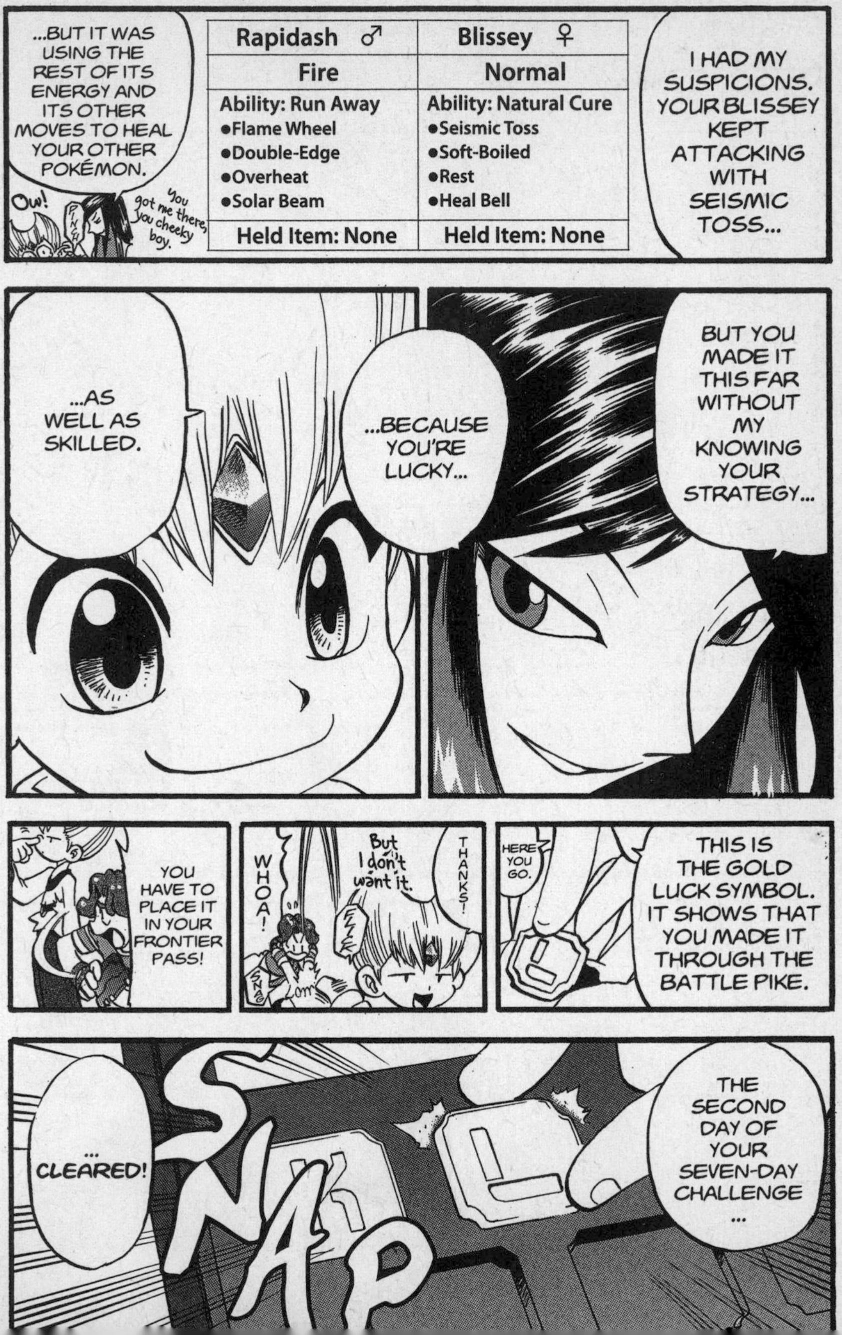
I HAD MY SUSPICIONS. YOUR BLISSEY KEPT ATTACKING WITH SEISMIC TOSS...
Rapidash ♂ | Blissey ♀
Fire | Normal
Ability: Run Away | Ability: Natural Cure
●Flame Wheel | ●Seismic Toss
●Double-Edge | ●Soft-Boiled
●Overheat | ●Rest
●Solar Beam | ●Heal Bell
Held Item: None | Held Item: None
...BUT IT WAS USING THE REST OF ITS ENERGY AND ITS OTHER MOVES TO HEAL YOUR OTHER POKÉMON.
You got me there, you cheeky boy.
Ow!
BUT YOU MADE IT THIS FAR WITHOUT MY KNOWING YOUR STRATEGY...
...BECAUSE YOU'RE LUCKY...
...AS WELL AS SKILLED.
THIS IS THE GOLD LUCK SYMBOL. IT SHOWS THAT YOU MADE IT THROUGH THE BATTLE PIKE.
HERE YOU GO.
THANKS!
But I don't want it.
WHOA!
YOU HAVE TO PLACE IT IN YOUR FRONTIER PASS!
THE SECOND DAY OF YOUR SEVEN-DAY CHALLENGE...
...CLEARED!
SNAP

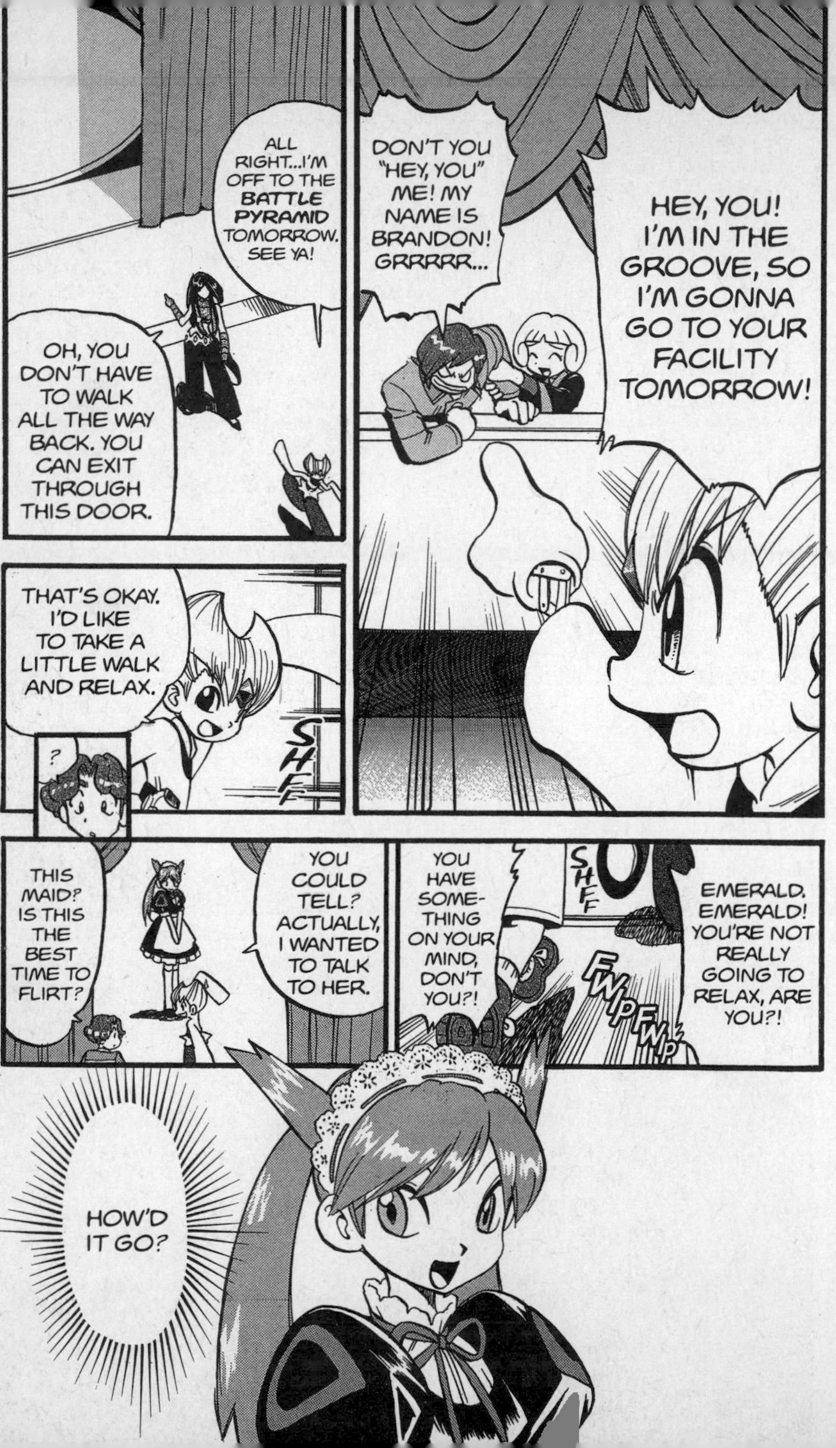
HEY, YOU! I'M IN THE GROOVE, SO I'M GONNA GO TO YOUR FACILITY TOMORROW!
DON'T YOU "HEY, YOU" ME! MY NAME IS BRANDON! GRRRRR...
ALL RIGHT...I'M OFF TO THE **BATTLE PYRAMID** TOMORROW. SEE YA!
OH, YOU DON'T HAVE TO WALK ALL THE WAY BACK. YOU CAN EXIT THROUGH THIS DOOR.
THAT'S OKAY. I'D LIKE TO TAKE A LITTLE WALK AND RELAX.
SHFF
?
EMERALD. EMERALD! YOU'RE NOT REALLY GOING TO RELAX, ARE YOU?!
SHFF
FWIPFWIP
YOU HAVE SOME-THING ON YOUR MIND, DON'T YOU?!
YOU COULD TELL? ACTUALLY, I WANTED TO TALK TO HER.
THIS MAID? IS THIS THE BEST TIME TO FLIRT?
HOW'D IT GO?

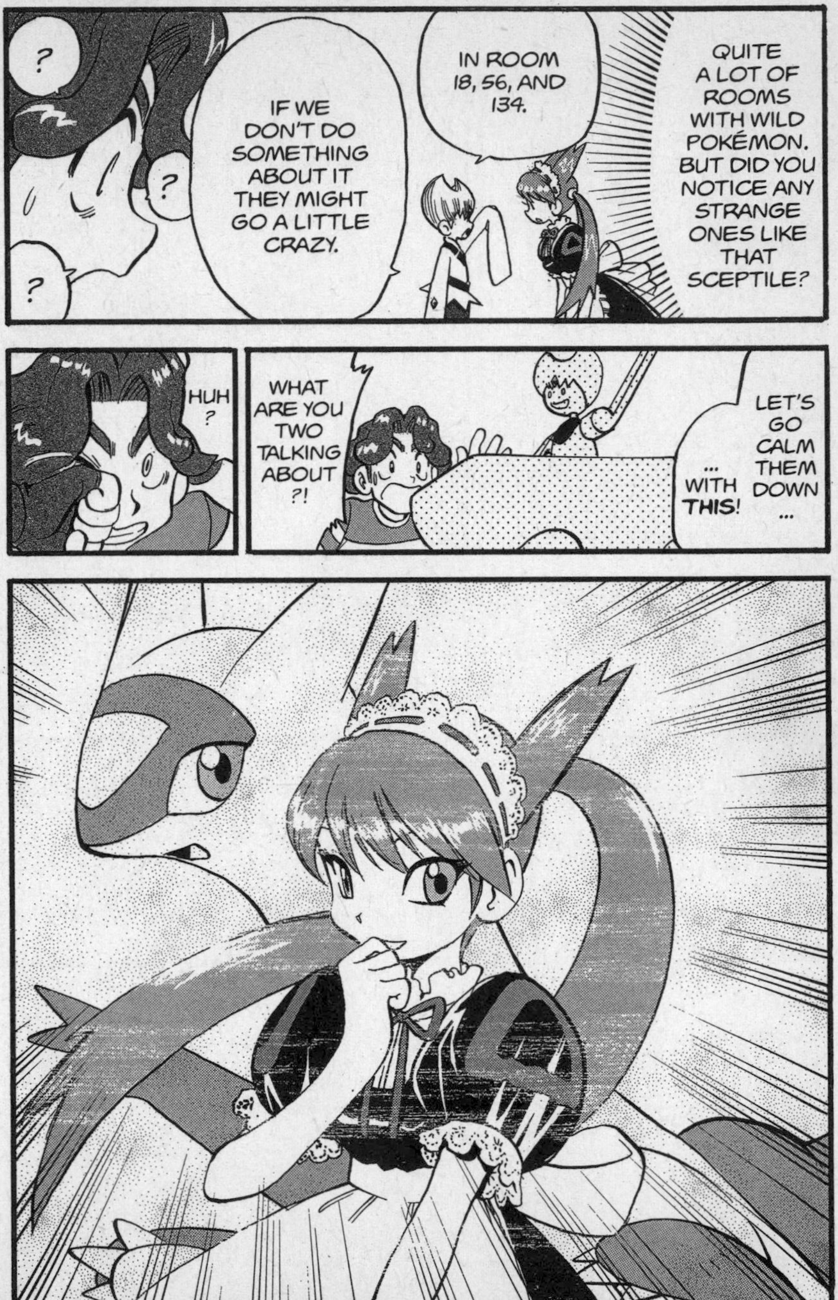
QUITE A LOT OF ROOMS WITH WILD POKÉMON. BUT DID YOU NOTICE ANY STRANGE ONES LIKE THAT SCEPTILE?
IN ROOM 18, 56, AND 134.
IF WE DON'T DO SOMETHING ABOUT IT THEY MIGHT GO A LITTLE CRAZY.
?
?
?
LET'S GO CALM THEM DOWN ...
... WITH THIS!
WHAT ARE YOU TWO TALKING ABOUT ?!
HUH ?

DEAR MEMBERS OF THE PRESS...

Thank you for visiting the Battle Frontier today. Permit me to continue explaining the rules of this facility...

OWNER: SCOTT

FACILITY RULES

BATTLE PYRAMID

Battle-type	Number of Pokémon	Type of Symbol	Wins needed to attain the Symbol
•Single •Double •Wild	3 Pokémon	Brave	Seven Floors X 10 Rounds = 70 Floors

The Trainer must go through a pyramid with changing floor patterns and climb to the top. It is dark inside the pyramid, but the floor will gradually light up as you win battles against wild Pokémon and Trainers. There are also Trainers inside who will provide hints to aid challengers in finding their goal.

There is a warp tile on each floor of the pyramid which transports the challenger up to the next floor. The challenger must climb up seven floors and reach the top floor of a level to complete one round.

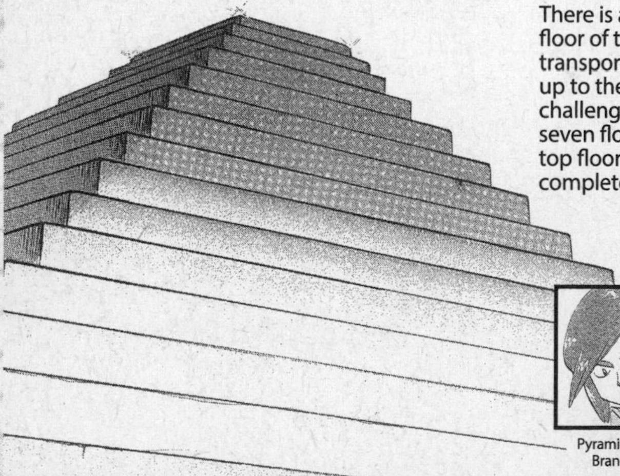

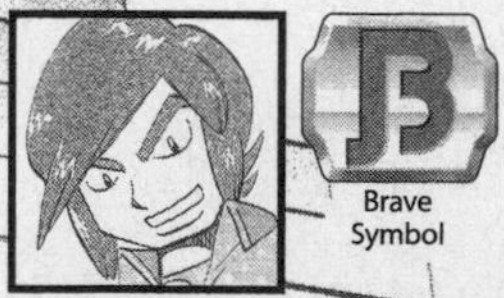

Pyramid King Brandon

Brave Symbol

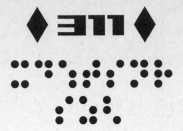

A Dust-Up with Dusclops

POKÉMON ADVENTURES•THE SIXTH CHAPTER•EMERALD

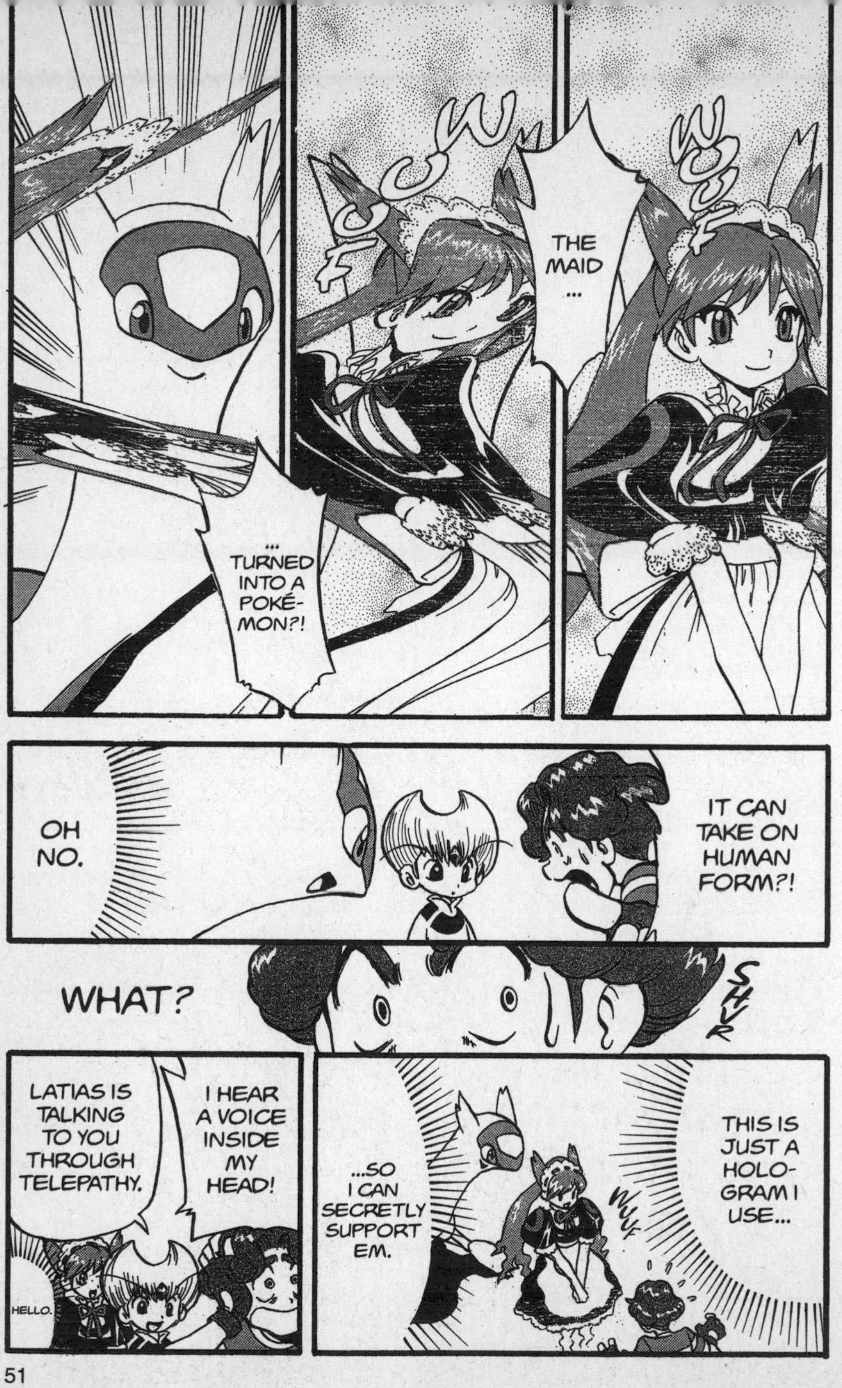
WOOF
THE MAID ...
... TURNED INTO A POKÉMON?!
IT CAN TAKE ON HUMAN FORM?!
OH NO.
WHAT?
THIS IS JUST A HOLOGRAM I USE...
...SO I CAN SECRETLY SUPPORT EM.
I HEAR A VOICE INSIDE MY HEAD!
LATIAS IS TALKING TO YOU THROUGH TELEPATHY.
HELLO.

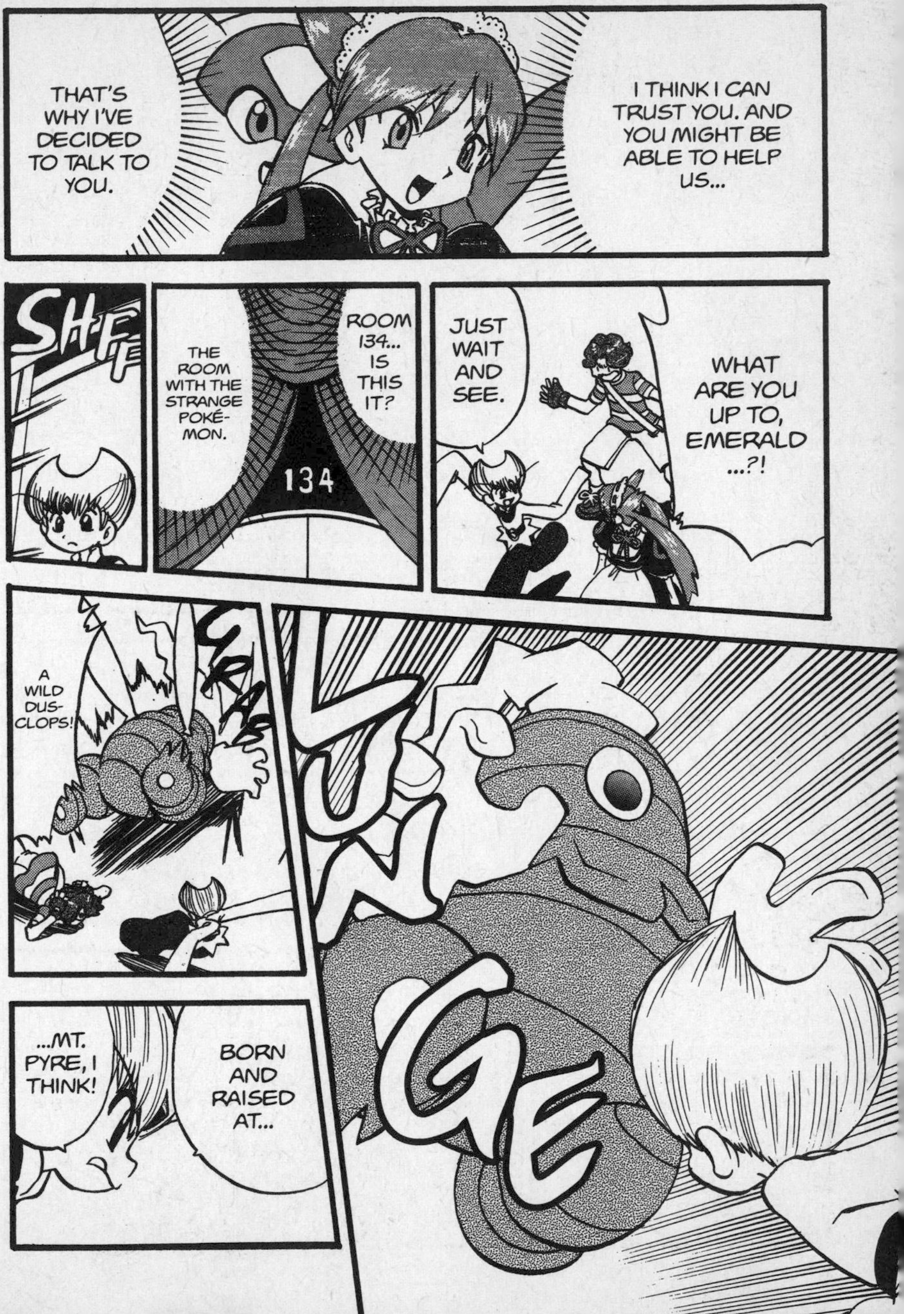

I THINK I CAN TRUST YOU. AND YOU MIGHT BE ABLE TO HELP US...
THAT'S WHY I'VE DECIDED TO TALK TO YOU.
WHAT ARE YOU UP TO, EMERALD ...?!
JUST WAIT AND SEE.
ROOM 134... IS THIS IT?
THE ROOM WITH THE STRANGE POKÉMON.
134
SHFF
LUNGE
A WILD DUS-CLOPS!
BORN AND RAISED AT...
...MT. PYRE, I THINK!

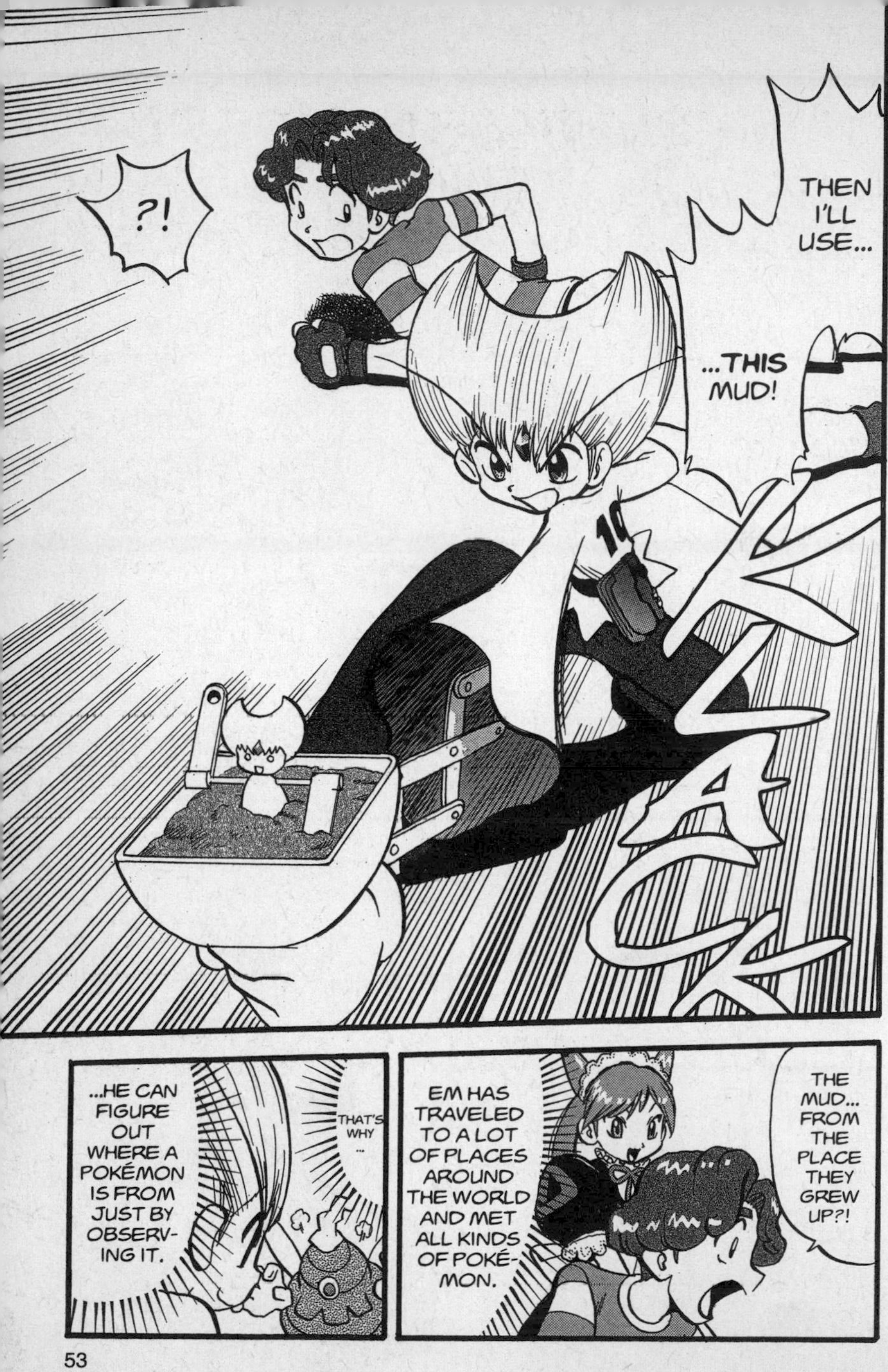
THEN I'LL USE...
...THIS MUD!
?!
THE MUD... FROM THE PLACE THEY GREW UP?!
EM HAS TRAVELED TO A LOT OF PLACES AROUND THE WORLD AND MET ALL KINDS OF POKÉMON.
THAT'S WHY...
...HE CAN FIGURE OUT WHERE A POKÉMON IS FROM JUST BY OBSERVING IT.

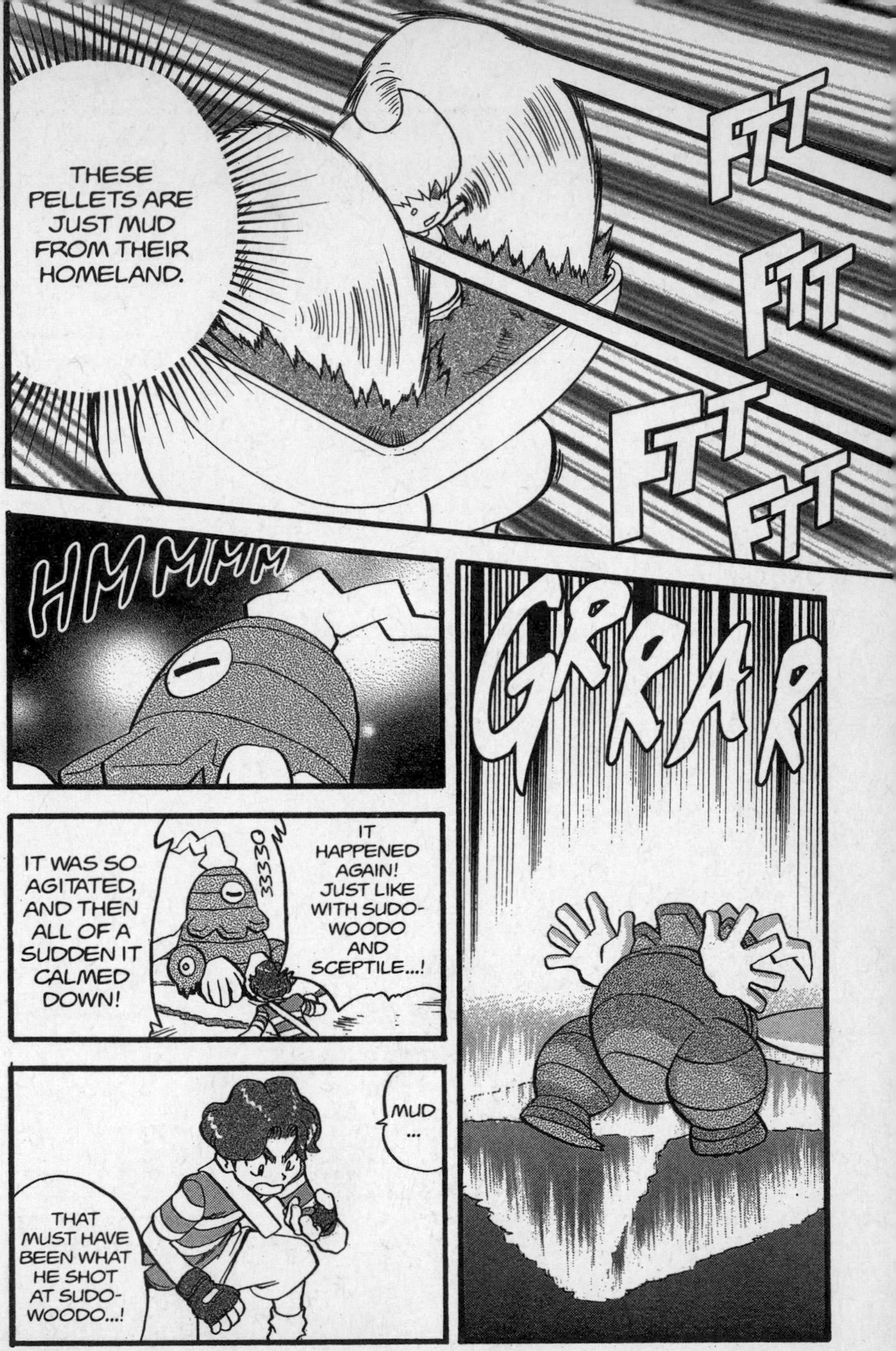
THESE PELLETS ARE JUST MUD FROM THEIR HOMELAND.
FTT
FTT
FTT
FTT
GRRAR
HMMMM
IT HAPPENED AGAIN! JUST LIKE WITH SUDO-WOODO AND SCEPTILE...!
MMMM
IT WAS SO AGITATED, AND THEN ALL OF A SUDDEN IT CALMED DOWN!
MUD...
THAT MUST HAVE BEEN WHAT HE SHOT AT SUDO-WOODO...!

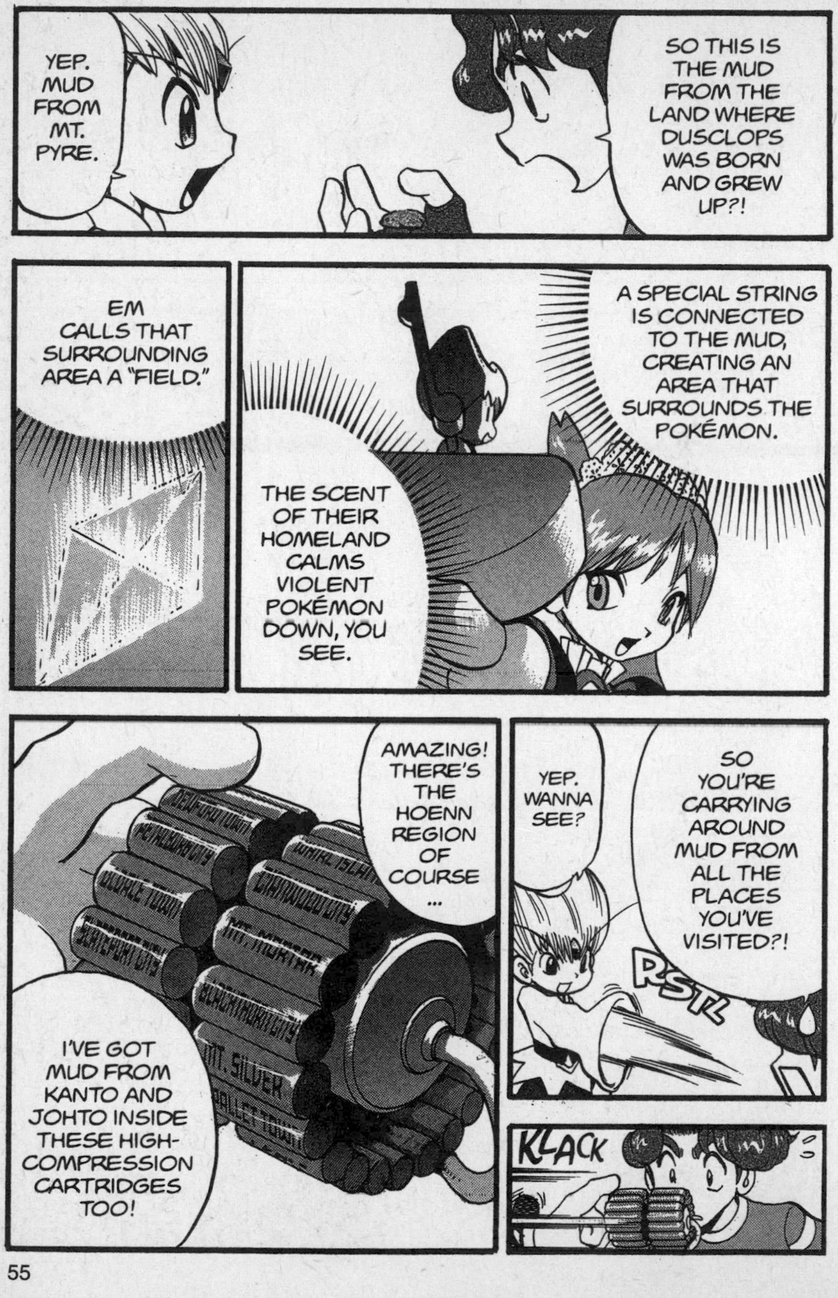
SO THIS IS THE MUD FROM THE LAND WHERE DUSCLOPS WAS BORN AND GREW UP?!
YEP. MUD FROM MT. PYRE.
A SPECIAL STRING IS CONNECTED TO THE MUD, CREATING AN AREA THAT SURROUNDS THE POKÉMON.
THE SCENT OF THEIR HOMELAND CALMS VIOLENT POKÉMON DOWN, YOU SEE.
EM CALLS THAT SURROUNDING AREA A "FIELD."
SO YOU'RE CARRYING AROUND MUD FROM ALL THE PLACES YOU'VE VISITED?!
YEP. WANNA SEE?
RSTL
KLACK
AMAZING! THERE'S THE HOENN REGION OF COURSE ...
MT. MORTAR
MT. SILVER
I'VE GOT MUD FROM KANTO AND JOHTO INSIDE THESE HIGH-COMPRESSION CARTRIDGES TOO!

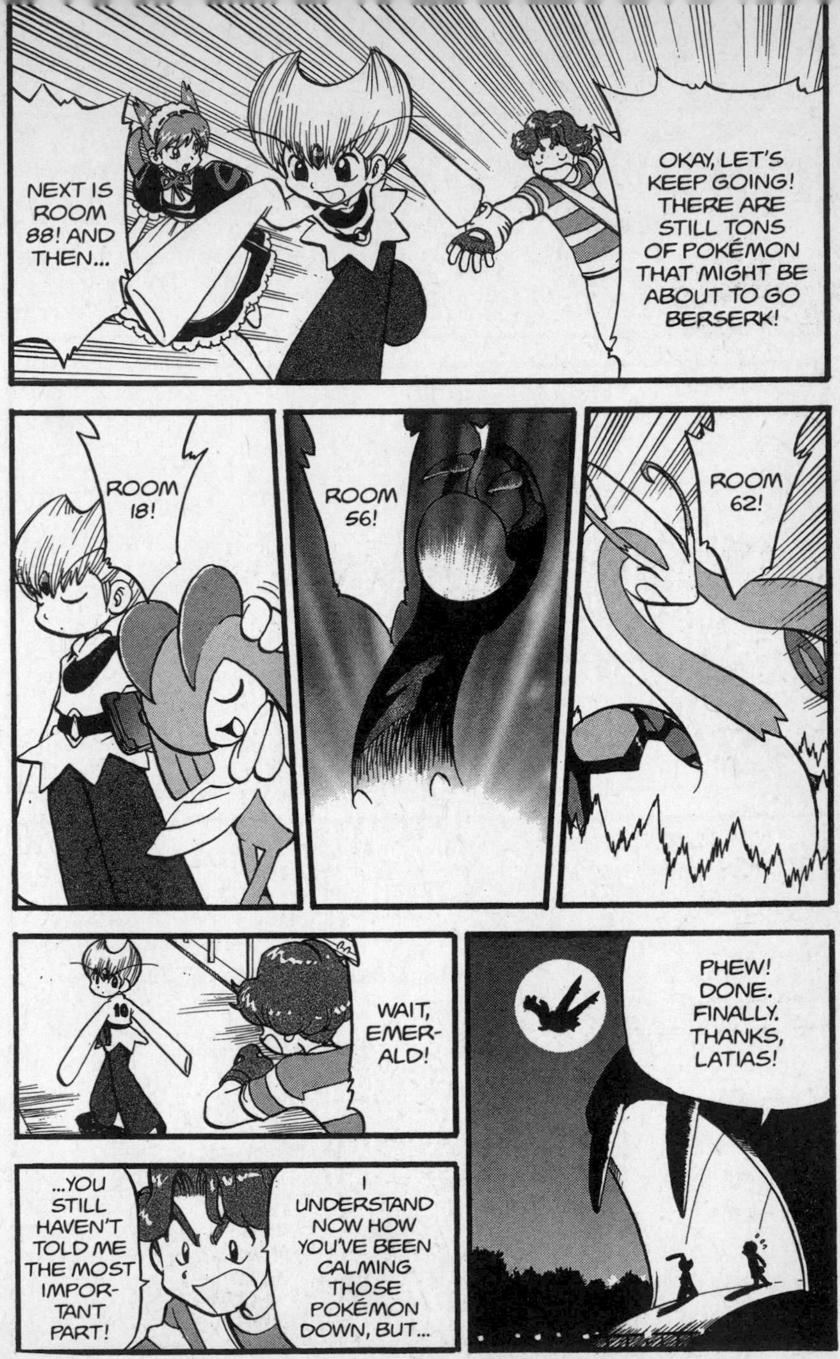
OKAY, LET'S KEEP GOING! THERE ARE STILL TONS OF POKÉMON THAT MIGHT BE ABOUT TO GO BERSERK!
NEXT IS ROOM 88! AND THEN...
ROOM 62!
ROOM 56!
ROOM 18!
PHEW! DONE. FINALLY. THANKS, LATIAS!
WAIT, EMERALD!
I UNDERSTAND NOW HOW YOU'VE BEEN CALMING THOSE POKÉMON DOWN, BUT...
...YOU STILL HAVEN'T TOLD ME THE MOST IMPORTANT PART!

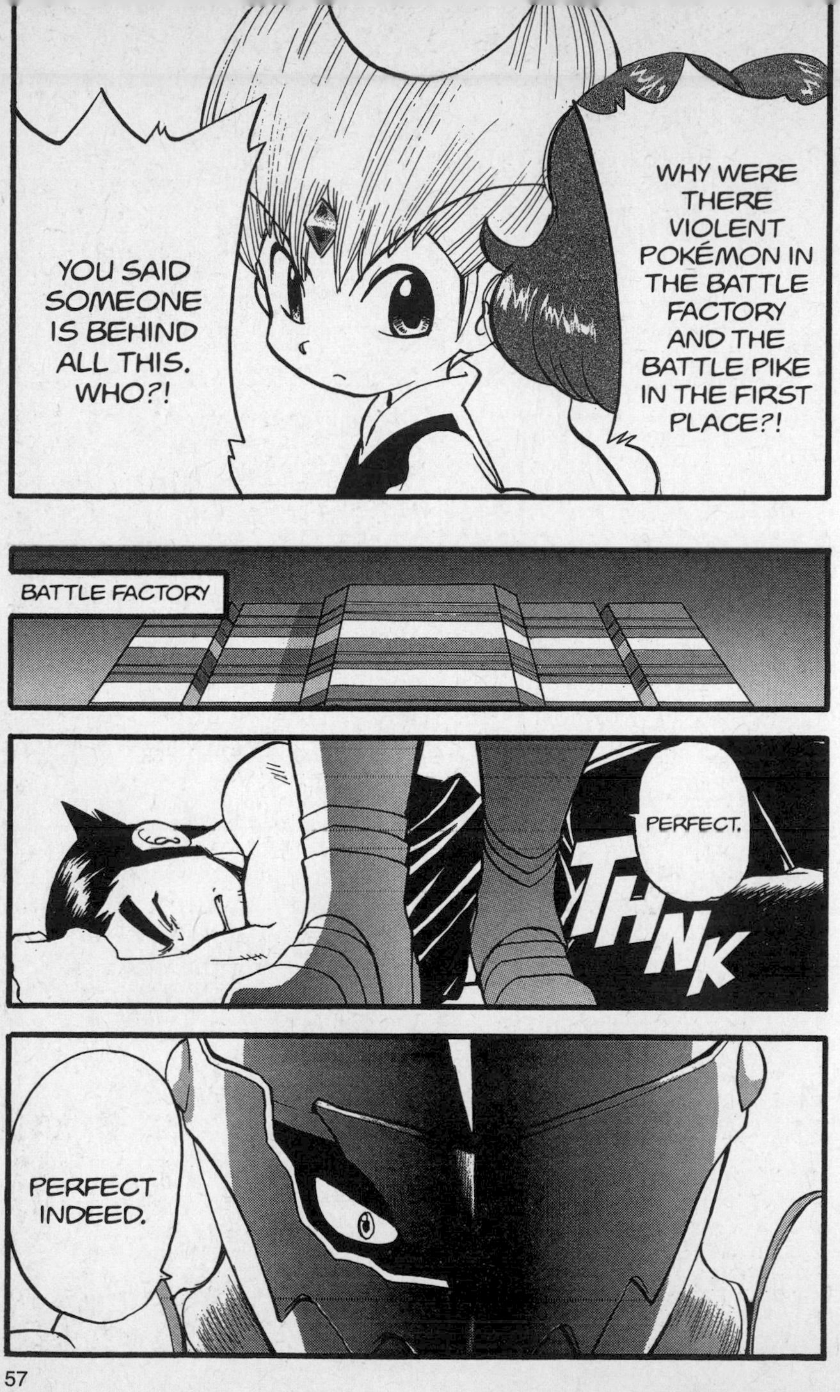
WHY WERE THERE VIOLENT POKÉMON IN THE BATTLE FACTORY AND THE BATTLE PIKE IN THE FIRST PLACE?!
YOU SAID SOMEONE IS BEHIND ALL THIS. WHO?!
BATTLE FACTORY
PERFECT.
THNK
PERFECT INDEED.

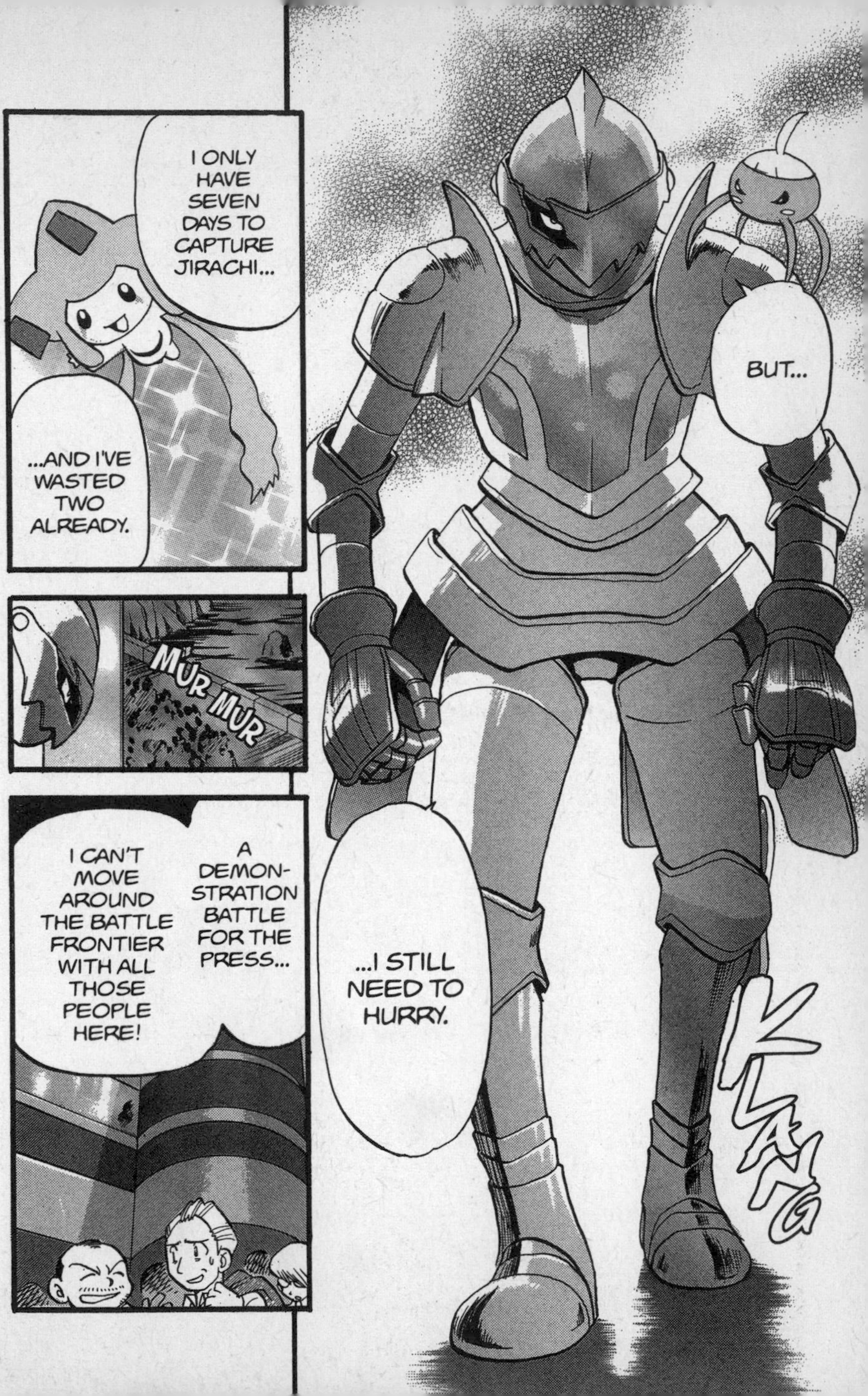
I ONLY HAVE SEVEN DAYS TO CAPTURE JIRACHI...
...AND I'VE WASTED TWO ALREADY.
MUR MUR
A DEMONSTRATION BATTLE FOR THE PRESS...
I CAN'T MOVE AROUND THE BATTLE FRONTIER WITH ALL THOSE PEOPLE HERE!
BUT...
...I STILL NEED TO HURRY.
KLANG

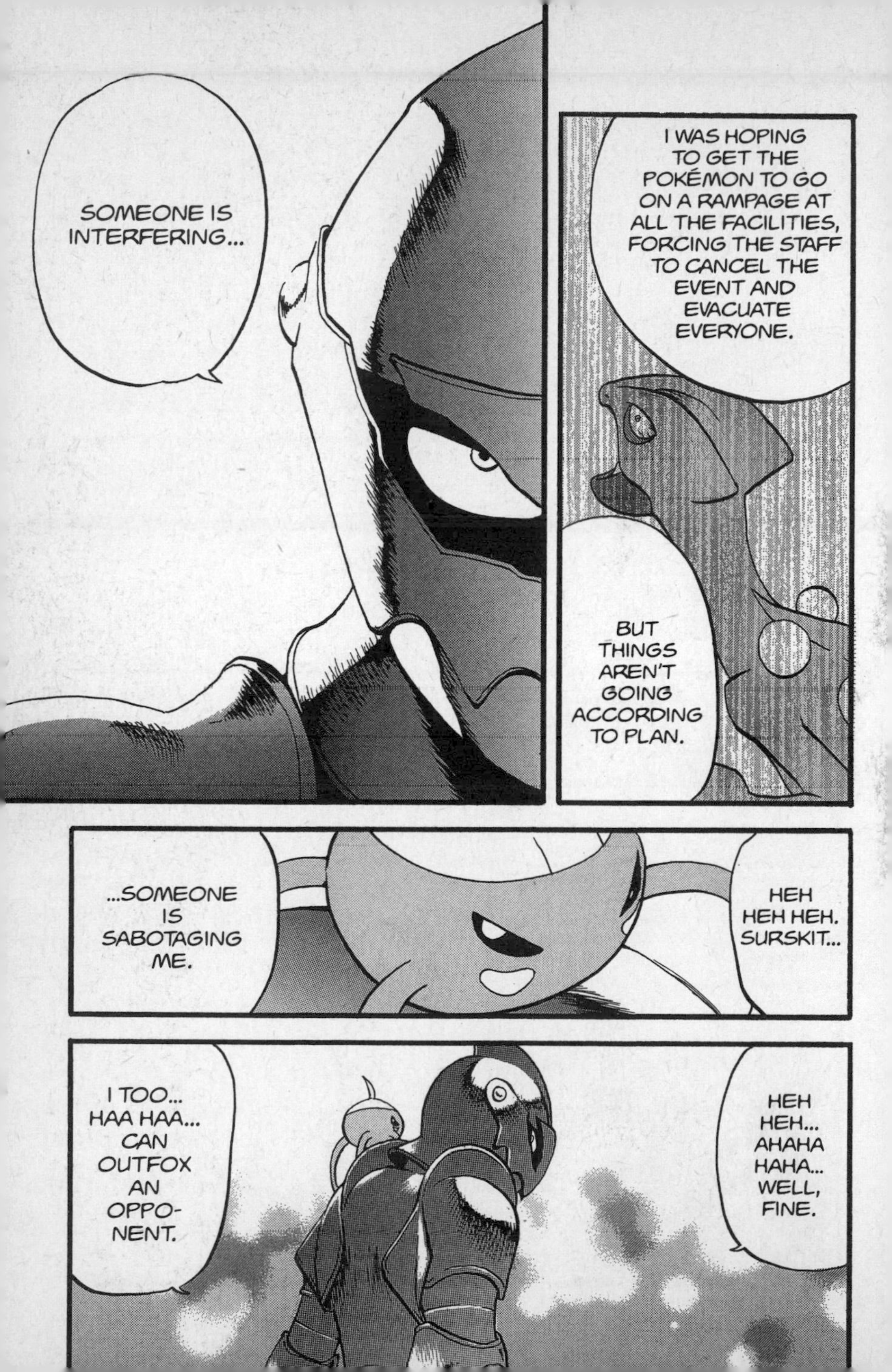
I WAS HOPING TO GET THE POKÉMON TO GO ON A RAMPAGE AT ALL THE FACILITIES, FORCING THE STAFF TO CANCEL THE EVENT AND EVACUATE EVERYONE.
BUT THINGS AREN'T GOING ACCORDING TO PLAN.
SOMEONE IS INTERFERING...
HEH HEH HEH. SURSKIT...
...SOMEONE IS SABOTAGING ME.
HEH HEH... AHAHA HAHA... WELL, FINE.
I TOO... HAA HAA... CAN OUTFOX AN OPPO-NENT.

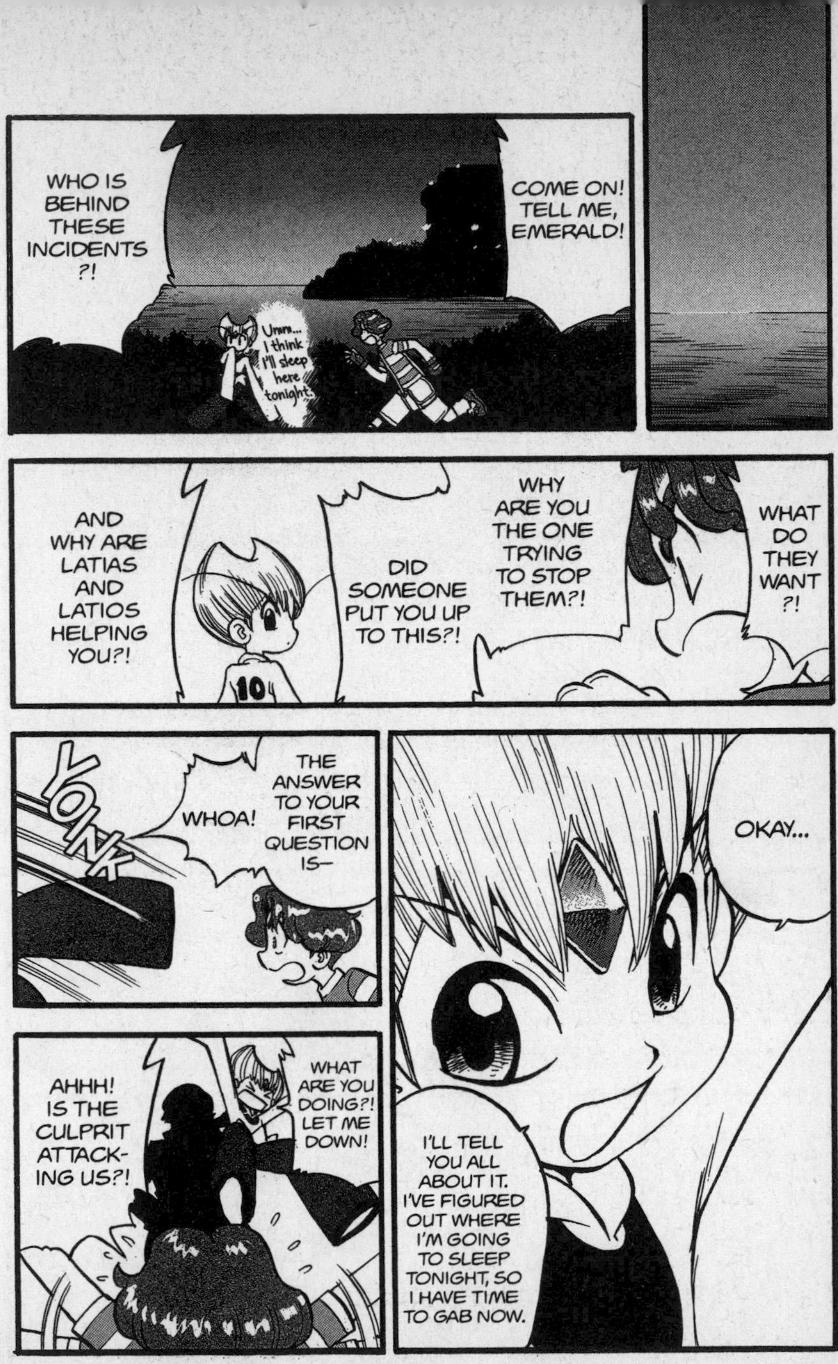
COME ON! TELL ME, EMERALD!
WHO IS BEHIND THESE INCIDENTS ?!
Umm... I think I'll sleep here tonight.
WHAT DO THEY WANT ?!
WHY ARE YOU THE ONE TRYING TO STOP THEM?!
DID SOMEONE PUT YOU UP TO THIS?!
AND WHY ARE LATIAS AND LATIOS HELPING YOU?!
OKAY...
I'LL TELL YOU ALL ABOUT IT. I'VE FIGURED OUT WHERE I'M GOING TO SLEEP TONIGHT, SO I HAVE TIME TO GAB NOW.
THE ANSWER TO YOUR FIRST QUESTION IS—
WHOA!
YOINK
WHAT ARE YOU DOING?! LET ME DOWN!
AHHH! IS THE CULPRIT ATTACKING US?!

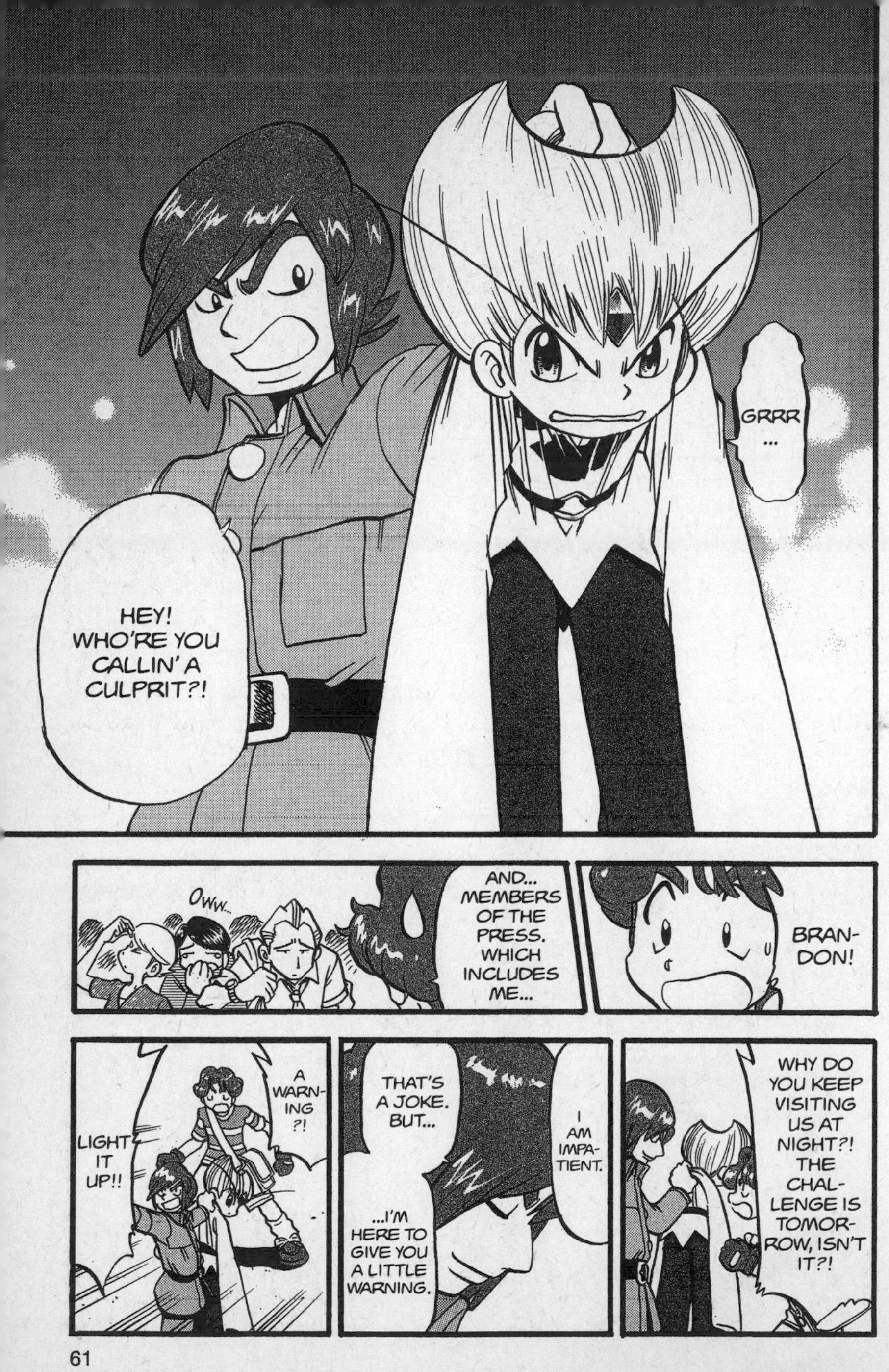
GRRR...
HEY! WHO'RE YOU CALLIN' A CULPRIT?!
BRAN-DON!
AND... MEMBERS OF THE PRESS. WHICH INCLUDES ME...
OWW...
WHY DO YOU KEEP VISITING US AT NIGHT?! THE CHAL-LENGE IS TOMOR-ROW, ISN'T IT?!
I AM IMPA-TIENT.
THAT'S A JOKE. BUT...
...I'M HERE TO GIVE YOU A LITTLE WARNING.
A WARN-ING?!
LIGHT IT UP!!

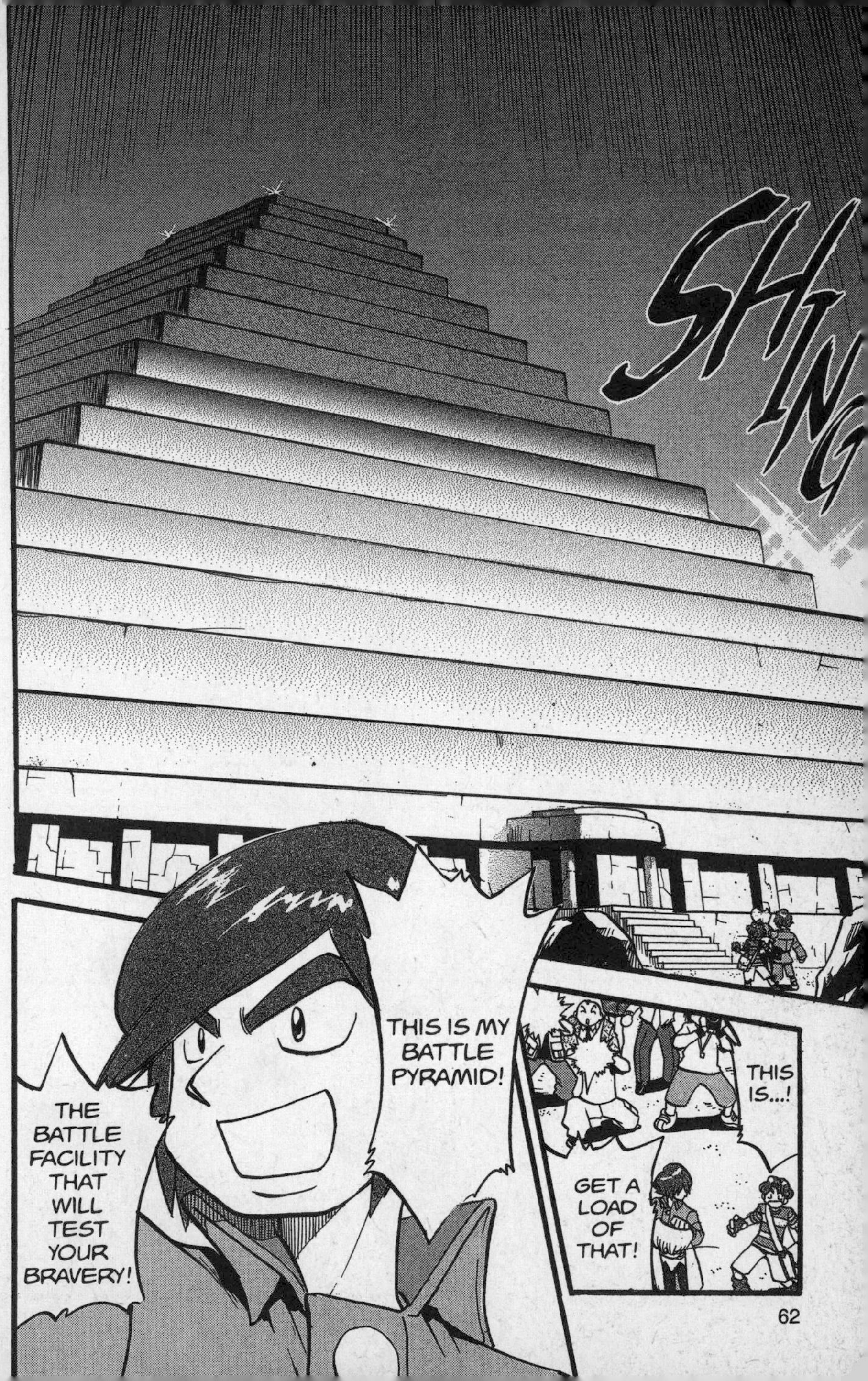
SHING
THIS IS...!
GET A LOAD OF THAT!
THIS IS MY BATTLE PYRAMID!
THE BATTLE FACILITY THAT WILL TEST YOUR BRAVERY!

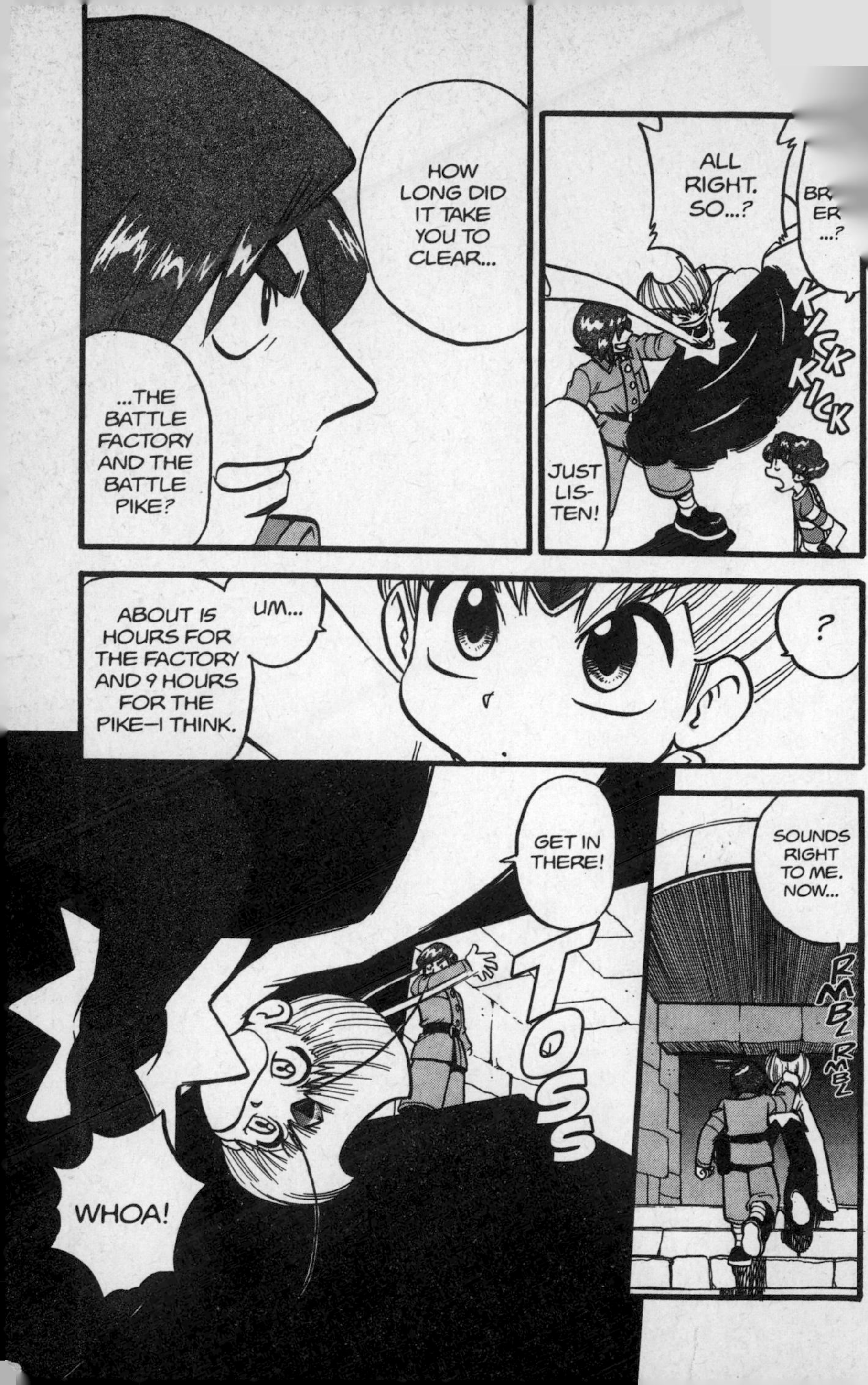
BR
ER
...?
ALL RIGHT. SO...?
KICK KICK
JUST LISTEN!
HOW LONG DID IT TAKE YOU TO CLEAR...
...THE BATTLE FACTORY AND THE BATTLE PIKE?
?
UM...
ABOUT 15 HOURS FOR THE FACTORY AND 9 HOURS FOR THE PIKE—I THINK.
SOUNDS RIGHT TO ME. NOW...
RMBL RMBL
GET IN THERE!
TOSS
WHOA!

THUNK
OW!
?!
THIS IS WHAT IT'S LIKE INSIDE THE PYRAMID?!
IT'S PITCH BLACK IN HERE!
OKAY.
COME BACK HERE NOW.
YOU DON'T HAVE TO TELL ME TWICE!
HUH?! A DEAD-END!
THIS WAY...?
WHA—?
PHEW! I FINALLY FOUND THE WAY OUT.
NICE WORK.
ONE MORE TIME.
TOSS
AHHHHH!

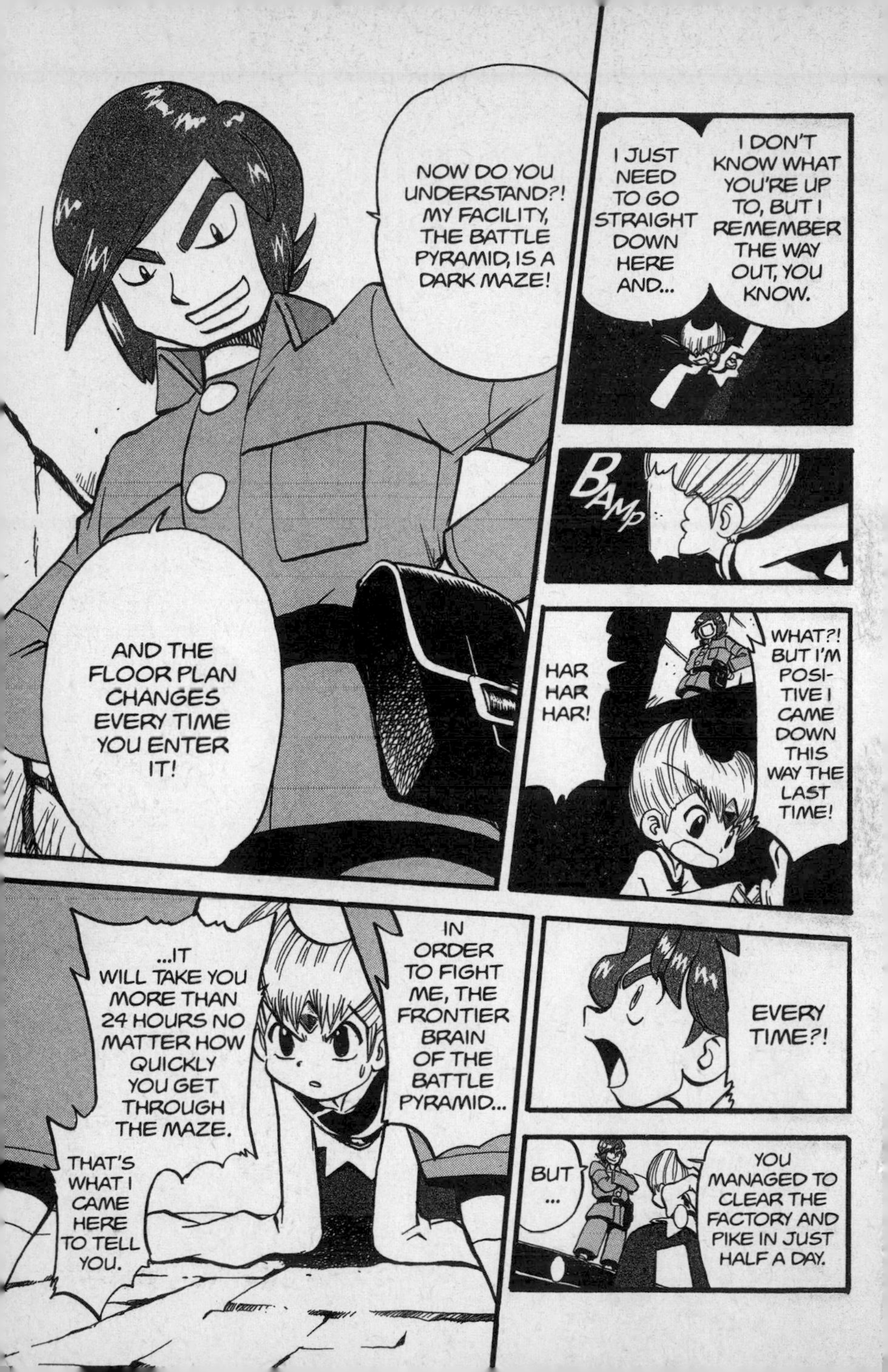
I DON'T KNOW WHAT YOU'RE UP TO, BUT I REMEMBER THE WAY OUT, YOU KNOW.
I JUST NEED TO GO STRAIGHT DOWN HERE AND...
BAMP
WHAT?! BUT I'M POSI-TIVE I CAME DOWN THIS WAY THE LAST TIME!
HAR HAR HAR!
NOW DO YOU UNDERSTAND?! MY FACILITY, THE BATTLE PYRAMID, IS A DARK MAZE!
AND THE FLOOR PLAN CHANGES EVERY TIME YOU ENTER IT!
EVERY TIME?!
YOU MANAGED TO CLEAR THE FACTORY AND PIKE IN JUST HALF A DAY.
BUT ...
IN ORDER TO FIGHT ME, THE FRONTIER BRAIN OF THE BATTLE PYRAMID...
...IT WILL TAKE YOU MORE THAN 24 HOURS NO MATTER HOW QUICKLY YOU GET THROUGH THE MAZE.
THAT'S WHAT I CAME HERE TO TELL YOU.

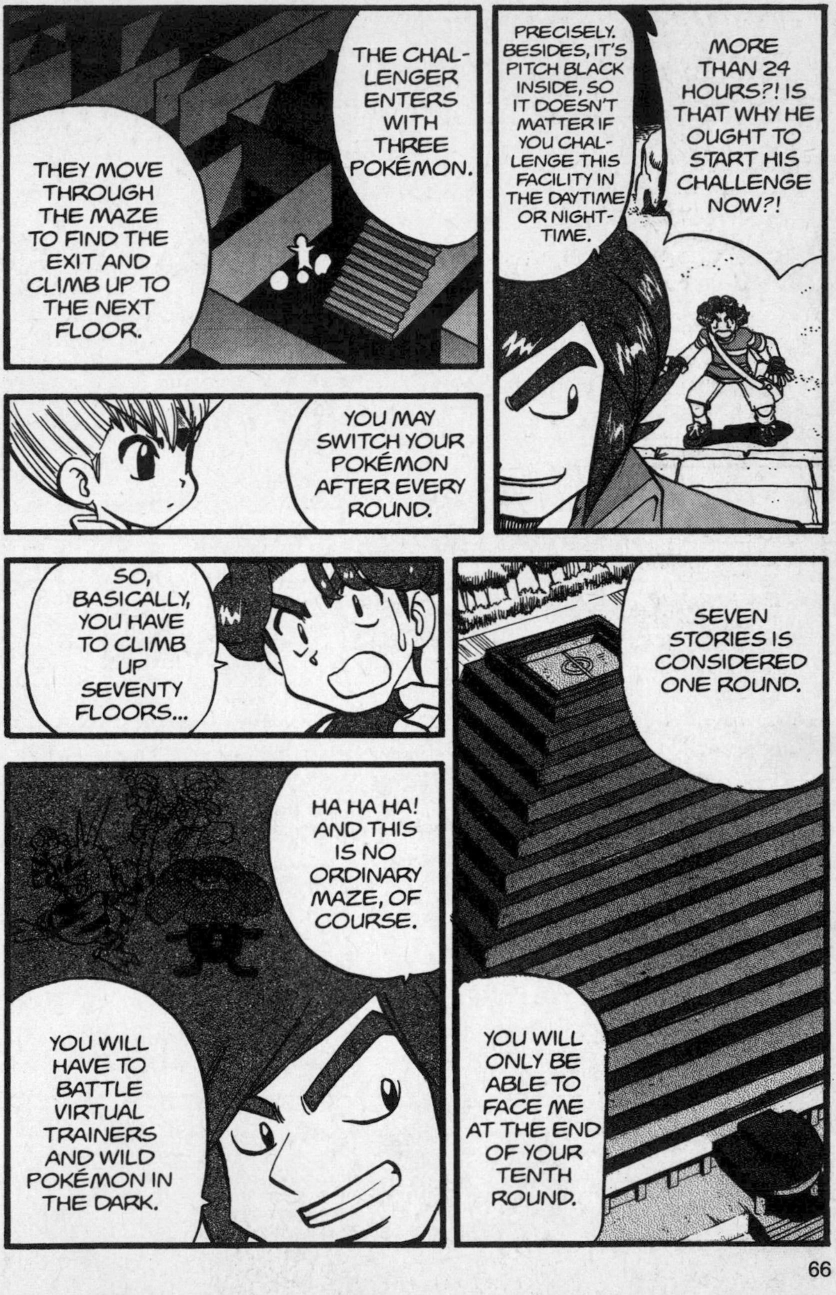
MORE THAN 24 HOURS?! IS THAT WHY HE OUGHT TO START HIS CHALLENGE NOW?!
PRECISELY. BESIDES, IT'S PITCH BLACK INSIDE, SO IT DOESN'T MATTER IF YOU CHALLENGE THIS FACILITY IN THE DAYTIME OR NIGHTTIME.
THE CHALLENGER ENTERS WITH THREE POKÉMON.
THEY MOVE THROUGH THE MAZE TO FIND THE EXIT AND CLIMB UP TO THE NEXT FLOOR.
YOU MAY SWITCH YOUR POKÉMON AFTER EVERY ROUND.
SEVEN STORIES IS CONSIDERED ONE ROUND.
YOU WILL ONLY BE ABLE TO FACE ME AT THE END OF YOUR TENTH ROUND.
SO, BASICALLY, YOU HAVE TO CLIMB UP SEVENTY FLOORS...
HA HA HA! AND THIS IS NO ORDINARY MAZE, OF COURSE.
YOU WILL HAVE TO BATTLE VIRTUAL TRAINERS AND WILD POKÉMON IN THE DARK.

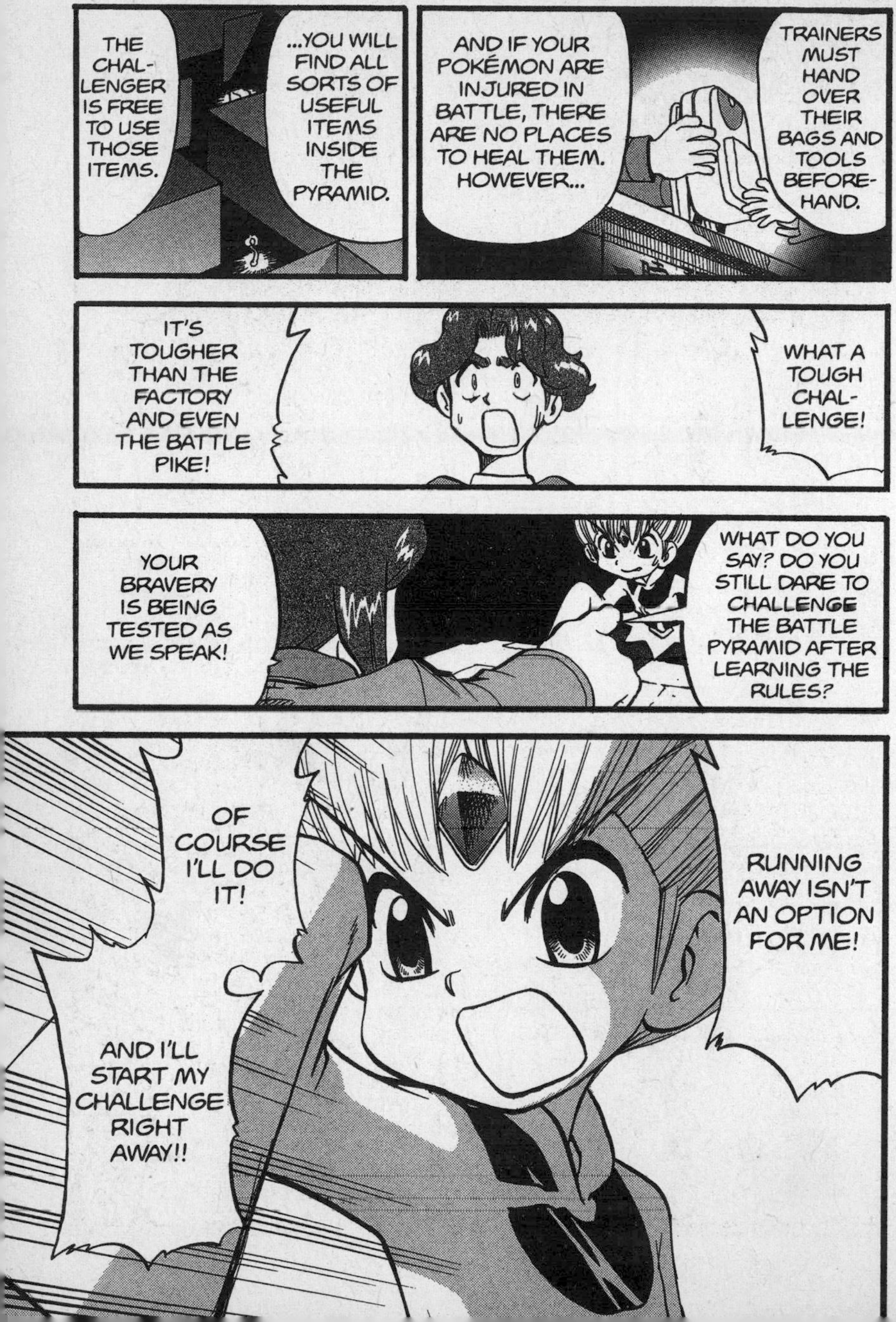

TRAINERS MUST HAND OVER THEIR BAGS AND TOOLS BEFOREHAND.
AND IF YOUR POKÉMON ARE INJURED IN BATTLE, THERE ARE NO PLACES TO HEAL THEM. HOWEVER...
...YOU WILL FIND ALL SORTS OF USEFUL ITEMS INSIDE THE PYRAMID.
THE CHALLENGER IS FREE TO USE THOSE ITEMS.
WHAT A TOUGH CHALLENGE!
IT'S TOUGHER THAN THE FACTORY AND EVEN THE BATTLE PIKE!
WHAT DO YOU SAY? DO YOU STILL DARE TO CHALLENGE THE BATTLE PYRAMID AFTER LEARNING THE RULES?
YOUR BRAVERY IS BEING TESTED AS WE SPEAK!
RUNNING AWAY ISN'T AN OPTION FOR ME!
OF COURSE I'LL DO IT!
AND I'LL START MY CHALLENGE RIGHT AWAY!!

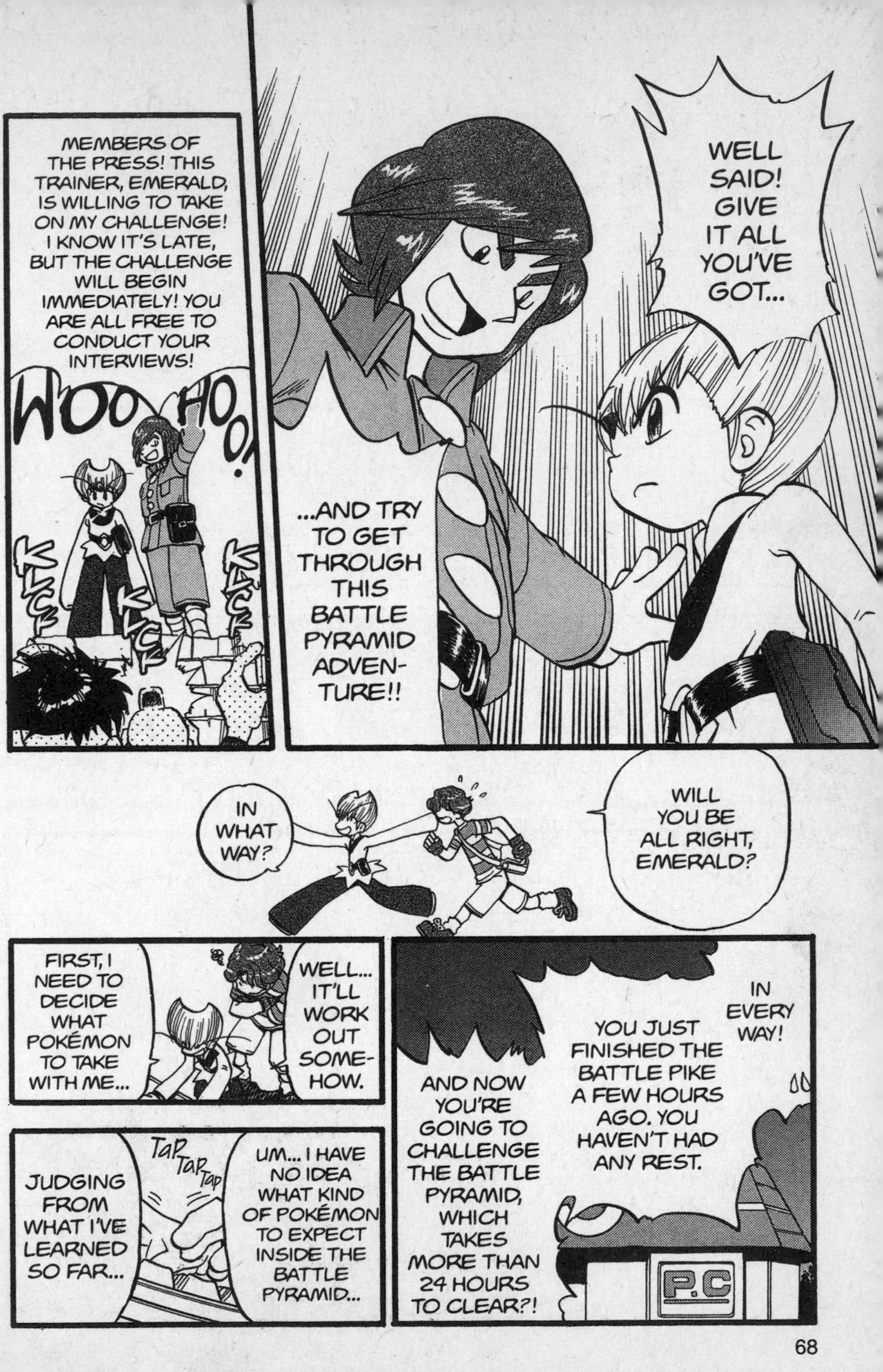

WELL SAID! GIVE IT ALL YOU'VE GOT...
...AND TRY TO GET THROUGH THIS BATTLE PYRAMID ADVEN-TURE!!
MEMBERS OF THE PRESS! THIS TRAINER, EMERALD, IS WILLING TO TAKE ON MY CHALLENGE! I KNOW IT'S LATE, BUT THE CHALLENGE WILL BEGIN IMMEDIATELY! YOU ARE ALL FREE TO CONDUCT YOUR INTERVIEWS!
WOO HOO!
KLICK
KLICK
KLICK
KLICK
WILL YOU BE ALL RIGHT, EMERALD?
IN WHAT WAY?
IN EVERY WAY!
YOU JUST FINISHED THE BATTLE PIKE A FEW HOURS AGO. YOU HAVEN'T HAD ANY REST.
AND NOW YOU'RE GOING TO CHALLENGE THE BATTLE PYRAMID, WHICH TAKES MORE THAN 24 HOURS TO CLEAR?!
P.C
WELL... IT'LL WORK OUT SOME-HOW.
FIRST, I NEED TO DECIDE WHAT POKÉMON TO TAKE WITH ME...
UM... I HAVE NO IDEA WHAT KIND OF POKÉMON TO EXPECT INSIDE THE BATTLE PYRAMID...
TAP TAP TAP
JUDGING FROM WHAT I'VE LEARNED SO FAR...

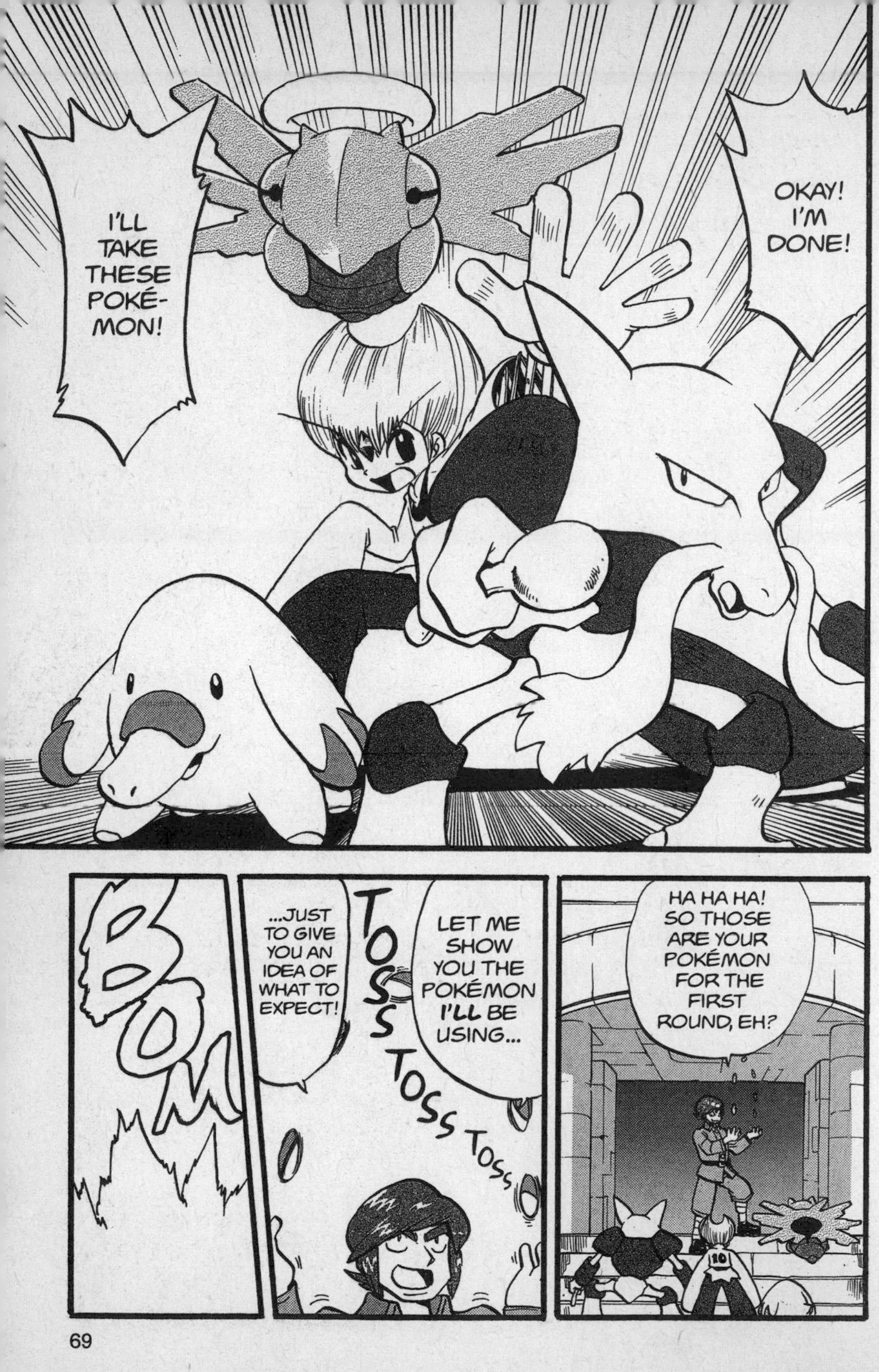
OKAY! I'M DONE!
I'LL TAKE THESE POKÉ-MON!
HA HA HA! SO THOSE ARE YOUR POKÉMON FOR THE FIRST ROUND, EH?
LET ME SHOW YOU THE POKÉMON **I'LL** BE USING...
...JUST TO GIVE YOU AN IDEA OF WHAT TO EXPECT!
TOSS TOSS TOSS TOSS
BOOM

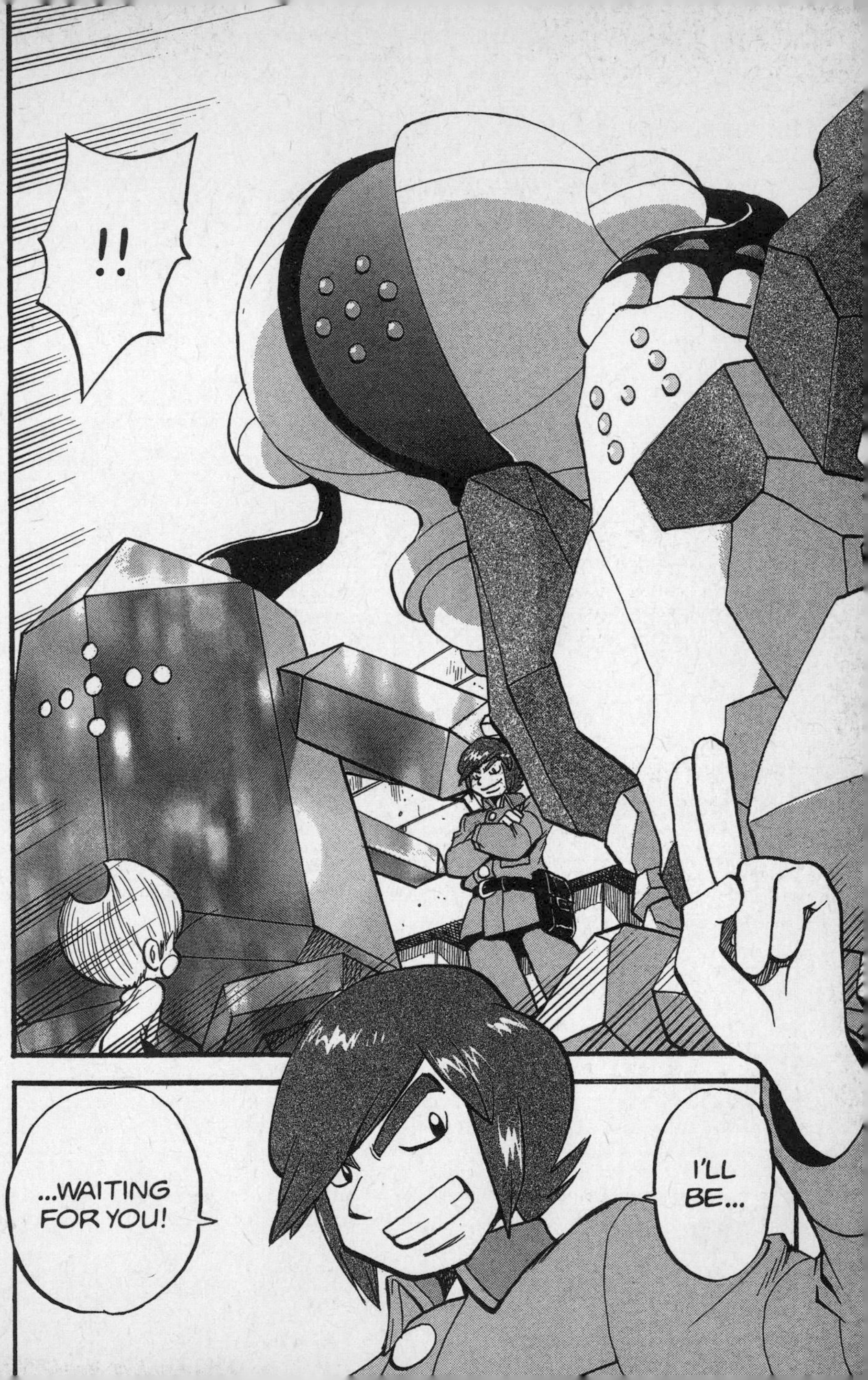
!!
I'LL BE...
...WAITING FOR YOU!

DEAR MEMBERS OF THE PRESS...

Thank you for visiting the Battle Frontier today. Permit me to continue explaining the rules of this facility...

OWNER: SCOTT

FACILITY RULES
BATTLE PYRAMID 2

The Battle Pyramid is the only facility where the trainer is allowed to use items. This bulletin explains how the items may be used.

■ ITEMS WHICH CAN BE FOUND INSIDE THE FACILITY ■

The challenger will be provided with a Battle Bag to stock items they find inside the pyramid. The bag already contains a Hyper Potion and Ether. The challenger may keep the items they find inside the pyramid once they reach the next floor for use in their next round. But if the challenger loses a round, the bag will be reset to its original state.

■ POKÉMON WHO APPEAR DURING THE VARIOUS ROUNDS ■

The challenger will be met by many Pokémon with paralyzing moves during the first round, poisoning moves in the second, burning moves in the third, and so on. In other words, the types of Pokémon that appear will vary depending on the round.

312

Chipping Away at Regirock

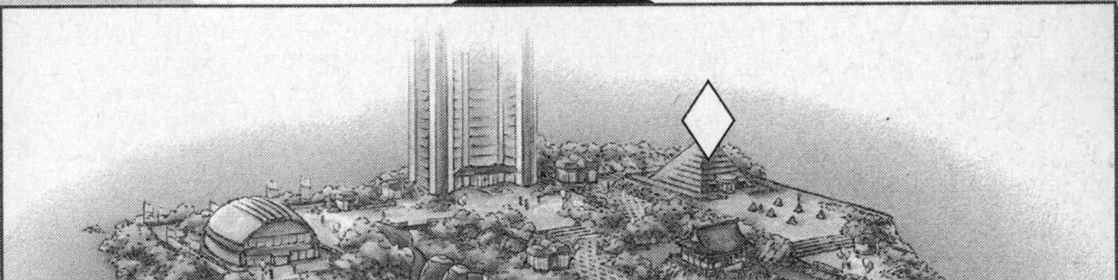

POKÉMON ADVENTURES•THE SIXTH CHAPTER•EMERALD

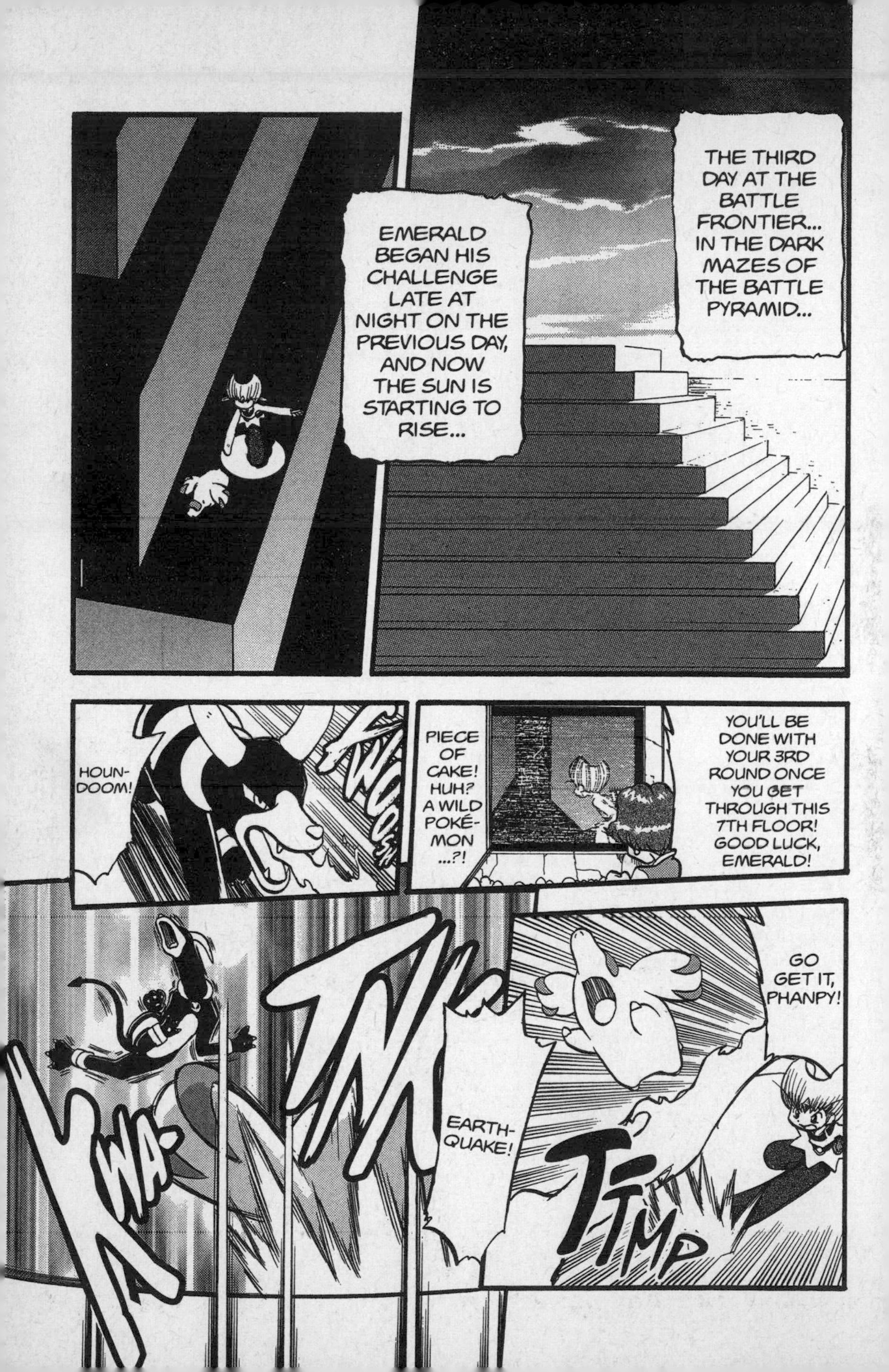
THE THIRD DAY AT THE BATTLE FRONTIER... IN THE DARK MAZES OF THE BATTLE PYRAMID...
EMERALD BEGAN HIS CHALLENGE LATE AT NIGHT ON THE PREVIOUS DAY, AND NOW THE SUN IS STARTING TO RISE...
YOU'LL BE DONE WITH YOUR 3RD ROUND ONCE YOU GET THROUGH THIS 7TH FLOOR! GOOD LUCK, EMERALD!
PIECE OF CAKE! HUH? A WILD POKÉMON ...?!
HOUN-DOOM!
GO GET IT, PHANPY!
EARTH-QUAKE!

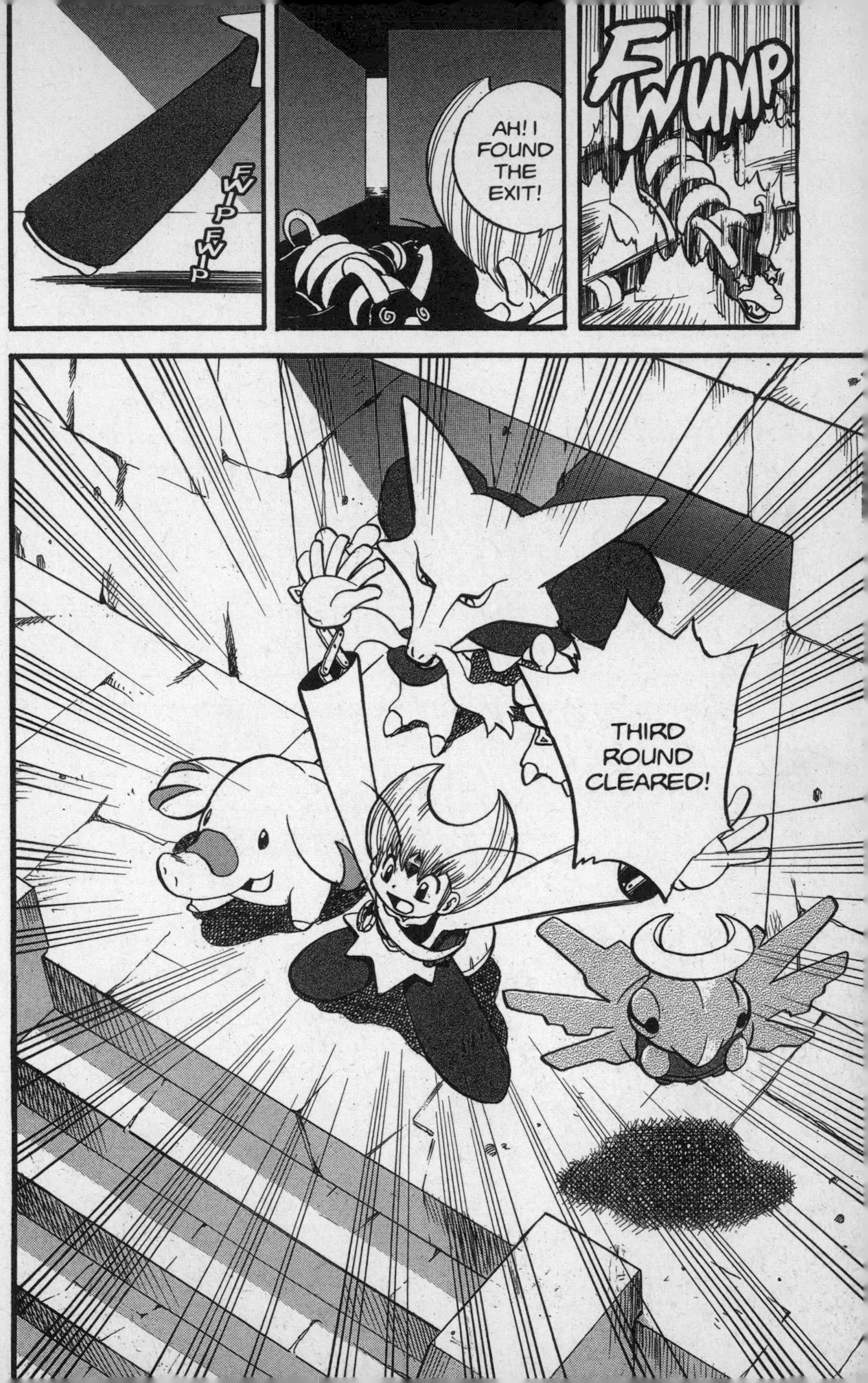
FWUMP
AH! I FOUND THE EXIT!
FWIP FWIP
THIRD ROUND CLEARED!

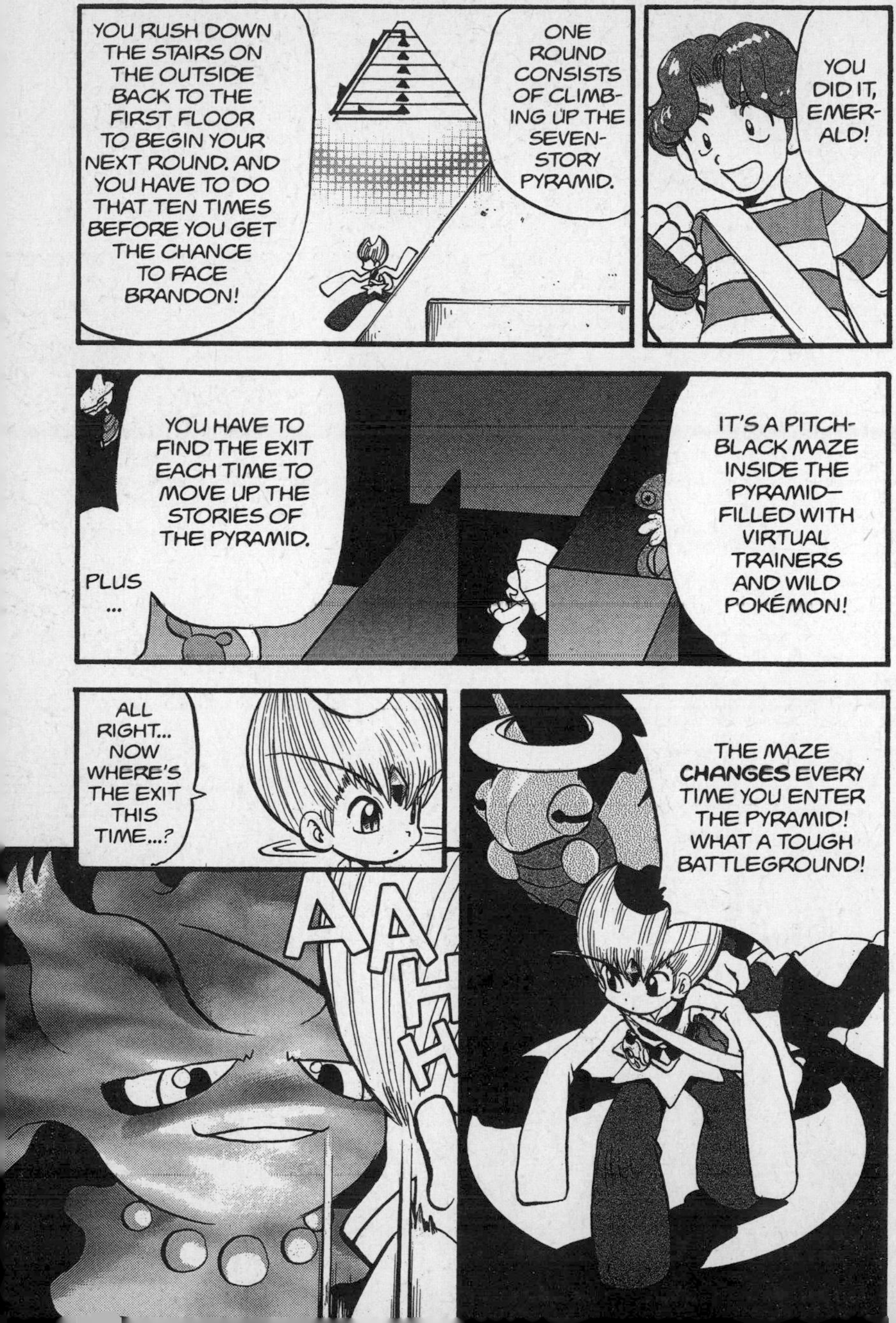
YOU DID IT, EMERALD!
ONE ROUND CONSISTS OF CLIMBING UP THE SEVEN-STORY PYRAMID.
YOU RUSH DOWN THE STAIRS ON THE OUTSIDE BACK TO THE FIRST FLOOR TO BEGIN YOUR NEXT ROUND. AND YOU HAVE TO DO THAT TEN TIMES BEFORE YOU GET THE CHANCE TO FACE BRANDON!
IT'S A PITCH-BLACK MAZE INSIDE THE PYRAMID—FILLED WITH VIRTUAL TRAINERS AND WILD POKÉMON!
YOU HAVE TO FIND THE EXIT EACH TIME TO MOVE UP THE STORIES OF THE PYRAMID.
PLUS ...
THE MAZE **CHANGES** EVERY TIME YOU ENTER THE PYRAMID! WHAT A TOUGH BATTLEGROUND!
ALL RIGHT... NOW WHERE'S THE EXIT THIS TIME...?
AAHHH

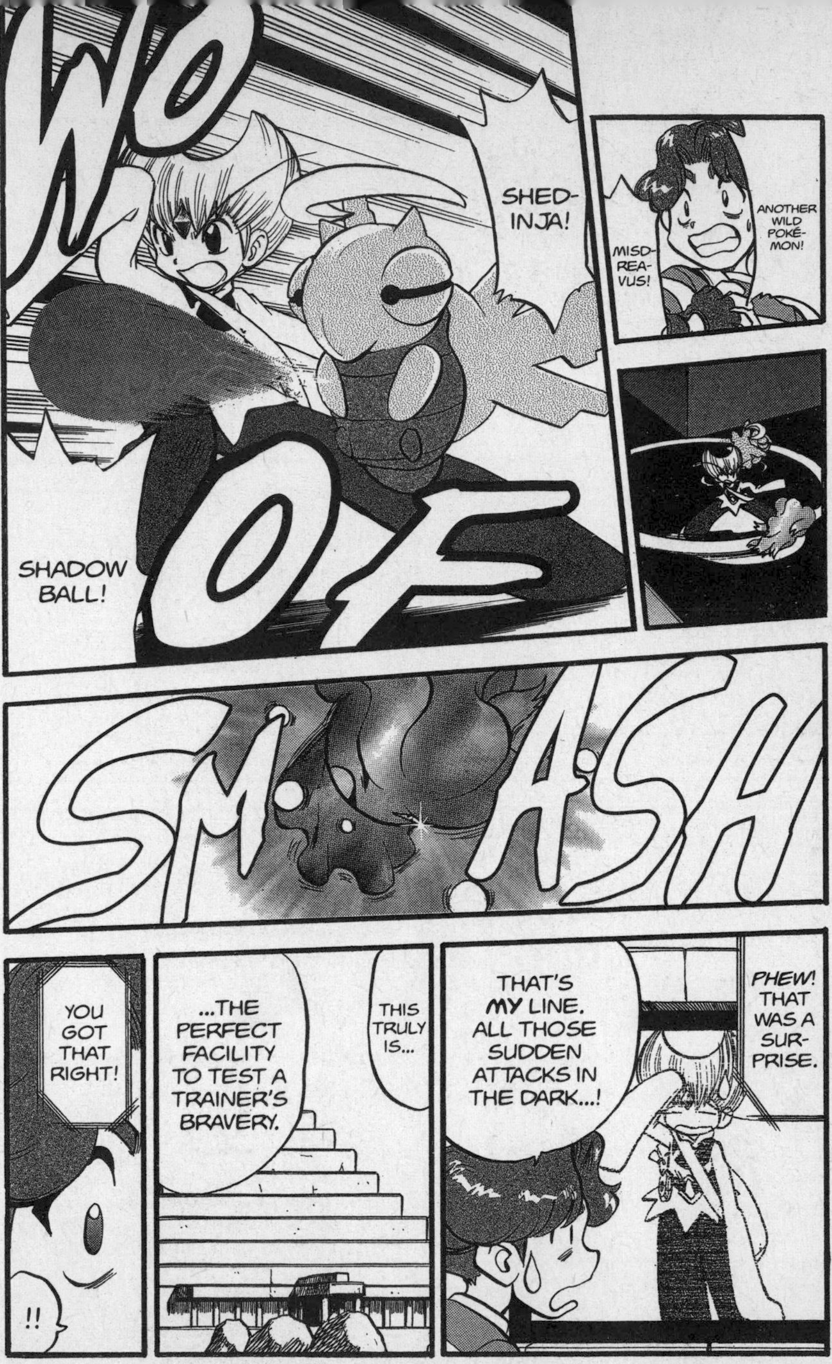
ANOTHER WILD POKÉMON!
MISDREAVUS!
SHEDINJA!
WO
SHADOW BALL!
OF
SMASH
PHEW! THAT WAS A SURPRISE.
THAT'S MY LINE. ALL THOSE SUDDEN ATTACKS IN THE DARK...!
THIS TRULY IS...
...THE PERFECT FACILITY TO TEST A TRAINER'S BRAVERY.
YOU GOT THAT RIGHT!
!!

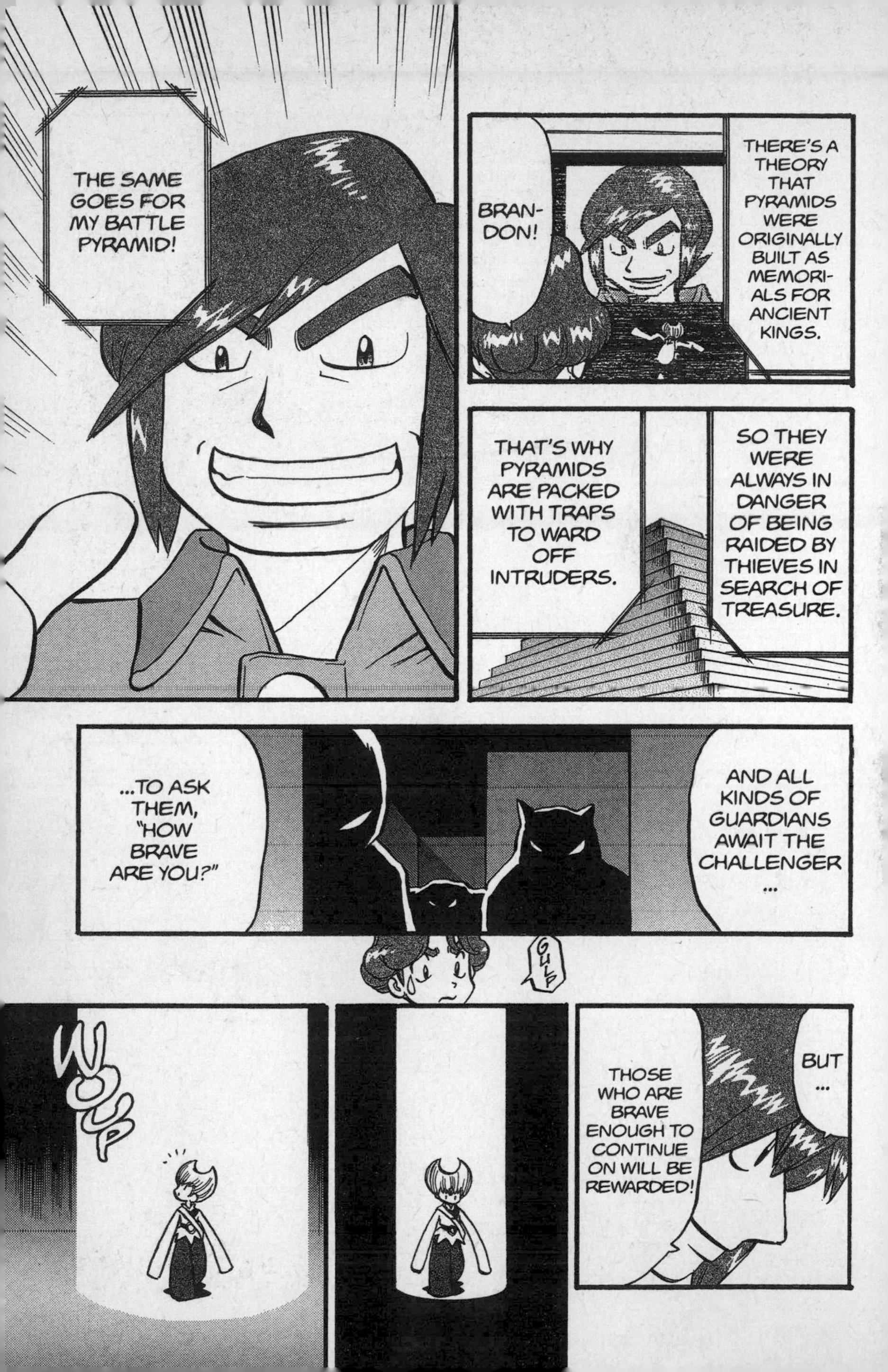
THERE'S A THEORY THAT PYRAMIDS WERE ORIGINALLY BUILT AS MEMORI-ALS FOR ANCIENT KINGS.
BRAN-DON!
SO THEY WERE ALWAYS IN DANGER OF BEING RAIDED BY THIEVES IN SEARCH OF TREASURE.
THAT'S WHY PYRAMIDS ARE PACKED WITH TRAPS TO WARD OFF INTRUDERS.
THE SAME GOES FOR MY BATTLE PYRAMID!
AND ALL KINDS OF GUARDIANS AWAIT THE CHALLENGER ...
...TO ASK THEM, "HOW BRAVE ARE YOU?"
GULP
BUT ...
THOSE WHO ARE BRAVE ENOUGH TO CONTINUE ON WILL BE REWARDED!
WOUP

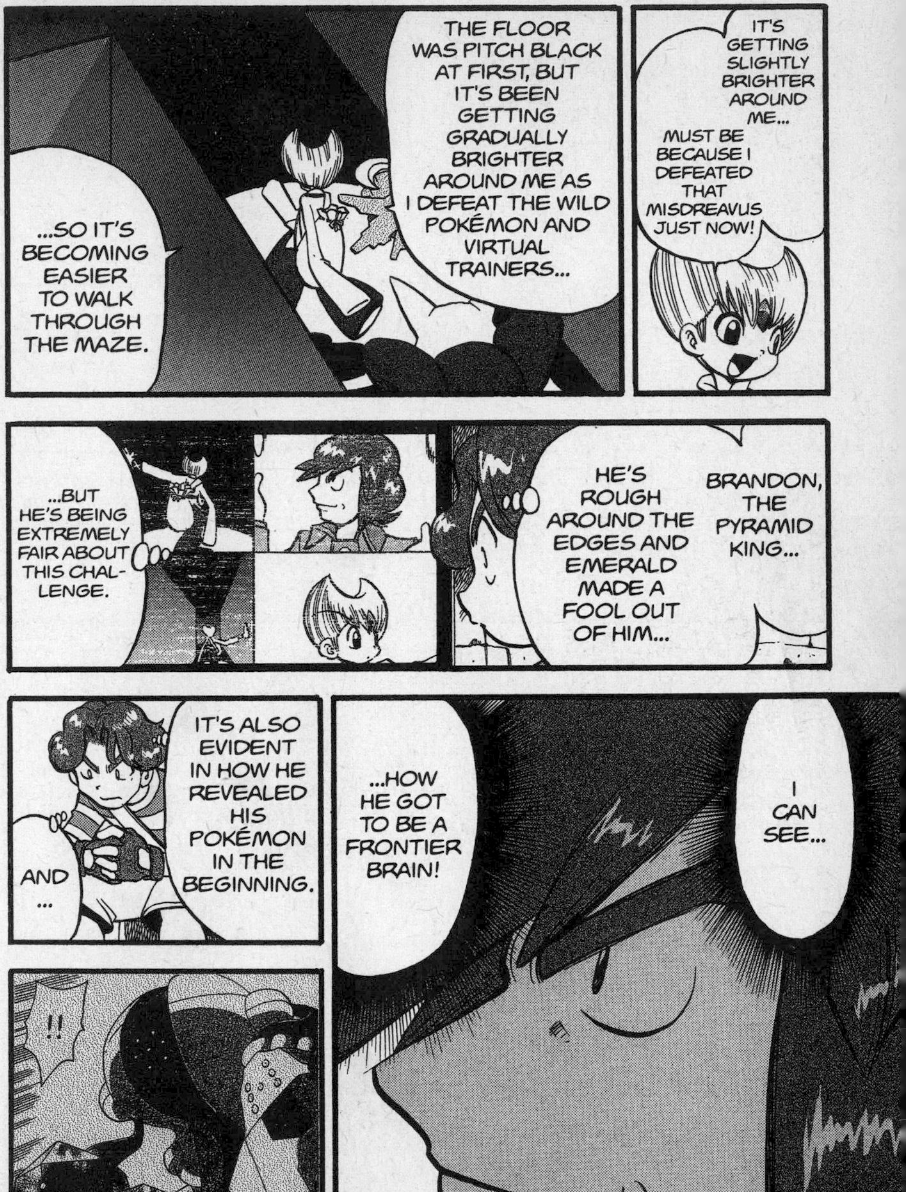
IT'S GETTING SLIGHTLY BRIGHTER AROUND ME...
MUST BE BECAUSE I DEFEATED THAT MISDREAVUS JUST NOW!
THE FLOOR WAS PITCH BLACK AT FIRST, BUT IT'S BEEN GETTING GRADUALLY BRIGHTER AROUND ME AS I DEFEAT THE WILD POKÉMON AND VIRTUAL TRAINERS...
...SO IT'S BECOMING EASIER TO WALK THROUGH THE MAZE.
BRANDON, THE PYRAMID KING...
HE'S ROUGH AROUND THE EDGES AND EMERALD MADE A FOOL OUT OF HIM...
...BUT HE'S BEING EXTREMELY FAIR ABOUT THIS CHALLENGE.
I CAN SEE...
...HOW HE GOT TO BE A FRONTIER BRAIN!
IT'S ALSO EVIDENT IN HOW HE REVEALED HIS POKÉMON IN THE BEGINNING.
AND ...
!!

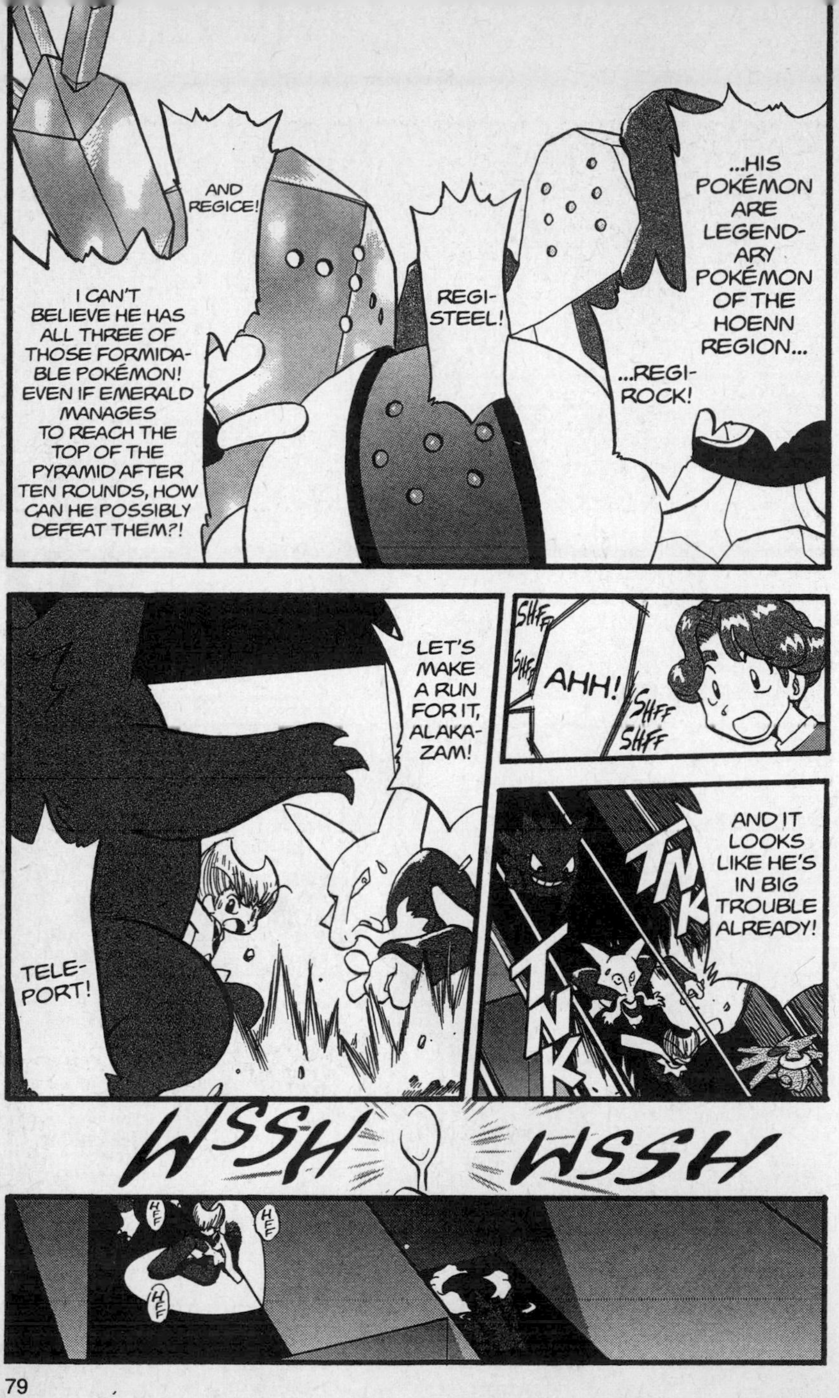
...HIS POKÉMON ARE LEGEND-ARY POKÉMON OF THE HOENN REGION...
...REGI-ROCK!
REGI-STEEL!
AND REGICE!
I CAN'T BELIEVE HE HAS ALL THREE OF THOSE FORMIDA-BLE POKÉMON! EVEN IF EMERALD MANAGES TO REACH THE TOP OF THE PYRAMID AFTER TEN ROUNDS, HOW CAN HE POSSIBLY DEFEAT THEM?!
SHFF
SHFF
AHH!
SHFF
SHFF
AND IT LOOKS LIKE HE'S IN BIG TROUBLE ALREADY!
TNK
TNK
LET'S MAKE A RUN FOR IT, ALAKA-ZAM!
TELE-PORT!
WSSH
WSSH
HEF
HEF
HEF

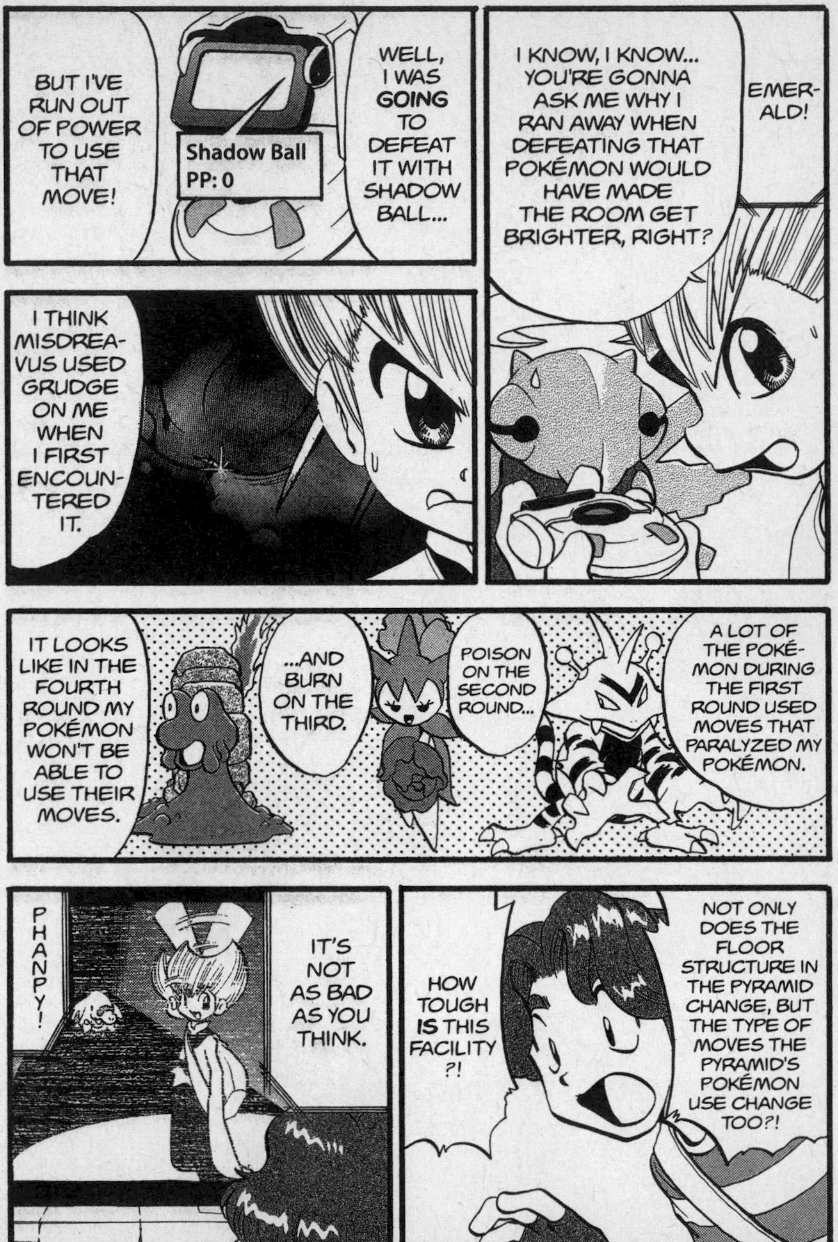
EMERALD!
I KNOW, I KNOW... YOU'RE GONNA ASK ME WHY I RAN AWAY WHEN DEFEATING THAT POKÉMON WOULD HAVE MADE THE ROOM GET BRIGHTER, RIGHT?
WELL, I WAS **GOING** TO DEFEAT IT WITH SHADOW BALL...
Shadow Ball
PP: 0
BUT I'VE RUN OUT OF POWER TO USE THAT MOVE!
I THINK MISDREAVUS USED GRUDGE ON ME WHEN I FIRST ENCOUNTERED IT.
A LOT OF THE POKÉMON DURING THE FIRST ROUND USED MOVES THAT PARALYZED MY POKÉMON.
POISON ON THE SECOND ROUND...
...AND BURN ON THE THIRD.
IT LOOKS LIKE IN THE FOURTH ROUND MY POKÉMON WON'T BE ABLE TO USE THEIR MOVES.
NOT ONLY DOES THE FLOOR STRUCTURE IN THE PYRAMID CHANGE, BUT THE TYPE OF MOVES THE PYRAMID'S POKÉMON USE CHANGE TOO?!
HOW TOUGH **IS** THIS FACILITY?!
IT'S NOT AS BAD AS YOU THINK.
PHANPY!

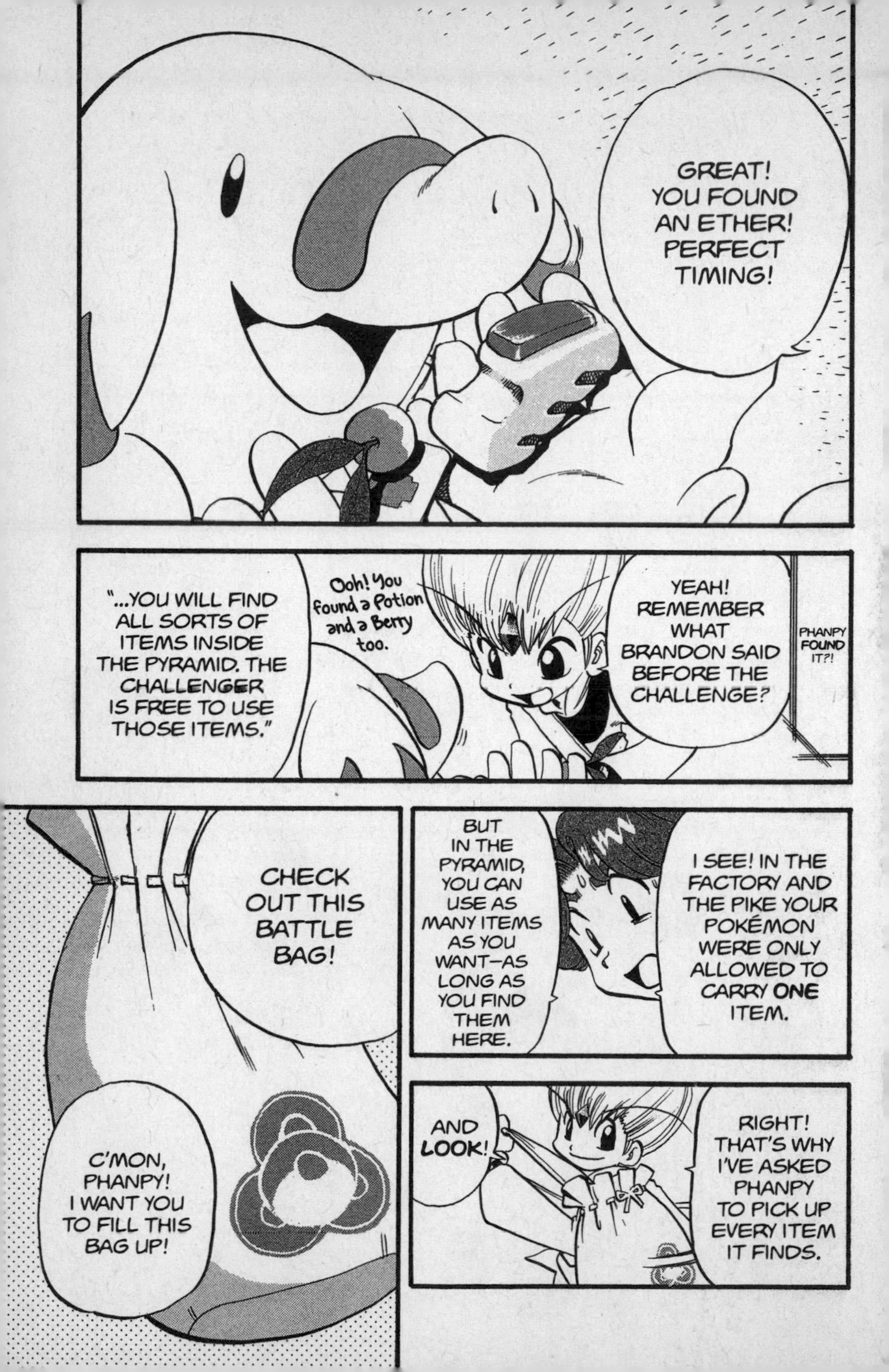
GREAT! YOU FOUND AN ETHER! PERFECT TIMING!
PHANPY FOUND IT?!
YEAH! REMEMBER WHAT BRANDON SAID BEFORE THE CHALLENGE?
Ooh! You found a Potion and a Berry too.
"...YOU WILL FIND ALL SORTS OF ITEMS INSIDE THE PYRAMID. THE CHALLENGER IS FREE TO USE THOSE ITEMS."
I SEE! IN THE FACTORY AND THE PIKE YOUR POKÉMON WERE ONLY ALLOWED TO CARRY **ONE** ITEM.
BUT IN THE PYRAMID, YOU CAN USE AS MANY ITEMS AS YOU WANT—AS LONG AS YOU FIND THEM HERE.
RIGHT! THAT'S WHY I'VE ASKED PHANPY TO PICK UP EVERY ITEM IT FINDS.
AND **LOOK**!
CHECK OUT THIS BATTLE BAG!
C'MON, PHANPY! I WANT YOU TO FILL THIS BAG UP!

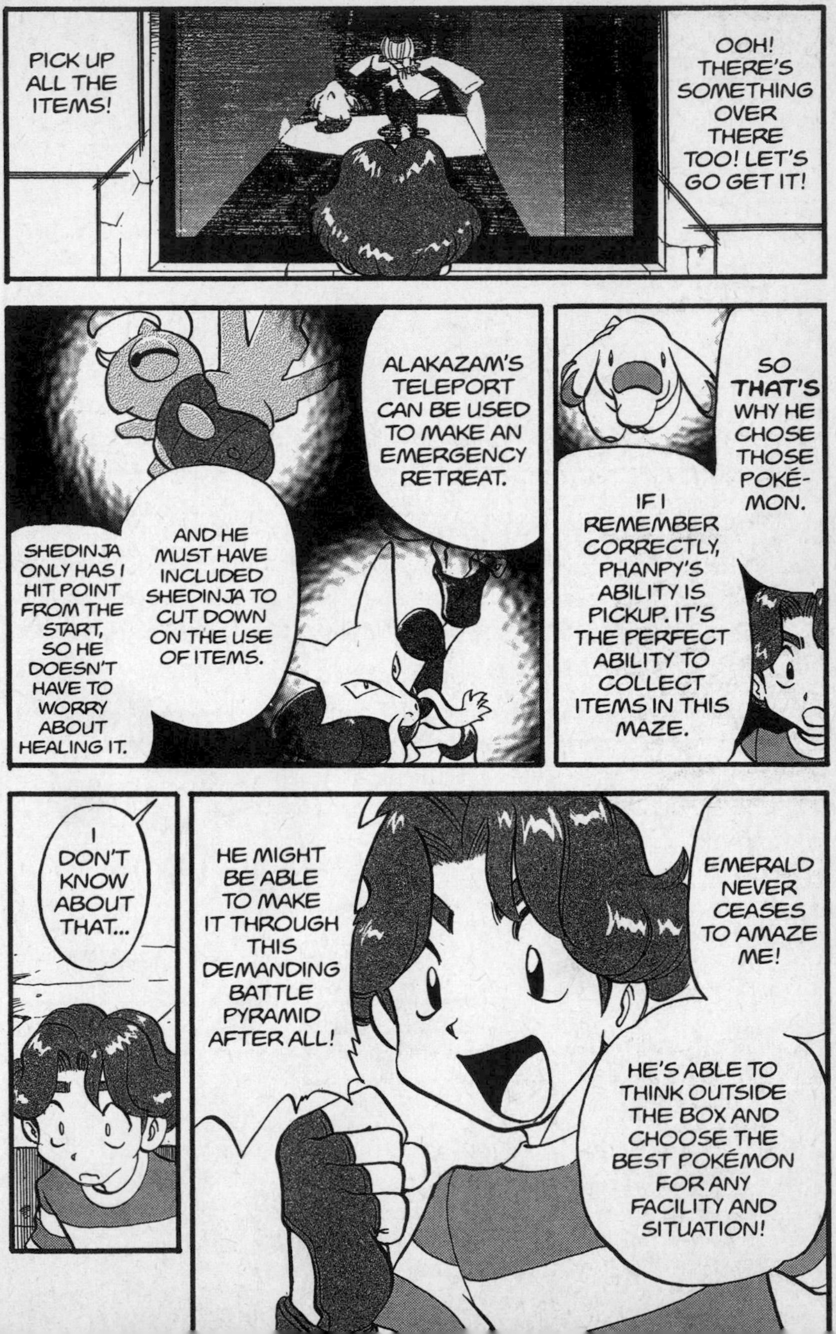
OOH! THERE'S SOMETHING OVER THERE TOO! LET'S GO GET IT!
PICK UP ALL THE ITEMS!
SO THAT'S WHY HE CHOSE THOSE POKÉMON.
IF I REMEMBER CORRECTLY, PHANPY'S ABILITY IS PICKUP. IT'S THE PERFECT ABILITY TO COLLECT ITEMS IN THIS MAZE.
ALAKAZAM'S TELEPORT CAN BE USED TO MAKE AN EMERGENCY RETREAT.
AND HE MUST HAVE INCLUDED SHEDINJA TO CUT DOWN ON THE USE OF ITEMS.
SHEDINJA ONLY HAS 1 HIT POINT FROM THE START, SO HE DOESN'T HAVE TO WORRY ABOUT HEALING IT.
EMERALD NEVER CEASES TO AMAZE ME!
HE'S ABLE TO THINK OUTSIDE THE BOX AND CHOOSE THE BEST POKÉMON FOR ANY FACILITY AND SITUATION!
HE MIGHT BE ABLE TO MAKE IT THROUGH THIS DEMANDING BATTLE PYRAMID AFTER ALL!
I DON'T KNOW ABOUT THAT...

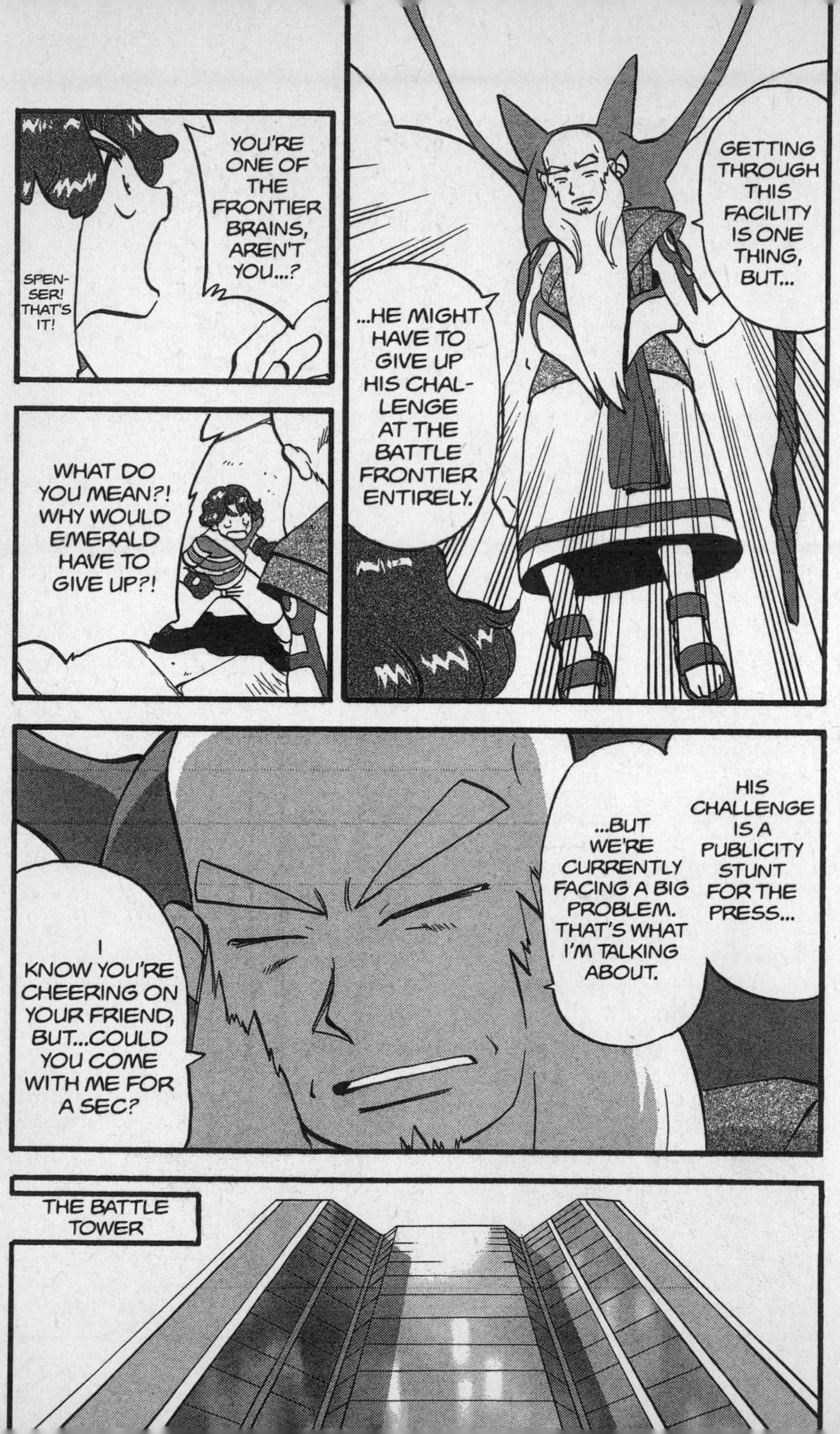
GETTING THROUGH THIS FACILITY IS ONE THING, BUT...
...HE MIGHT HAVE TO GIVE UP HIS CHAL-LENGE AT THE BATTLE FRONTIER ENTIRELY.
YOU'RE ONE OF THE FRONTIER BRAINS, AREN'T YOU...?
SPEN-SER! THAT'S IT!
WHAT DO YOU MEAN?! WHY WOULD EMERALD HAVE TO GIVE UP?!
HIS CHALLENGE IS A PUBLICITY STUNT FOR THE PRESS...
...BUT WE'RE CURRENTLY FACING A BIG PROBLEM. THAT'S WHAT I'M TALKING ABOUT.
I KNOW YOU'RE CHEERING ON YOUR FRIEND, BUT...COULD YOU COME WITH ME FOR A SEC?
THE BATTLE TOWER

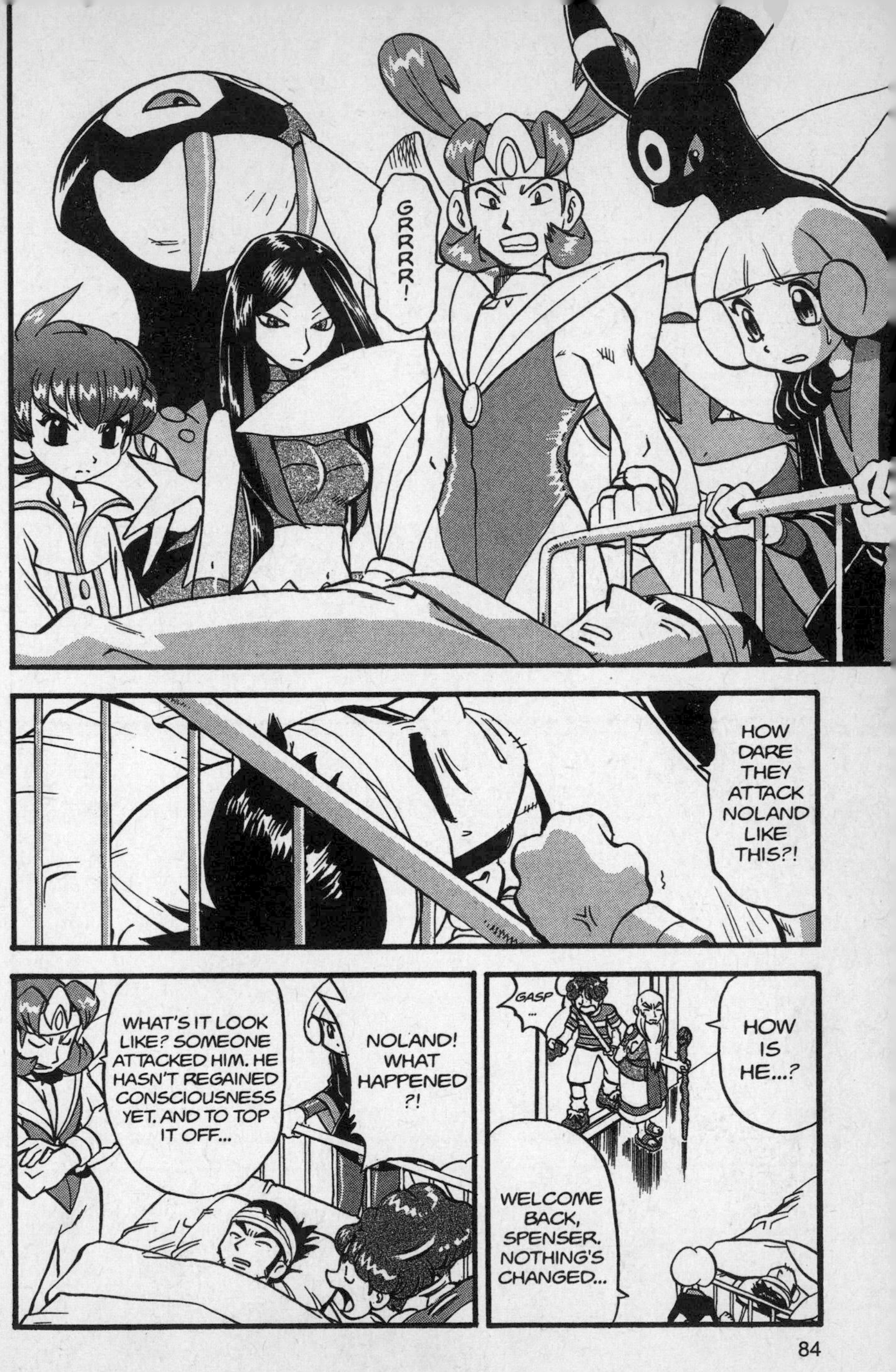
GRRRR!
HOW DARE THEY ATTACK NOLAND LIKE THIS?!
HOW IS HE...?
GASP...
WELCOME BACK, SPENSER. NOTHING'S CHANGED...
NOLAND! WHAT HAPPENED?!
WHAT'S IT LOOK LIKE? SOMEONE ATTACKED HIM. HE HASN'T REGAINED CONSCIOUSNESS YET. AND TO TOP IT OFF...

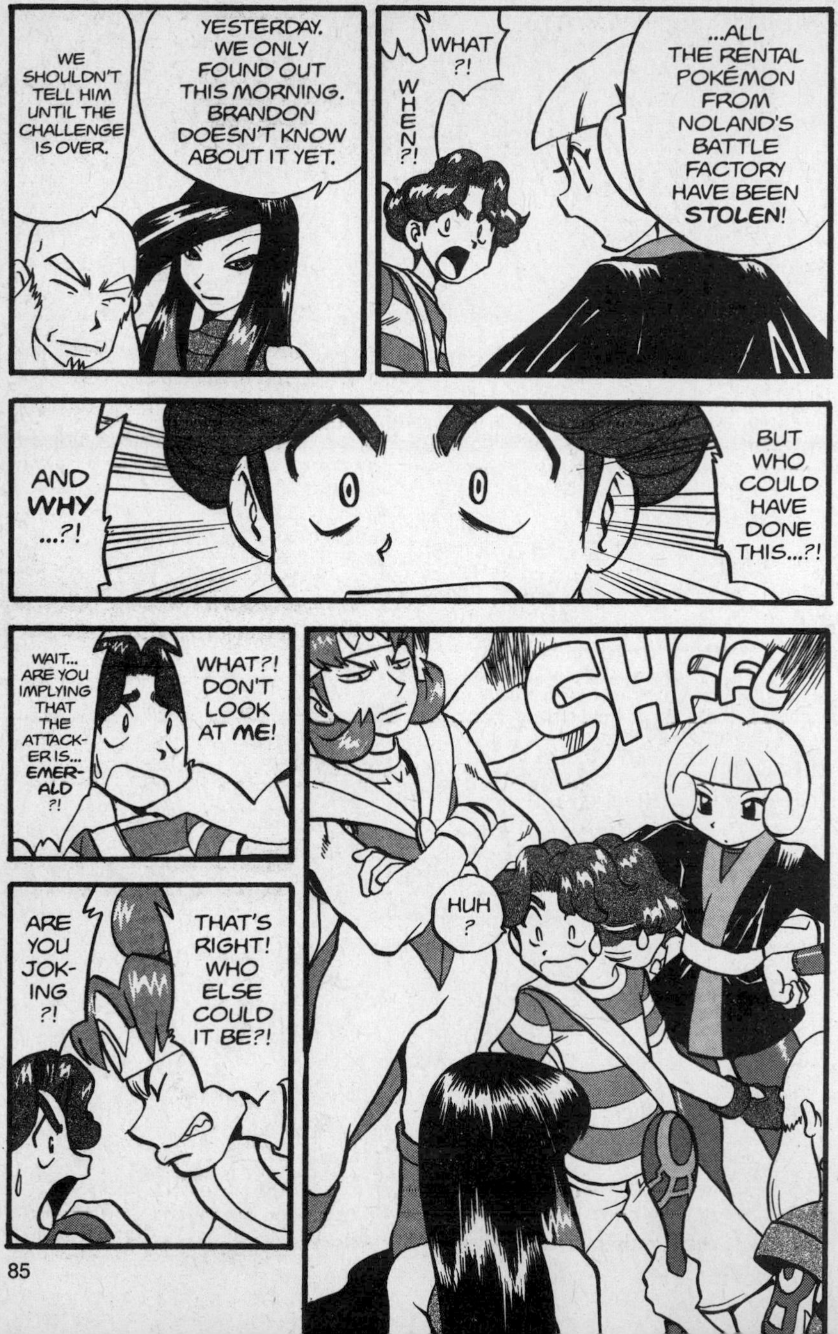
...ALL THE RENTAL POKÉMON FROM NOLAND'S BATTLE FACTORY HAVE BEEN STOLEN!
WHAT?!
WHEN?!
YESTERDAY. WE ONLY FOUND OUT THIS MORNING. BRANDON DOESN'T KNOW ABOUT IT YET.
WE SHOULDN'T TELL HIM UNTIL THE CHALLENGE IS OVER.
BUT WHO COULD HAVE DONE THIS...?!
AND WHY ...?!
SHFFL
HUH?
WHAT?! DON'T LOOK AT ME!
WAIT... ARE YOU IMPLYING THAT THE ATTACKER IS... EMERALD?!
THAT'S RIGHT! WHO ELSE COULD IT BE?!
ARE YOU JOKING?!

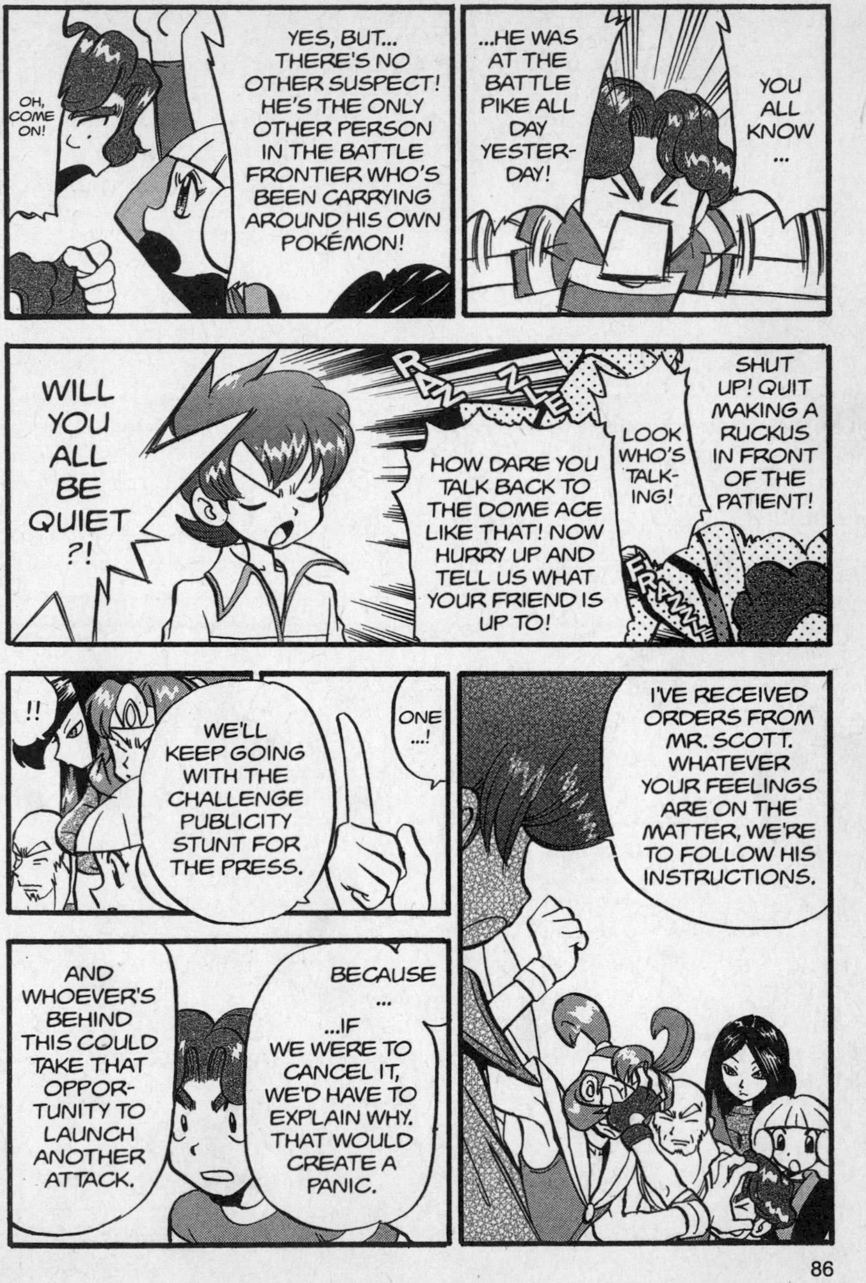
YOU ALL KNOW ...
...HE WAS AT THE BATTLE PIKE ALL DAY YESTER-DAY!
YES, BUT... THERE'S NO OTHER SUSPECT! HE'S THE ONLY OTHER PERSON IN THE BATTLE FRONTIER WHO'S BEEN CARRYING AROUND HIS OWN POKÉMON!
OH, COME ON!
SHUT UP! QUIT MAKING A RUCKUS IN FRONT OF THE PATIENT!
LOOK WHO'S TALK-ING!
FRAZZLE
HOW DARE YOU TALK BACK TO THE DOME ACE LIKE THAT! NOW HURRY UP AND TELL US WHAT YOUR FRIEND IS UP TO!
WILL YOU ALL BE QUIET ?!
I'VE RECEIVED ORDERS FROM MR. SCOTT. WHATEVER YOUR FEELINGS ARE ON THE MATTER, WE'RE TO FOLLOW HIS INSTRUCTIONS.
ONE ...!
WE'LL KEEP GOING WITH THE CHALLENGE PUBLICITY STUNT FOR THE PRESS.
!!
BECAUSE ...
...IF WE WERE TO CANCEL IT, WE'D HAVE TO EXPLAIN WHY. THAT WOULD CREATE A PANIC.
AND WHOEVER'S BEHIND THIS COULD TAKE THAT OPPOR-TUNITY TO LAUNCH ANOTHER ATTACK.

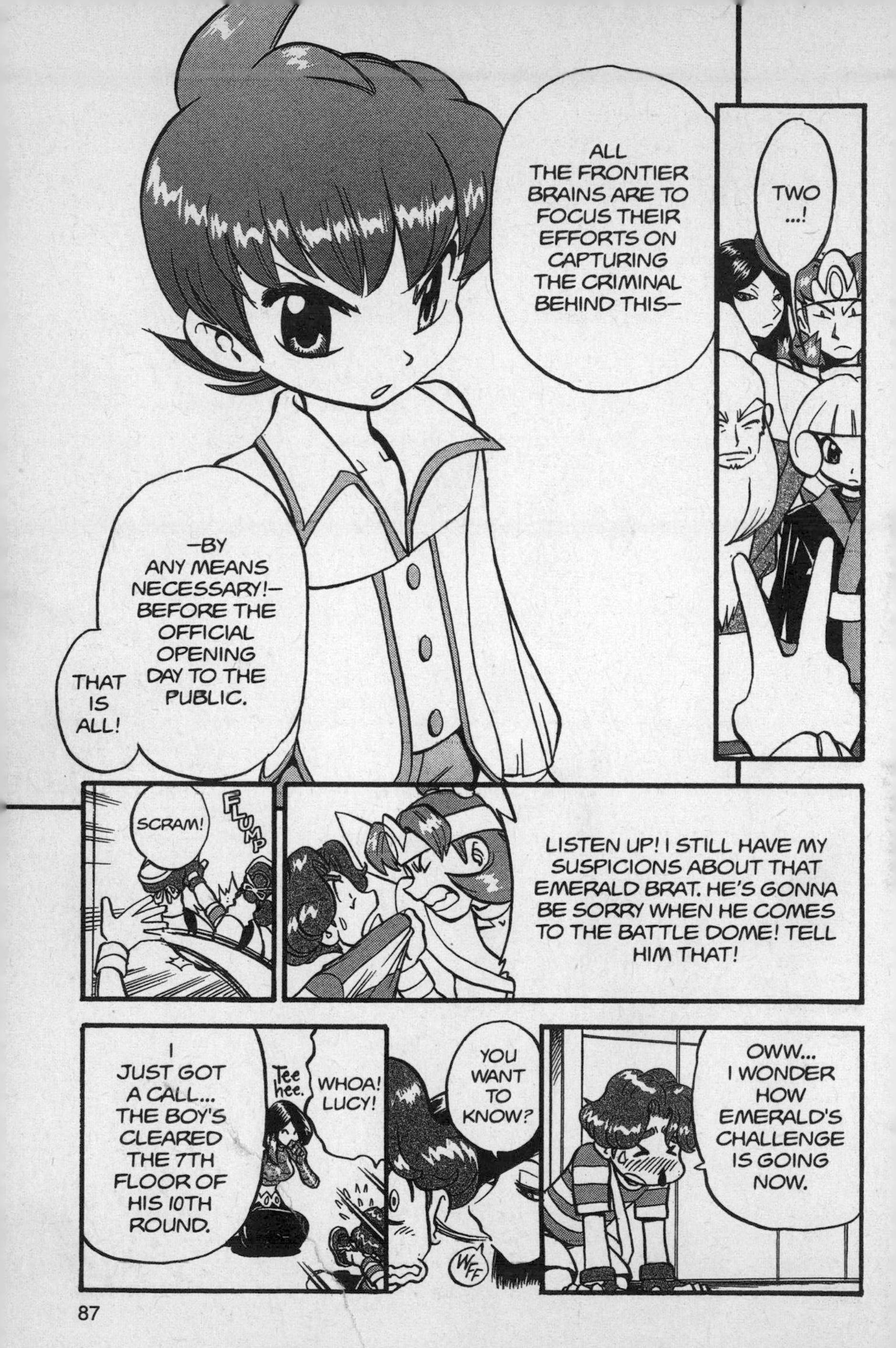
TWO ...!
ALL THE FRONTIER BRAINS ARE TO FOCUS THEIR EFFORTS ON CAPTURING THE CRIMINAL BEHIND THIS—
—BY ANY MEANS NECESSARY!— BEFORE THE OFFICIAL OPENING DAY TO THE PUBLIC.
THAT IS ALL!
LISTEN UP! I STILL HAVE MY SUSPICIONS ABOUT THAT EMERALD BRAT. HE'S GONNA BE SORRY WHEN HE COMES TO THE BATTLE DOME! TELL HIM THAT!
SCRAM!
FLUMP
OWW... I WONDER HOW EMERALD'S CHALLENGE IS GOING NOW.
YOU WANT TO KNOW?
WFF
WHOA! LUCY!
Tee hee.
I JUST GOT A CALL... THE BOY'S CLEARED THE 7TH FLOOR OF HIS 10TH ROUND.

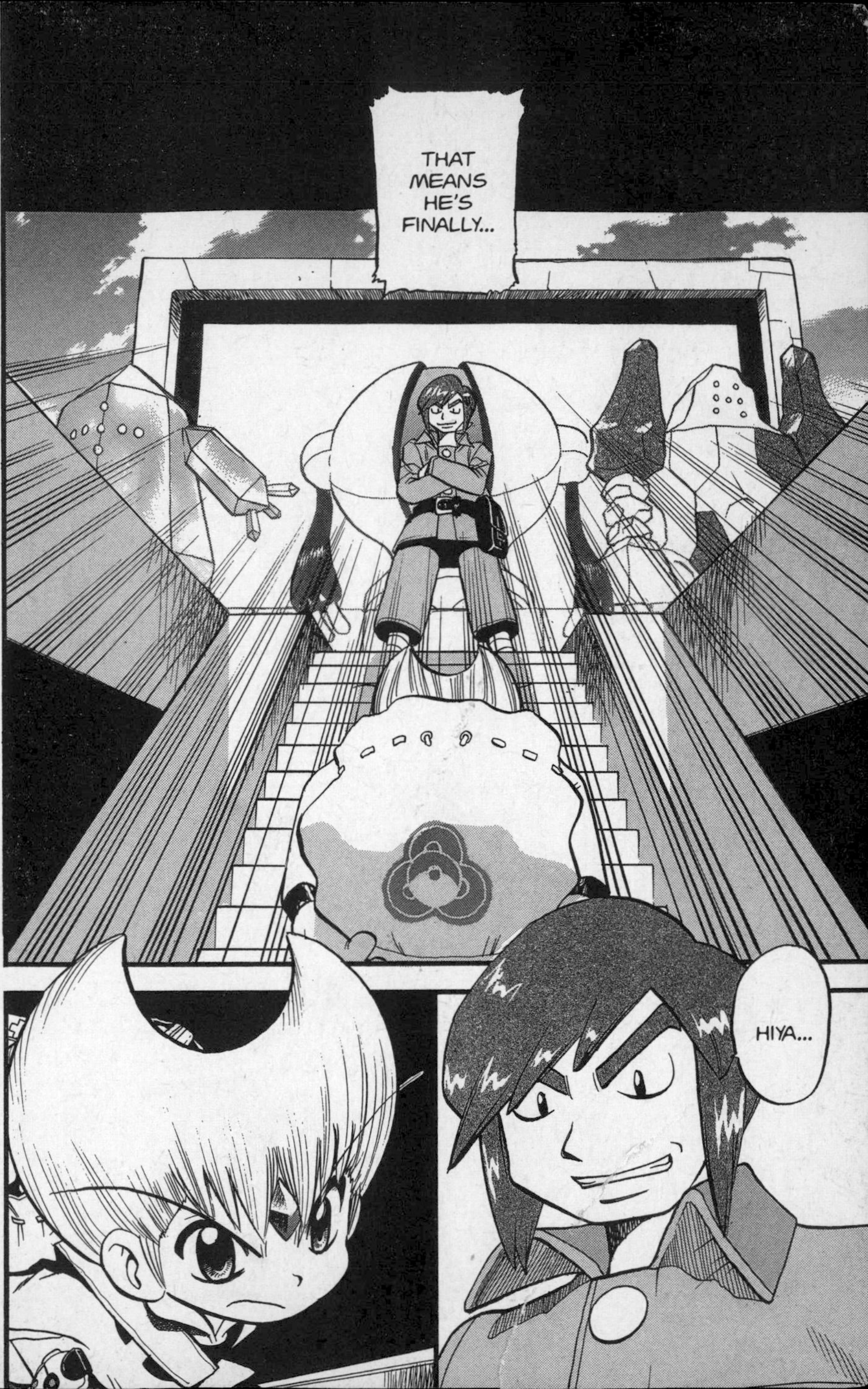
THAT MEANS HE'S FINALLY...
HIYA...

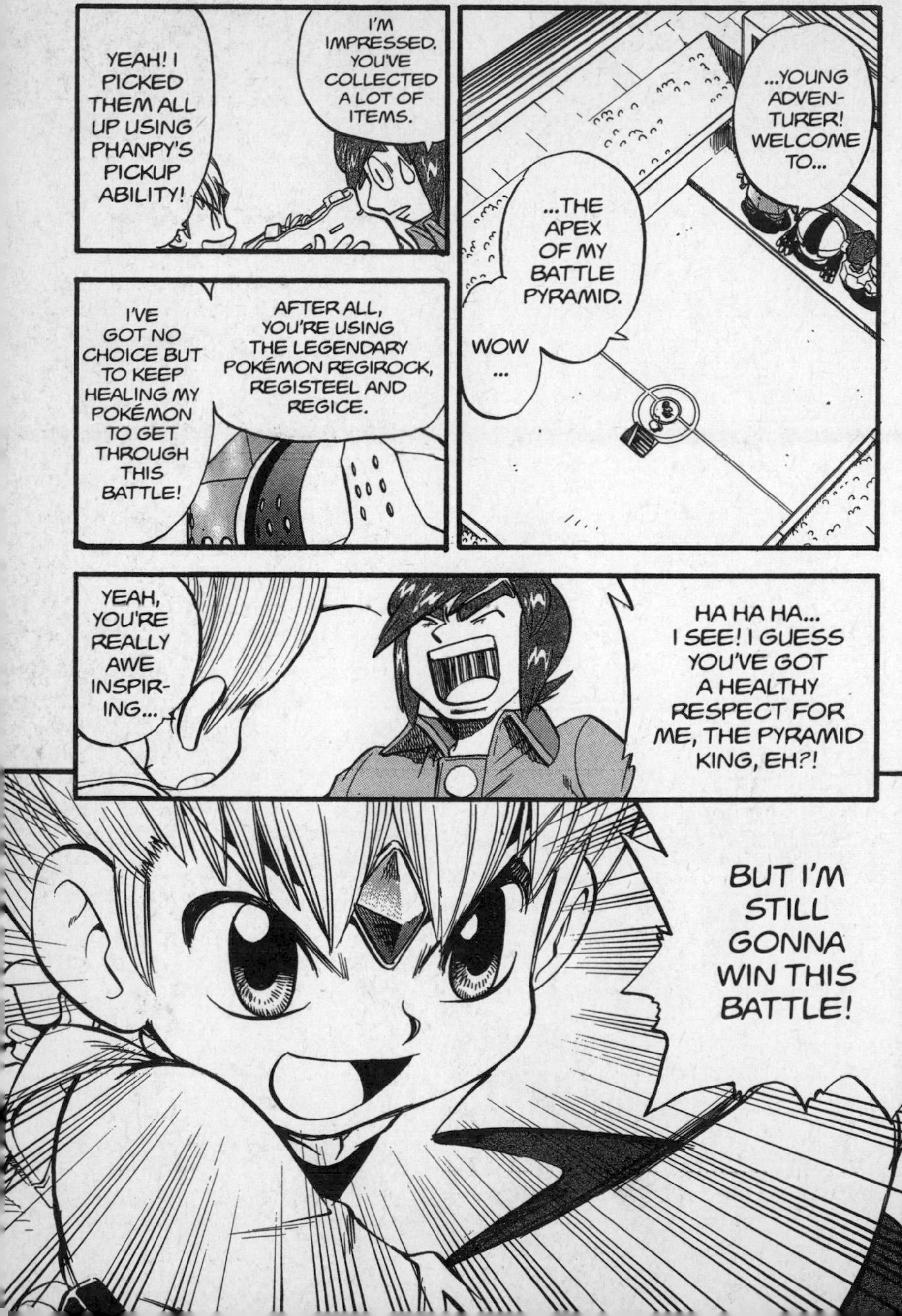
...YOUNG ADVEN-TURER! WELCOME TO...
...THE APEX OF MY BATTLE PYRAMID.
WOW...
I'M IMPRESSED. YOU'VE COLLECTED A LOT OF ITEMS.
YEAH! I PICKED THEM ALL UP USING PHANPY'S PICKUP ABILITY!
AFTER ALL, YOU'RE USING THE LEGENDARY POKÉMON REGIROCK, REGISTEEL AND REGICE.
I'VE GOT NO CHOICE BUT TO KEEP HEALING MY POKÉMON TO GET THROUGH THIS BATTLE!
HA HA HA... I SEE! I GUESS YOU'VE GOT A HEALTHY RESPECT FOR ME, THE PYRAMID KING, EH?!
YEAH, YOU'RE REALLY AWE INSPIR-ING...
BUT I'M STILL GONNA WIN THIS BATTLE!

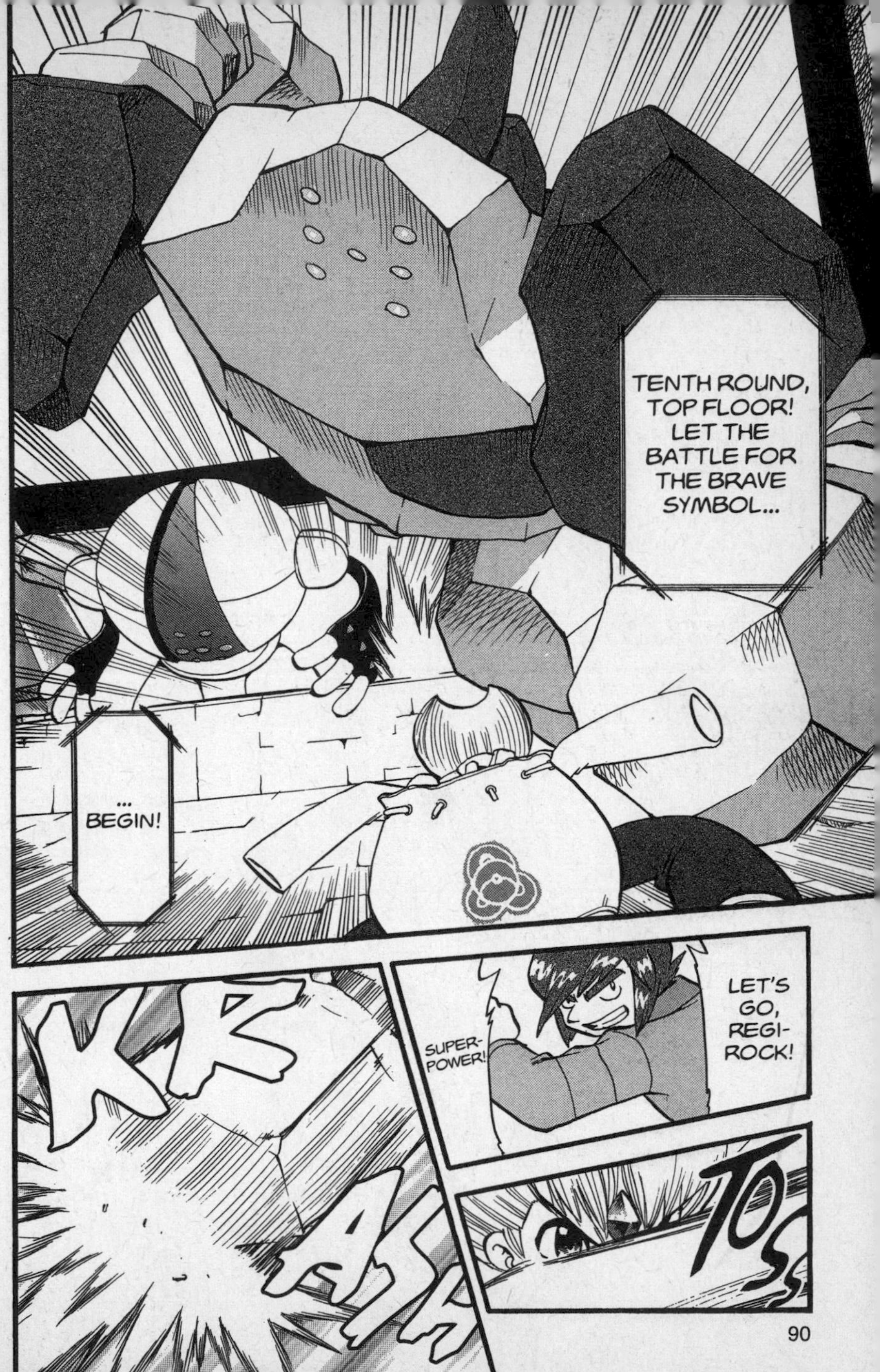
TENTH ROUND, TOP FLOOR! LET THE BATTLE FOR THE BRAVE SYMBOL...
... BEGIN!
LET'S GO, REGI-ROCK!
SUPER-POWER!
TOSS
KRASH

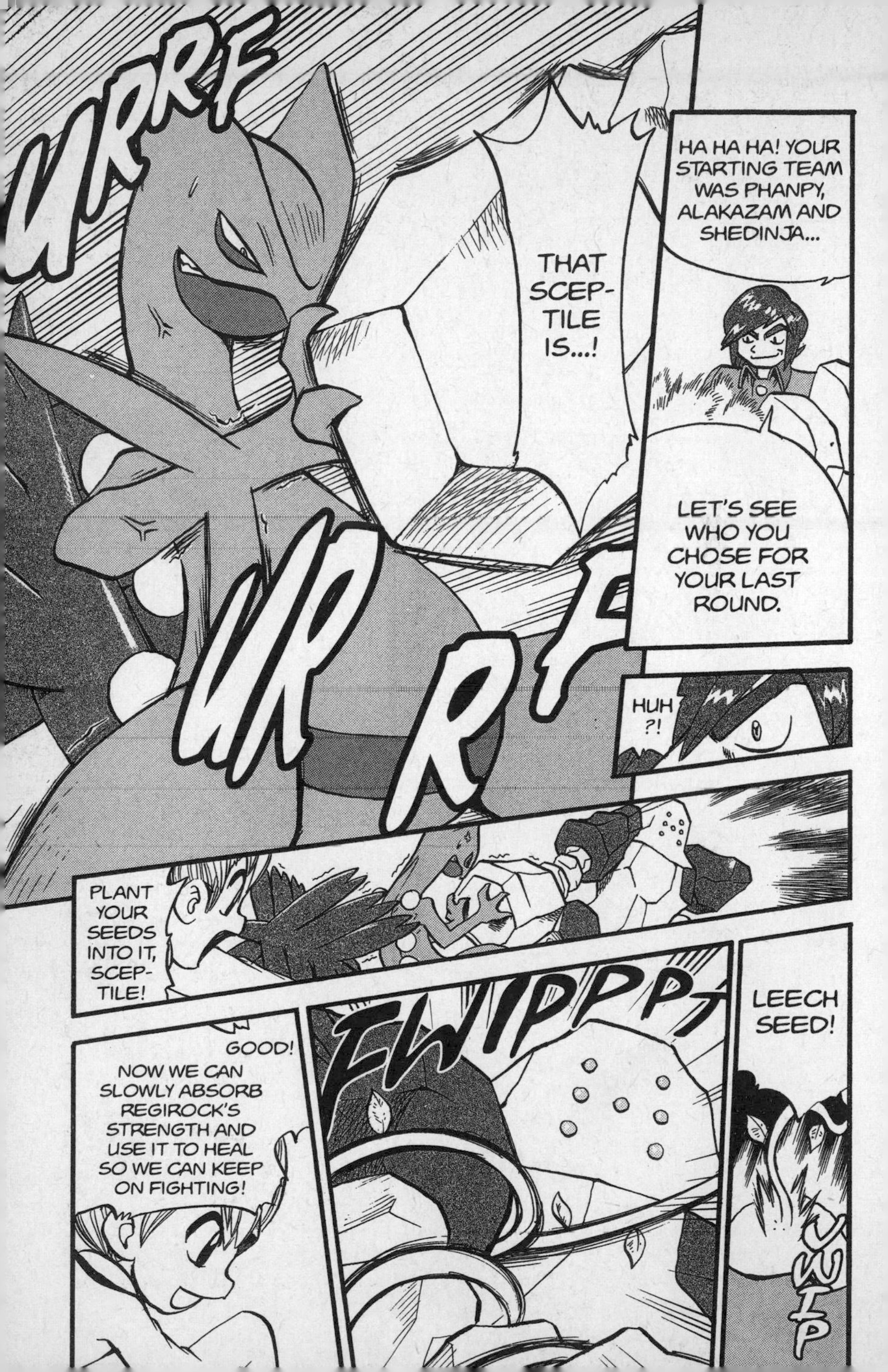
HA HA HA! YOUR STARTING TEAM WAS PHANPY, ALAKAZAM AND SHEDINJA...
LET'S SEE WHO YOU CHOSE FOR YOUR LAST ROUND.
HUH ?!
URRF
THAT SCEP-TILE IS...!
URRF
PLANT YOUR SEEDS INTO IT, SCEP-TILE!
LEECH SEED!
FWIPPPT
GOOD!
NOW WE CAN SLOWLY ABSORB REGIROCK'S STRENGTH AND USE IT TO HEAL SO WE CAN KEEP ON FIGHTING!

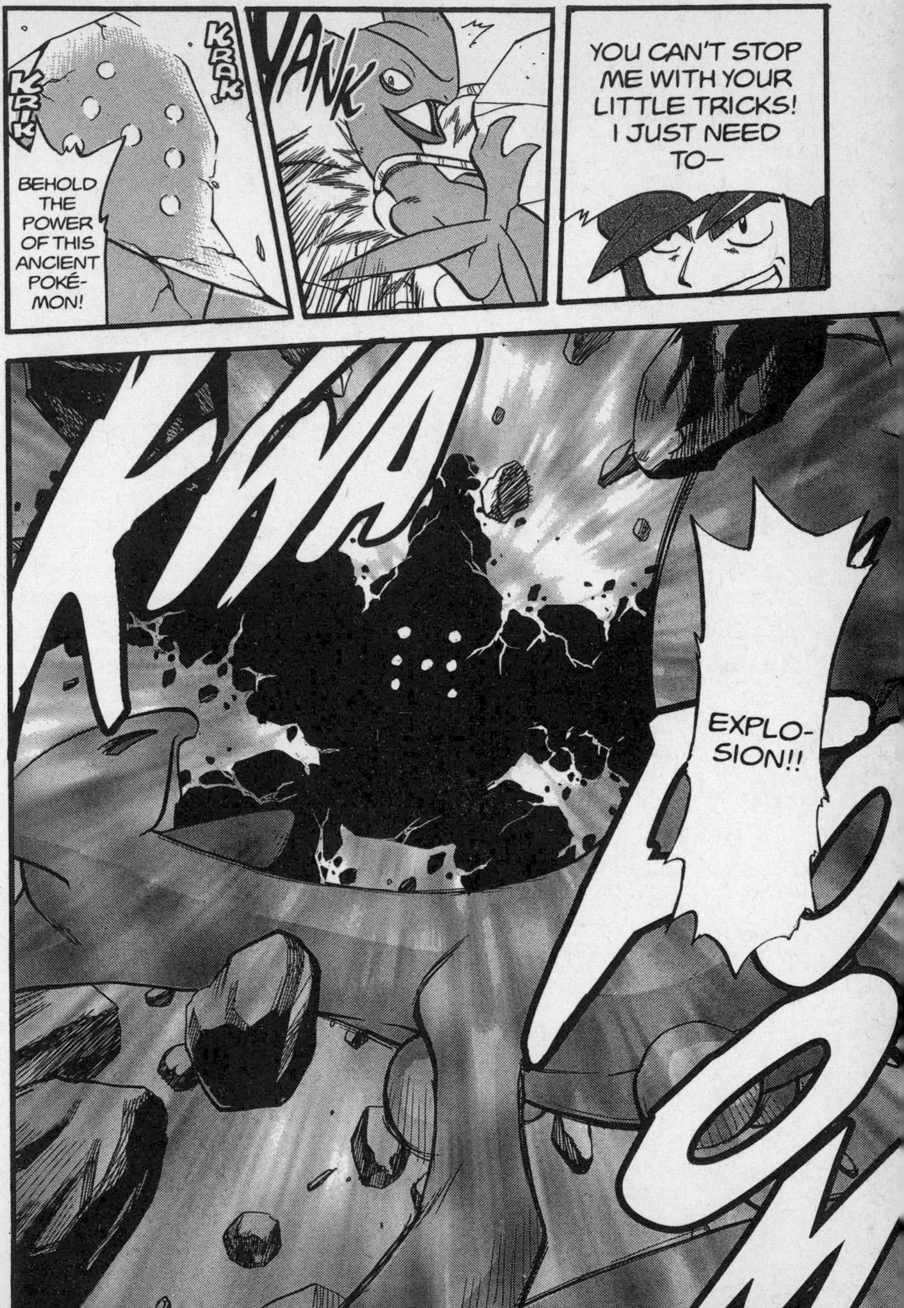
YOU CAN'T STOP ME WITH YOUR LITTLE TRICKS! I JUST NEED TO—
YANK
KRAK
KRIK
BEHOLD THE POWER OF THIS ANCIENT POKÉ-MON!
EXPLO-SION!!

DEAR MEMBERS OF THE PRESS...

Thank you for visiting the Battle Frontier today. Permit me to continue explaining the rules of this facility...

OWNER: SCOTT

FACILITY RULES **BATTLE ARENA 1**		Battle-type	Number of Pokémon	Type of Symbol	Wins needed to attain the Symbol
		• Single	3 Pokémon	Guts	Seven battles × 8 Rounds = 56 Consecutive Wins

The challenger is not allowed to change the order of their Pokémon at the Battle Arena and must fight a 3-on-3 Knockout Battle. If the battle is not over in three rounds, the trainers are rated on three scales: Mind, Skill and Body. The rating system is on a scale of three. You receive 2 points for a ○, 1 point for a △, and 0 points for an ×. The Pokémon who receives the highest score wins the battle.

Guts Symbol

Arena Tycoon
Greta

You Need to Chill Out, Regice

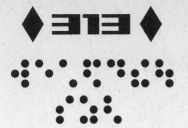

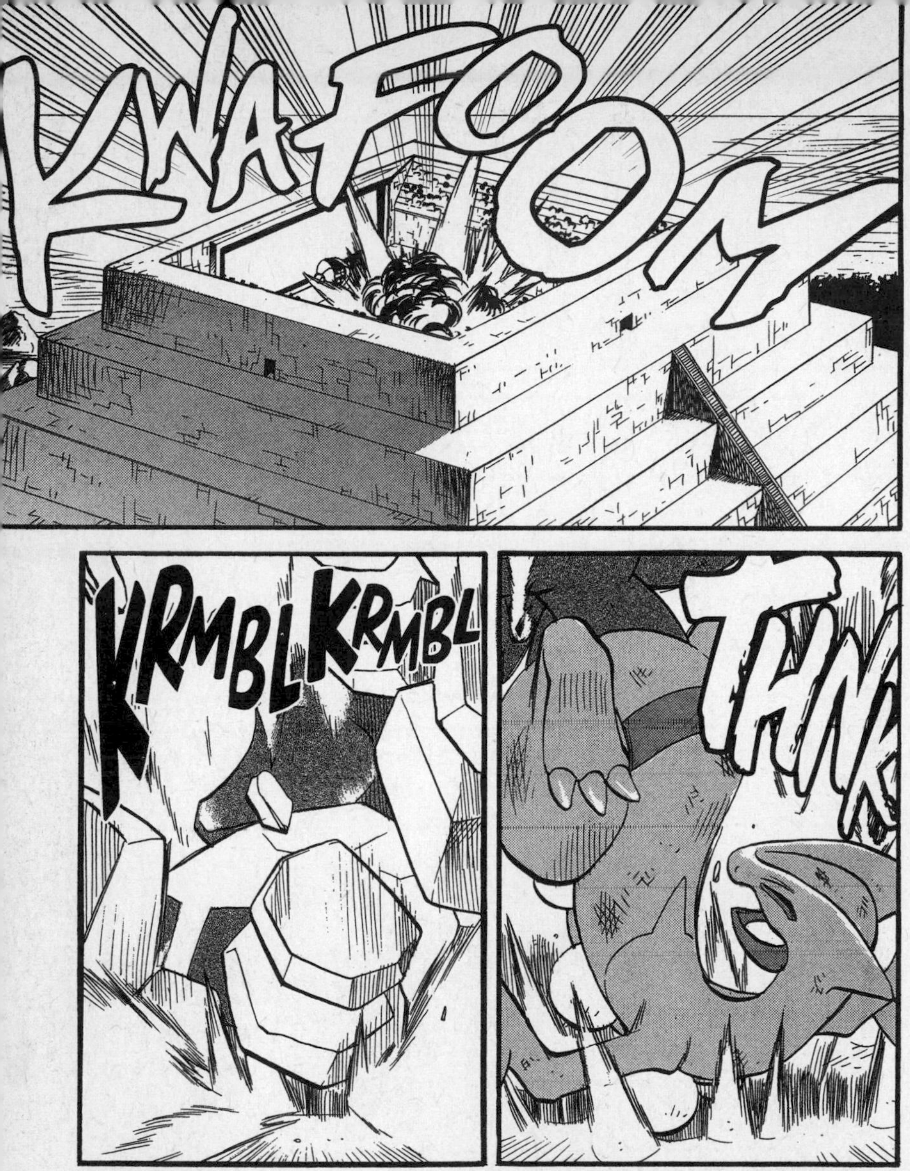
KWAFOOM
THNK
KRMBL KRMBL
ZLOOP
SCEP-TILE!
WELL DONE, REGI-ROCK!
HA HA HA! SEE?

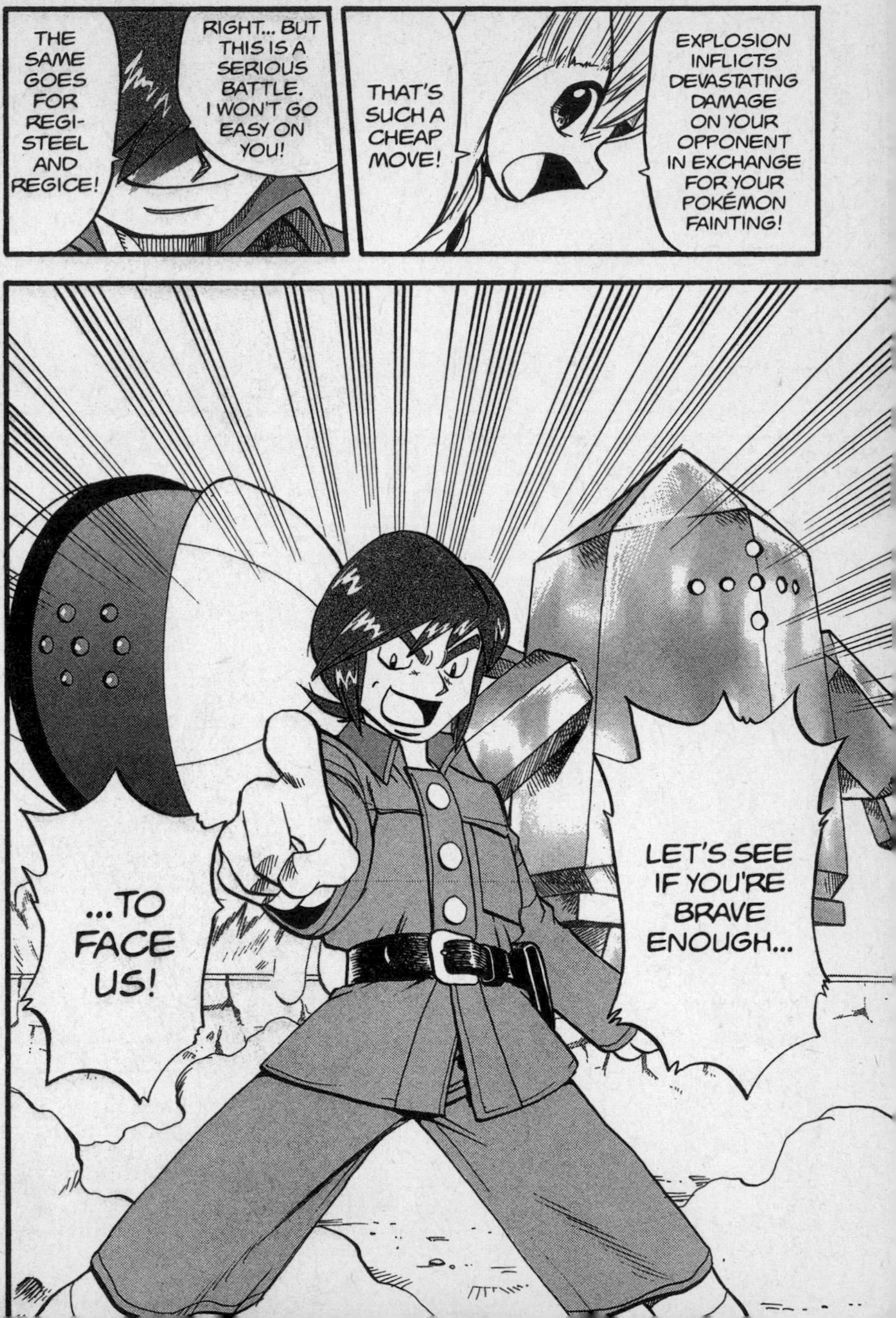
EXPLOSION INFLICTS DEVASTATING DAMAGE ON YOUR OPPONENT IN EXCHANGE FOR YOUR POKÉMON FAINTING!
THAT'S SUCH A CHEAP MOVE!
RIGHT... BUT THIS IS A SERIOUS BATTLE. I WON'T GO EASY ON YOU!
THE SAME GOES FOR REGI-STEEL AND REGICE!
LET'S SEE IF YOU'RE BRAVE ENOUGH...
...TO FACE US!

WHOAAA!

TING

SMASH

SO YOUR SECOND POKÉMON IS REGISTEEL!

SCEPTILE, CUBONE, HITMONCHAN.

THOSE ARE THE THREE POKÉMON YOU CHOSE FOR YOUR FINAL TEAM, HUH?

LET ME JUST GET SCEPTILE OUT OF THE WAY...

...AND THEN...

BOM

BOM

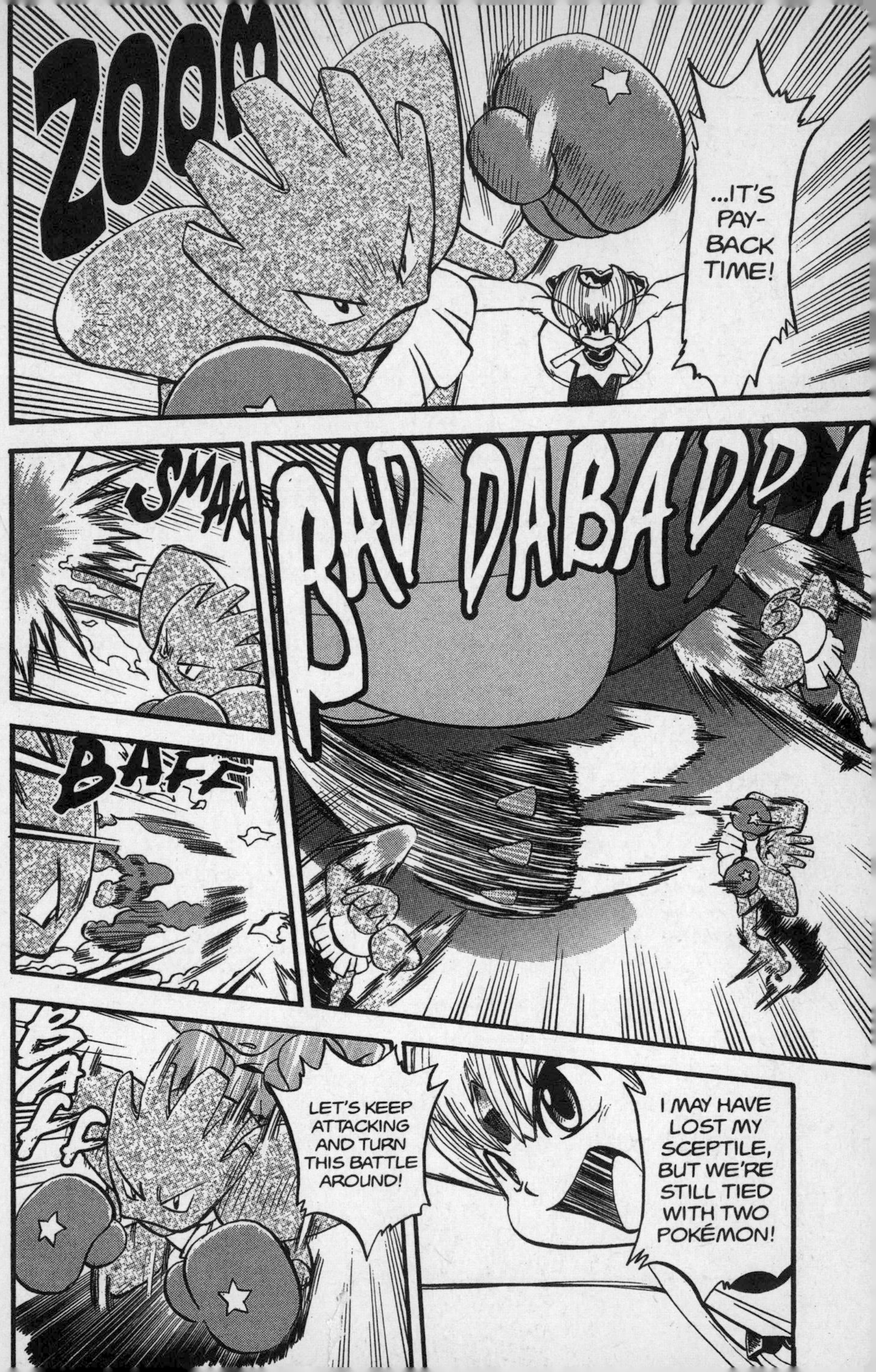

...IT'S PAY-BACK TIME!
ZOOM
BAD DABADDA
SMAK
BAFF
I MAY HAVE LOST MY SCEPTILE, BUT WE'RE STILL TIED WITH TWO POKÉMON!
LET'S KEEP ATTACKING AND TURN THIS BATTLE AROUND!
BAFF

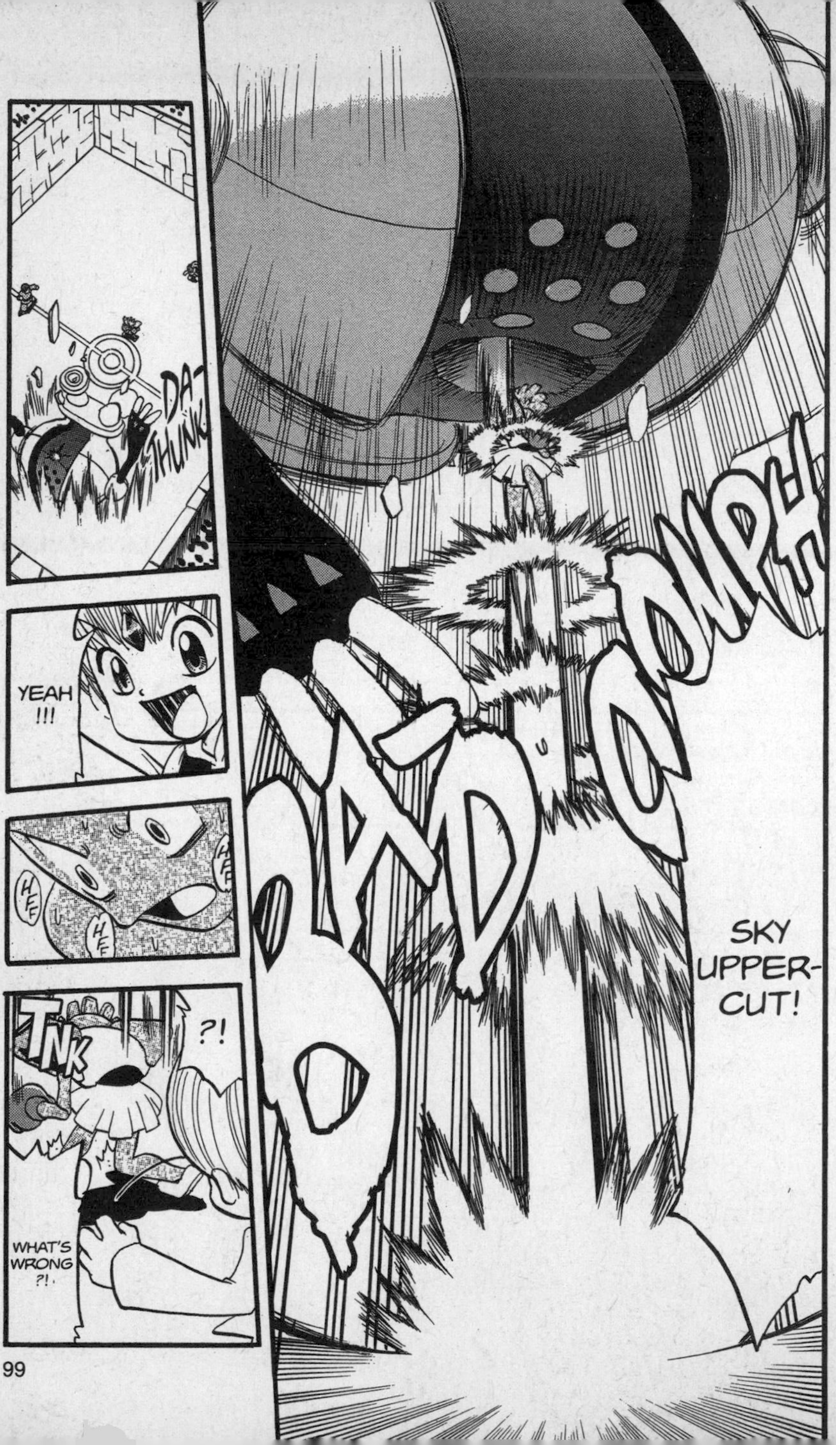
BADOOMPH
SKY UPPER-CUT!
DAT THUNK
YEAH !!!
HFF
HFF
HFF
TNK
?!
WHAT'S WRONG ?!

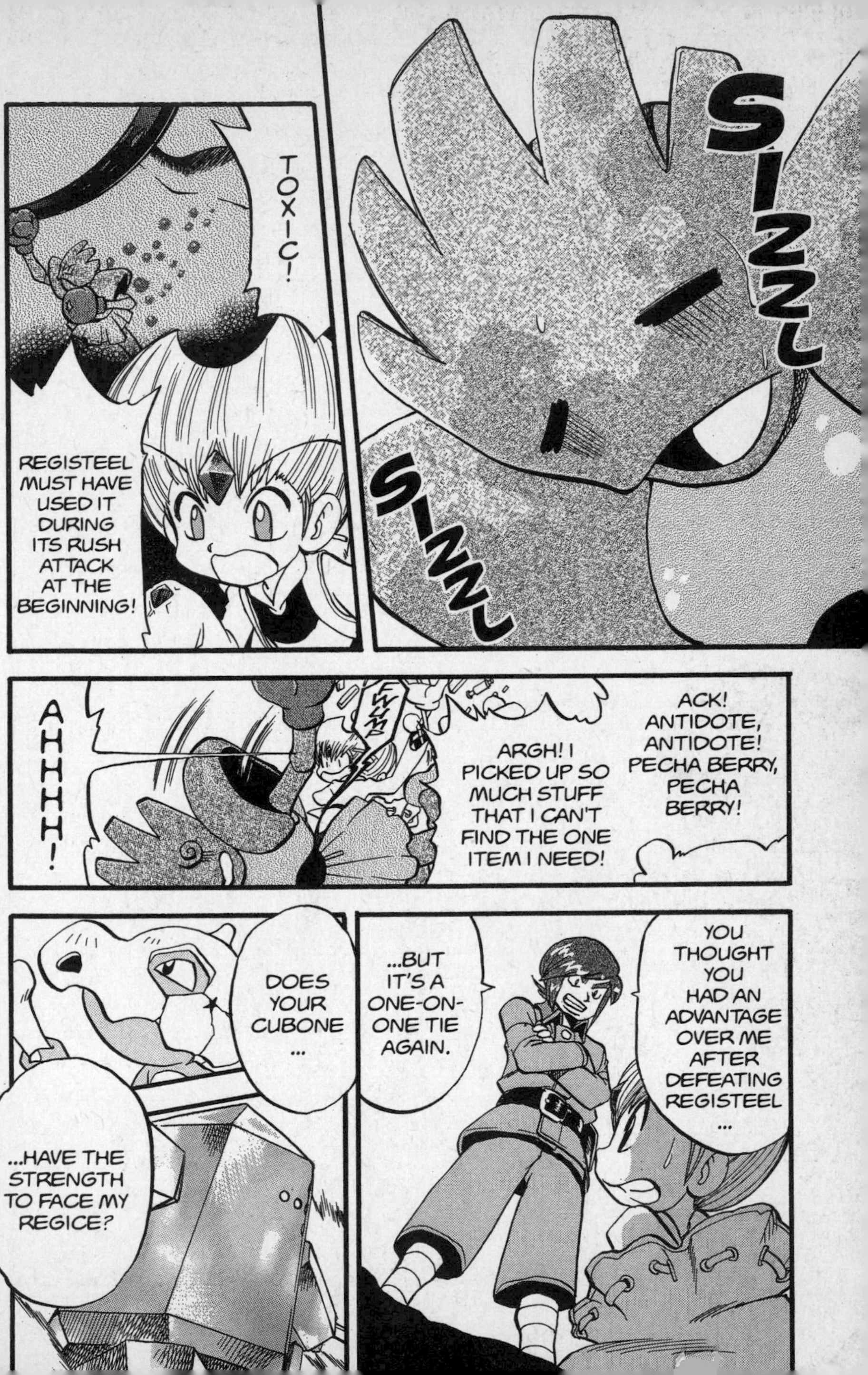
SIZZL
SIZZL
TOXIC!
REGISTEEL MUST HAVE USED IT DURING ITS RUSH ATTACK AT THE BEGINNING!
ACK! ANTIDOTE, ANTIDOTE! PECHA BERRY, PECHA BERRY!
ARGH! I PICKED UP SO MUCH STUFF THAT I CAN'T FIND THE ONE ITEM I NEED!
FWUMP
AHHHH!
YOU THOUGHT YOU HAD AN ADVANTAGE OVER ME AFTER DEFEATING REGISTEEL ...
...BUT IT'S A ONE-ON-ONE TIE AGAIN.
DOES YOUR CUBONE ...
...HAVE THE STRENGTH TO FACE MY REGICE?

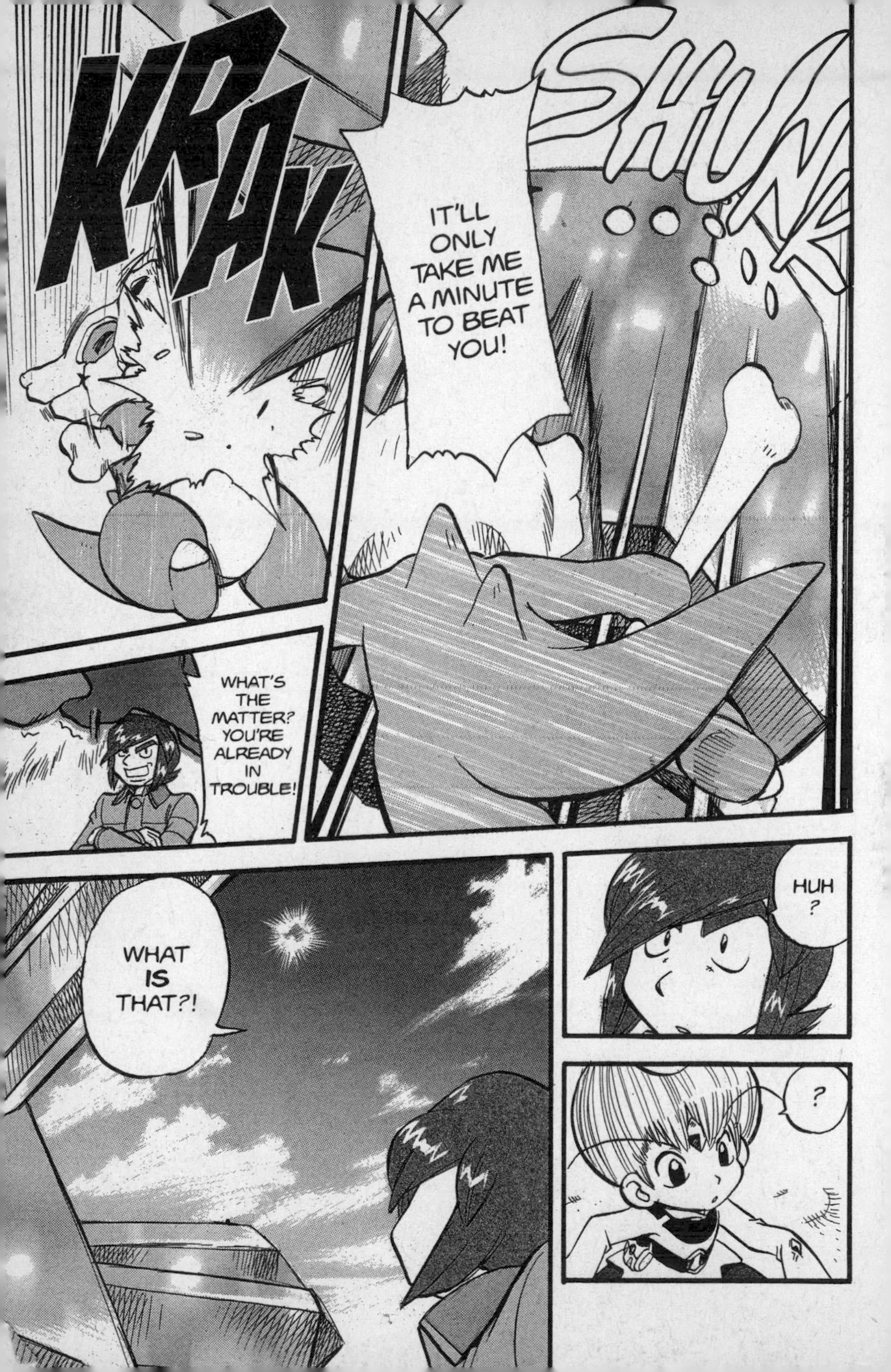
SHUNK
IT'LL ONLY TAKE ME A MINUTE TO BEAT YOU!
KRAK
WHAT'S THE MATTER? YOU'RE ALREADY IN TROUBLE!
HUH?
?
WHAT IS THAT?!

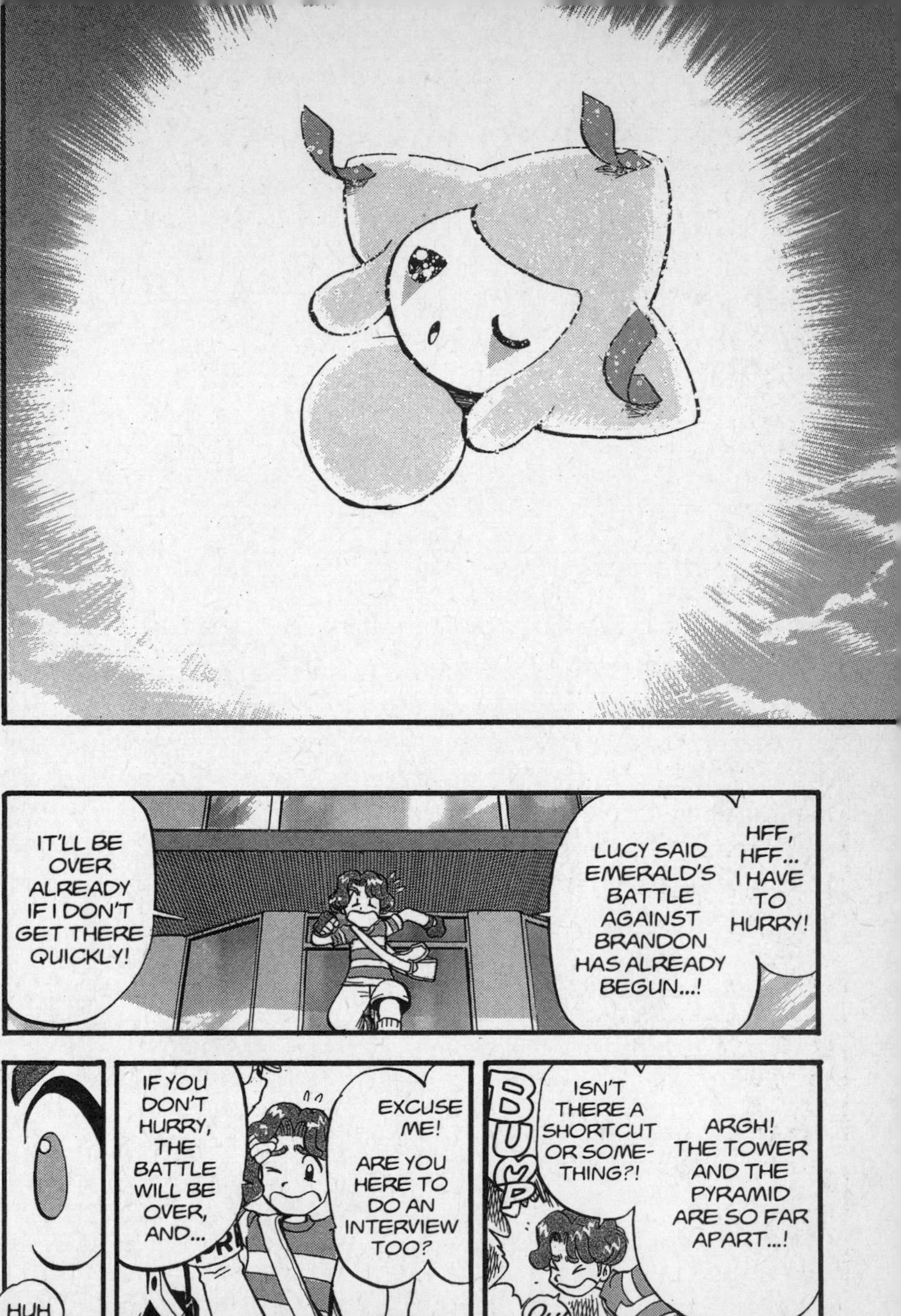
HFF, HFF... I HAVE TO HURRY!
LUCY SAID EMERALD'S BATTLE AGAINST BRANDON HAS ALREADY BEGUN...!
IT'LL BE OVER ALREADY IF I DON'T GET THERE QUICKLY!
ARGH! THE TOWER AND THE PYRAMID ARE SO FAR APART...!
ISN'T THERE A SHORTCUT OR SOME-THING?!
BUMP
OH!
EXCUSE ME!
ARE YOU HERE TO DO AN INTERVIEW TOO?
IF YOU DON'T HURRY, THE BATTLE WILL BE OVER, AND...
HUH?

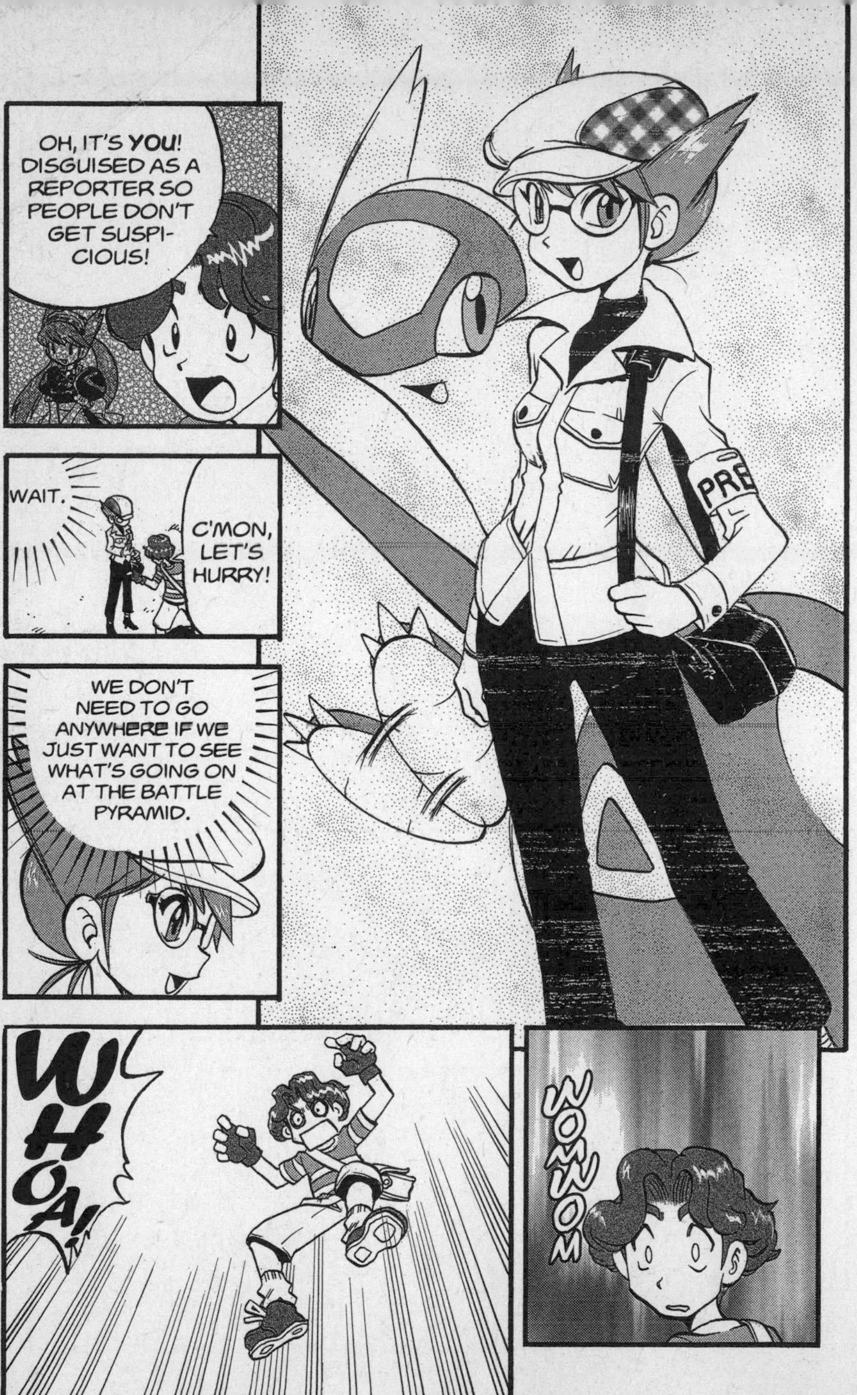
PRE
OH, IT'S **YOU**! DISGUISED AS A REPORTER SO PEOPLE DON'T GET SUSPICIOUS!
C'MON, LET'S HURRY!
WAIT.
WE DON'T NEED TO GO ANYWHERE IF WE JUST WANT TO SEE WHAT'S GOING ON AT THE BATTLE PYRAMID.
WOMWOM
WHOA!

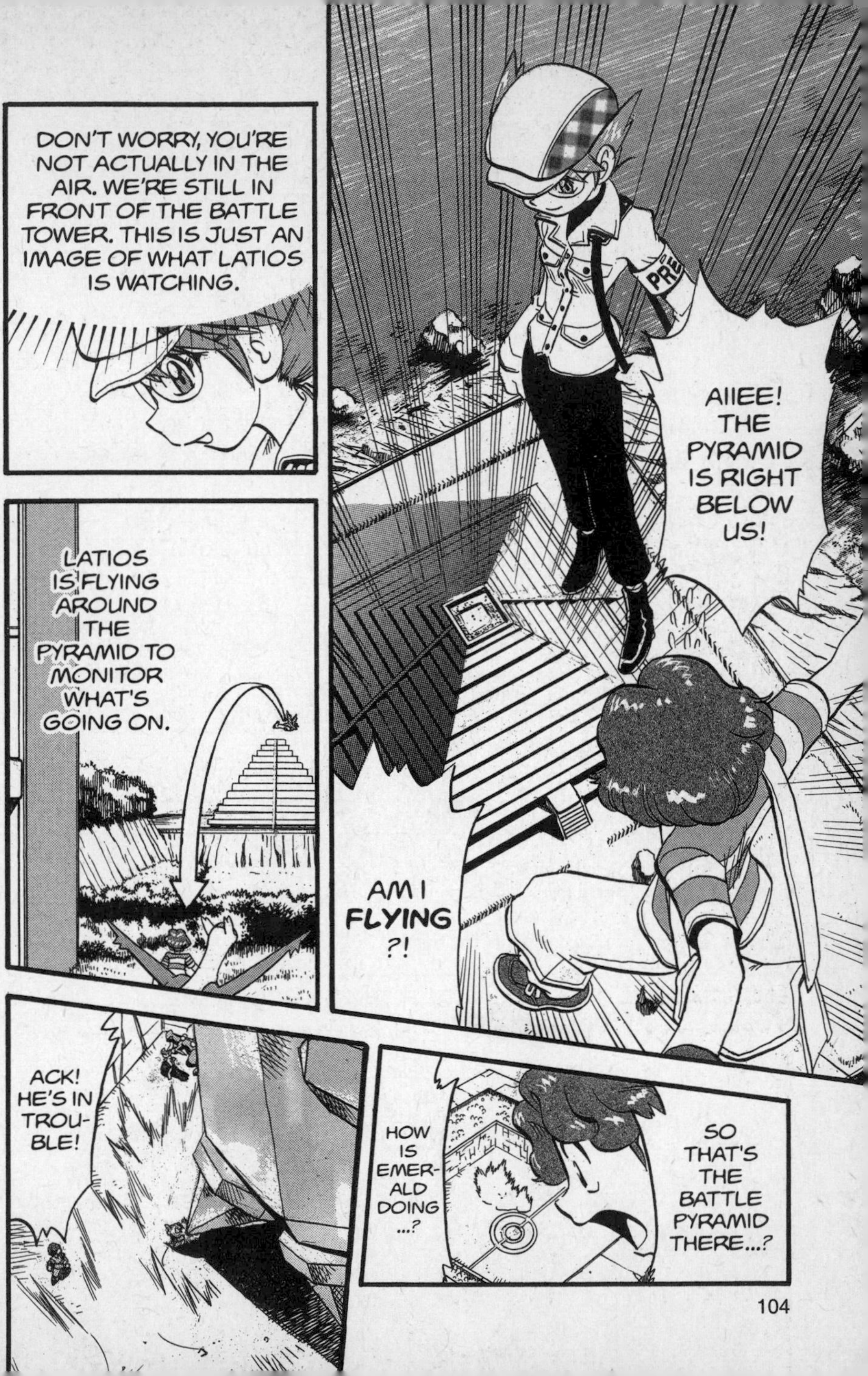
AIIEE! THE PYRAMID IS RIGHT BELOW US!
AM I FLYING?!
DON'T WORRY, YOU'RE NOT ACTUALLY IN THE AIR. WE'RE STILL IN FRONT OF THE BATTLE TOWER. THIS IS JUST AN IMAGE OF WHAT LATIOS IS WATCHING.
LATIOS IS FLYING AROUND THE PYRAMID TO MONITOR WHAT'S GOING ON.
SO THAT'S THE BATTLE PYRAMID THERE...?
HOW IS EMERALD DOING...?
ACK! HE'S IN TROUBLE!

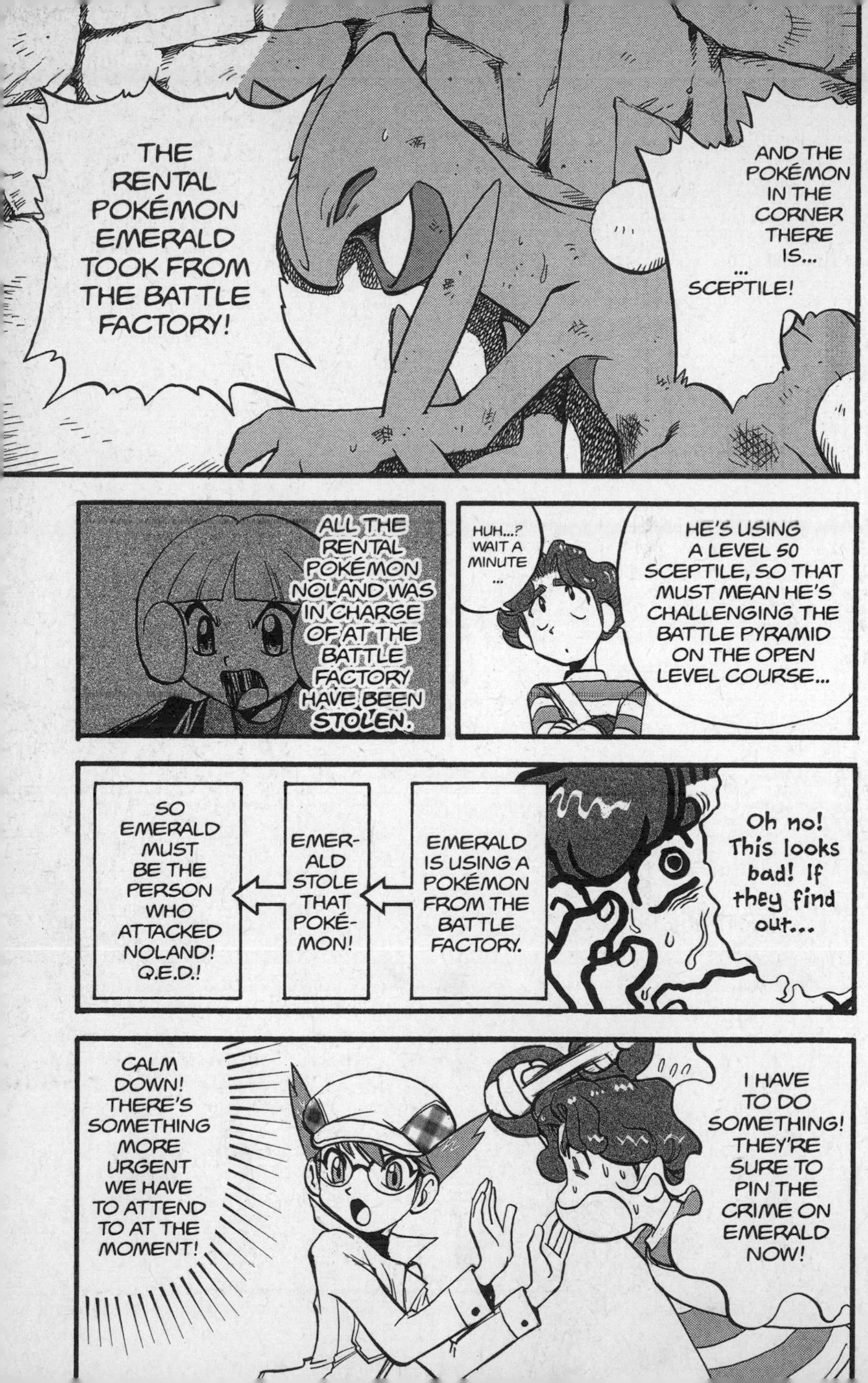
AND THE POKÉMON IN THE CORNER THERE IS... ... SCEPTILE!
THE RENTAL POKÉMON EMERALD TOOK FROM THE BATTLE FACTORY!
HUH...? WAIT A MINUTE ...
HE'S USING A LEVEL 50 SCEPTILE, SO THAT MUST MEAN HE'S CHALLENGING THE BATTLE PYRAMID ON THE OPEN LEVEL COURSE...
ALL THE RENTAL POKÉMON NOLAND WAS IN CHARGE OF AT THE BATTLE FACTORY HAVE BEEN STOLEN.
Oh no! This looks bad! If they find out...
EMERALD IS USING A POKÉMON FROM THE BATTLE FACTORY.
EMER-ALD STOLE THAT POKÉ-MON!
SO EMERALD MUST BE THE PERSON WHO ATTACKED NOLAND! Q.E.D.!
I HAVE TO DO SOMETHING! THEY'RE SURE TO PIN THE CRIME ON EMERALD NOW!
CALM DOWN! THERE'S SOMETHING MORE URGENT WE HAVE TO ATTEND TO AT THE MOMENT!

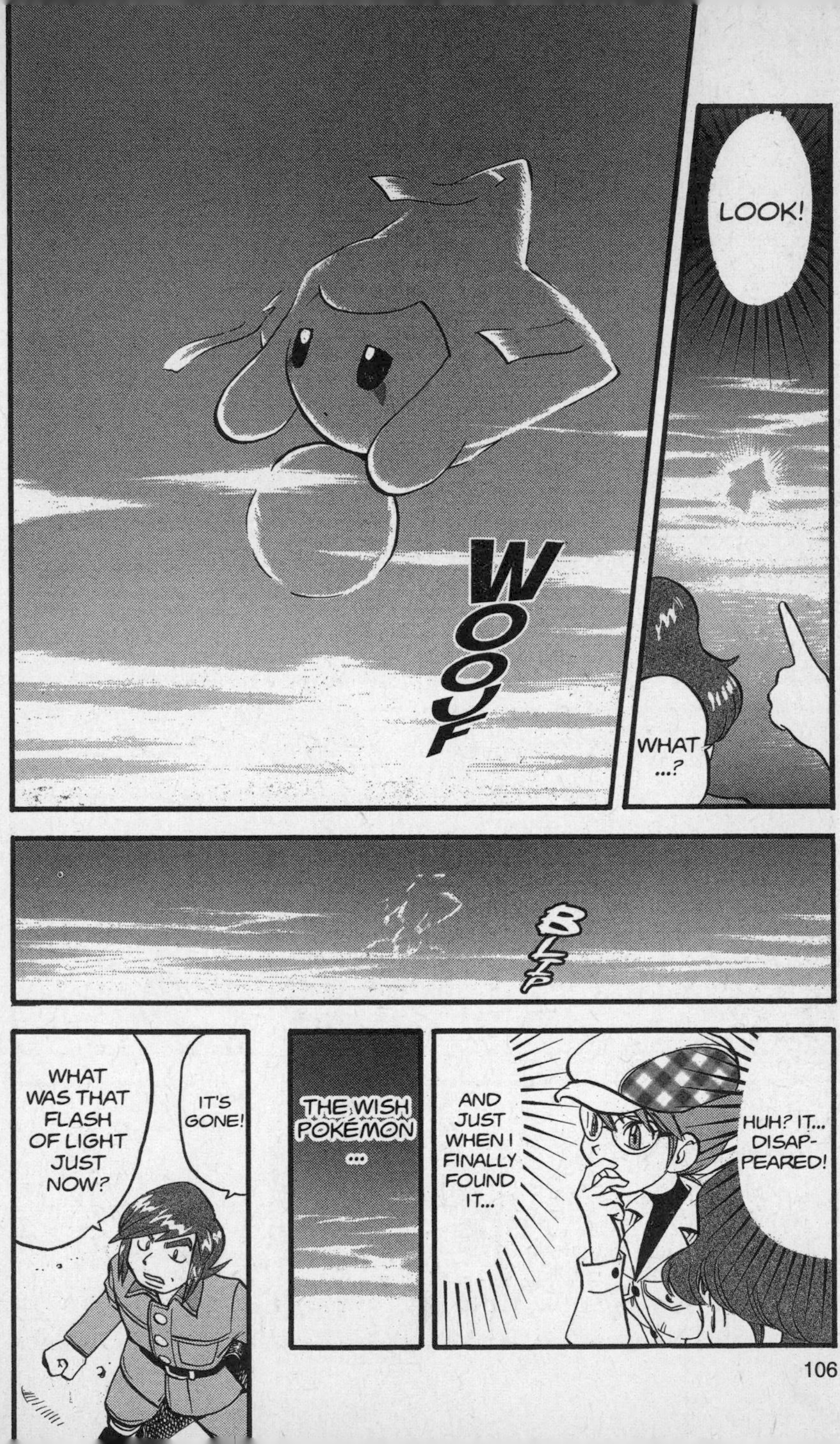

LOOK!
WHAT ...?
WOOUF
BLIP
HUH? IT... DISAP-PEARED!
AND JUST WHEN I FINALLY FOUND IT...
THE WISH POKÉMON ...
IT'S GONE!
WHAT WAS THAT FLASH OF LIGHT JUST NOW?

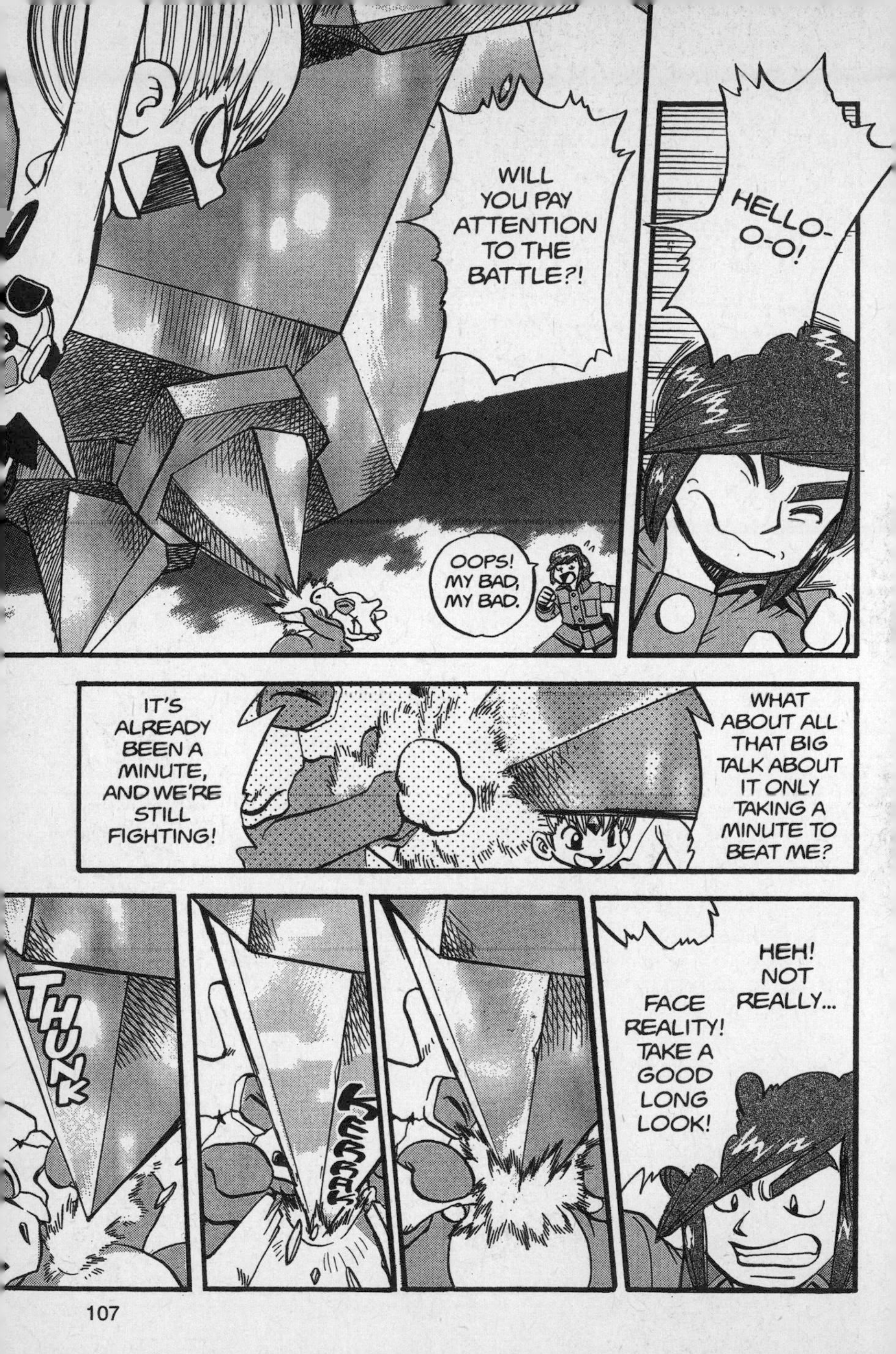
HELLO-O-O!
WILL YOU PAY ATTENTION TO THE BATTLE?!
OOPS! MY BAD, MY BAD.
WHAT ABOUT ALL THAT BIG TALK ABOUT IT ONLY TAKING A MINUTE TO BEAT ME?
IT'S ALREADY BEEN A MINUTE, AND WE'RE STILL FIGHTING!
HEH! NOT REALLY...
FACE REALITY! TAKE A GOOD LONG LOOK!
THUNK

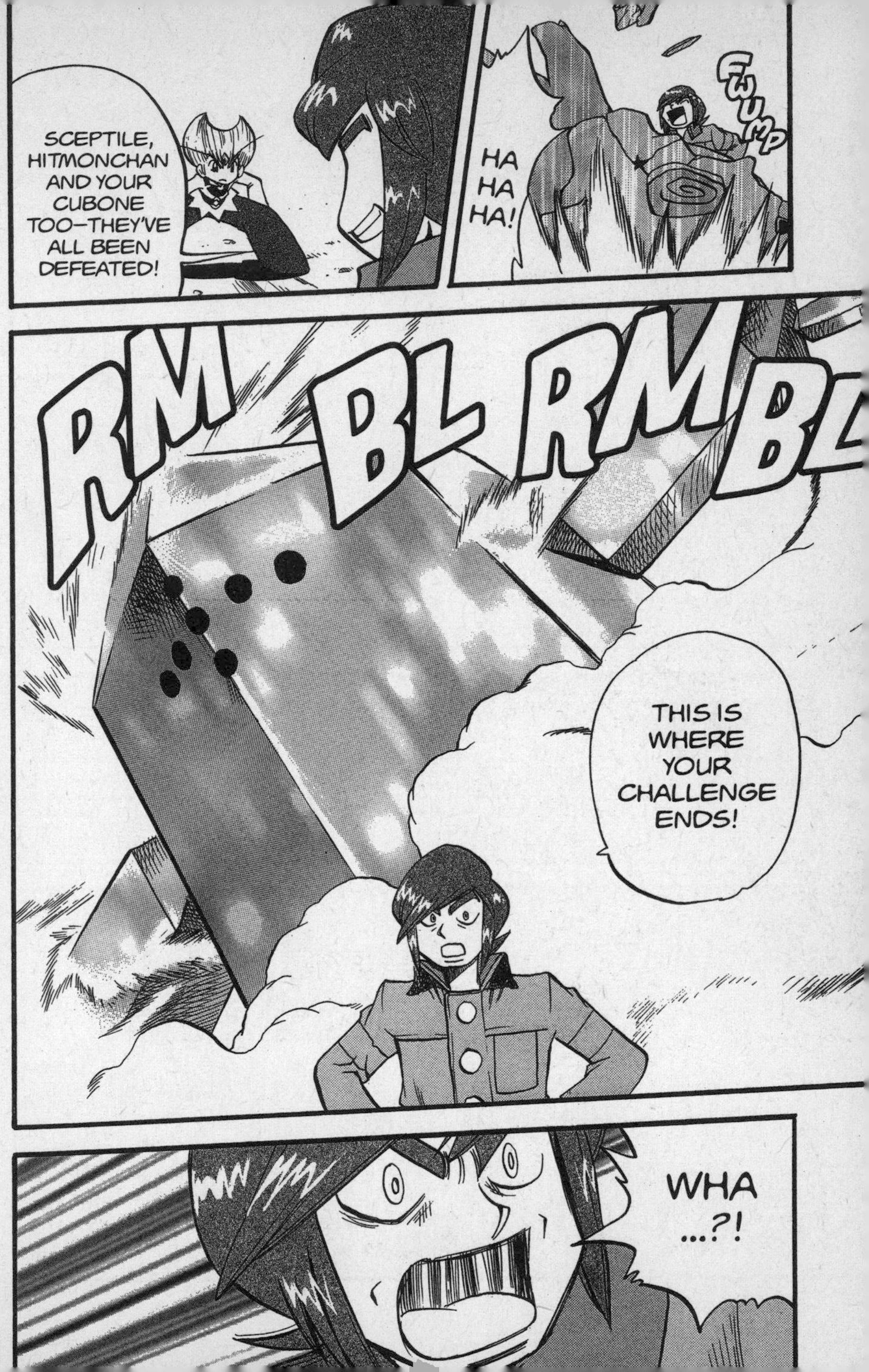
HA HA HA!
FWUMP
SCEPTILE, HITMONCHAN AND YOUR CUBONE TOO—THEY'VE ALL BEEN DEFEATED!
RM BL RM BL
THIS IS WHERE YOUR CHALLENGE ENDS!
WHA ...?!

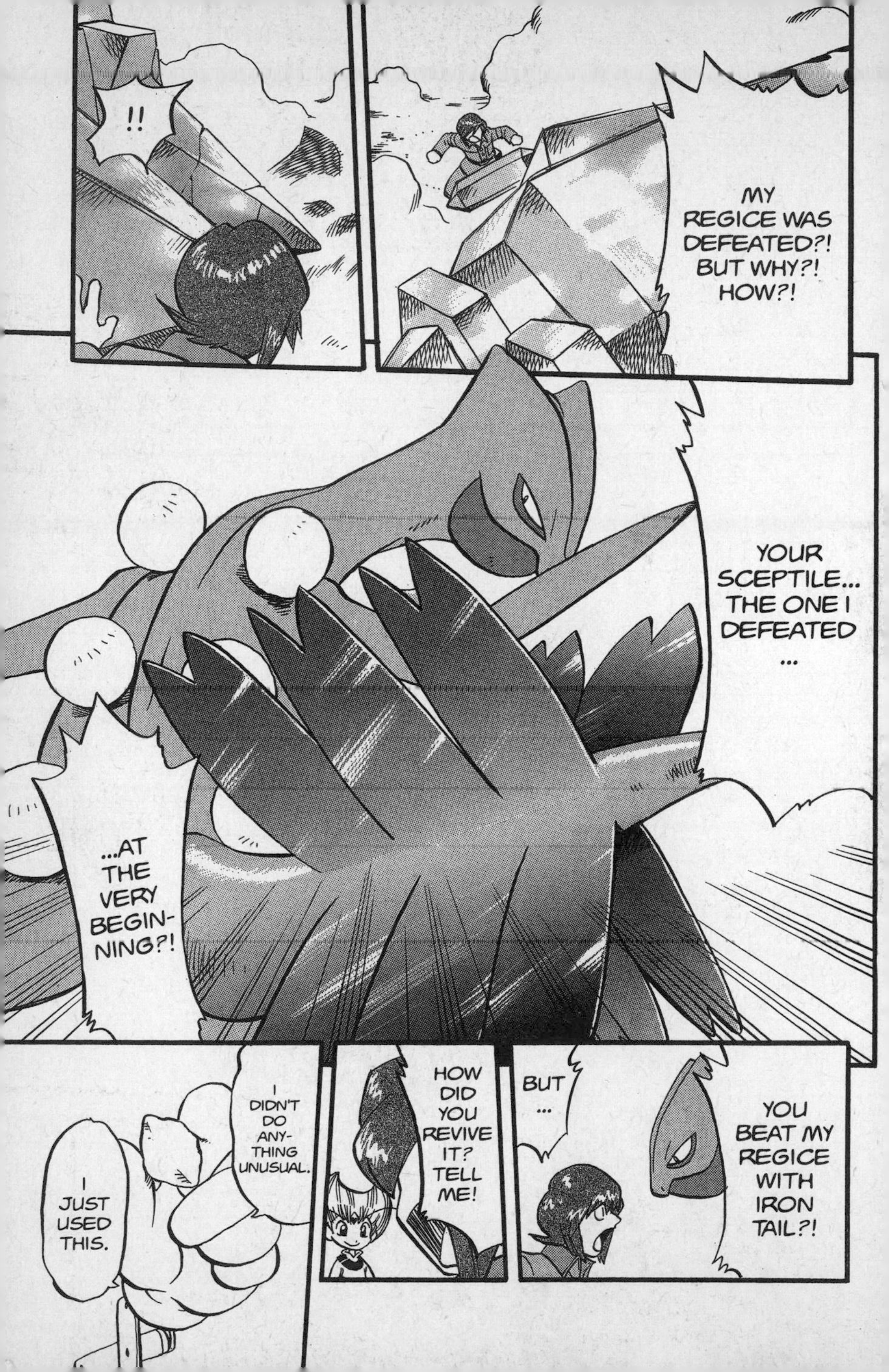
MY REGICE WAS DEFEATED?! BUT WHY?! HOW?!
!!
YOUR SCEPTILE... THE ONE I DEFEATED ...
...AT THE VERY BEGIN-NING?!
YOU BEAT MY REGICE WITH IRON TAIL?!
BUT ...
HOW DID YOU REVIVE IT? TELL ME!
I DIDN'T DO ANY-THING UNUSUAL.
I JUST USED THIS.

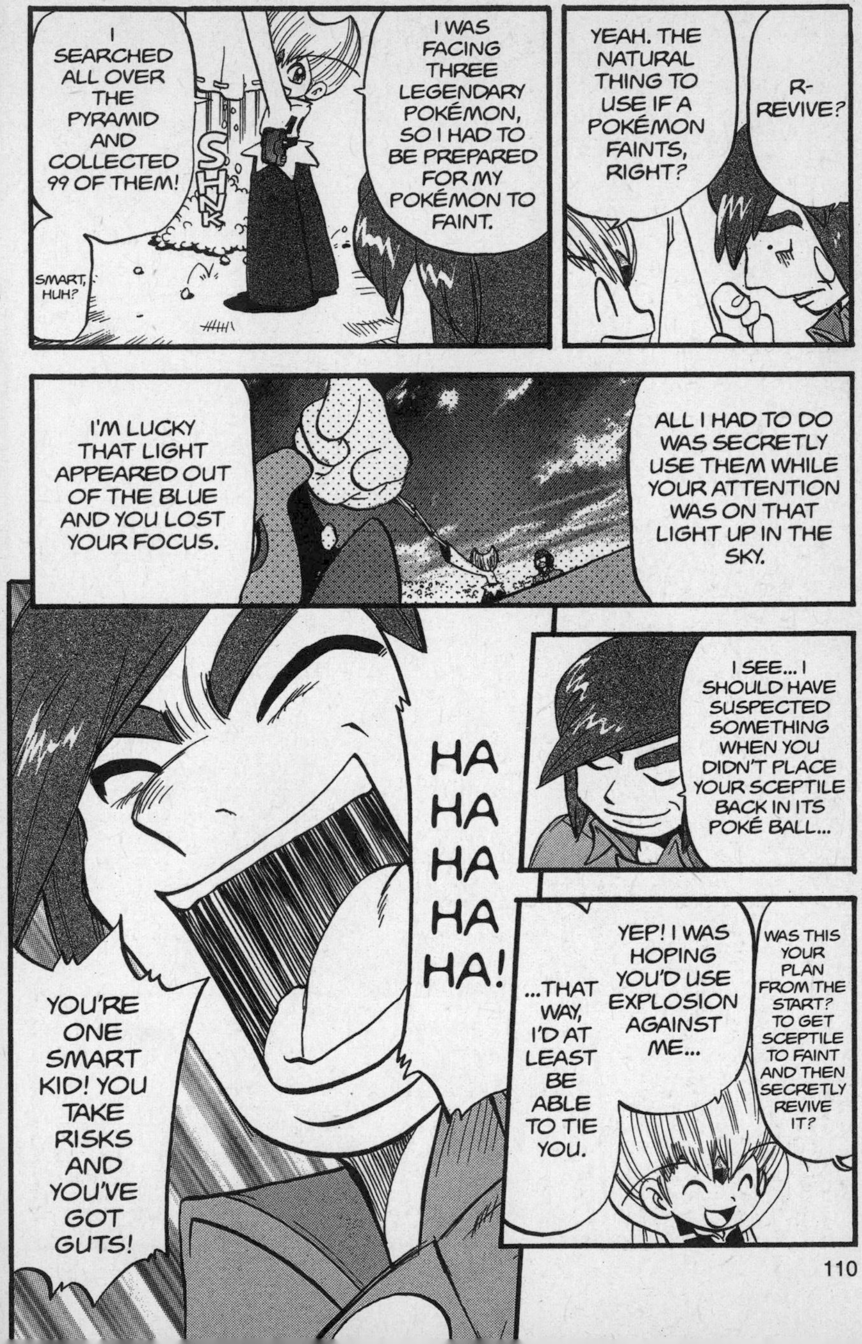
R-REVIVE?
YEAH. THE NATURAL THING TO USE IF A POKÉMON FAINTS, RIGHT?
I WAS FACING THREE LEGENDARY POKÉMON, SO I HAD TO BE PREPARED FOR MY POKÉMON TO FAINT.
SHNK
I SEARCHED ALL OVER THE PYRAMID AND COLLECTED 99 OF THEM!
SMART, HUH?
ALL I HAD TO DO WAS SECRETLY USE THEM WHILE YOUR ATTENTION WAS ON THAT LIGHT UP IN THE SKY.
I'M LUCKY THAT LIGHT APPEARED OUT OF THE BLUE AND YOU LOST YOUR FOCUS.
I SEE... I SHOULD HAVE SUSPECTED SOMETHING WHEN YOU DIDN'T PLACE YOUR SCEPTILE BACK IN ITS POKÉ BALL...
WAS THIS YOUR PLAN FROM THE START? TO GET SCEPTILE TO FAINT AND THEN SECRETLY REVIVE IT?
YEP! I WAS HOPING YOU'D USE EXPLOSION AGAINST ME...
...THAT WAY, I'D AT LEAST BE ABLE TO TIE YOU.
HA HA HA HA HA!
YOU'RE ONE SMART KID! YOU TAKE RISKS AND YOU'VE GOT GUTS!

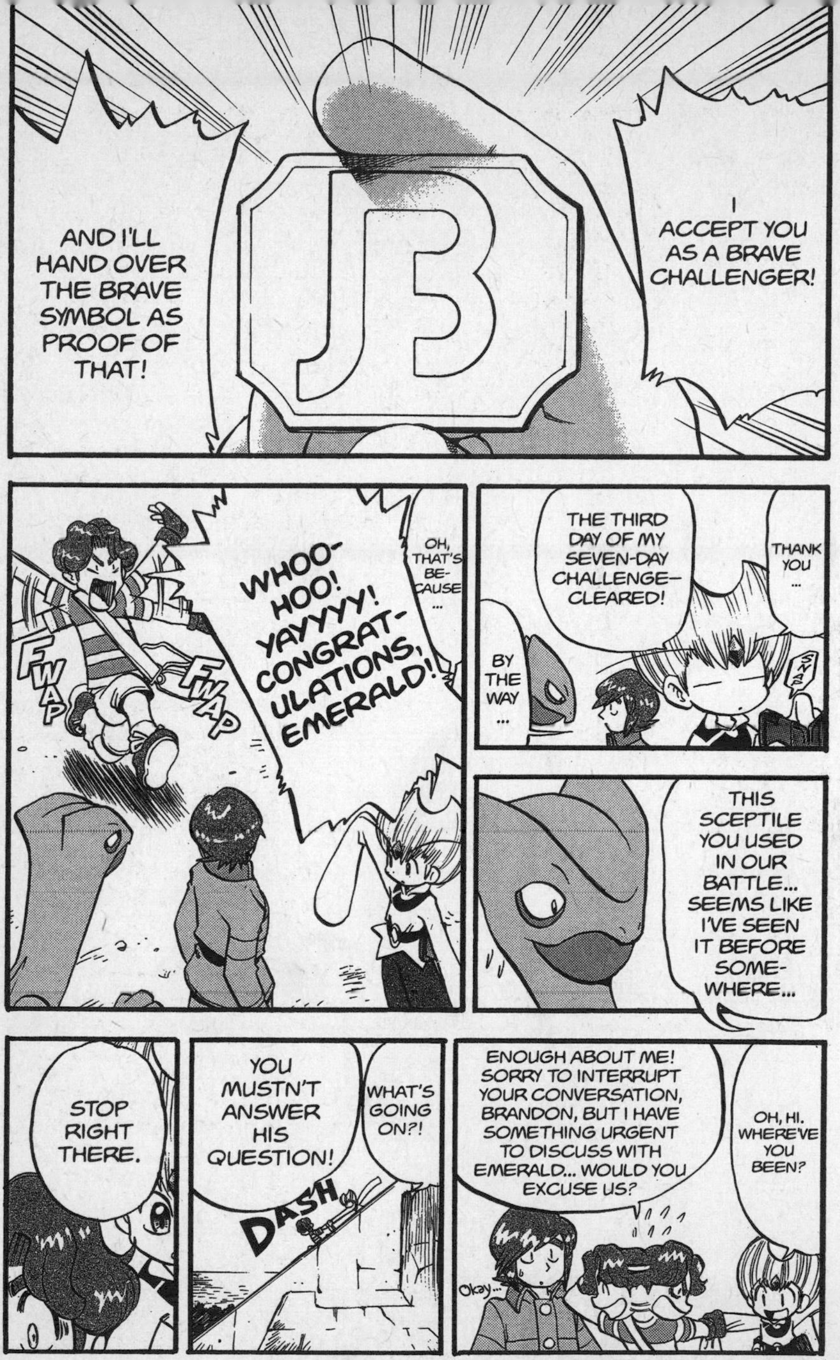
I ACCEPT YOU AS A BRAVE CHALLENGER!
AND I'LL HAND OVER THE BRAVE SYMBOL AS PROOF OF THAT!
THANK YOU ...
SNAP
THE THIRD DAY OF MY SEVEN-DAY CHALLENGE—CLEARED!
BY THE WAY ...
THIS SCEPTILE YOU USED IN OUR BATTLE... SEEMS LIKE I'VE SEEN IT BEFORE SOMEWHERE...
OH, THAT'S BE-CAUSE ...
WHOO-HOO! YAYYYY! CONGRAT-ULATIONS, EMERALD!
FWAP
FWAP
OH, HI. WHERE'VE YOU BEEN?
ENOUGH ABOUT ME! SORRY TO INTERRUPT YOUR CONVERSATION, BRANDON, BUT I HAVE SOMETHING URGENT TO DISCUSS WITH EMERALD... WOULD YOU EXCUSE US?
Okay...
WHAT'S GOING ON?!
YOU MUSTN'T ANSWER HIS QUESTION!
DASH
STOP RIGHT THERE.

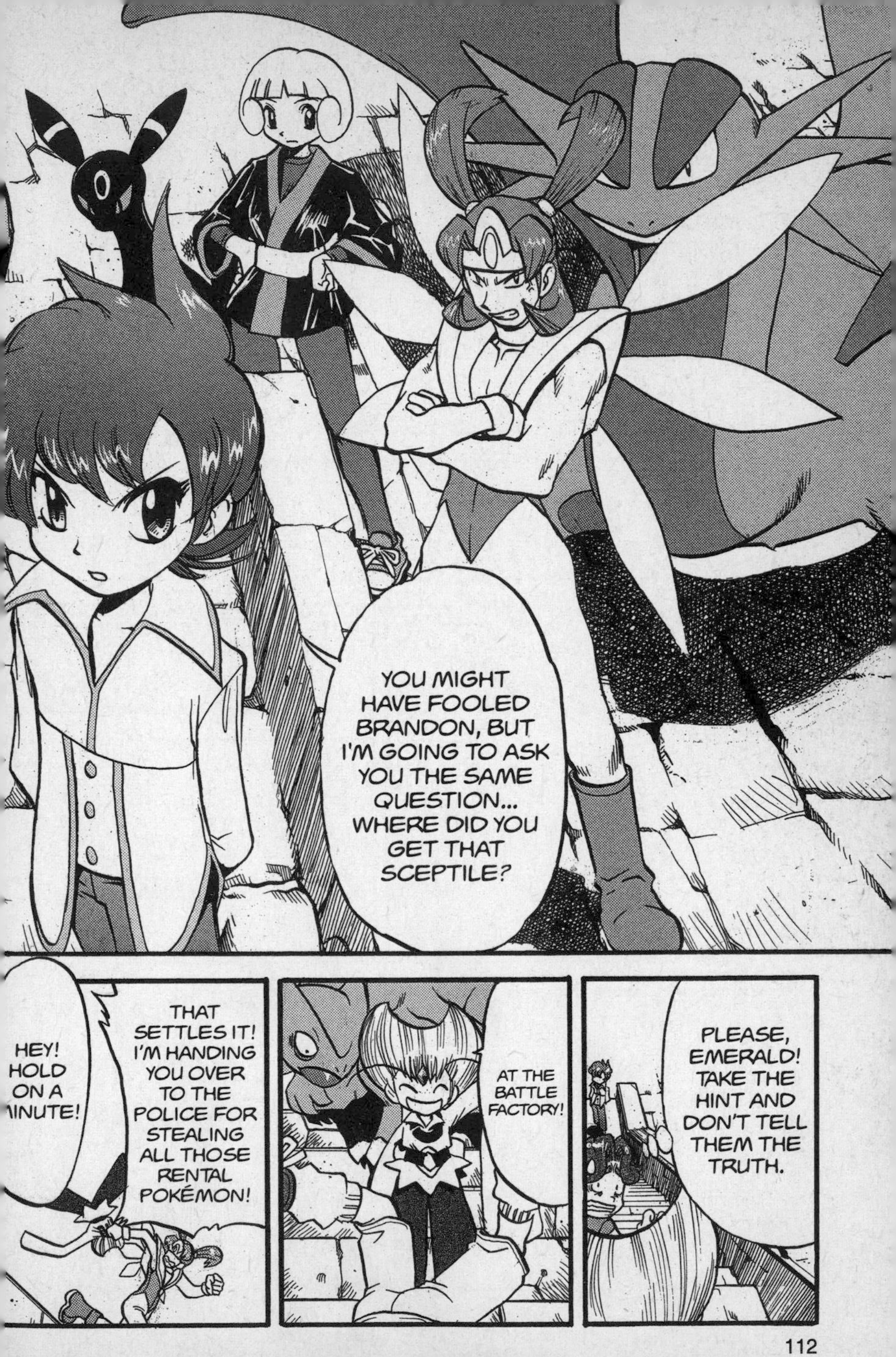

YOU MIGHT HAVE FOOLED BRANDON, BUT I'M GOING TO ASK YOU THE SAME QUESTION... WHERE DID YOU GET THAT SCEPTILE?
PLEASE, EMERALD! TAKE THE HINT AND DON'T TELL THEM THE TRUTH.
AT THE BATTLE FACTORY!
THAT SETTLES IT! I'M HANDING YOU OVER TO THE POLICE FOR STEALING ALL THOSE RENTAL POKÉMON!
HEY! HOLD ON A MINUTE!

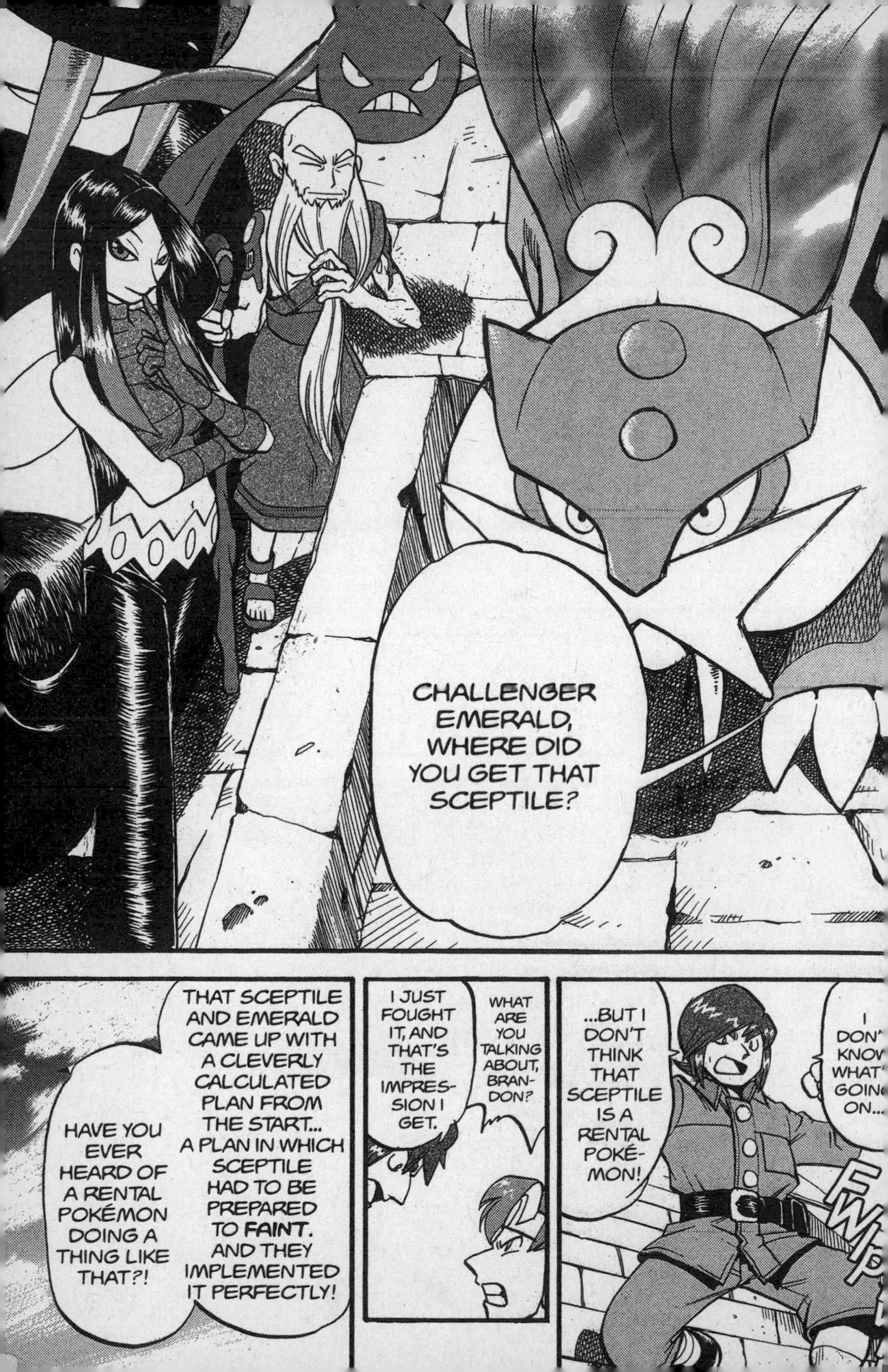
CHALLENGER EMERALD, WHERE DID YOU GET THAT SCEPTILE?
I DON' KNOW WHAT' GOIN ON...
...BUT I DON'T THINK THAT SCEPTILE IS A RENTAL POKÉMON!
FWIP
WHAT ARE YOU TALKING ABOUT, BRANDON?
I JUST FOUGHT IT, AND THAT'S THE IMPRESSION I GET.
THAT SCEPTILE AND EMERALD CAME UP WITH A CLEVERLY CALCULATED PLAN FROM THE START... A PLAN IN WHICH SCEPTILE HAD TO BE PREPARED TO **FAINT**. AND THEY IMPLEMENTED IT PERFECTLY!
HAVE YOU EVER HEARD OF A RENTAL POKÉMON DOING A THING LIKE THAT?!

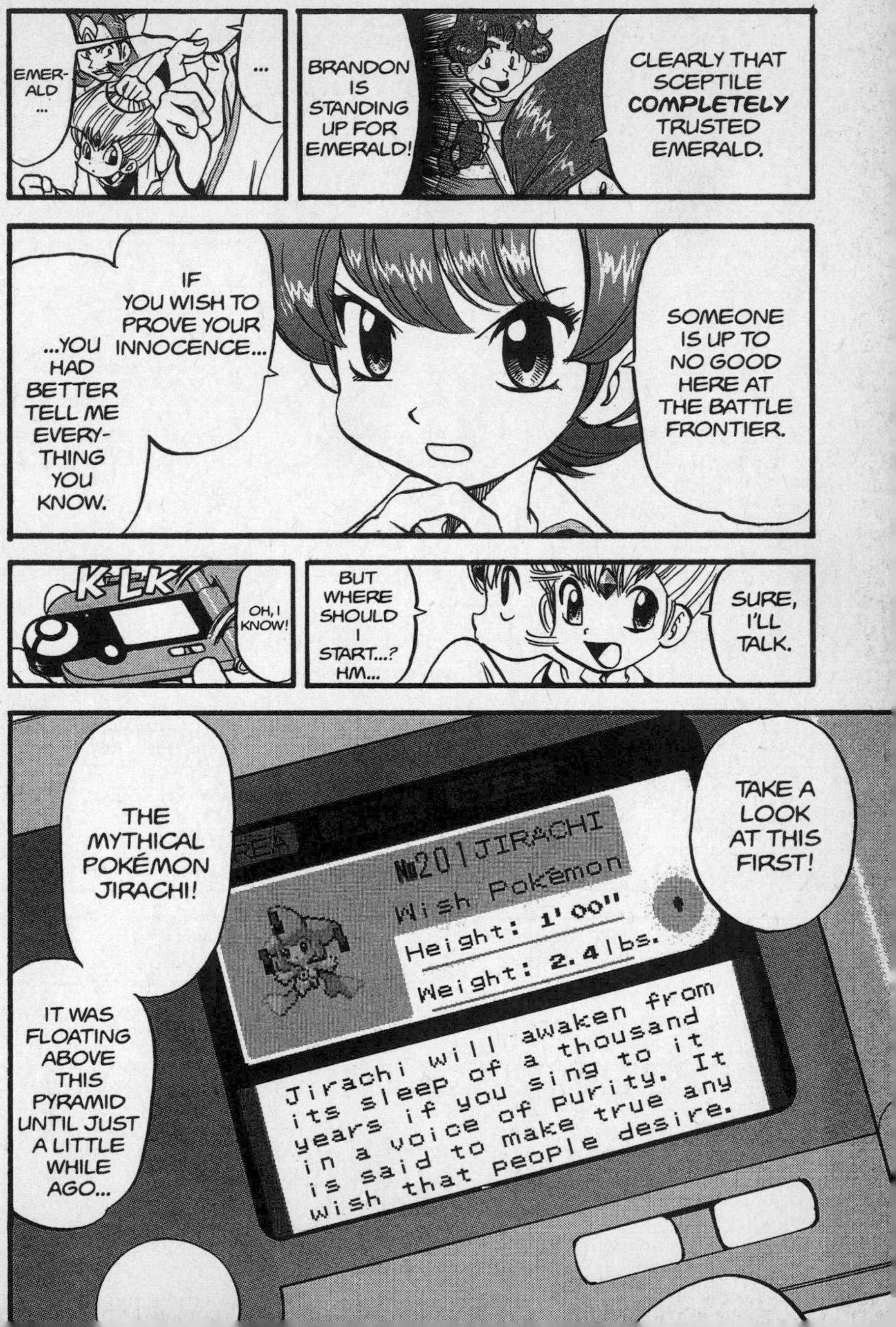
CLEARLY THAT SCEPTILE COMPLETELY TRUSTED EMERALD.
BRANDON IS STANDING UP FOR EMERALD!
...
EMERALD...
SOMEONE IS UP TO NO GOOD HERE AT THE BATTLE FRONTIER.
IF YOU WISH TO PROVE YOUR INNOCENCE...
...YOU HAD BETTER TELL ME EVERYTHING YOU KNOW.
SURE, I'LL TALK.
BUT WHERE SHOULD I START...? HM...
OH, I KNOW!
K-LK
TAKE A LOOK AT THIS FIRST!
No201 JIRACHI
Wish Pokémon
Height: 1'00"
Weight: 2.4 lbs.
Jirachi will awaken from its sleep of a thousand years if you sing to it in a voice of purity. It is said to make true any wish that people desire.
THE MYTHICAL POKÉMON JIRACHI!
IT WAS FLOATING ABOVE THIS PYRAMID UNTIL JUST A LITTLE WHILE AGO...

DEAR MEMBERS OF THE PRESS...

Thank you for visiting the Battle Frontier today. Permit me to continue explaining the rules of this facility...

OWNER: SCOTT

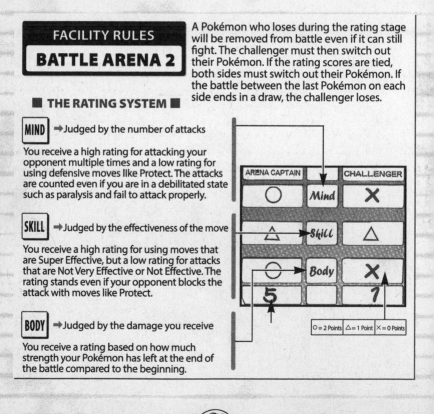

FACILITY RULES
BATTLE ARENA 2

A Pokémon who loses during the rating stage will be removed from battle even if it can still fight. The challenger must then switch out their Pokémon. If the rating scores are tied, both sides must switch out their Pokémon. If the battle between the last Pokémon on each side ends in a draw, the challenger loses.

■ THE RATING SYSTEM ■

MIND → Judged by the number of attacks

You receive a high rating for attacking your opponent multiple times and a low rating for using defensive moves like Protect. The attacks are counted even if you are in a debilitated state such as paralysis and fail to attack properly.

SKILL → Judged by the effectiveness of the move

You receive a high rating for using moves that are Super Effective, but a low rating for attacks that are Not Very Effective or Not Effective. The rating stands even if your opponent blocks the attack with moves like Protect.

BODY → Judged by the damage you receive

You receive a rating based on how much strength your Pokémon has left at the end of the battle compared to the beginning.

ARENA CAPTAIN		CHALLENGER
○	Mind	✕
△	Skill	△
○	Body	✕
5		**1**

○ = 2 Points △ = 1 Point ✕ = 0 Points

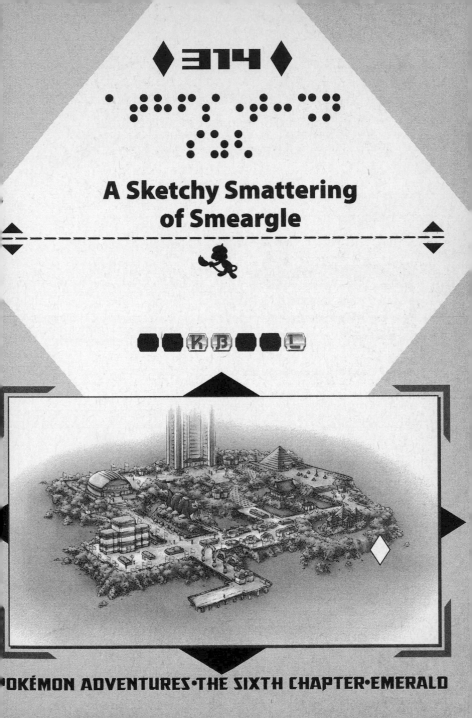

◆ 314 ◆

A Sketchy Smattering of Smeargle

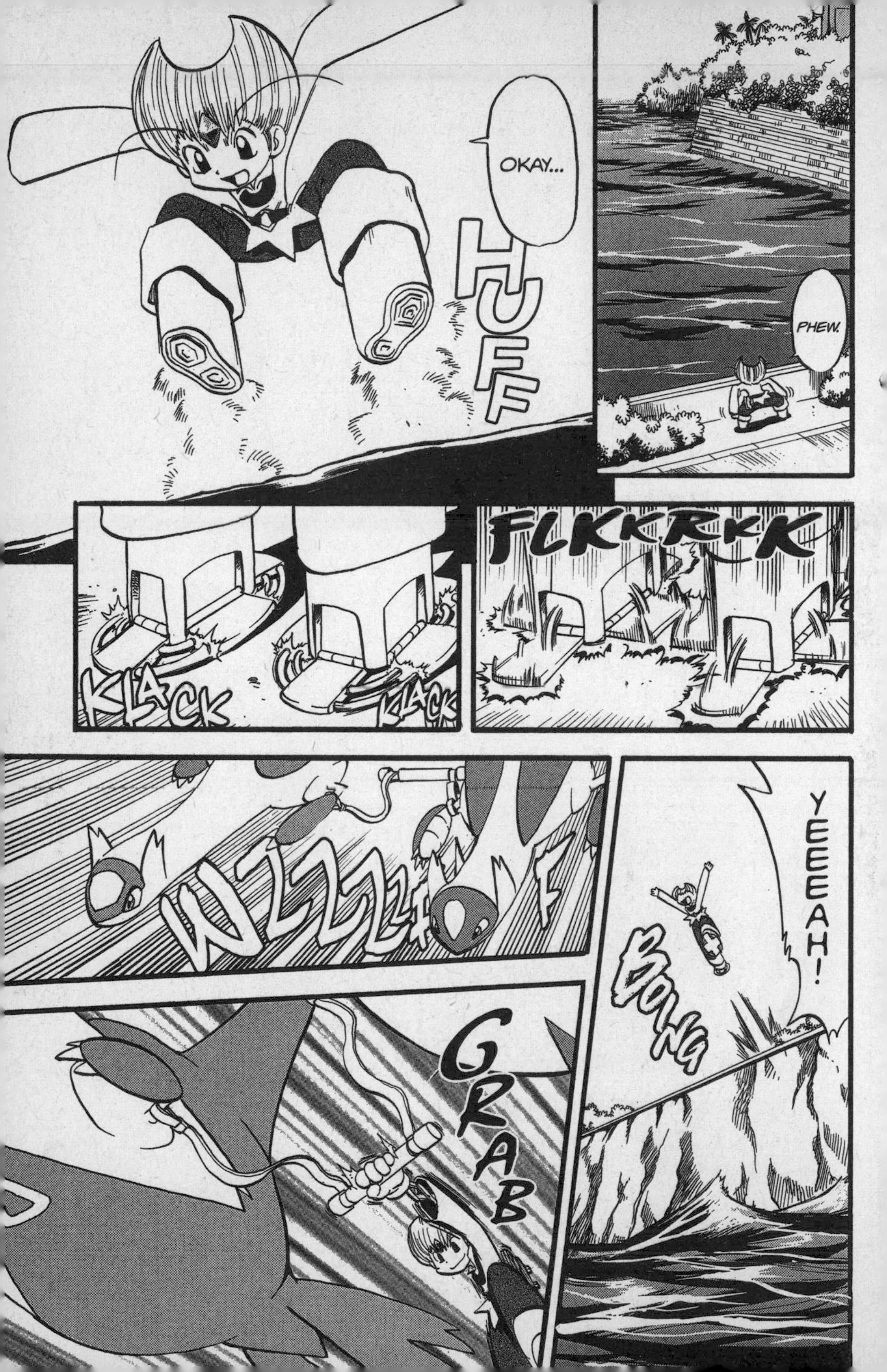
PHEW.
OKAY...
HUFF
FLKKRRKK
KLACK
KLACK
YEEEAH!
BOING
GRAB

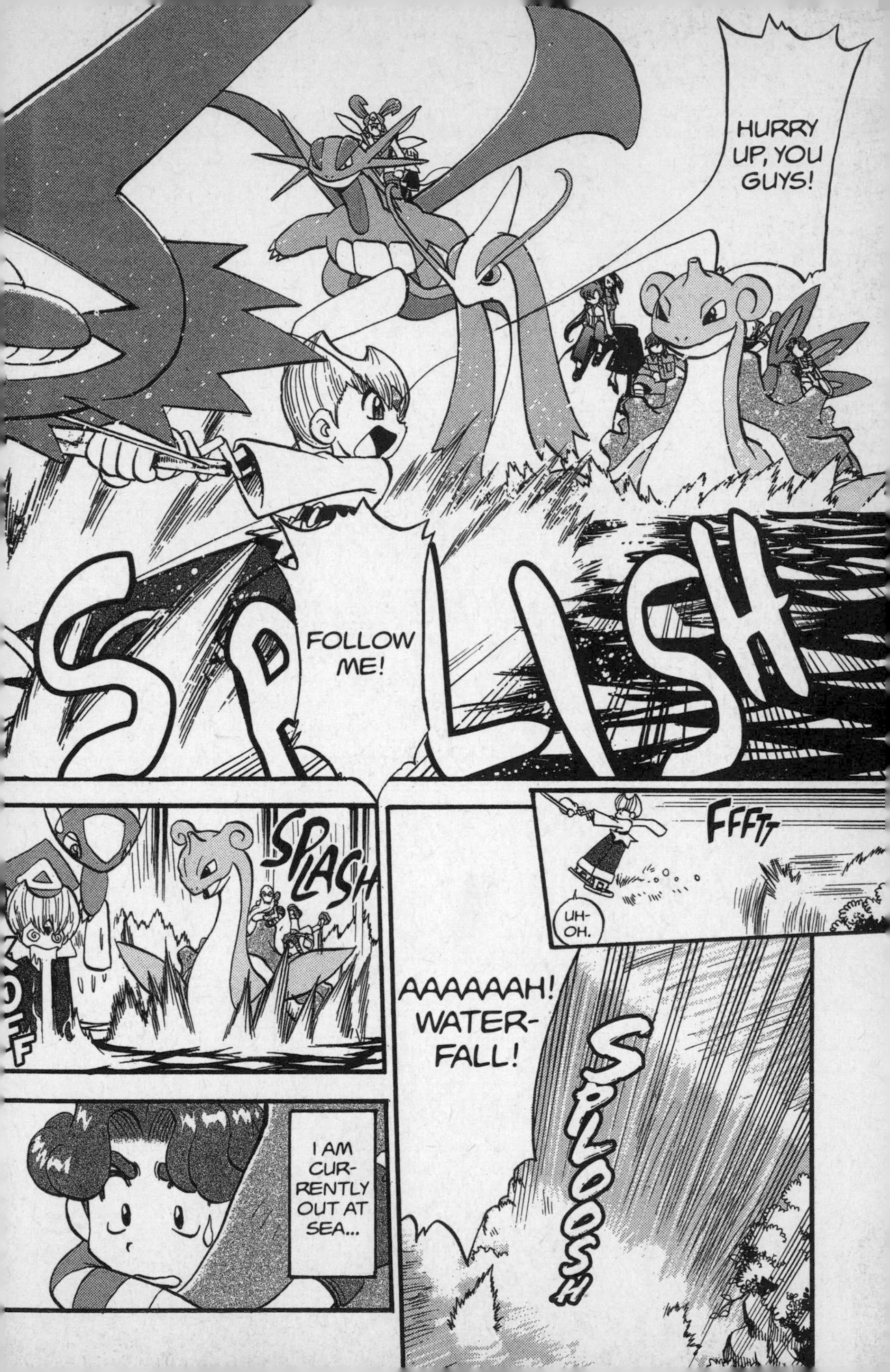
HURRY UP, YOU GUYS!
SPLASH
FOLLOW ME!
FFFTT
UH-OH.
AAAAAAH! WATER-FALL!
SPLOOSH
SPLASH
I AM CUR-RENTLY OUT AT SEA...

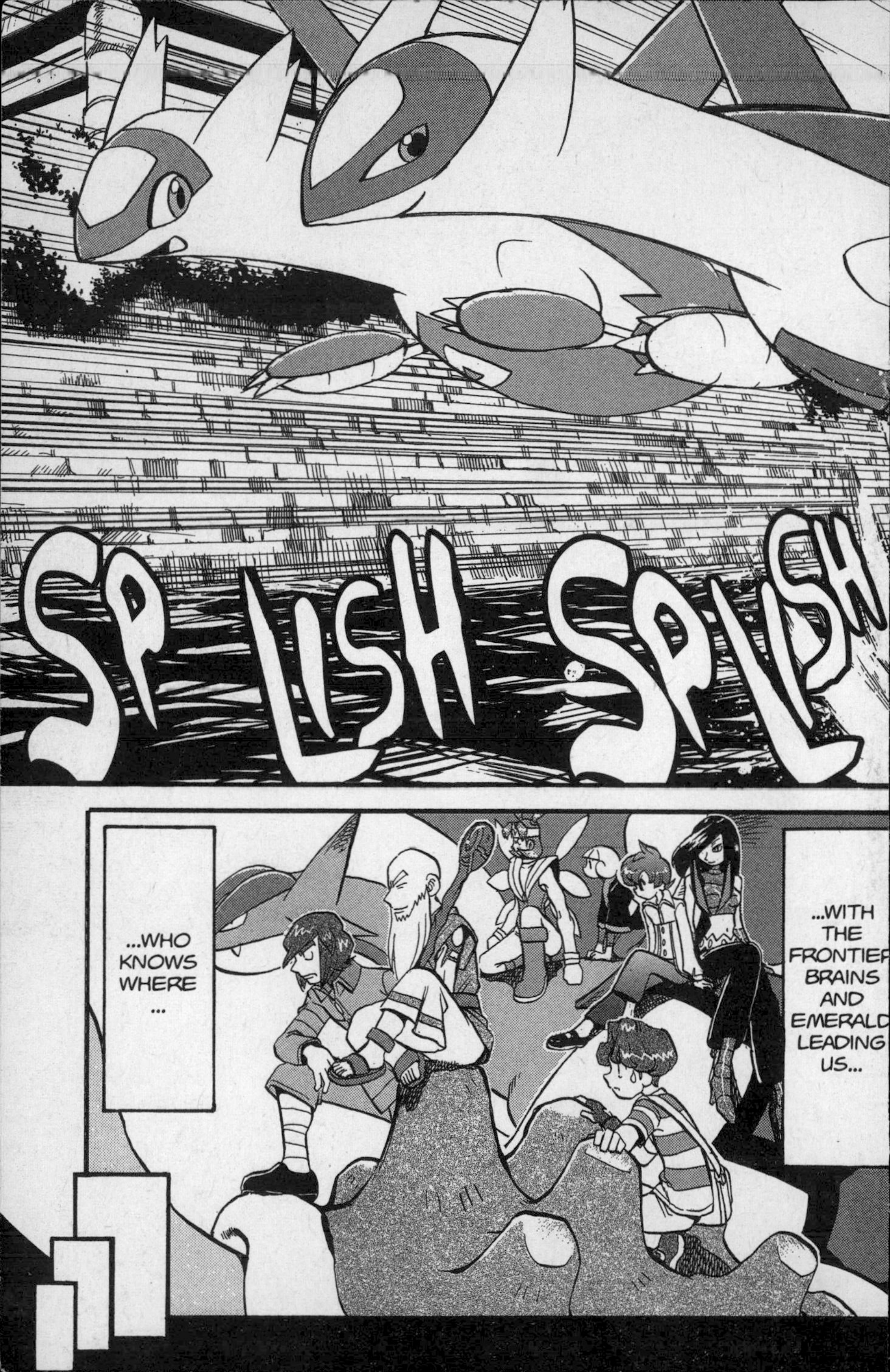
SPLISH SPLISH
...WITH THE FRONTIER BRAINS AND EMERALD LEADING US...
...WHO KNOWS WHERE ...

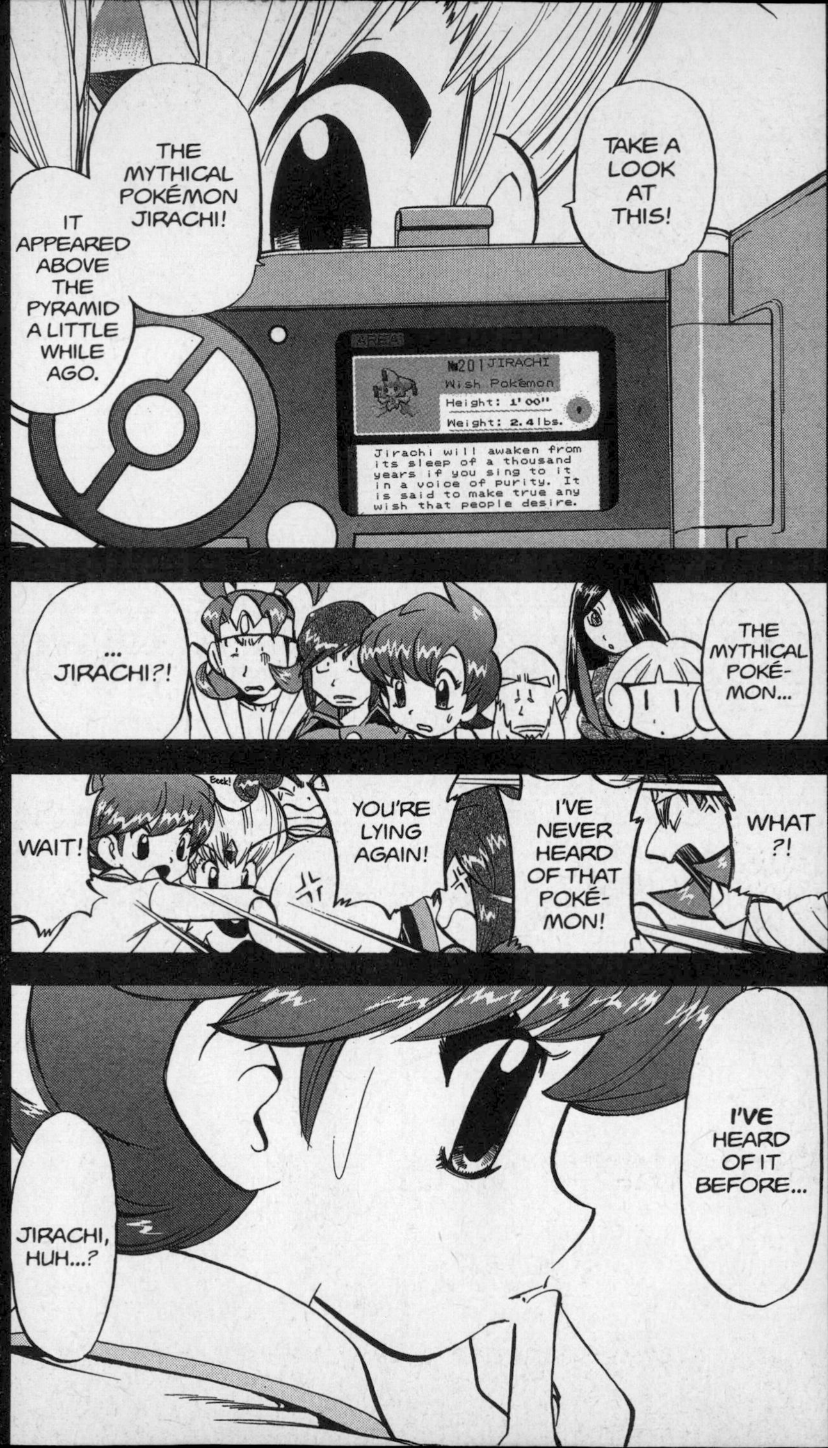

TAKE A LOOK AT THIS!
THE MYTHICAL POKÉMON JIRACHI!
IT APPEARED ABOVE THE PYRAMID A LITTLE WHILE AGO.
AREA
№201 JIRACHI
Wish Pokémon
Height: 1'00"
Weight: 2.4lbs.
Jirachi will awaken from its sleep of a thousand years if you sing to it in a voice of purity. It is said to make true any wish that people desire.
THE MYTHICAL POKÉ-MON...
...JIRACHI?!
WHAT?!
I'VE NEVER HEARD OF THAT POKÉ-MON!
YOU'RE LYING AGAIN!
Eeek!
WAIT!
I'VE HEARD OF IT BEFORE...
JIRACHI, HUH...?

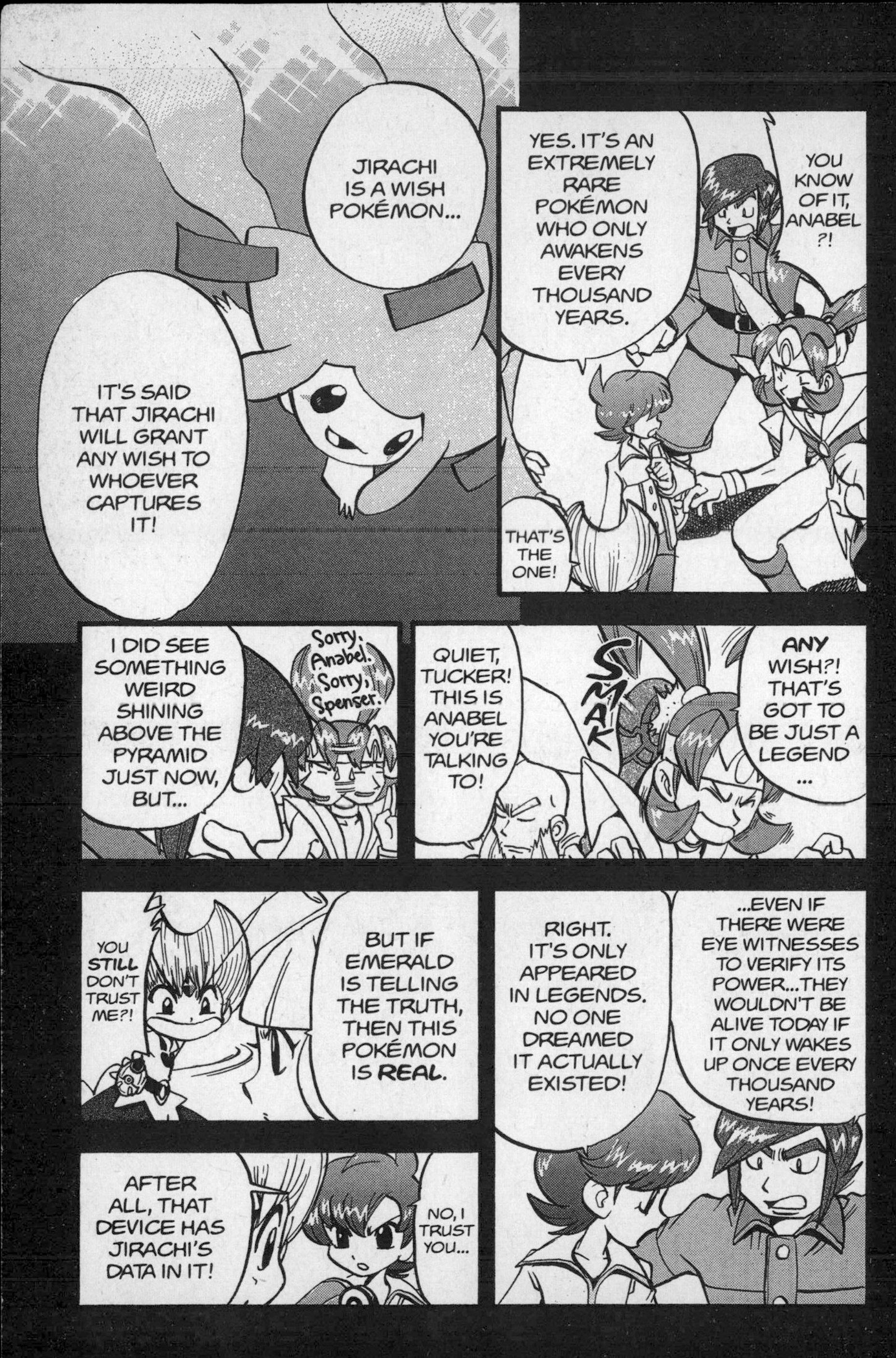
YOU KNOW OF IT, ANABEL?!
YES. IT'S AN EXTREMELY RARE POKÉMON WHO ONLY AWAKENS EVERY THOUSAND YEARS.
THAT'S THE ONE!
JIRACHI IS A WISH POKÉMON...
IT'S SAID THAT JIRACHI WILL GRANT ANY WISH TO WHOEVER CAPTURES IT!
ANY WISH?! THAT'S GOT TO BE JUST A LEGEND...
SMAK
QUIET, TUCKER! THIS IS ANABEL YOU'RE TALKING TO!
Sorry, Anabel. Sorry, Spenser.
I DID SEE SOMETHING WEIRD SHINING ABOVE THE PYRAMID JUST NOW, BUT...
RIGHT. IT'S ONLY APPEARED IN LEGENDS. NO ONE DREAMED IT ACTUALLY EXISTED!
...EVEN IF THERE WERE EYE WITNESSES TO VERIFY ITS POWER...THEY WOULDN'T BE ALIVE TODAY IF IT ONLY WAKES UP ONCE EVERY THOUSAND YEARS!
BUT IF EMERALD IS TELLING THE TRUTH, THEN THIS POKÉMON IS **REAL**.
YOU **STILL** DON'T TRUST ME?!
NO, I TRUST YOU...
AFTER ALL, THAT DEVICE HAS JIRACHI'S DATA IN IT!

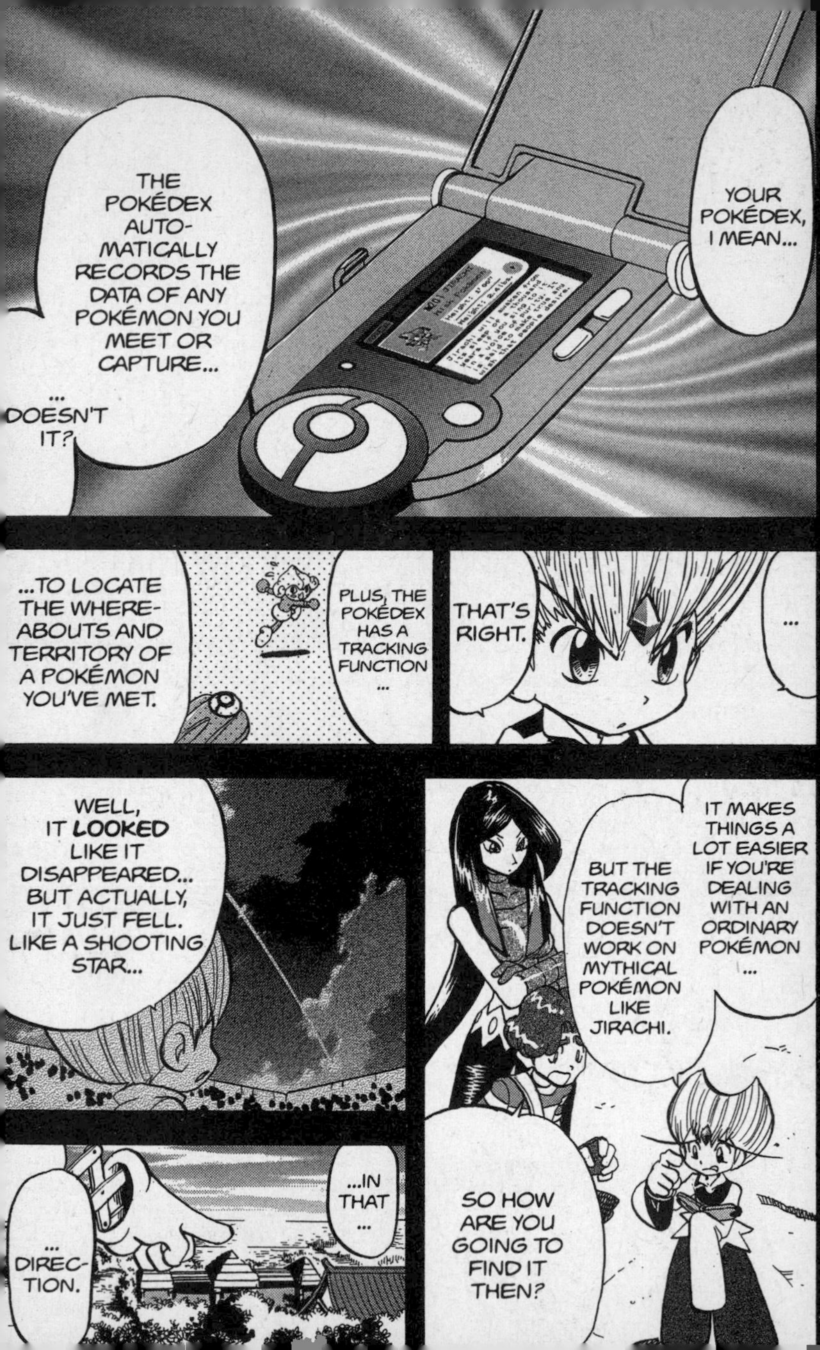
YOUR POKÉDEX, I MEAN...
THE POKÉDEX AUTO-MATICALLY RECORDS THE DATA OF ANY POKÉMON YOU MEET OR CAPTURE...
...DOESN'T IT?
...
THAT'S RIGHT.
PLUS, THE POKÉDEX HAS A TRACKING FUNCTION...
...TO LOCATE THE WHERE-ABOUTS AND TERRITORY OF A POKÉMON YOU'VE MET.
IT MAKES THINGS A LOT EASIER IF YOU'RE DEALING WITH AN ORDINARY POKÉMON...
BUT THE TRACKING FUNCTION DOESN'T WORK ON MYTHICAL POKÉMON LIKE JIRACHI.
SO HOW ARE YOU GOING TO FIND IT THEN?
WELL, IT **LOOKED** LIKE IT DISAPPEARED... BUT ACTUALLY, IT JUST FELL. LIKE A SHOOTING STAR...
...IN THAT...
...DIRECTION.

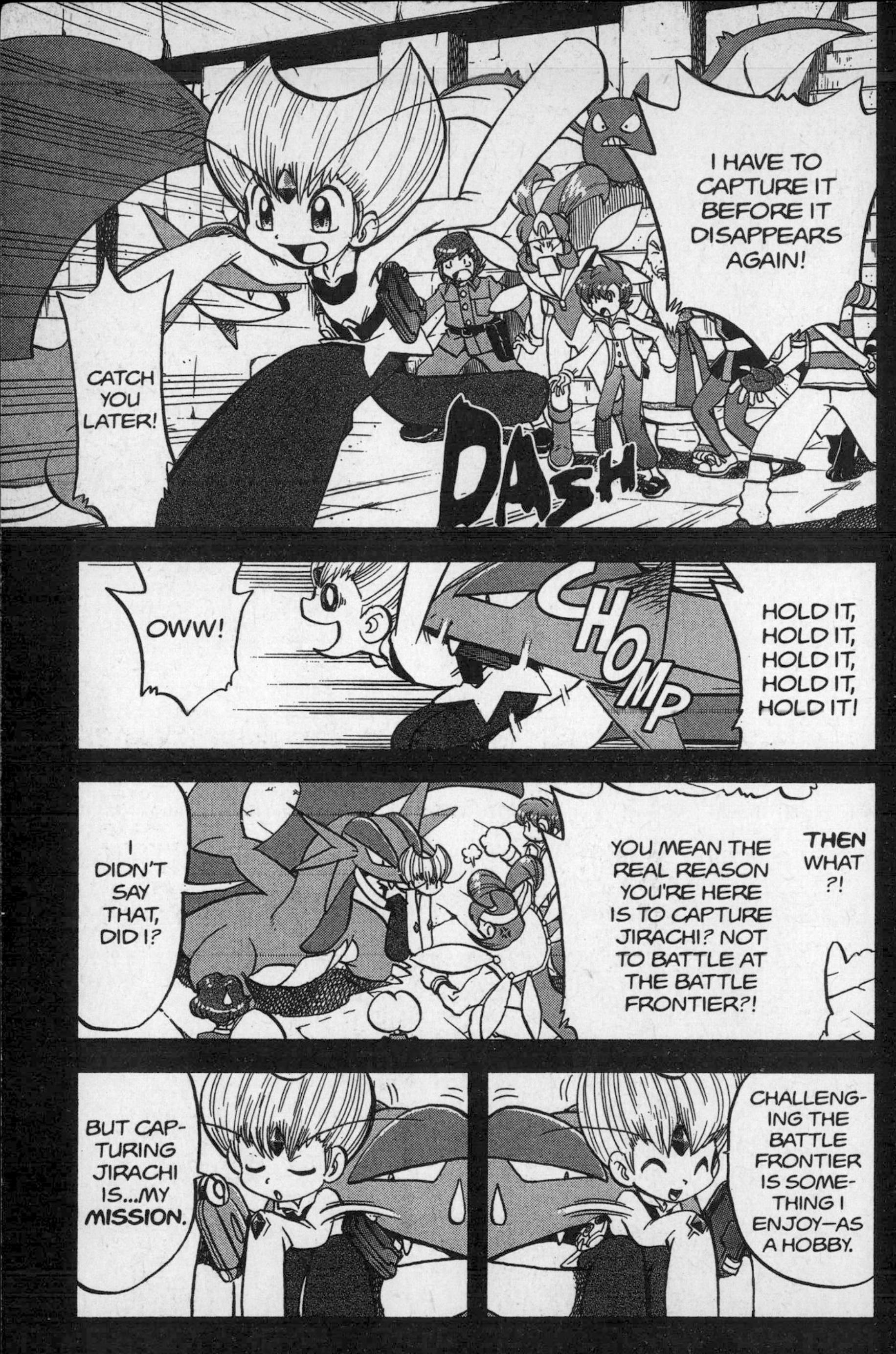
I HAVE TO CAPTURE IT BEFORE IT DISAPPEARS AGAIN!
CATCH YOU LATER!
DASH
HOLD IT, HOLD IT, HOLD IT, HOLD IT, HOLD IT!
CHOMP
OWW!
THEN WHAT?!
YOU MEAN THE REAL REASON YOU'RE HERE IS TO CAPTURE JIRACHI? NOT TO BATTLE AT THE BATTLE FRONTIER?!
I DIDN'T SAY THAT, DID I?
CHALLENGING THE BATTLE FRONTIER IS SOMETHING I ENJOY—AS A HOBBY.
BUT CAPTURING JIRACHI IS...MY MISSION.

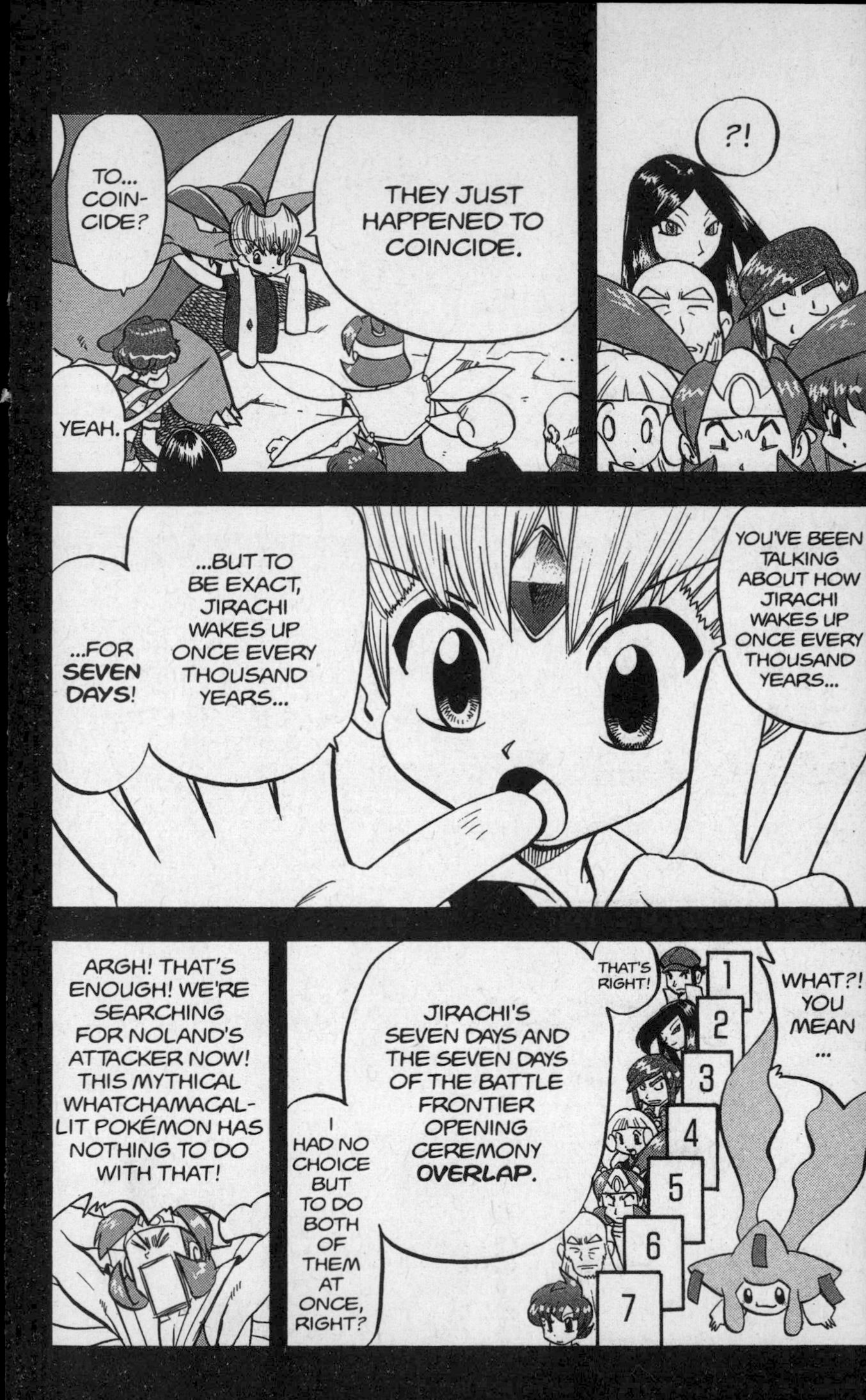
?!
THEY JUST HAPPENED TO COINCIDE.
TO... COIN-CIDE?
YEAH.
YOU'VE BEEN TALKING ABOUT HOW JIRACHI WAKES UP ONCE EVERY THOUSAND YEARS...
...BUT TO BE EXACT, JIRACHI WAKES UP ONCE EVERY THOUSAND YEARS...
...FOR **SEVEN DAYS**!
WHAT?! YOU MEAN ...
THAT'S RIGHT!
1
2
3
4
5
6
7
JIRACHI'S SEVEN DAYS AND THE SEVEN DAYS OF THE BATTLE FRONTIER OPENING CEREMONY **OVERLAP**.
I HAD NO CHOICE BUT TO DO BOTH OF THEM AT ONCE, RIGHT?
ARGH! THAT'S ENOUGH! WE'RE SEARCHING FOR NOLAND'S ATTACKER NOW! THIS MYTHICAL WHATCHAMACAL-LIT POKÉMON HAS NOTHING TO DO WITH THAT!

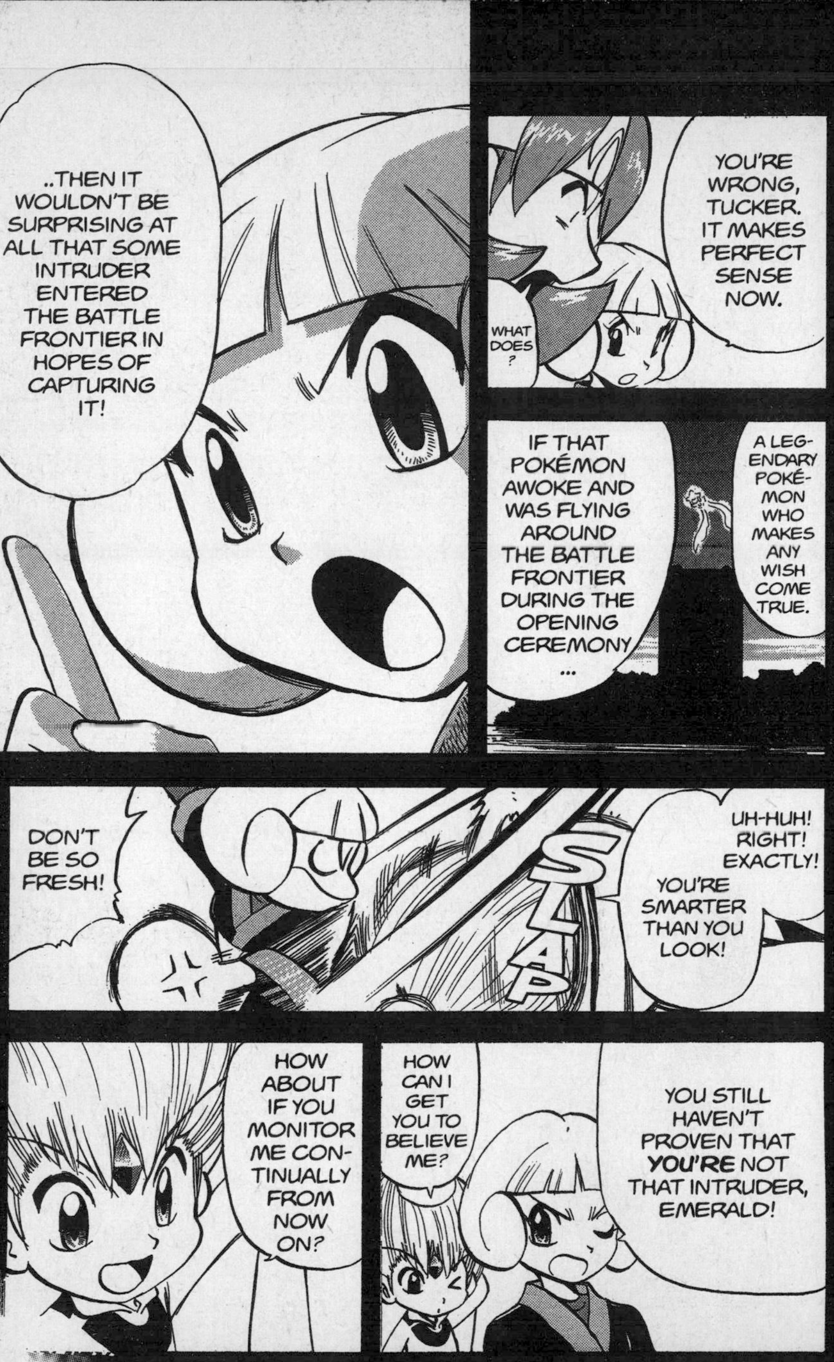
YOU'RE WRONG, TUCKER. IT MAKES PERFECT SENSE NOW.
WHAT DOES ?
A LEG-ENDARY POKÉ-MON WHO MAKES ANY WISH COME TRUE.
IF THAT POKÉMON AWOKE AND WAS FLYING AROUND THE BATTLE FRONTIER DURING THE OPENING CEREMONY ...
..THEN IT WOULDN'T BE SURPRISING AT ALL THAT SOME INTRUDER ENTERED THE BATTLE FRONTIER IN HOPES OF CAPTURING IT!
UH-HUH! RIGHT! EXACTLY!
YOU'RE SMARTER THAN YOU LOOK!
SLAP
DON'T BE SO FRESH!
YOU STILL HAVEN'T PROVEN THAT **YOU'RE** NOT THAT INTRUDER, EMERALD!
HOW CAN I GET YOU TO BELIEVE ME?
HOW ABOUT IF YOU MONITOR ME CON-TINUALLY FROM NOW ON?

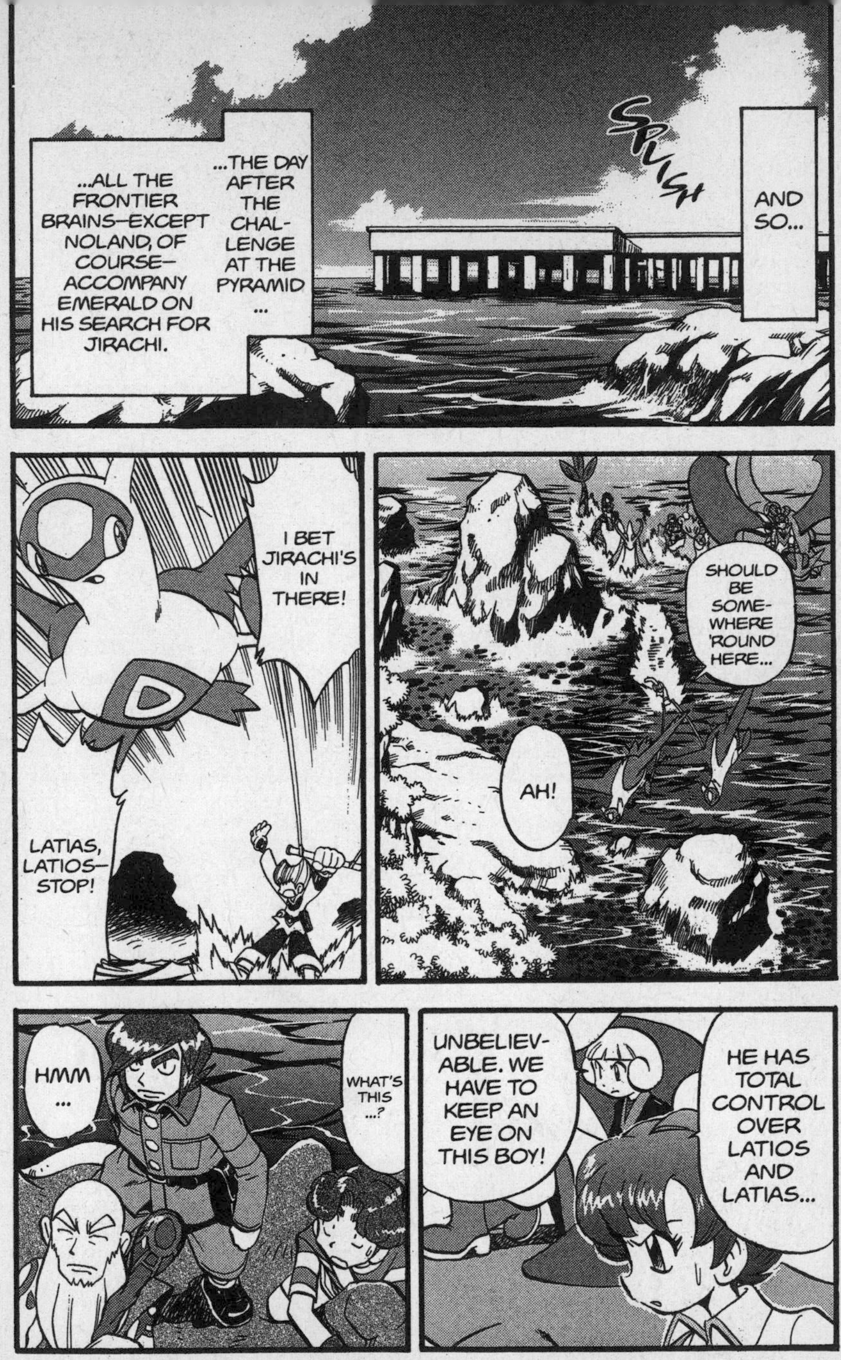
AND SO...
SPLISH
...THE DAY AFTER THE CHAL-LENGE AT THE PYRAMID...
...ALL THE FRONTIER BRAINS—EXCEPT NOLAND, OF COURSE—ACCOMPANY EMERALD ON HIS SEARCH FOR JIRACHI.
SHOULD BE SOME-WHERE 'ROUND HERE...
AH!
I BET JIRACHI'S IN THERE!
LATIAS, LATIOS—STOP!
HE HAS TOTAL CONTROL OVER LATIOS AND LATIAS...
UNBELIEV-ABLE. WE HAVE TO KEEP AN EYE ON THIS BOY!
WHAT'S THIS ...?
HMM ...

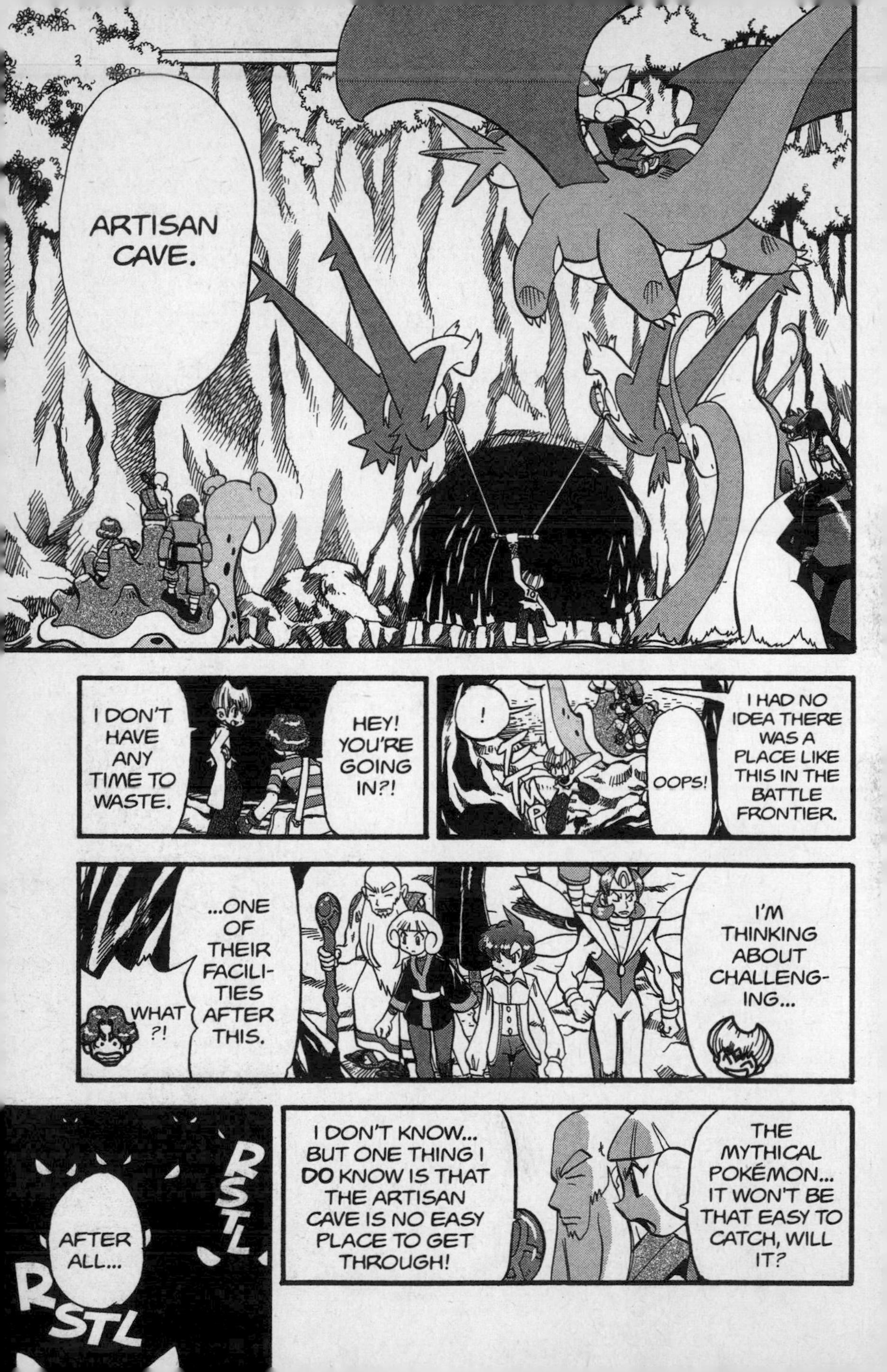
ARTISAN CAVE.
I HAD NO IDEA THERE WAS A PLACE LIKE THIS IN THE BATTLE FRONTIER.
OOPS!
!
HEY! YOU'RE GOING IN?!
I DON'T HAVE ANY TIME TO WASTE.
I'M THINKING ABOUT CHALLENGING...
...ONE OF THEIR FACILITIES AFTER THIS.
WHAT?!
THE MYTHICAL POKÉMON... IT WON'T BE THAT EASY TO CATCH, WILL IT?
I DON'T KNOW... BUT ONE THING I DO KNOW IS THAT THE ARTISAN CAVE IS NO EASY PLACE TO GET THROUGH!
RSTL
AFTER ALL...
RSTL

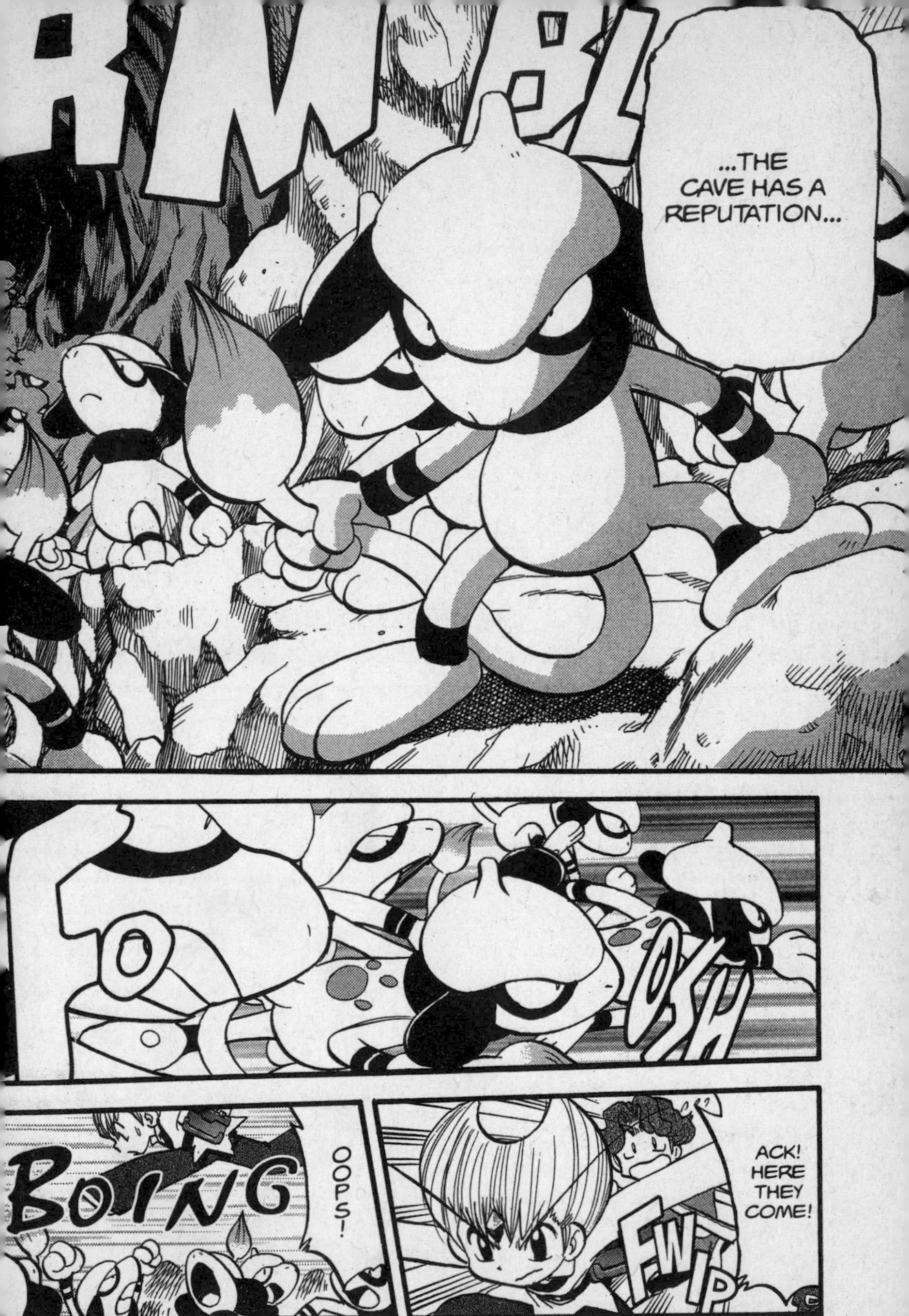
RUMBL
...THE CAVE HAS A REPUTATION...
OSH
ACK! HERE THEY COME!
FWIP
OOPS!
BOING

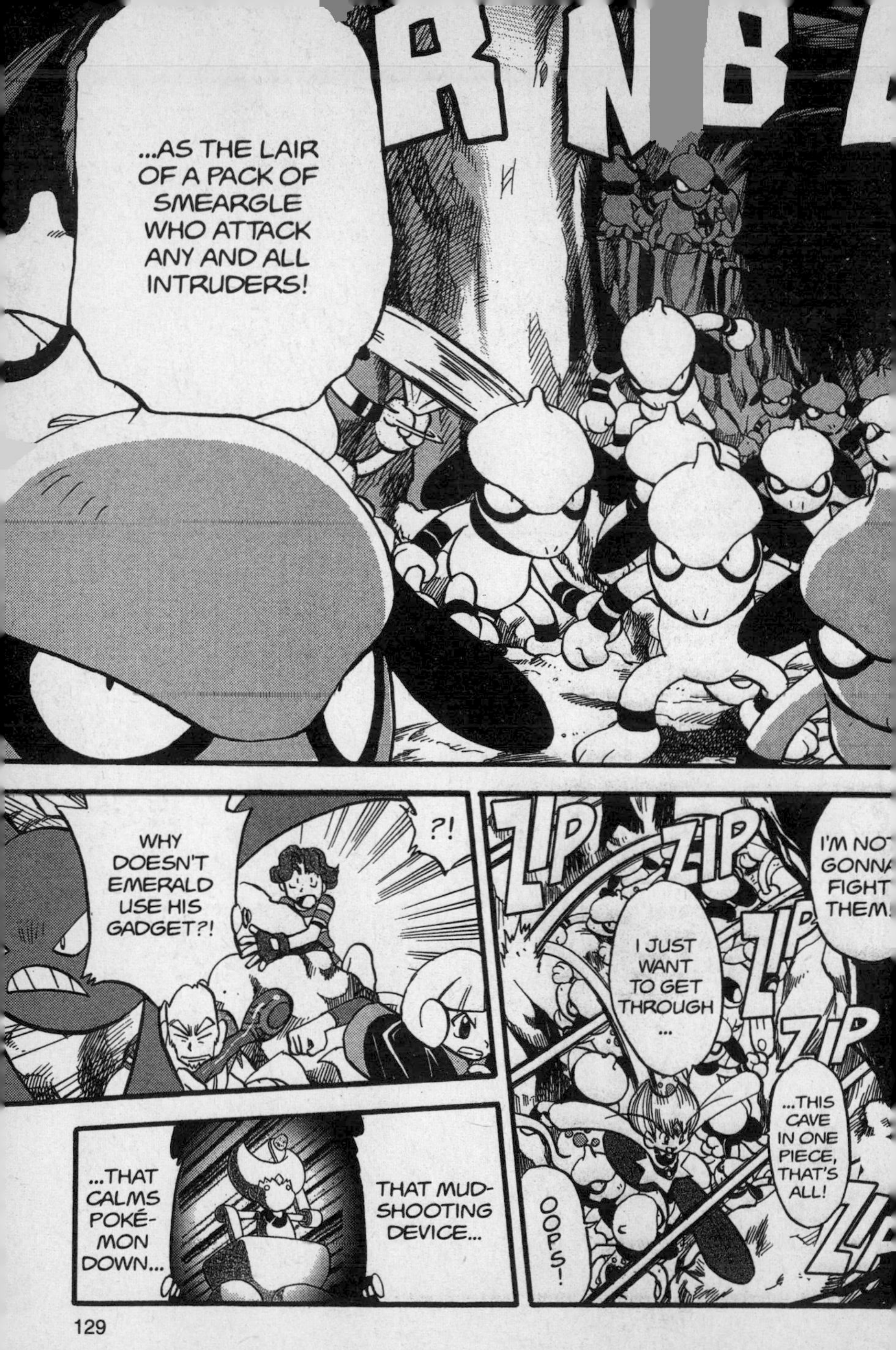
...AS THE LAIR OF A PACK OF SMEARGLE WHO ATTACK ANY AND ALL INTRUDERS!
ZIP
ZIP
I'M NOT GONNA FIGHT THEM.
I JUST WANT TO GET THROUGH ...
ZIP
ZIP
...THIS CAVE IN ONE PIECE, THAT'S ALL!
OOPS!
?!
WHY DOESN'T EMERALD USE HIS GADGET?!
THAT MUD-SHOOTING DEVICE...
...THAT CALMS POKÉMON DOWN...

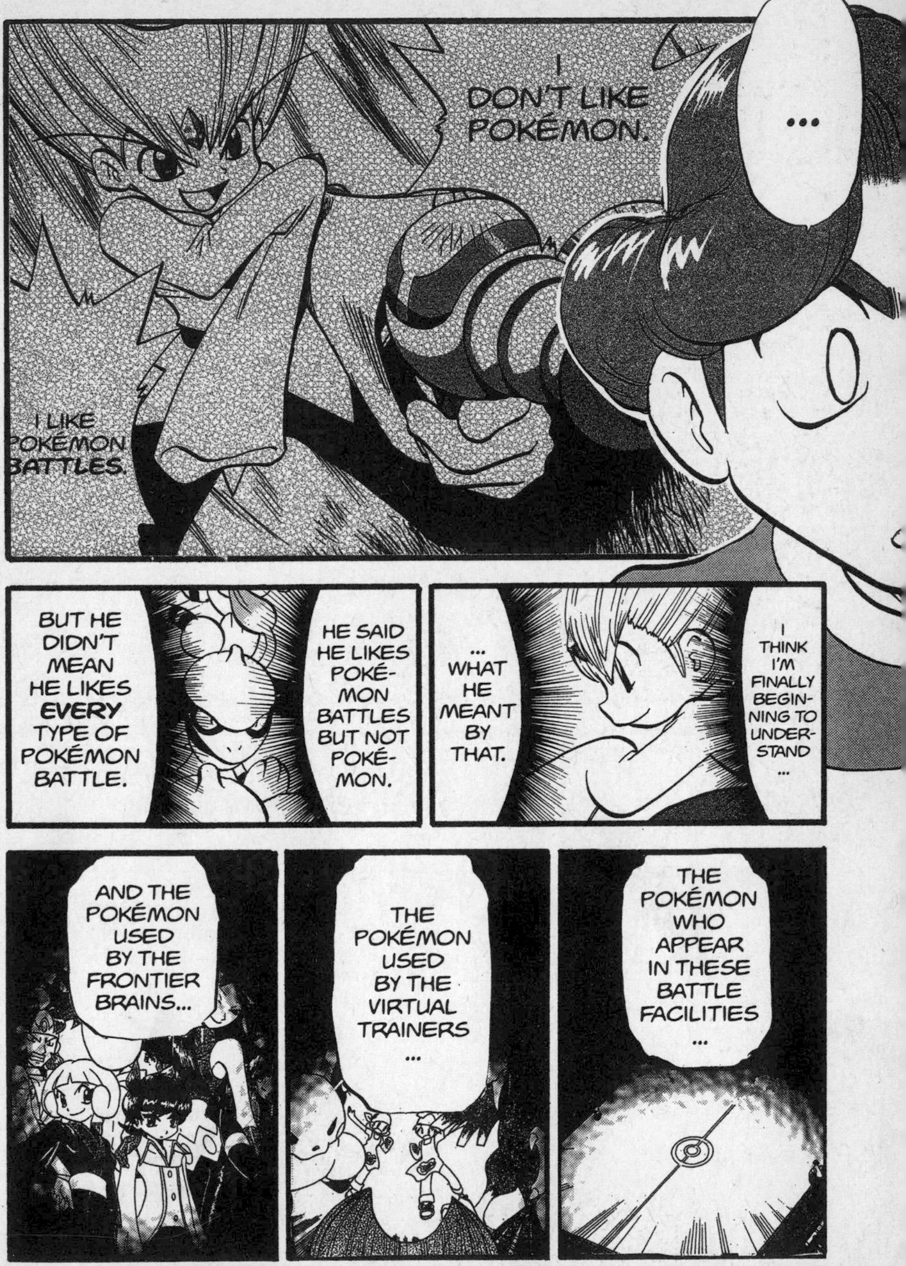
...
I DON'T LIKE POKÉMON.
I LIKE POKÉMON BATTLES.
I THINK I'M FINALLY BEGINNING TO UNDERSTAND ...
... WHAT HE MEANT BY THAT.
HE SAID HE LIKES POKÉMON BATTLES BUT NOT POKÉMON.
BUT HE DIDN'T MEAN HE LIKES **EVERY** TYPE OF POKÉMON BATTLE.
THE POKÉMON WHO APPEAR IN THESE BATTLE FACILITIES ...
THE POKÉMON USED BY THE VIRTUAL TRAINERS ...
AND THE POKÉMON USED BY THE FRONTIER BRAINS...

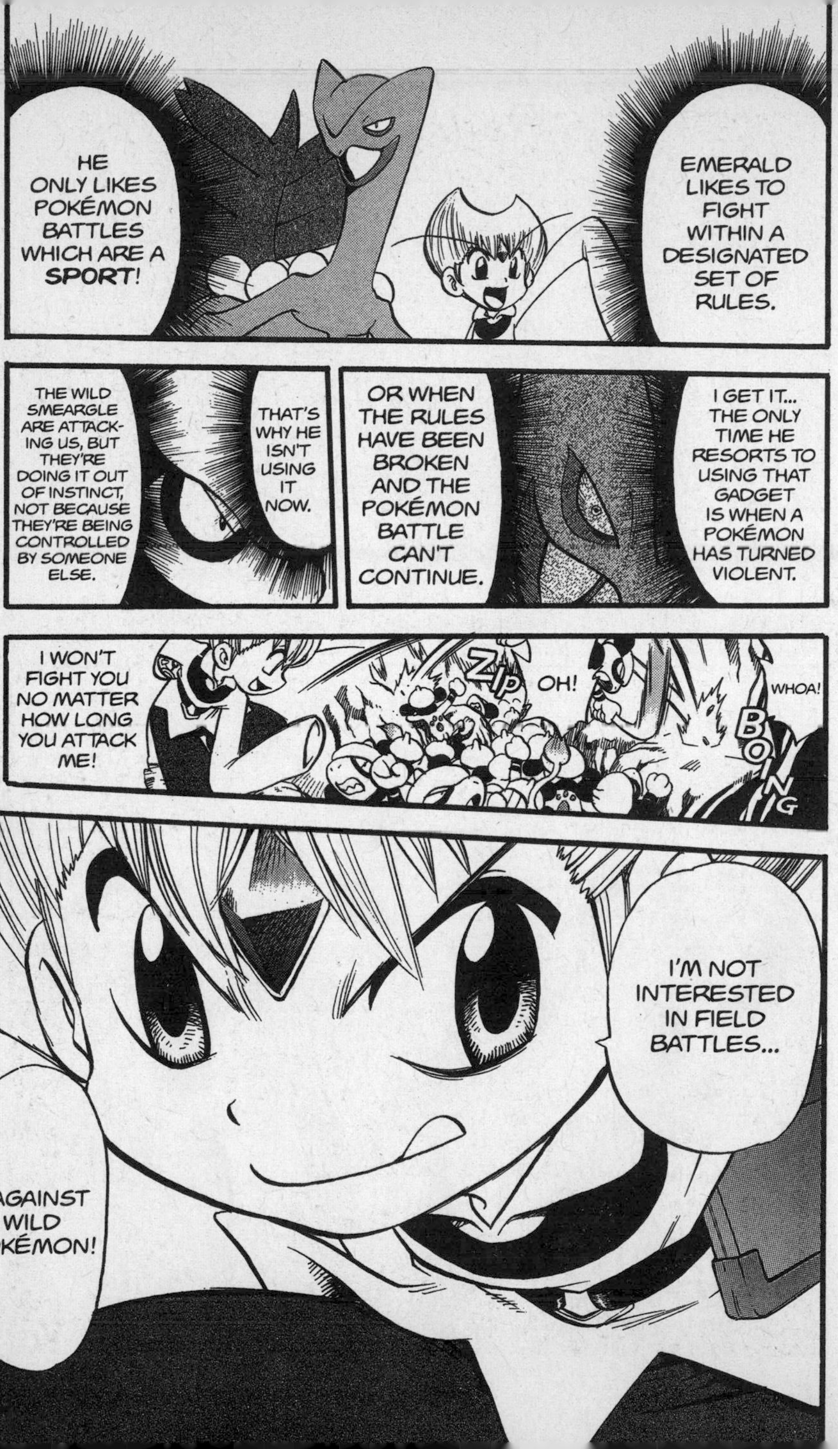
EMERALD LIKES TO FIGHT WITHIN A DESIGNATED SET OF RULES.
HE ONLY LIKES POKÉMON BATTLES WHICH ARE A **SPORT**!
I GET IT... THE ONLY TIME HE RESORTS TO USING THAT GADGET IS WHEN A POKÉMON HAS TURNED VIOLENT.
OR WHEN THE RULES HAVE BEEN BROKEN AND THE POKÉMON BATTLE CAN'T CONTINUE.
THAT'S WHY HE ISN'T USING IT NOW.
THE WILD SMEARGLE ARE ATTACKING US, BUT THEY'RE DOING IT OUT OF INSTINCT, NOT BECAUSE THEY'RE BEING CONTROLLED BY SOMEONE ELSE.
WHOA!
BOING
OH!
ZIP
I WON'T FIGHT YOU NO MATTER HOW LONG YOU ATTACK ME!
I'M NOT INTERESTED IN FIELD BATTLES...
...AGAINST WILD POKÉMON!

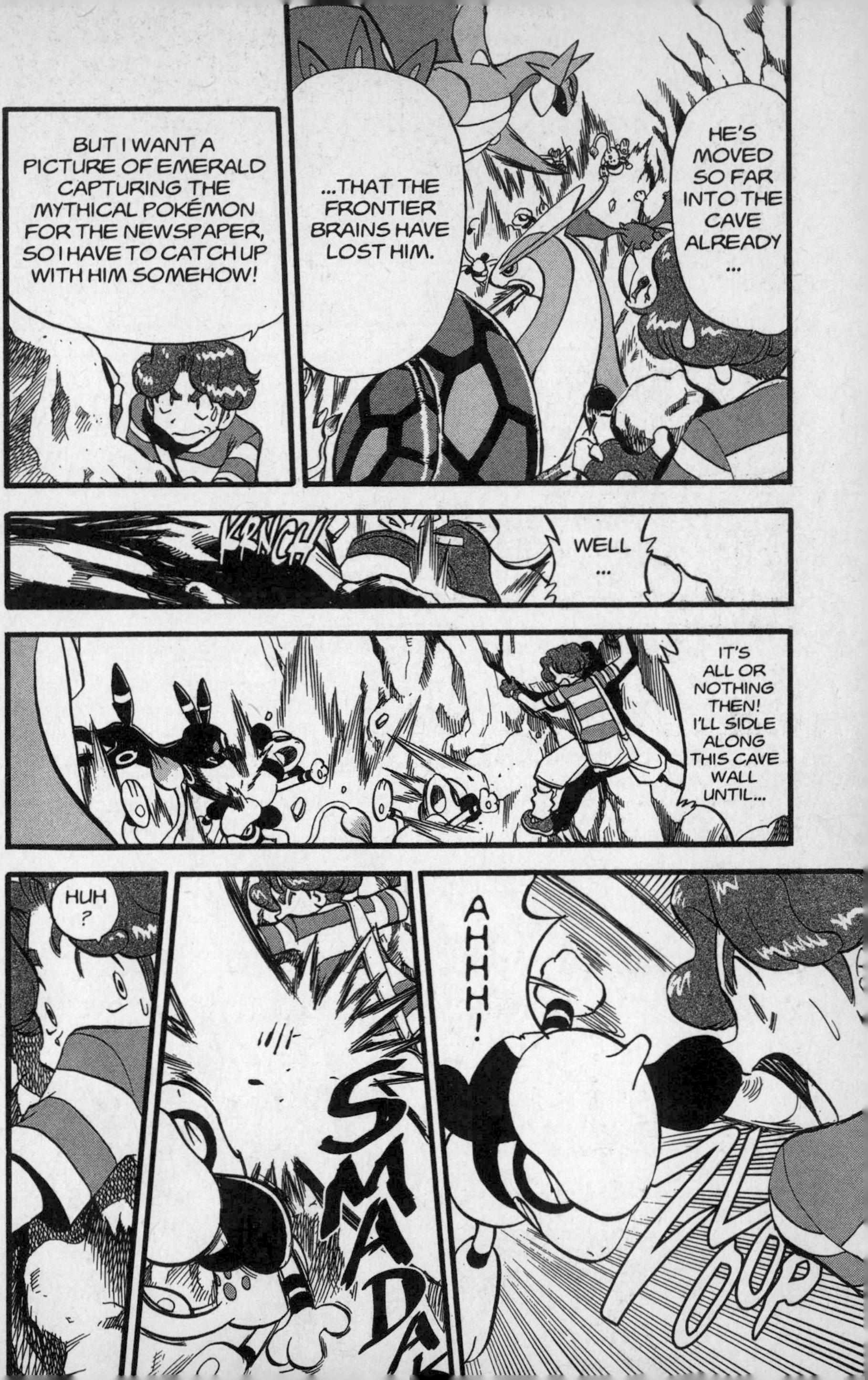
HE'S MOVED SO FAR INTO THE CAVE ALREADY...
...THAT THE FRONTIER BRAINS HAVE LOST HIM.
BUT I WANT A PICTURE OF EMERALD CAPTURING THE MYTHICAL POKÉMON FOR THE NEWSPAPER, SO I HAVE TO CATCH UP WITH HIM SOMEHOW!
WELL...
KRNCH
IT'S ALL OR NOTHING THEN! I'LL SIDLE ALONG THIS CAVE WALL UNTIL...
AHHH!
ZOOP
SMADAK
HUH?

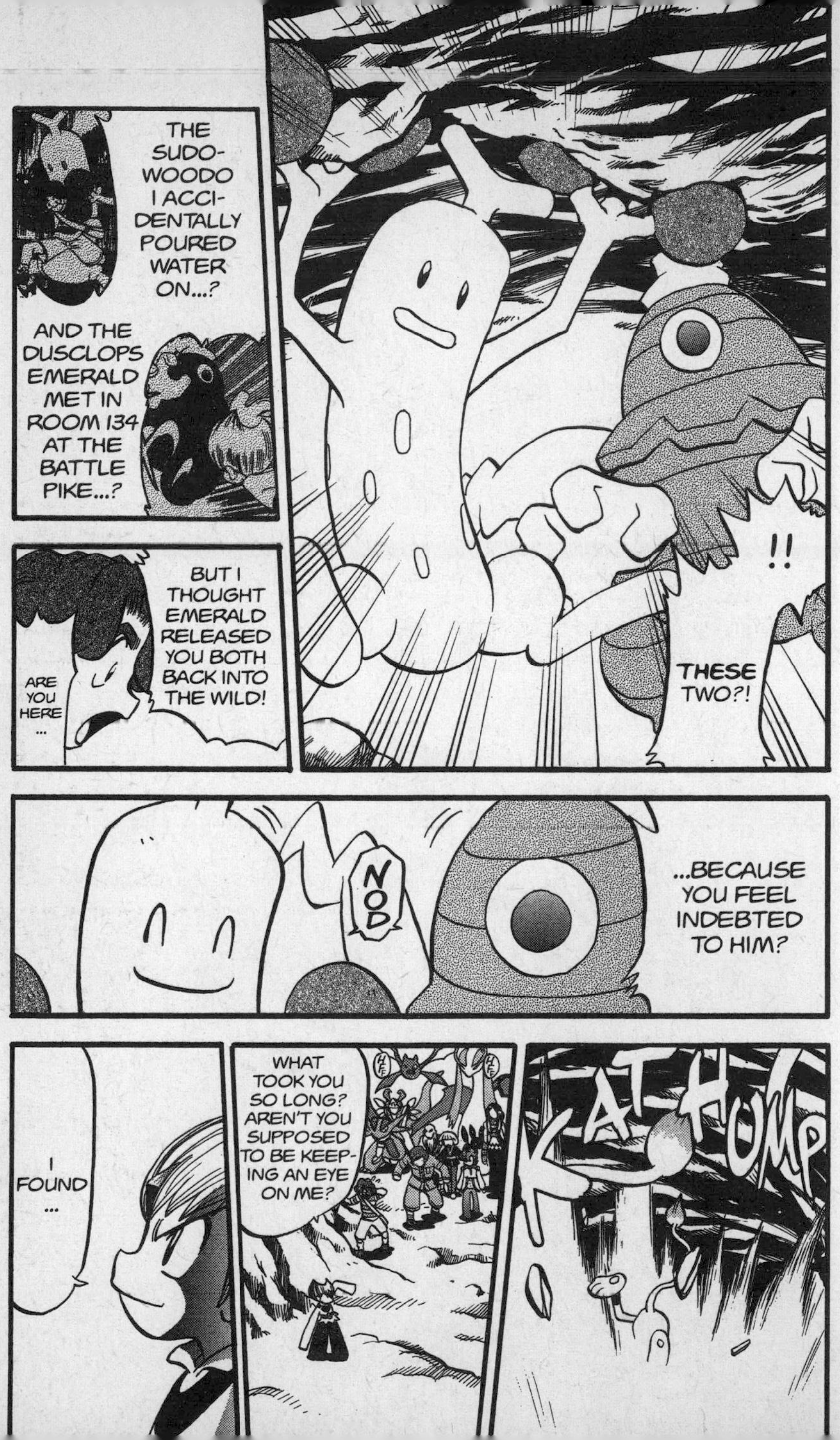
!!
THESE TWO?!
THE SUDO-WOODO I ACCI-DENTALLY POURED WATER ON...?
AND THE DUSCLOPS EMERALD MET IN ROOM 134 AT THE BATTLE PIKE...?
BUT I THOUGHT EMERALD RELEASED YOU BOTH BACK INTO THE WILD!
ARE YOU HERE...
...BECAUSE YOU FEEL INDEBTED TO HIM?
NOD
KATHOMP
HE
HE
WHAT TOOK YOU SO LONG? AREN'T YOU SUPPOSED TO BE KEEP-ING AN EYE ON ME?
I FOUND...

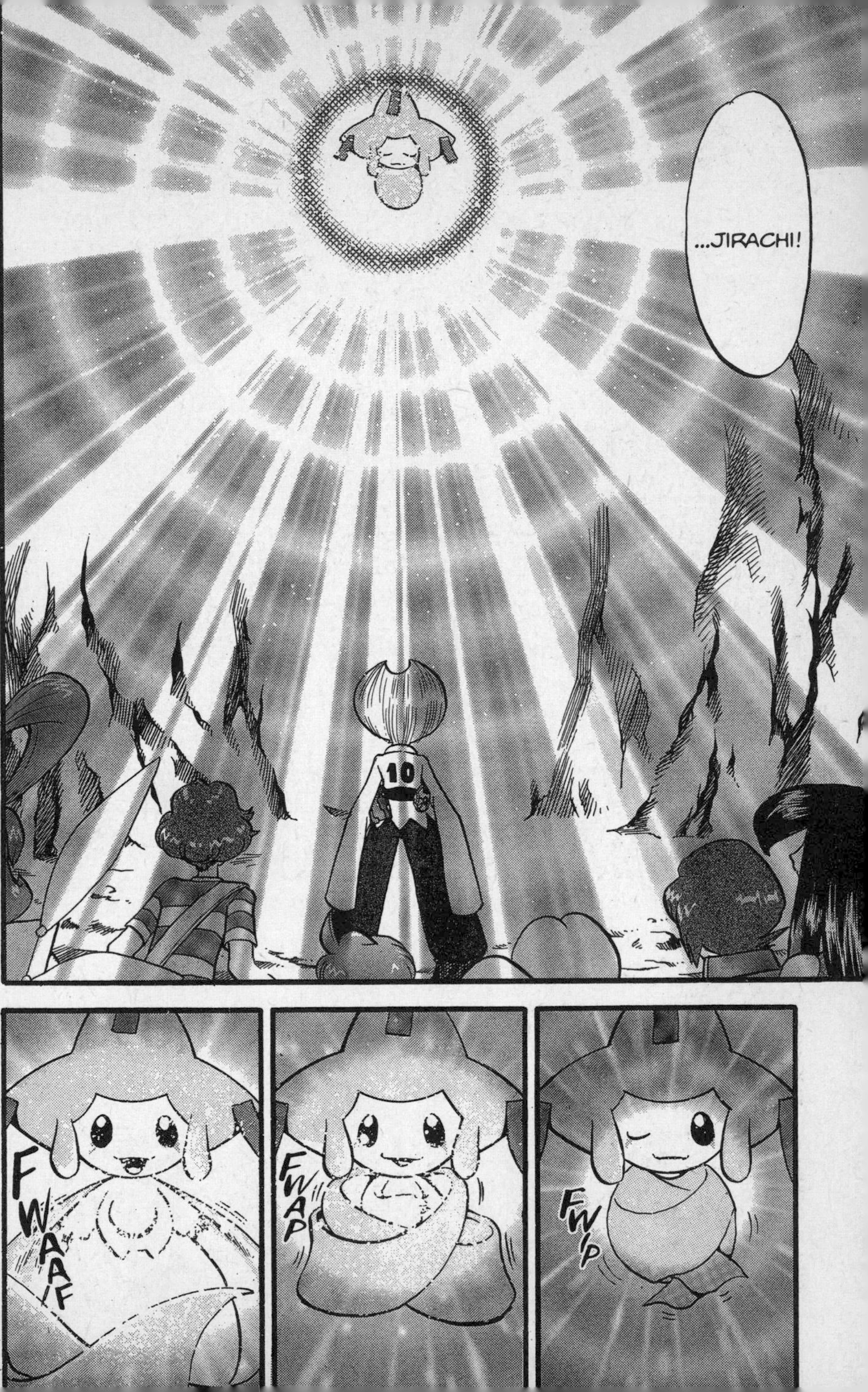
...JIRACHI!
FWIP
FWAP
FWAAF

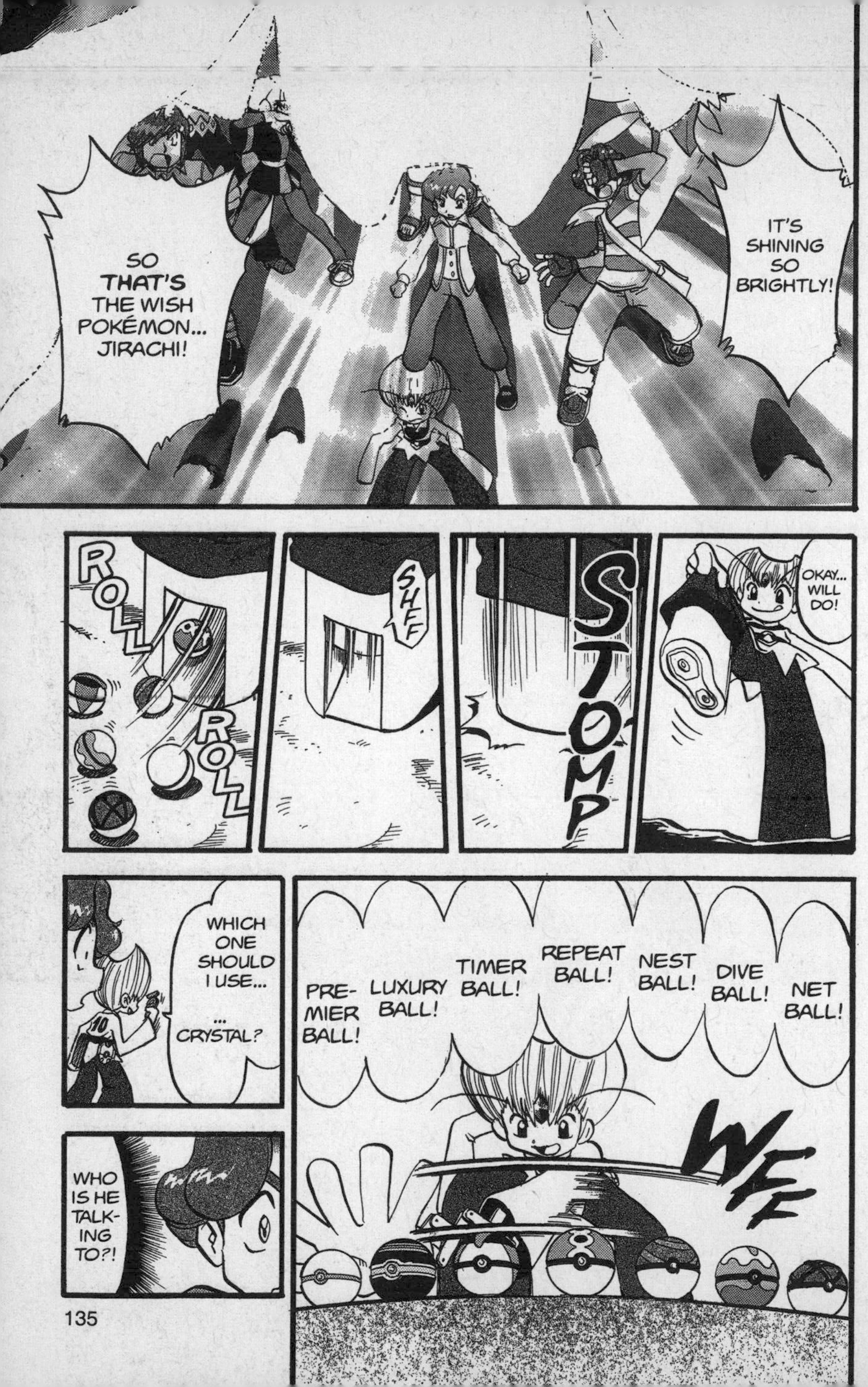
IT'S SHINING SO BRIGHTLY!
SO **THAT'S** THE WISH POKÉMON... JIRACHI!
OKAY... WILL DO!
STOMP
SHFF
ROLL
ROLL
NET BALL!
DIVE BALL!
NEST BALL!
REPEAT BALL!
TIMER BALL!
LUXURY BALL!
PRE-MIER BALL!
WFF
WHICH ONE SHOULD I USE...
...CRYSTAL?
WHO IS HE TALK-ING TO?!

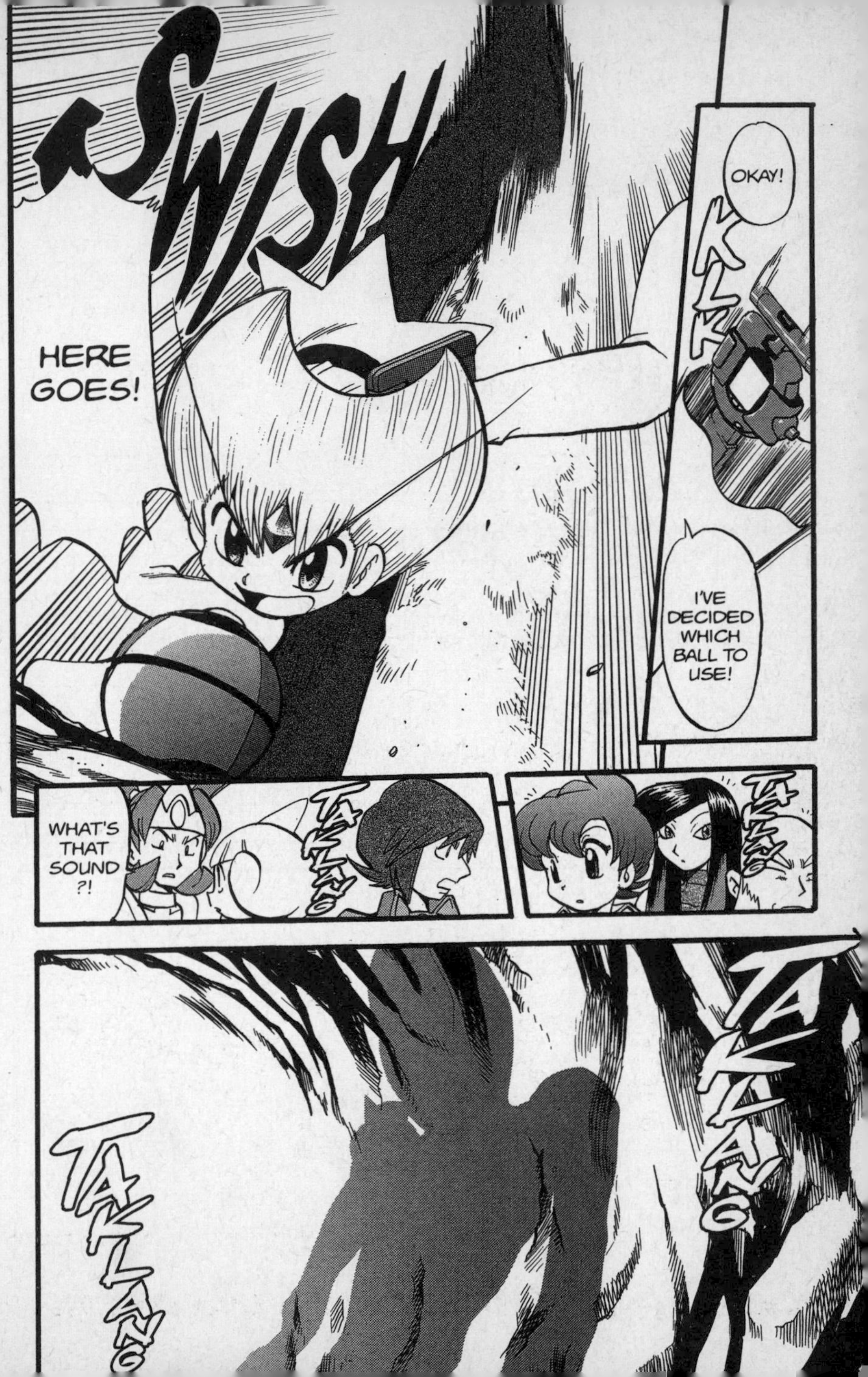
OKAY!
KLIK
I'VE DECIDED WHICH BALL TO USE!
SWISH
HERE GOES!
TAKLANG
WHAT'S THAT SOUND?!
TAKLANG
TAKLANG
TAKLANG

◆375◆

Skirting Around Surskit
I

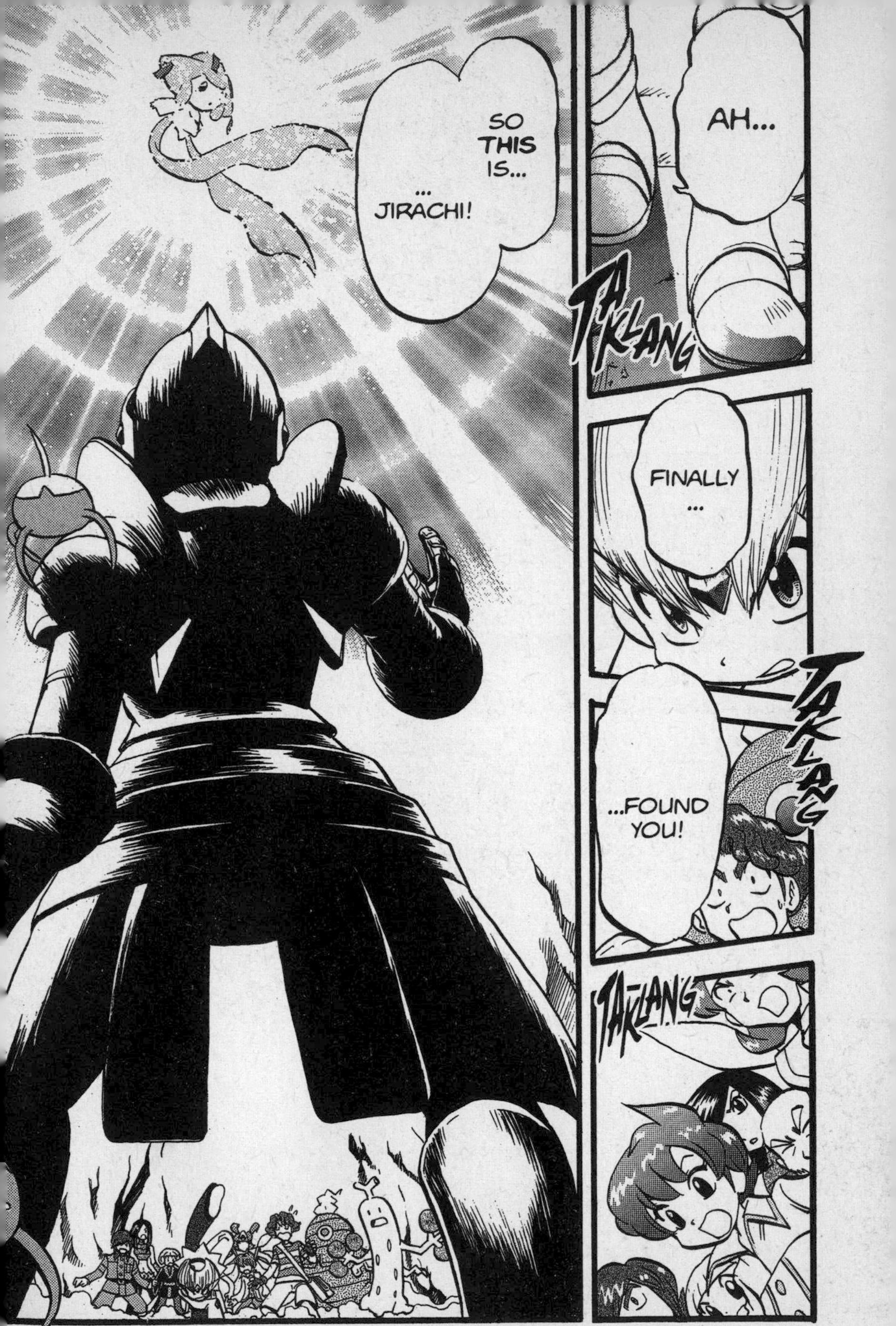
AH...
TAKLANG
FINALLY ...
...FOUND YOU!
TAKLANG
TAKLANG
SO THIS IS...
... JIRACHI!

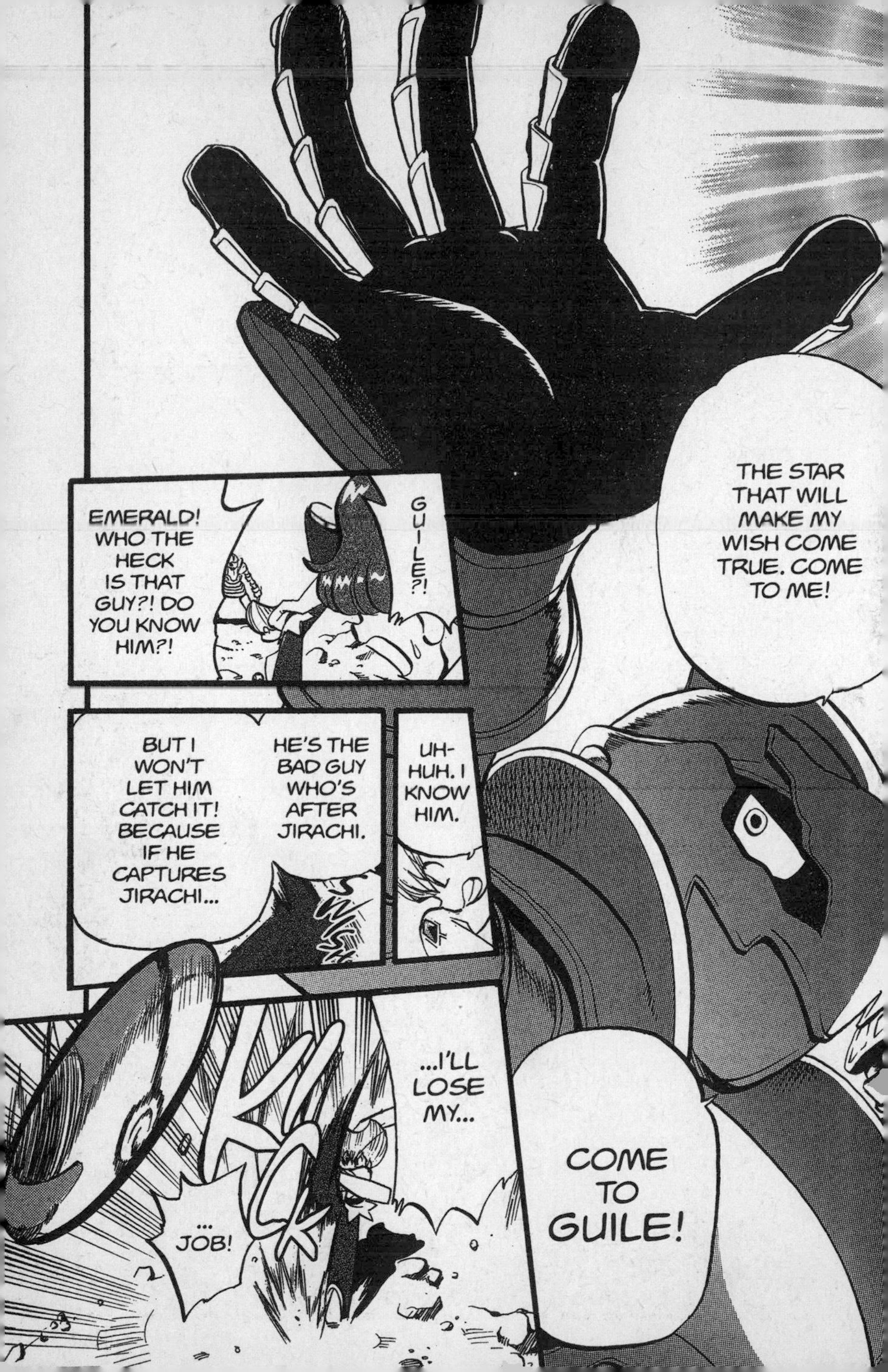
THE STAR THAT WILL MAKE MY WISH COME TRUE. COME TO ME!
COME TO GUILE!
GUILE?!
EMERALD! WHO THE HECK IS THAT GUY?! DO YOU KNOW HIM?!
UH-HUH. I KNOW HIM.
HE'S THE BAD GUY WHO'S AFTER JIRACHI.
BUT I WON'T LET HIM CATCH IT! BECAUSE IF HE CAPTURES JIRACHI...
...I'LL LOSE MY...
...JOB!

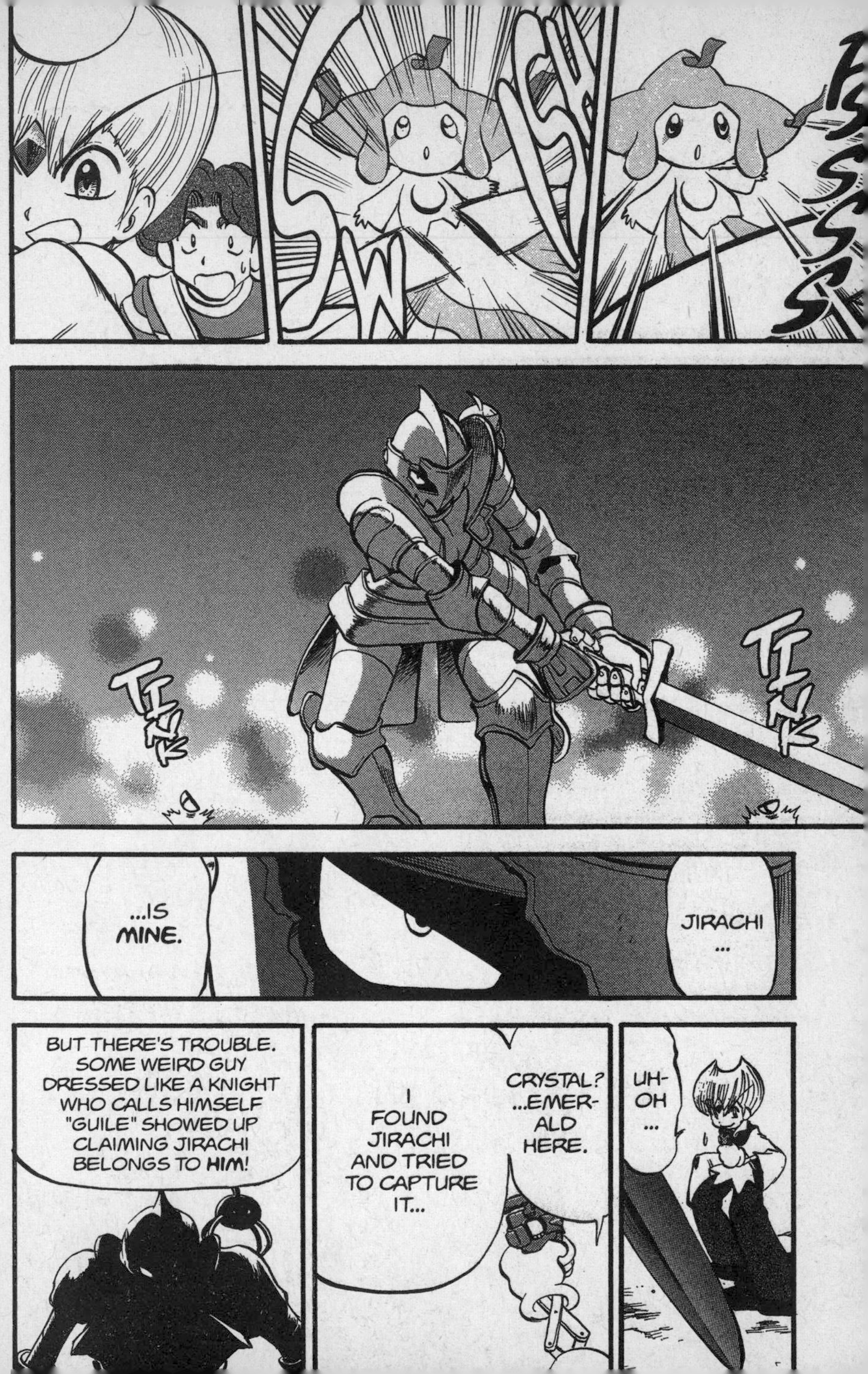
FSSSSS
SWISH
TINK
TINK
JIRACHI ...
...IS MINE.
UH-OH ...
CRYSTAL? ...EMER-ALD HERE.
I FOUND JIRACHI AND TRIED TO CAPTURE IT...
BUT THERE'S TROUBLE. SOME WEIRD GUY DRESSED LIKE A KNIGHT WHO CALLS HIMSELF "GUILE" SHOWED UP CLAIMING JIRACHI BELONGS TO HIM!

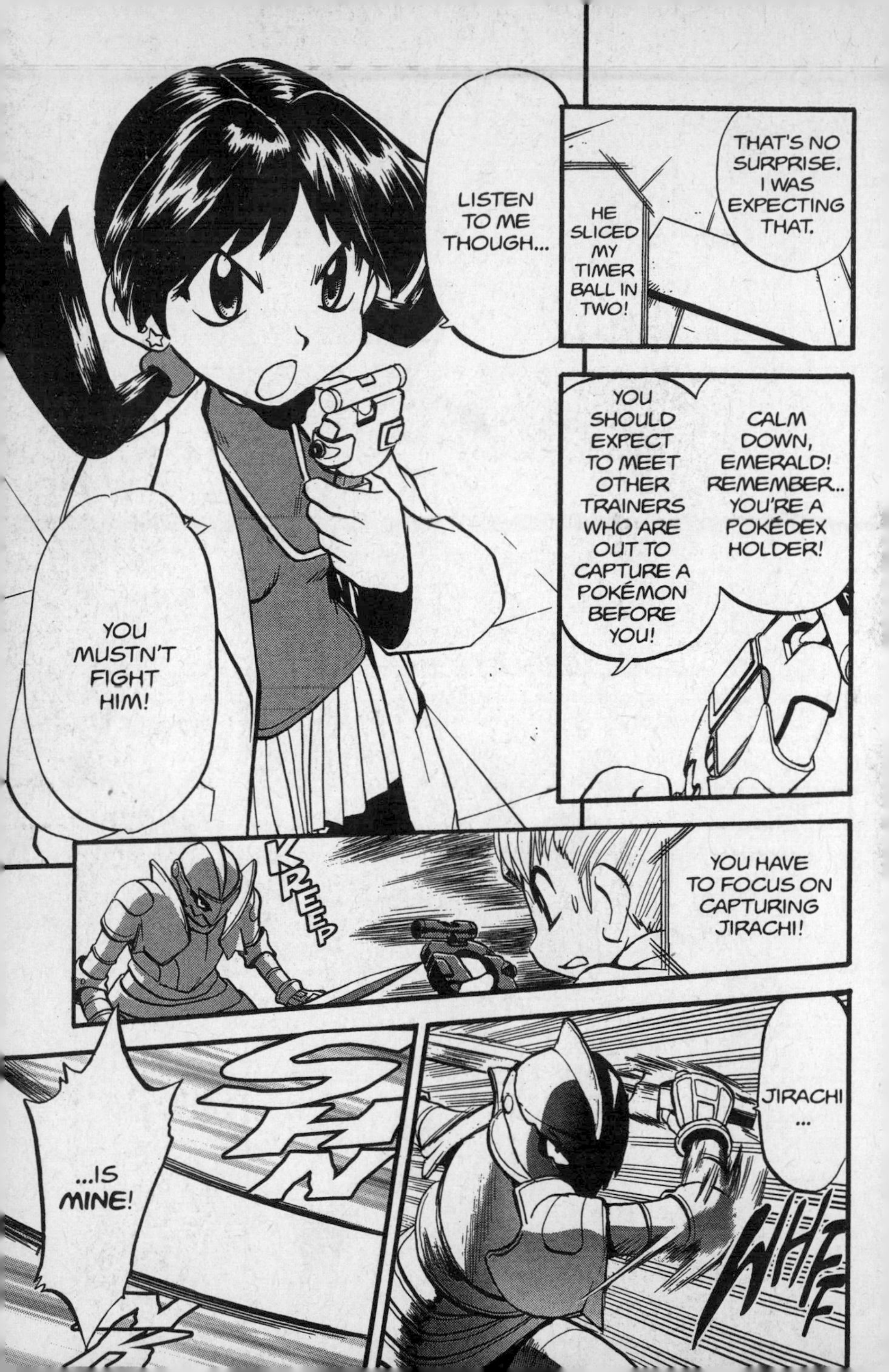
THAT'S NO SURPRISE. I WAS EXPECTING THAT.
HE SLICED MY TIMER BALL IN TWO!
CALM DOWN, EMERALD! REMEMBER... YOU'RE A POKÉDEX HOLDER!
YOU SHOULD EXPECT TO MEET OTHER TRAINERS WHO ARE OUT TO CAPTURE A POKÉMON BEFORE YOU!
LISTEN TO ME THOUGH...
YOU MUSTN'T FIGHT HIM!
YOU HAVE TO FOCUS ON CAPTURING JIRACHI!
KREEP
JIRACHI ...
WHF
...IS MINE!

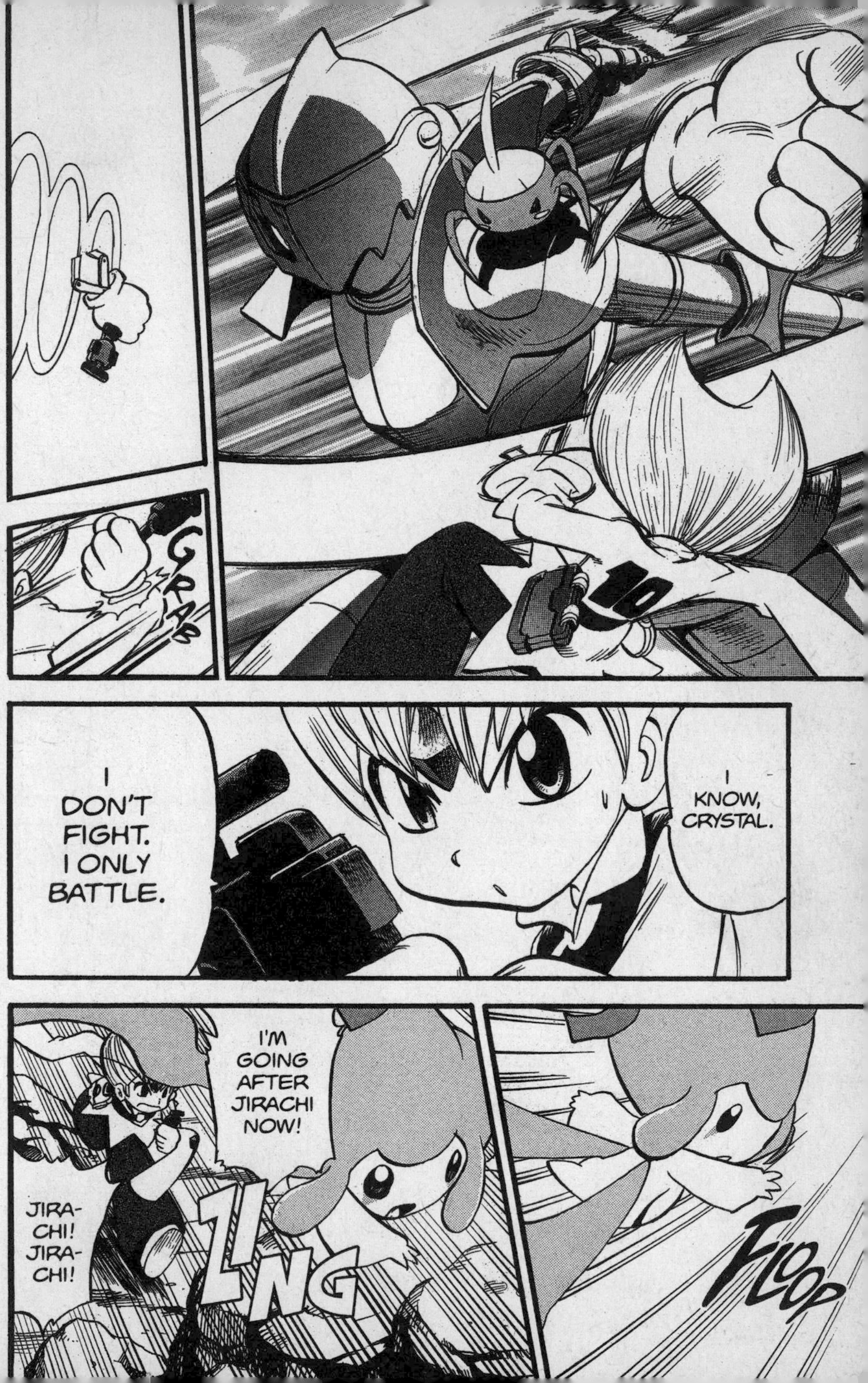
GRAB
I KNOW, CRYSTAL.
I DON'T FIGHT. I ONLY BATTLE.
FLOOP
I'M GOING AFTER JIRACHI NOW!
ZING
JIRA-CHI! JIRA-CHI!

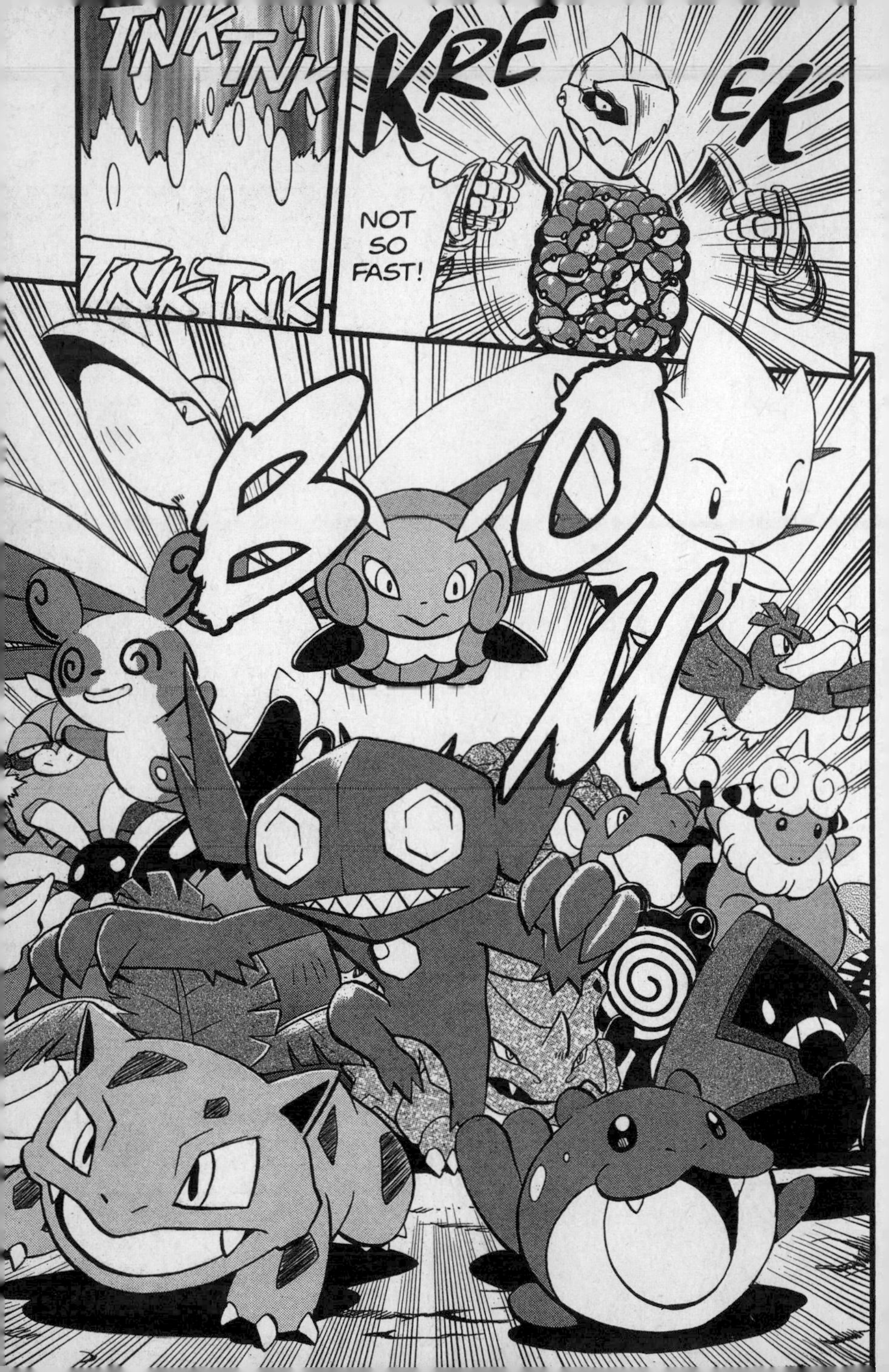
KRE EK
NOT SO FAST!
TNK TNK
TNK TNK
BOM

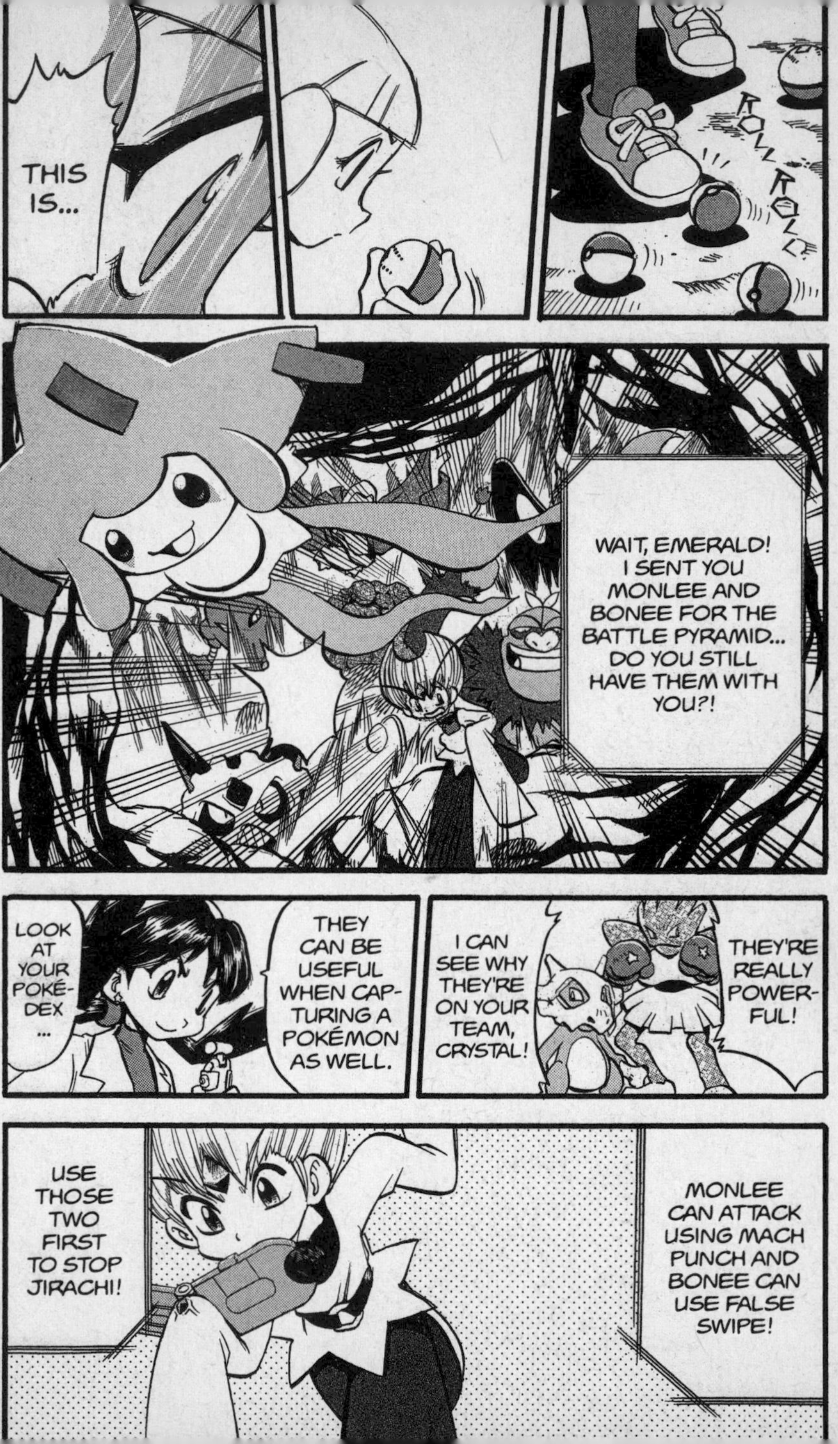
ROLL ROLL
THIS IS...
WAIT, EMERALD! I SENT YOU MONLEE AND BONEE FOR THE BATTLE PYRAMID... DO YOU STILL HAVE THEM WITH YOU?!
THEY'RE REALLY POWERFUL!
I CAN SEE WHY THEY'RE ON YOUR TEAM, CRYSTAL!
THEY CAN BE USEFUL WHEN CAPTURING A POKÉMON AS WELL.
LOOK AT YOUR POKÉDEX...
MONLEE CAN ATTACK USING MACH PUNCH AND BONEE CAN USE FALSE SWIPE!
USE THOSE TWO FIRST TO STOP JIRACHI!

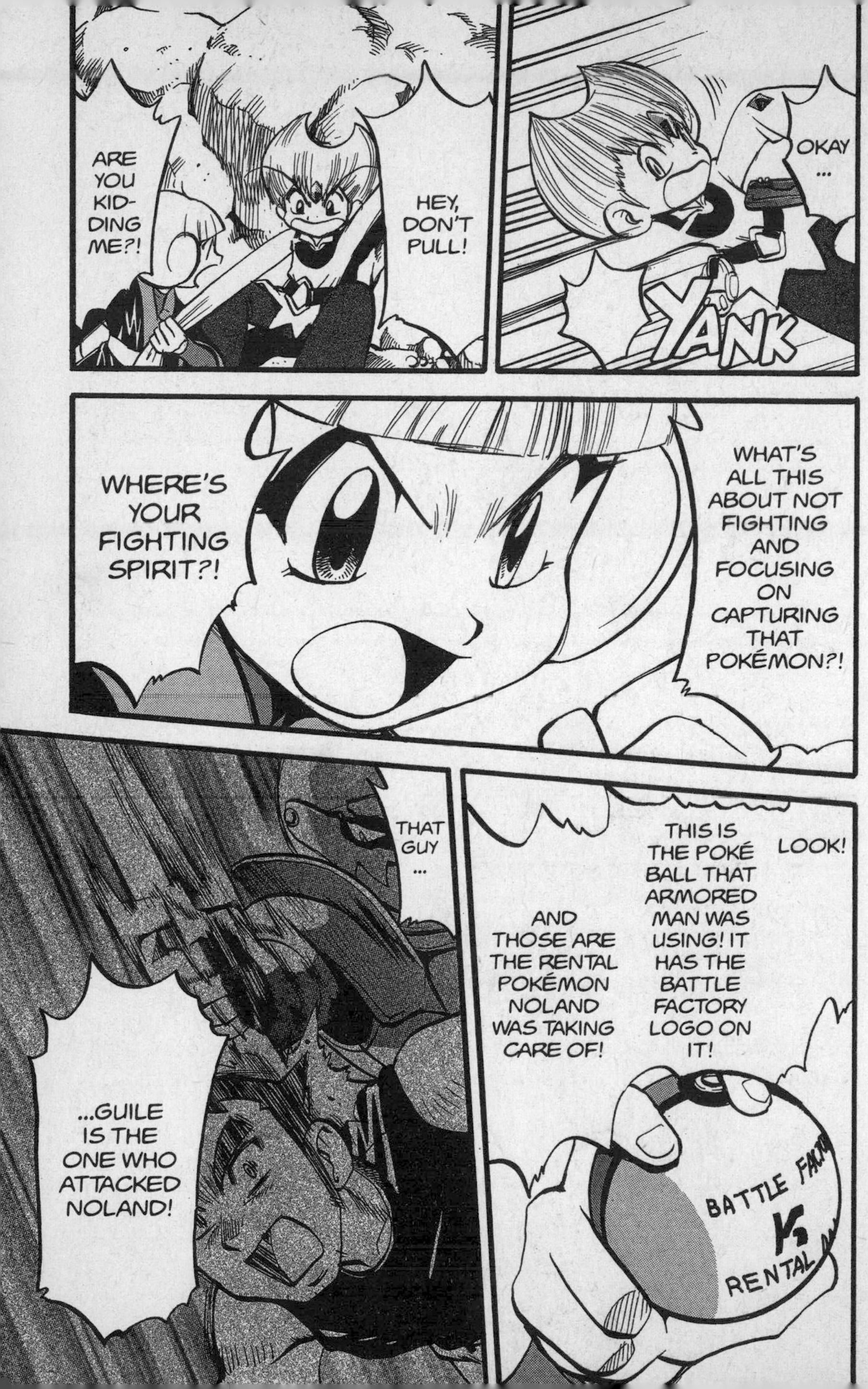
OKAY ...
YANK
HEY, DON'T PULL!
ARE YOU KIDDING ME?!
WHAT'S ALL THIS ABOUT NOT FIGHTING AND FOCUSING ON CAPTURING THAT POKÉMON?!
WHERE'S YOUR FIGHTING SPIRIT?!
LOOK!
THIS IS THE POKÉ BALL THAT ARMORED MAN WAS USING! IT HAS THE BATTLE FACTORY LOGO ON IT!
AND THOSE ARE THE RENTAL POKÉMON NOLAND WAS TAKING CARE OF!
BATTLE
RENTAL
THAT GUY ...
...GUILE IS THE ONE WHO ATTACKED NOLAND!

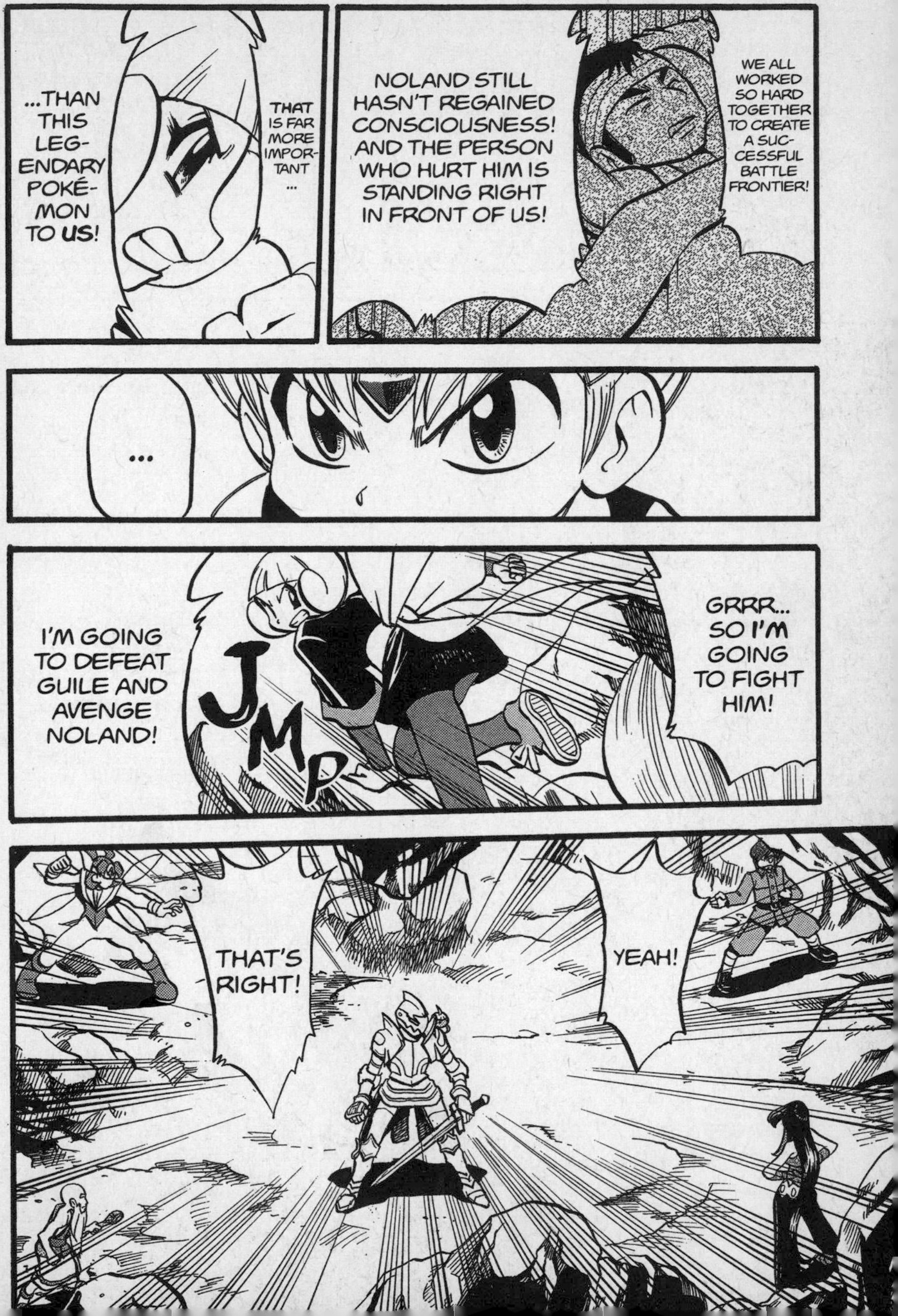
WE ALL WORKED SO HARD TOGETHER TO CREATE A SUCCESSFUL BATTLE FRONTIER!
NOLAND STILL HASN'T REGAINED CONSCIOUSNESS! AND THE PERSON WHO HURT HIM IS STANDING RIGHT IN FRONT OF US!
THAT IS FAR MORE IMPORTANT...
...THAN THIS LEGENDARY POKÉMON TO US!
...
GRRR... SO I'M GOING TO FIGHT HIM!
I'M GOING TO DEFEAT GUILE AND AVENGE NOLAND!
JMP
YEAH!
THAT'S RIGHT!

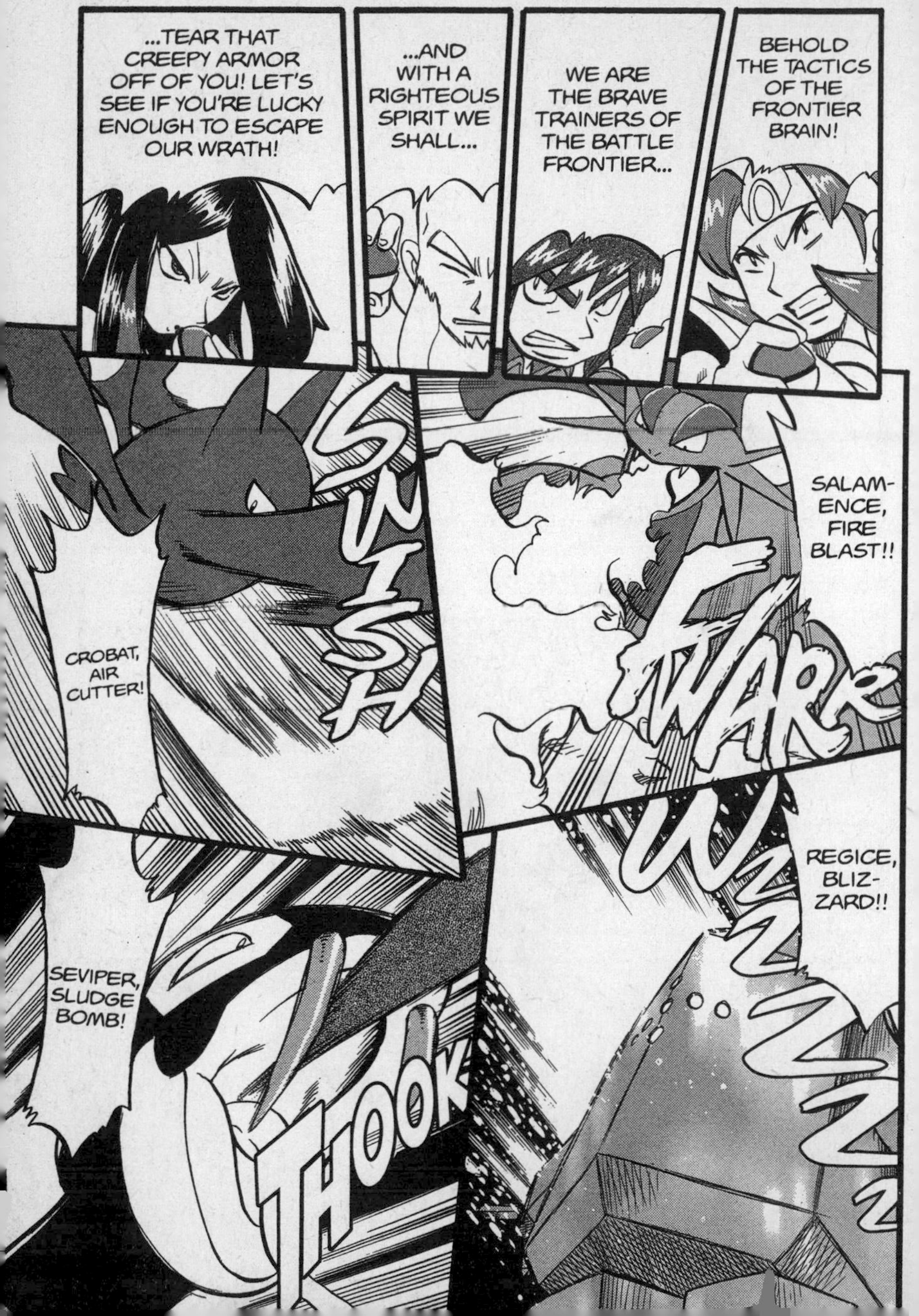
BEHOLD THE TACTICS OF THE FRONTIER BRAIN!
WE ARE THE BRAVE TRAINERS OF THE BATTLE FRONTIER...
...AND WITH A RIGHTEOUS SPIRIT WE SHALL...
...TEAR THAT CREEPY ARMOR OFF OF YOU! LET'S SEE IF YOU'RE LUCKY ENOUGH TO ESCAPE OUR WRATH!
SALAMENCE, FIRE BLAST!!
CROBAT, AIR CUTTER!
SWISH
REGICE, BLIZZARD!!
SEVIPER, SLUDGE BOMB!
THOOK

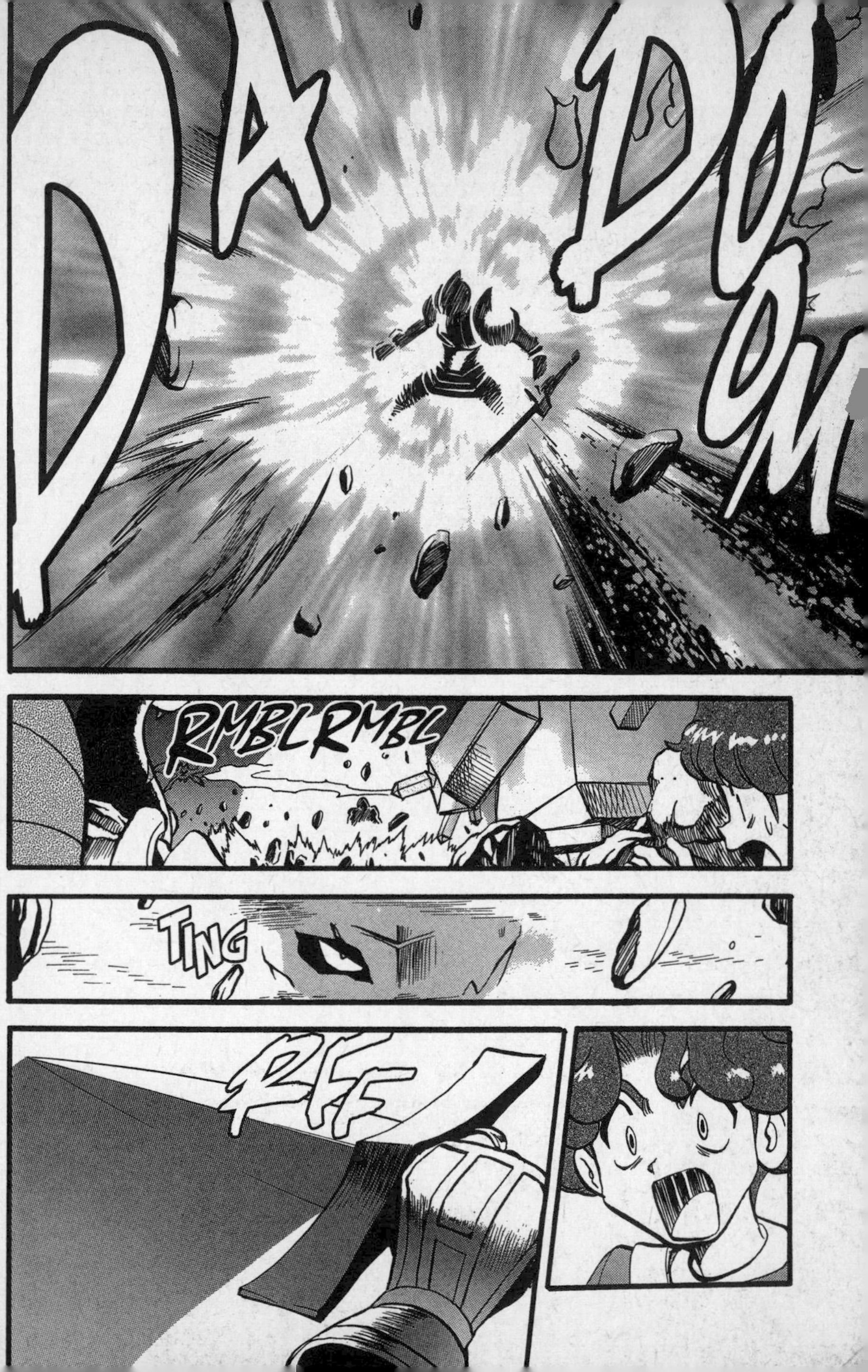
DADOOM
RMBLRMBL
TING
RFF

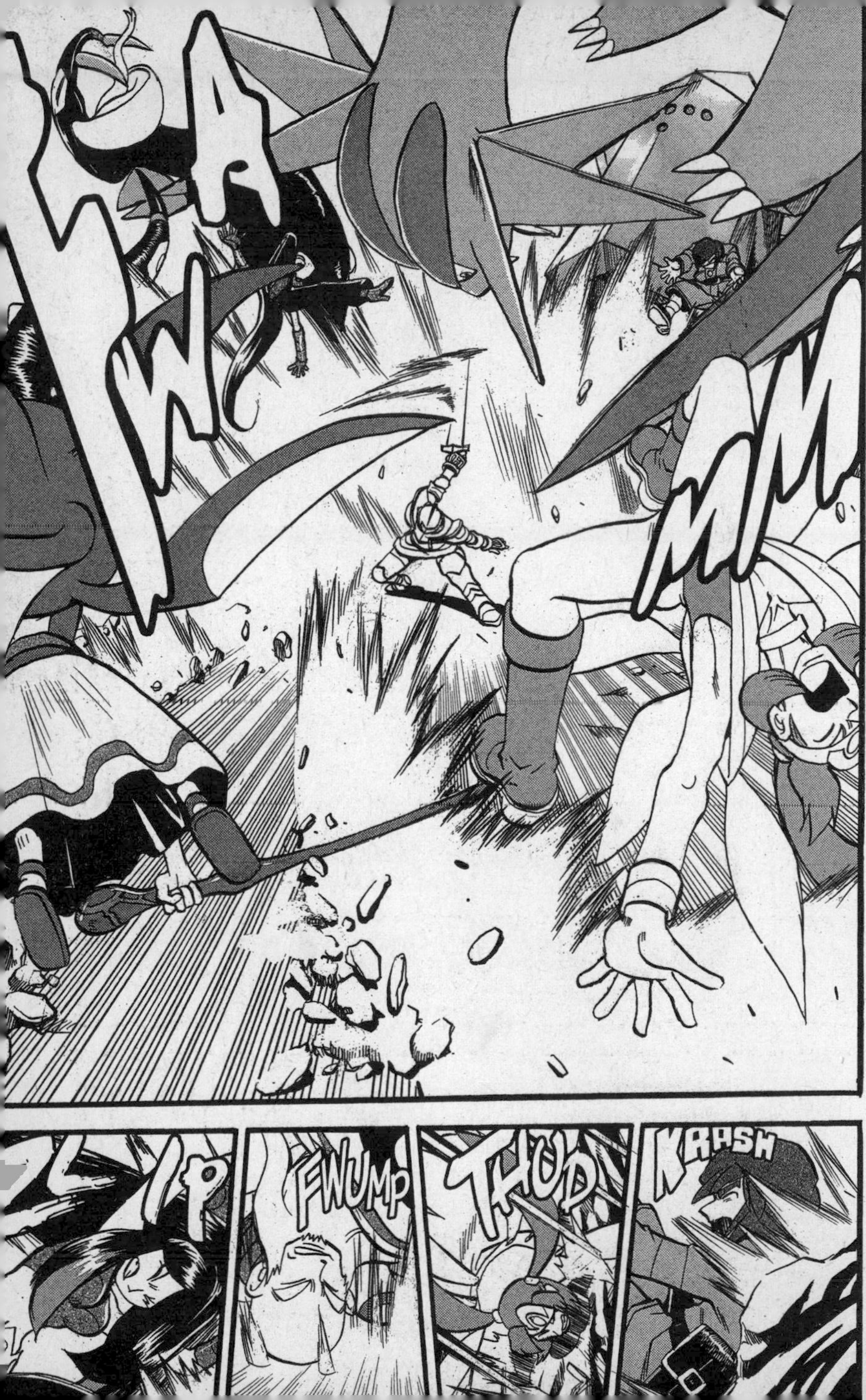
KRASH
THUD
FWUMP

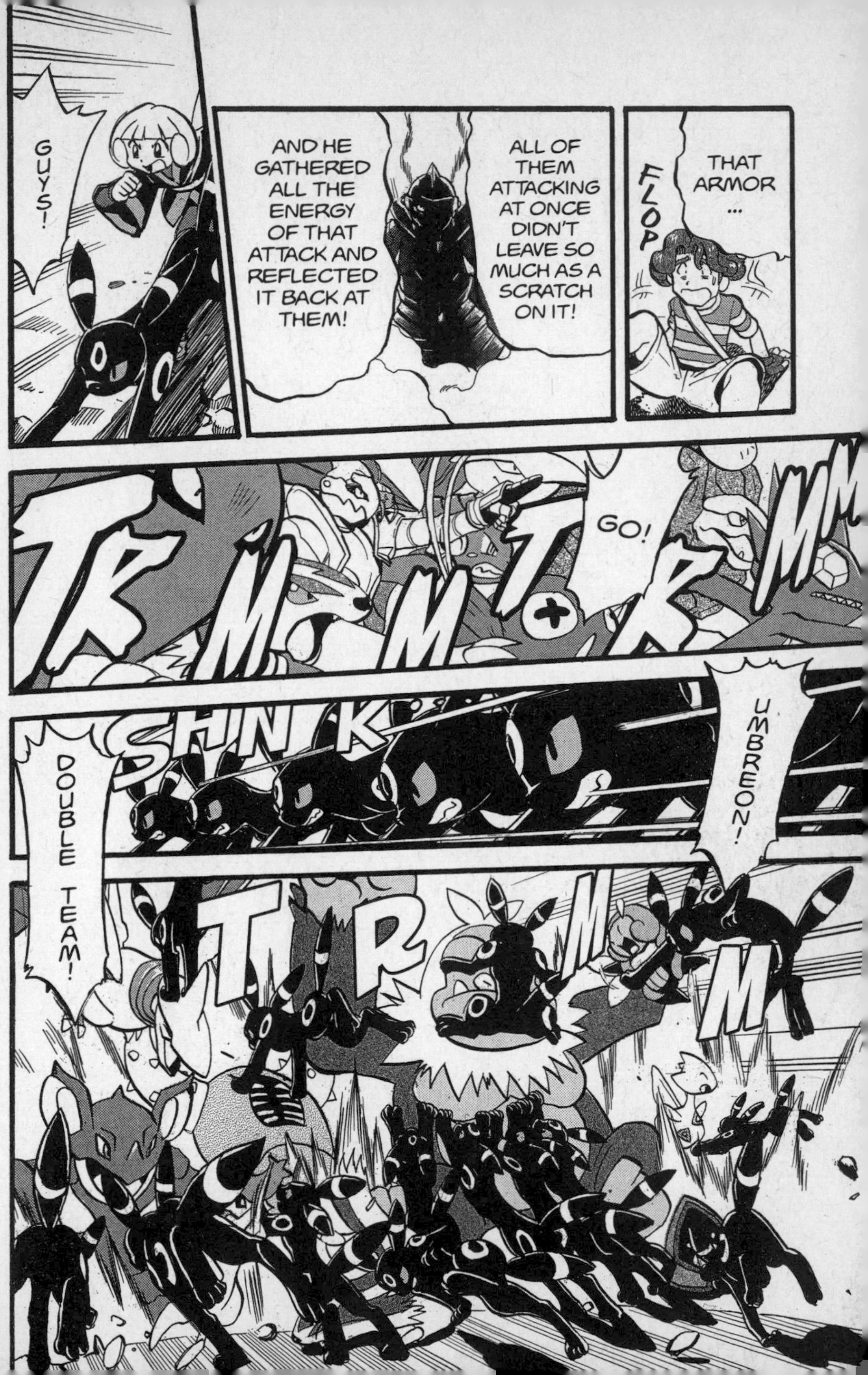
FLOP
THAT ARMOR ...
ALL OF THEM ATTACKING AT ONCE DIDN'T LEAVE SO MUCH AS A SCRATCH ON IT!
AND HE GATHERED ALL THE ENERGY OF THAT ATTACK AND REFLECTED IT BACK AT THEM!
GUYS!
GO!
TRMM TRMMM
UMBREON!
SHNK
DOUBLE TEAM!
TRMM

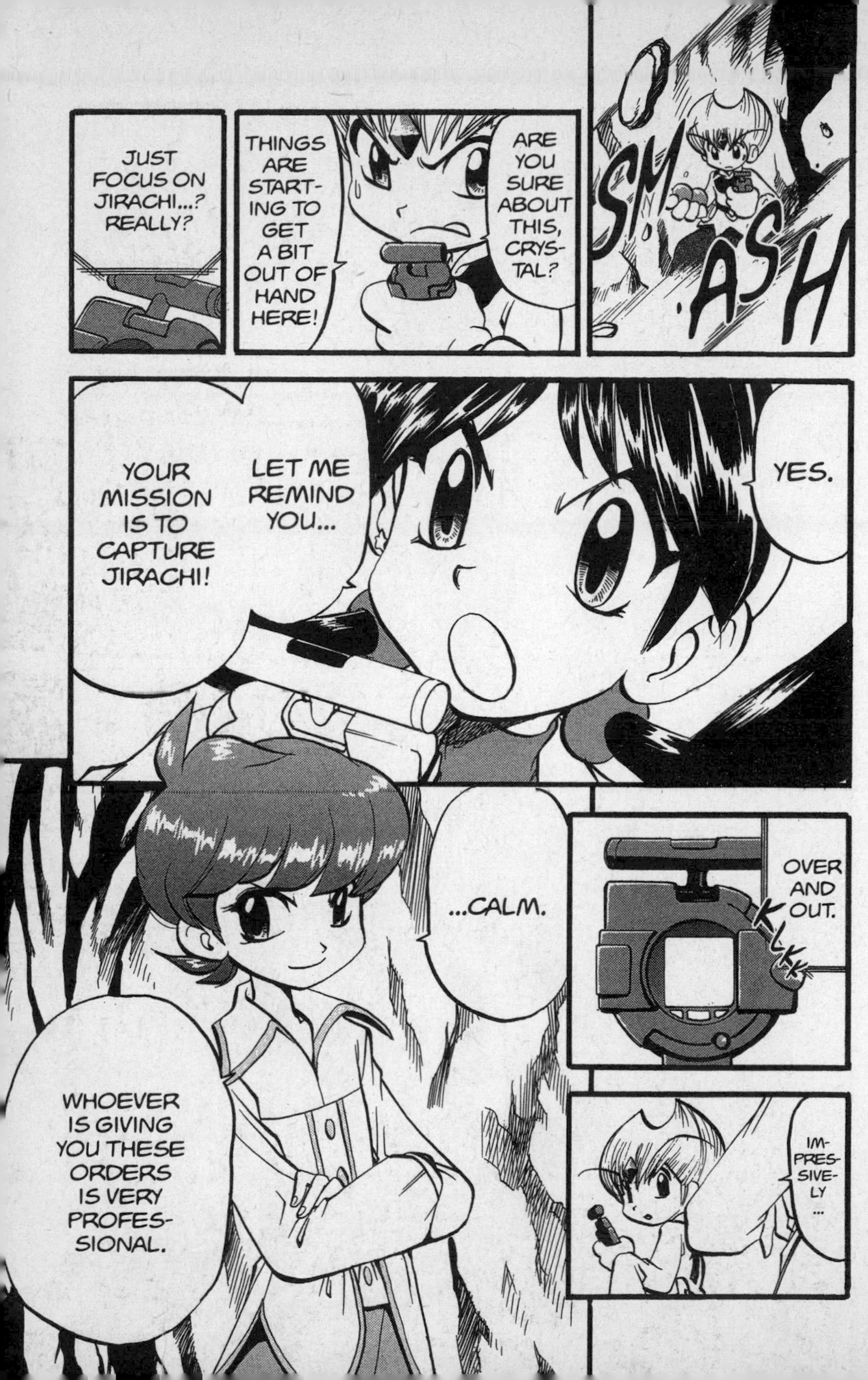
SMASH
ARE YOU SURE ABOUT THIS, CRYSTAL?
THINGS ARE STARTING TO GET A BIT OUT OF HAND HERE!
JUST FOCUS ON JIRACHI...? REALLY?
YES.
LET ME REMIND YOU...
YOUR MISSION IS TO CAPTURE JIRACHI!
OVER AND OUT.
IMPRESSIVELY...
...CALM.
WHOEVER IS GIVING YOU THESE ORDERS IS VERY PROFESSIONAL.

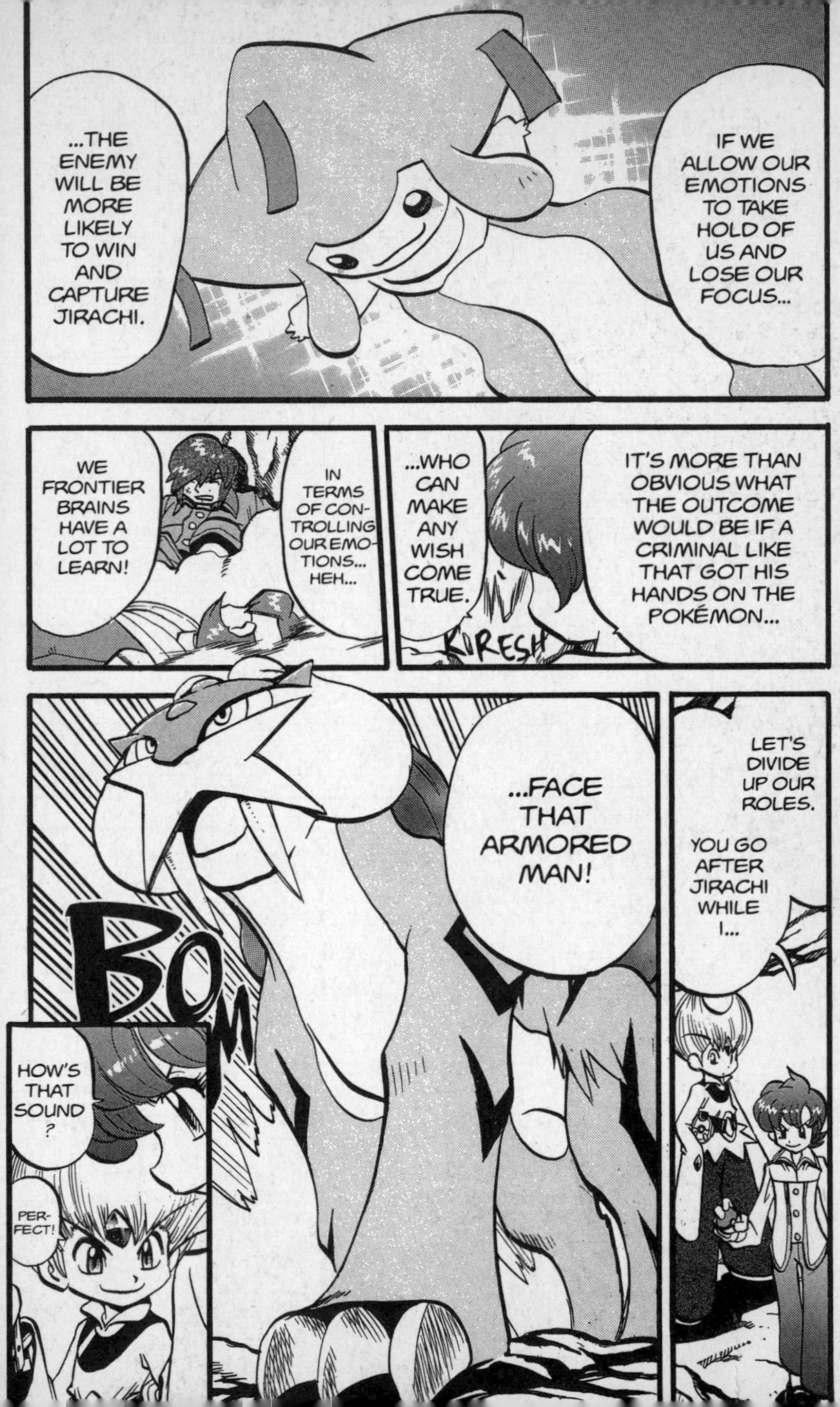
IF WE ALLOW OUR EMOTIONS TO TAKE HOLD OF US AND LOSE OUR FOCUS...
...THE ENEMY WILL BE MORE LIKELY TO WIN AND CAPTURE JIRACHI.
IT'S MORE THAN OBVIOUS WHAT THE OUTCOME WOULD BE IF A CRIMINAL LIKE THAT GOT HIS HANDS ON THE POKÉMON...
...WHO CAN MAKE ANY WISH COME TRUE.
KRESH
IN TERMS OF CONTROLLING OUR EMOTIONS... HEH...
WE FRONTIER BRAINS HAVE A LOT TO LEARN!
LET'S DIVIDE UP OUR ROLES.
YOU GO AFTER JIRACHI WHILE I...
...FACE THAT ARMORED MAN!
BOOM
HOW'S THAT SOUND?
PERFECT!

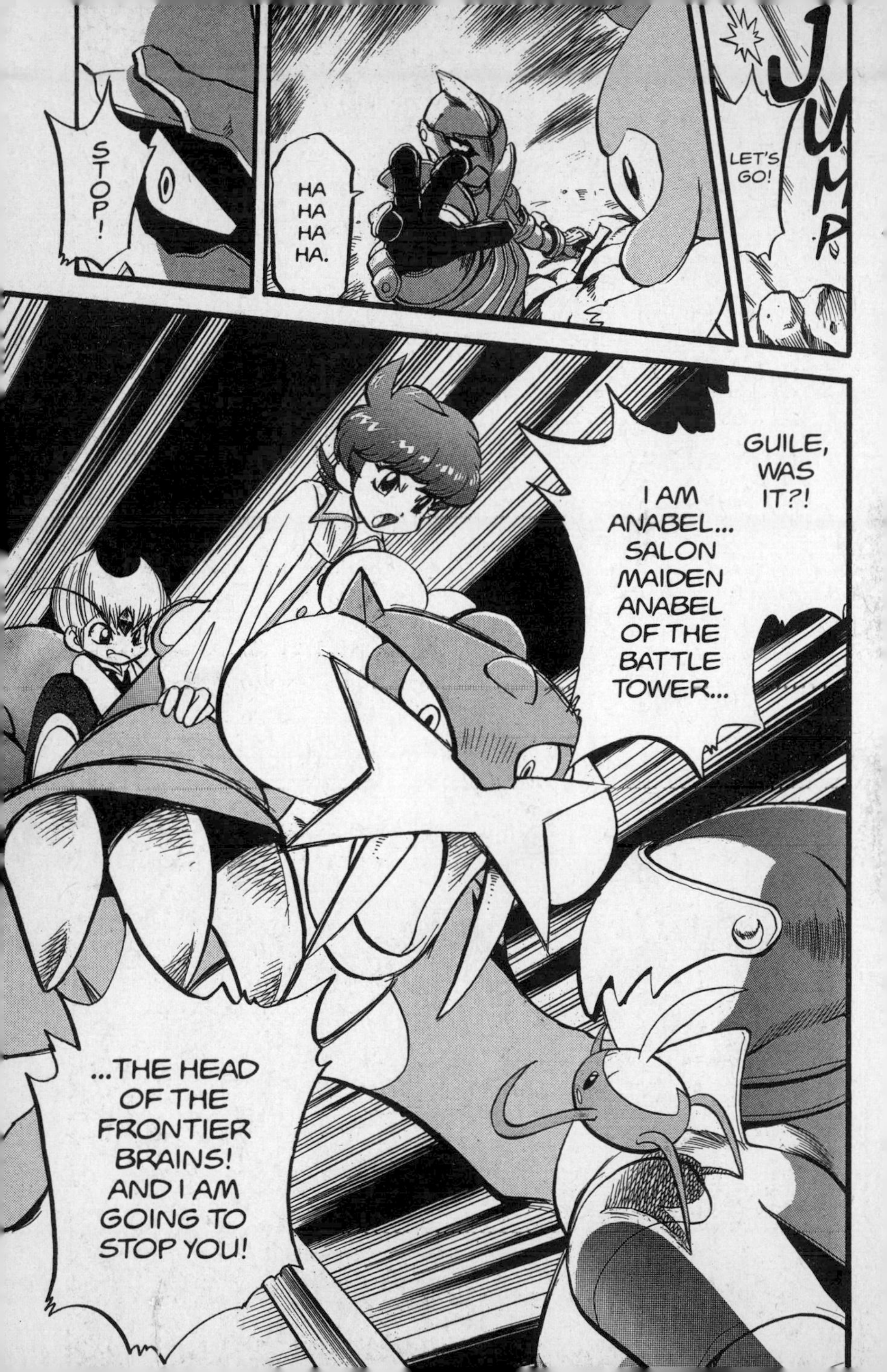
JUMP
LET'S GO!
HA HA HA HA.
STOP!
GUILE, WAS IT?!
I AM ANABEL... SALON MAIDEN ANABEL OF THE BATTLE TOWER...
...THE HEAD OF THE FRONTIER BRAINS! AND I AM GOING TO STOP YOU!

316

Skirting Around Surskit II

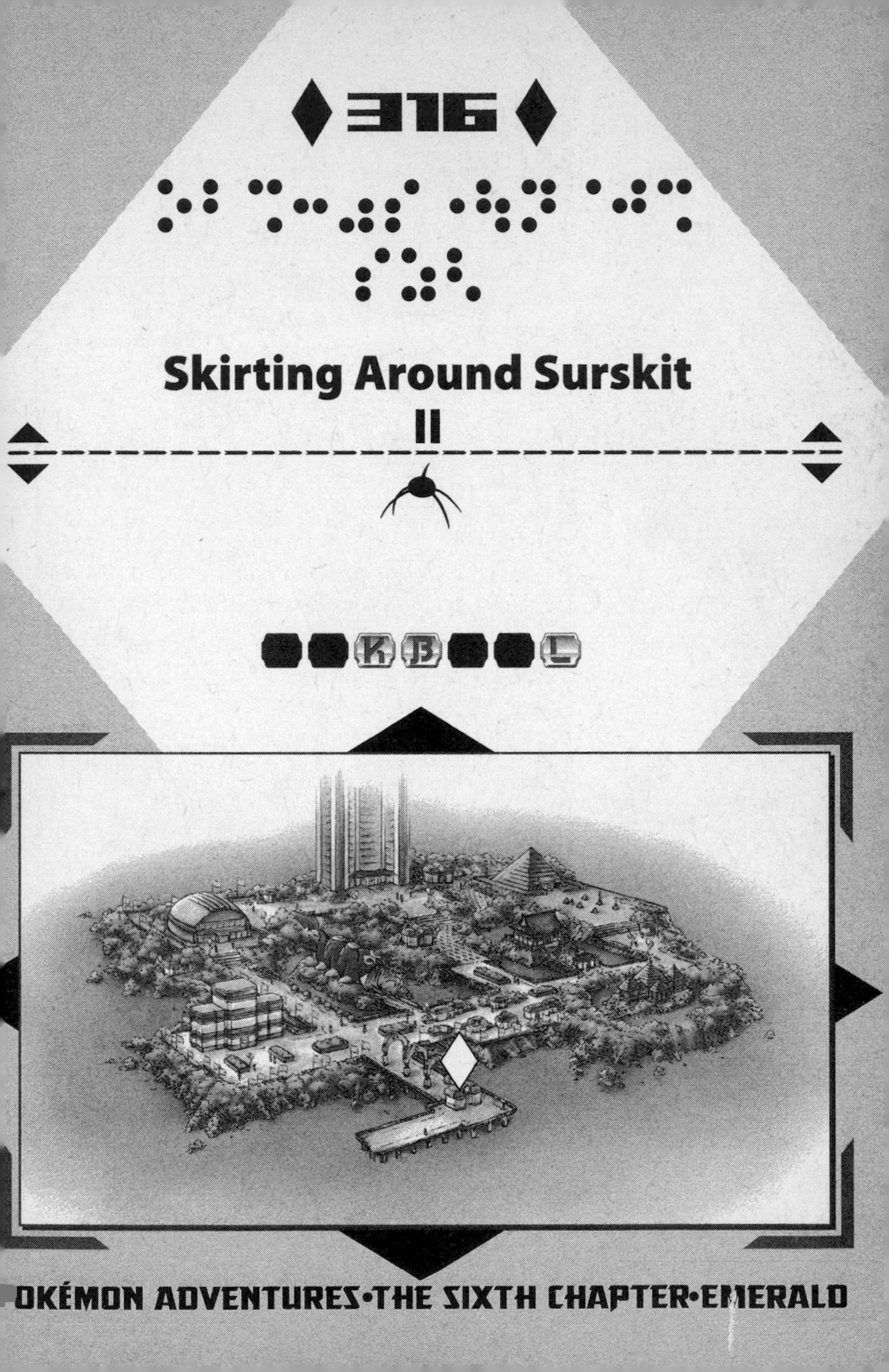

OKÉMON ADVENTURES•THE SIXTH CHAPTER•EMERALD

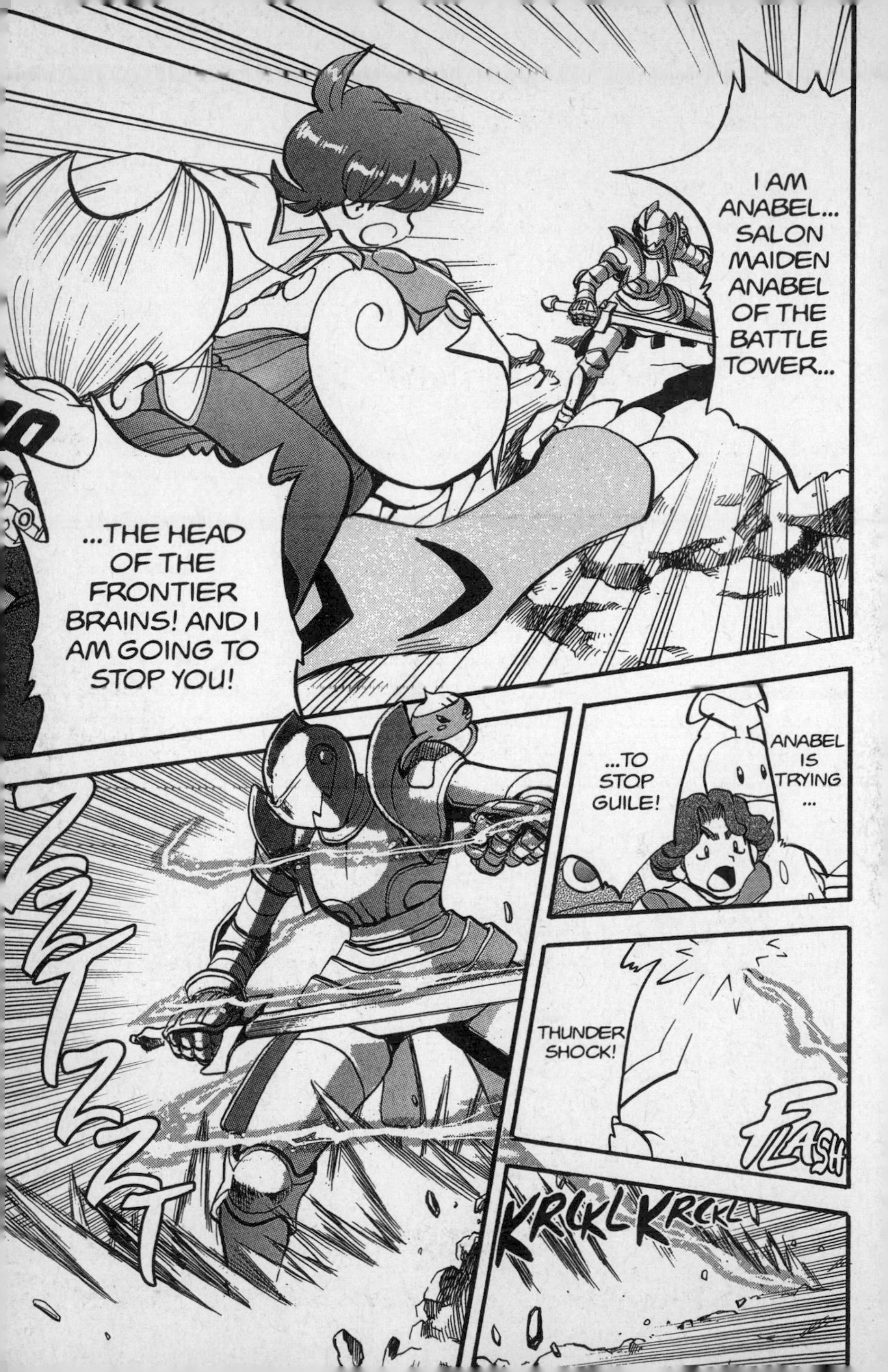
I AM ANABEL... SALON MAIDEN ANABEL OF THE BATTLE TOWER...
...THE HEAD OF THE FRONTIER BRAINS! AND I AM GOING TO STOP YOU!
ANABEL IS TRYING ...
...TO STOP GUILE!
THUNDER SHOCK!
FLASH
KRCKL KRCKL
ZZZZZT

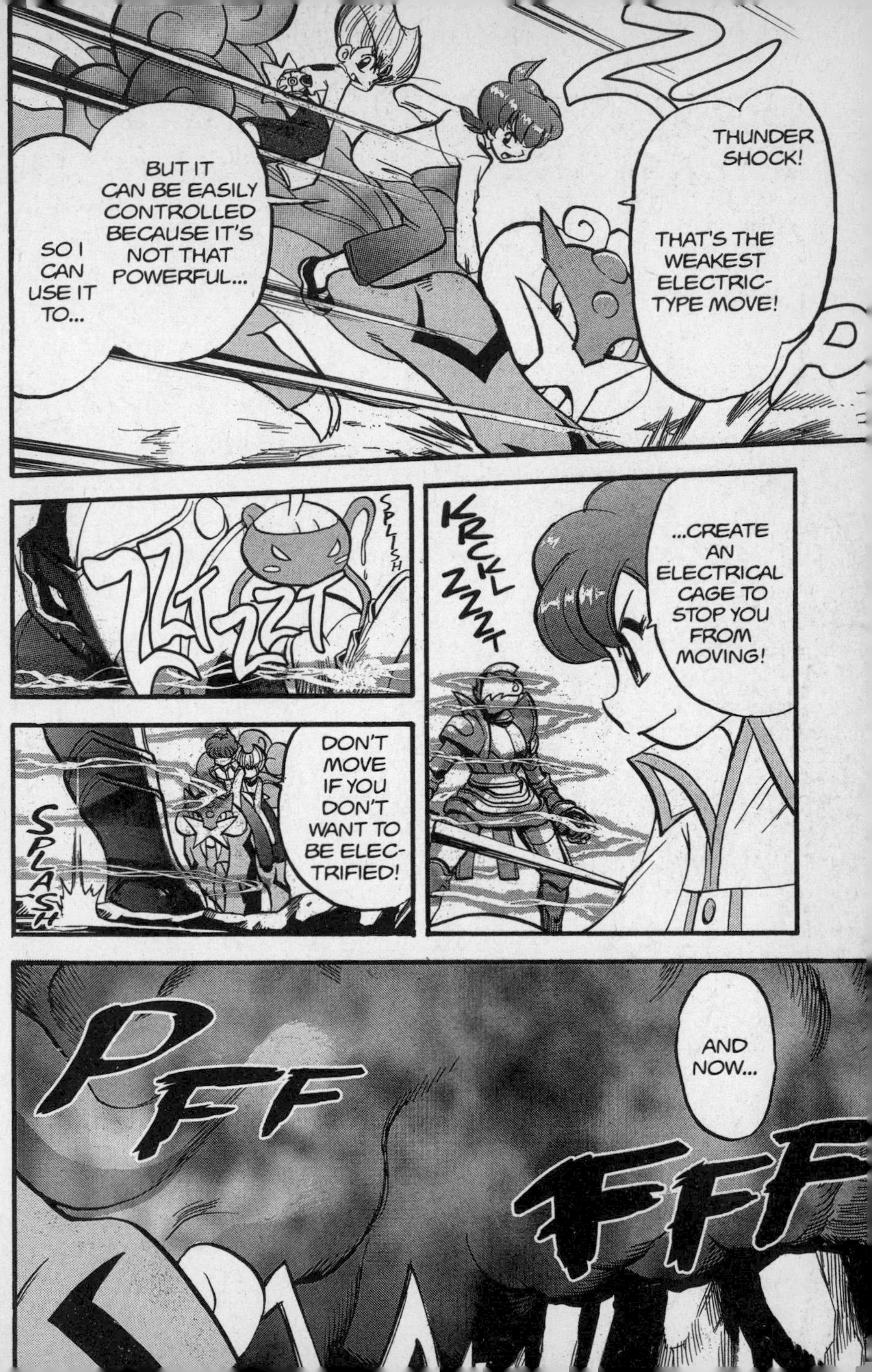

THUNDER SHOCK!
THAT'S THE WEAKEST ELECTRIC-TYPE MOVE!
BUT IT CAN BE EASILY CONTROLLED BECAUSE IT'S NOT THAT POWERFUL...
SO I CAN USE IT TO...
KRCKL ZZZZT
...CREATE AN ELECTRICAL CAGE TO STOP YOU FROM MOVING!
SPLISH
ZZT ZZT
DON'T MOVE IF YOU DON'T WANT TO BE ELEC-TRIFIED!
SPLASH
AND NOW...
PFFFFF

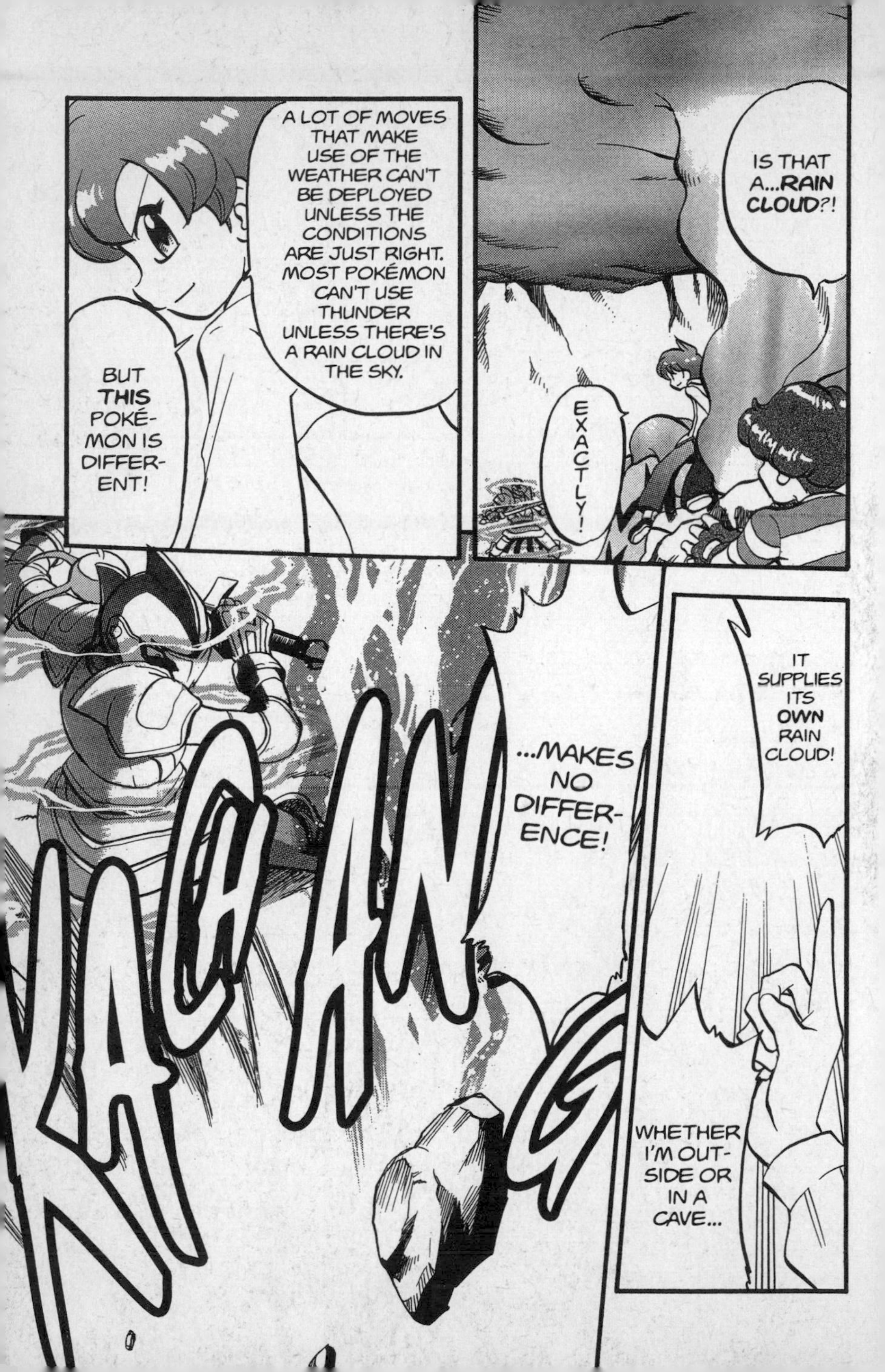
IS THAT A...**RAIN CLOUD**?!
EXACTLY!
A LOT OF MOVES THAT MAKE USE OF THE WEATHER CAN'T BE DEPLOYED UNLESS THE CONDITIONS ARE JUST RIGHT. MOST POKÉMON CAN'T USE THUNDER UNLESS THERE'S A RAIN CLOUD IN THE SKY.
BUT **THIS** POKÉMON IS DIFFERENT!
IT SUPPLIES ITS **OWN** RAIN CLOUD!
WHETHER I'M OUTSIDE OR IN A CAVE...
...MAKES NO DIFFERENCE!

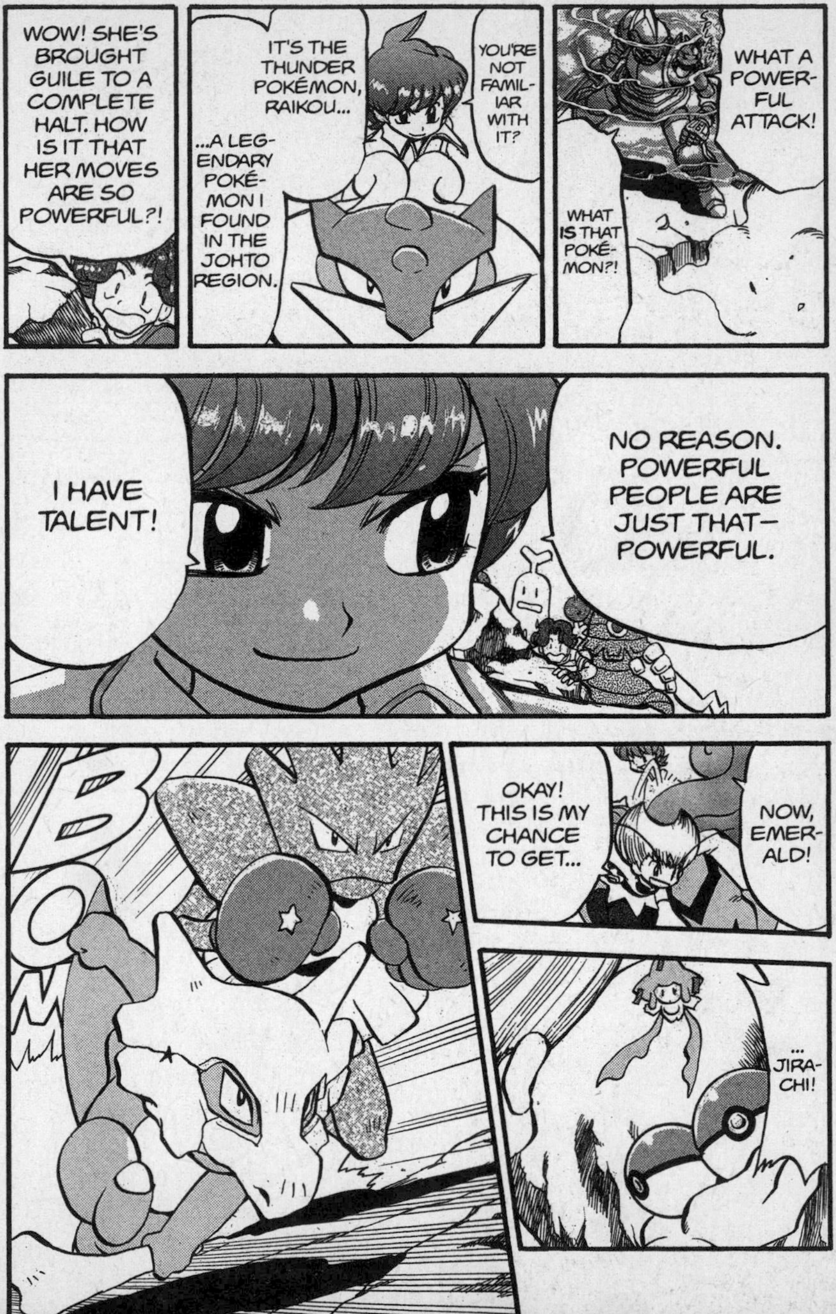
WHAT A POWERFUL ATTACK!
WHAT IS THAT POKÉMON?!
YOU'RE NOT FAMILIAR WITH IT?
IT'S THE THUNDER POKÉMON, RAIKOU...
...A LEGENDARY POKÉMON I FOUND IN THE JOHTO REGION.
WOW! SHE'S BROUGHT GUILE TO A COMPLETE HALT. HOW IS IT THAT HER MOVES ARE SO POWERFUL?!
NO REASON. POWERFUL PEOPLE ARE JUST THAT—POWERFUL.
I HAVE TALENT!
NOW, EMERALD!
OKAY! THIS IS MY CHANCE TO GET...
...JIRACHI!

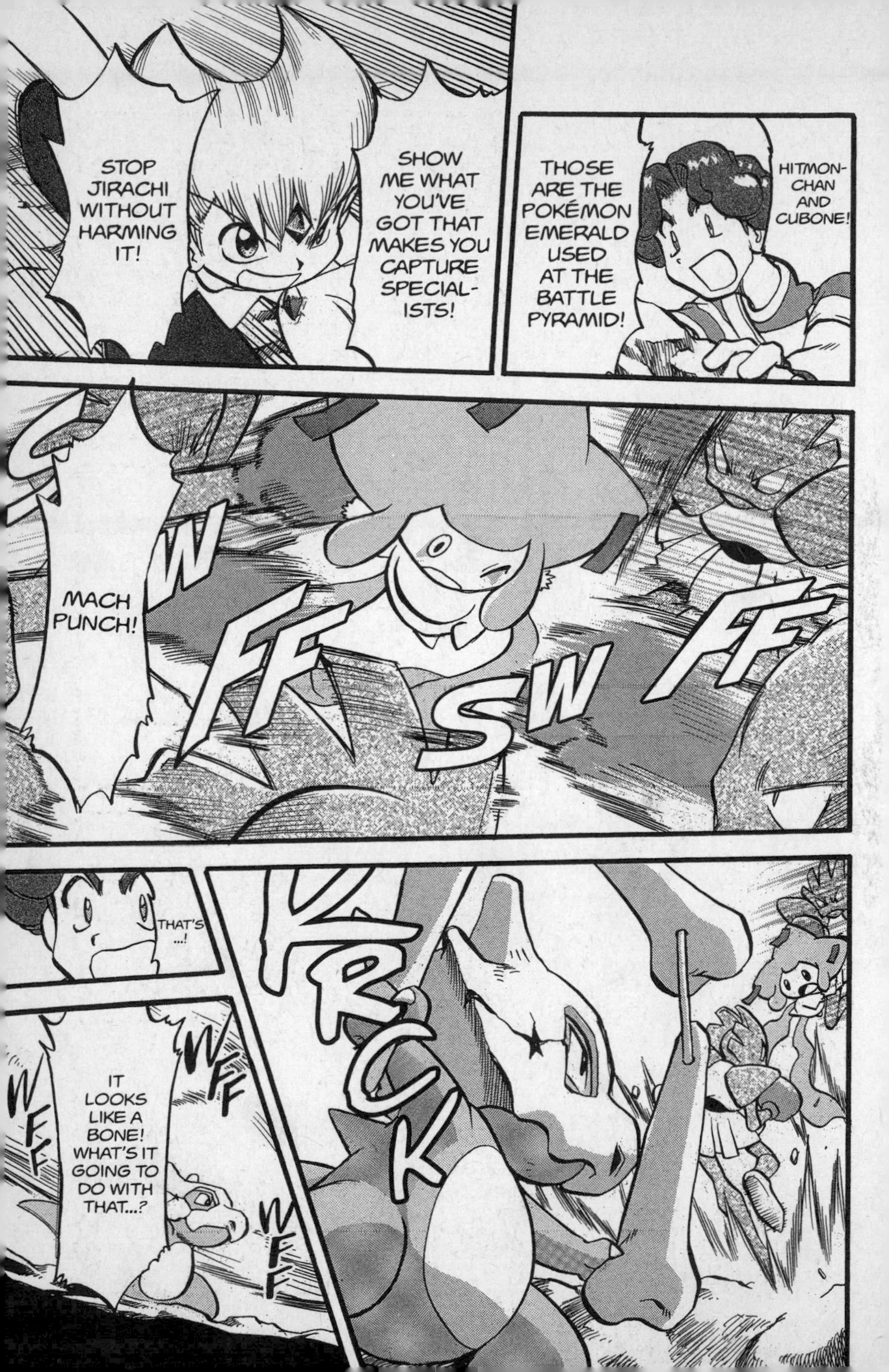
HITMON-CHAN AND CUBONE!
THOSE ARE THE POKÉMON EMERALD USED AT THE BATTLE PYRAMID!
SHOW ME WHAT YOU'VE GOT THAT MAKES YOU CAPTURE SPECIAL-ISTS!
STOP JIRACHI WITHOUT HARMING IT!
SWFF
SWFF
MACH PUNCH!
KRRCK
THAT'S ...!
WFF
IT LOOKS LIKE A BONE! WHAT'S IT GOING TO DO WITH THAT...?
WFF
WFF

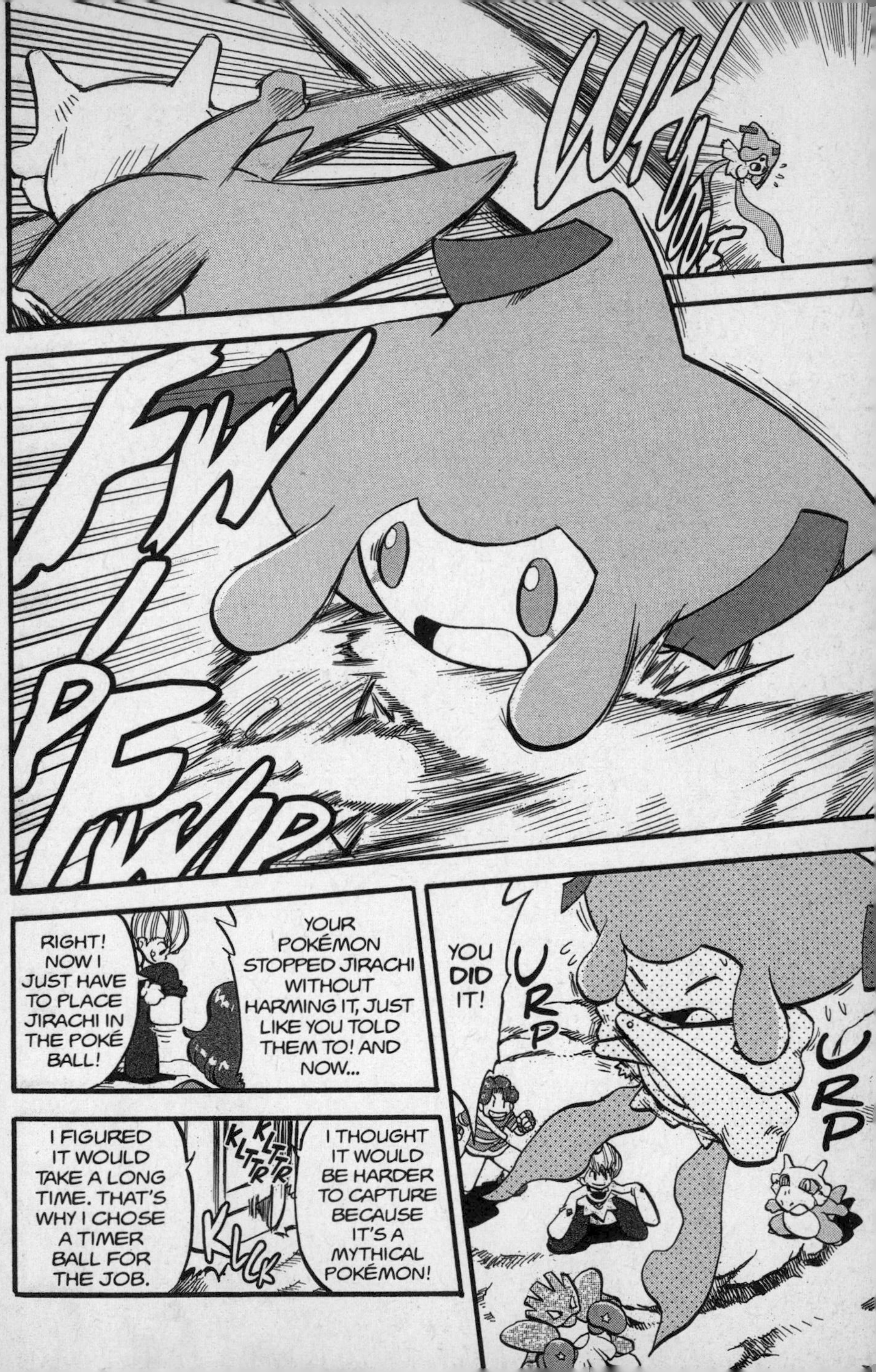
FWIP
FWIP
YOU DID IT!
URP
URP
YOUR POKÉMON STOPPED JIRACHI WITHOUT HARMING IT, JUST LIKE YOU TOLD THEM TO! AND NOW...
RIGHT! NOW I JUST HAVE TO PLACE JIRACHI IN THE POKÉ BALL!
I THOUGHT IT WOULD BE HARDER TO CAPTURE BECAUSE IT'S A MYTHICAL POKÉMON!
KLTTR KLTTR
KLIK
I FIGURED IT WOULD TAKE A LONG TIME. THAT'S WHY I CHOSE A TIMER BALL FOR THE JOB.

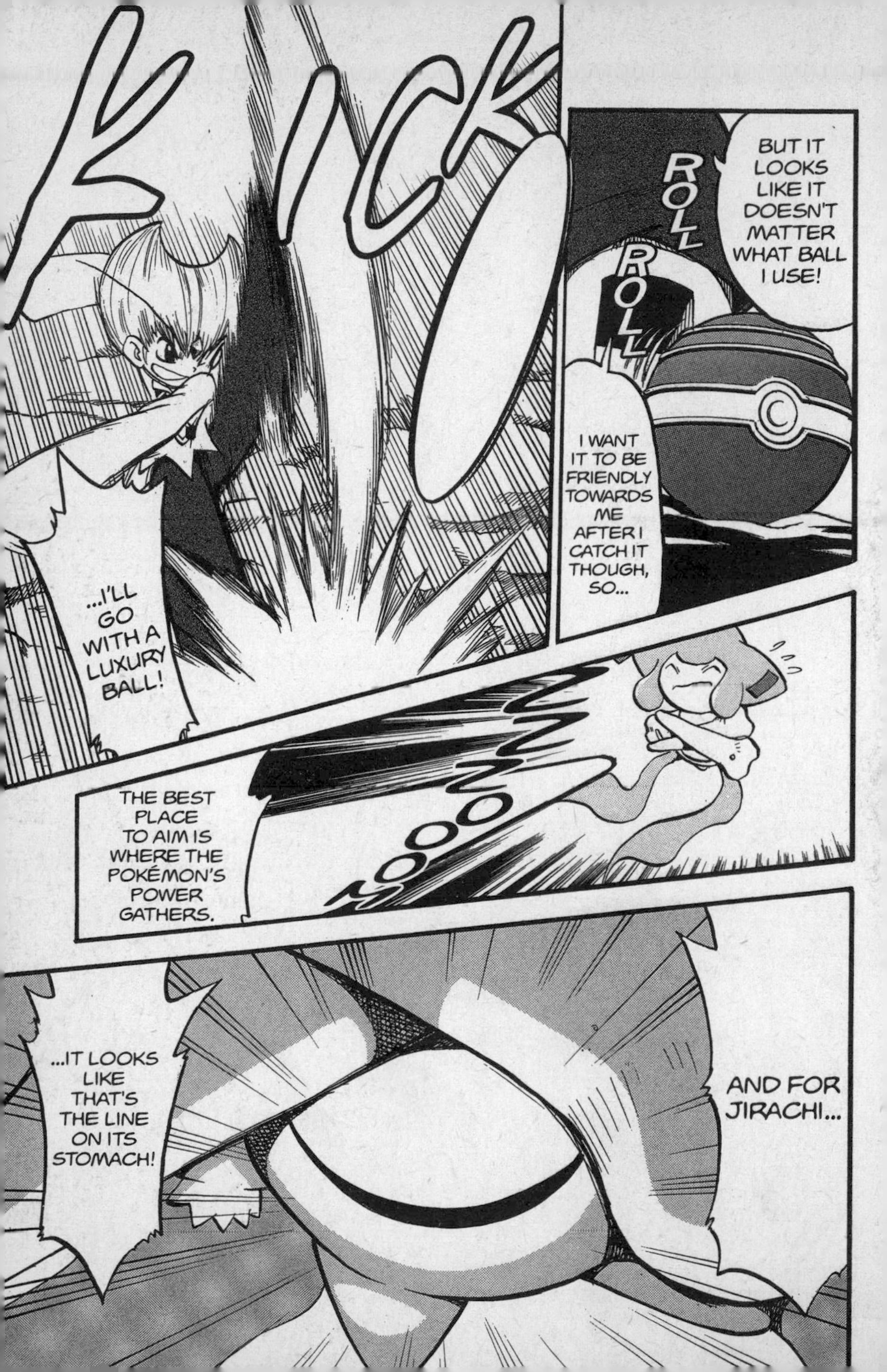
BUT IT LOOKS LIKE IT DOESN'T MATTER WHAT BALL I USE!
ROLL ROLL
I WANT IT TO BE FRIENDLY TOWARDS ME AFTER I CATCH IT THOUGH, SO...
KICK
...I'LL GO WITH A LUXURY BALL!
THE BEST PLACE TO AIM IS WHERE THE POKÉMON'S POWER GATHERS.
AND FOR JIRACHI...
...IT LOOKS LIKE THAT'S THE LINE ON ITS STOMACH!

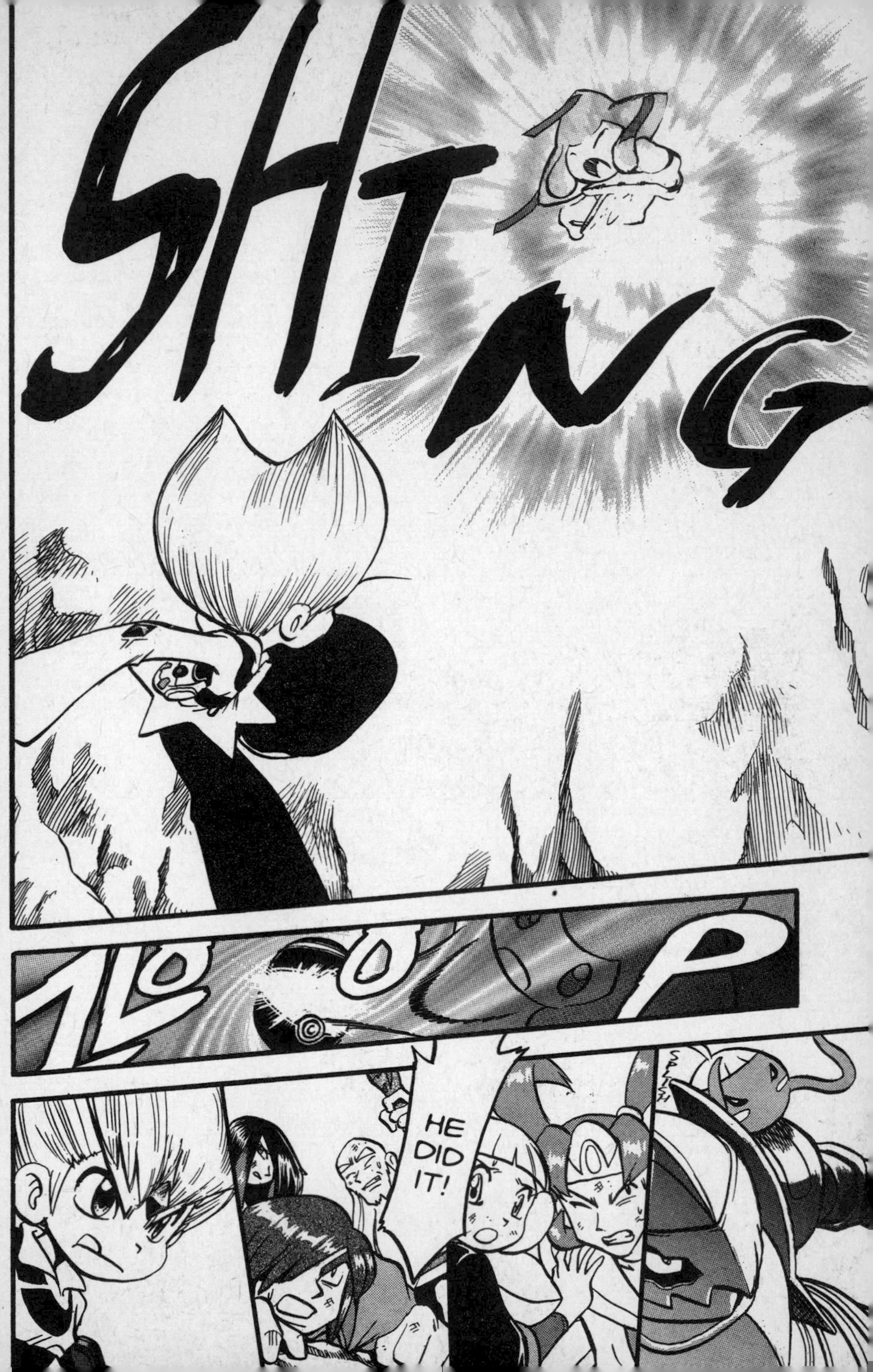

SHING
ZOOP
HE DID IT!
SPLISH

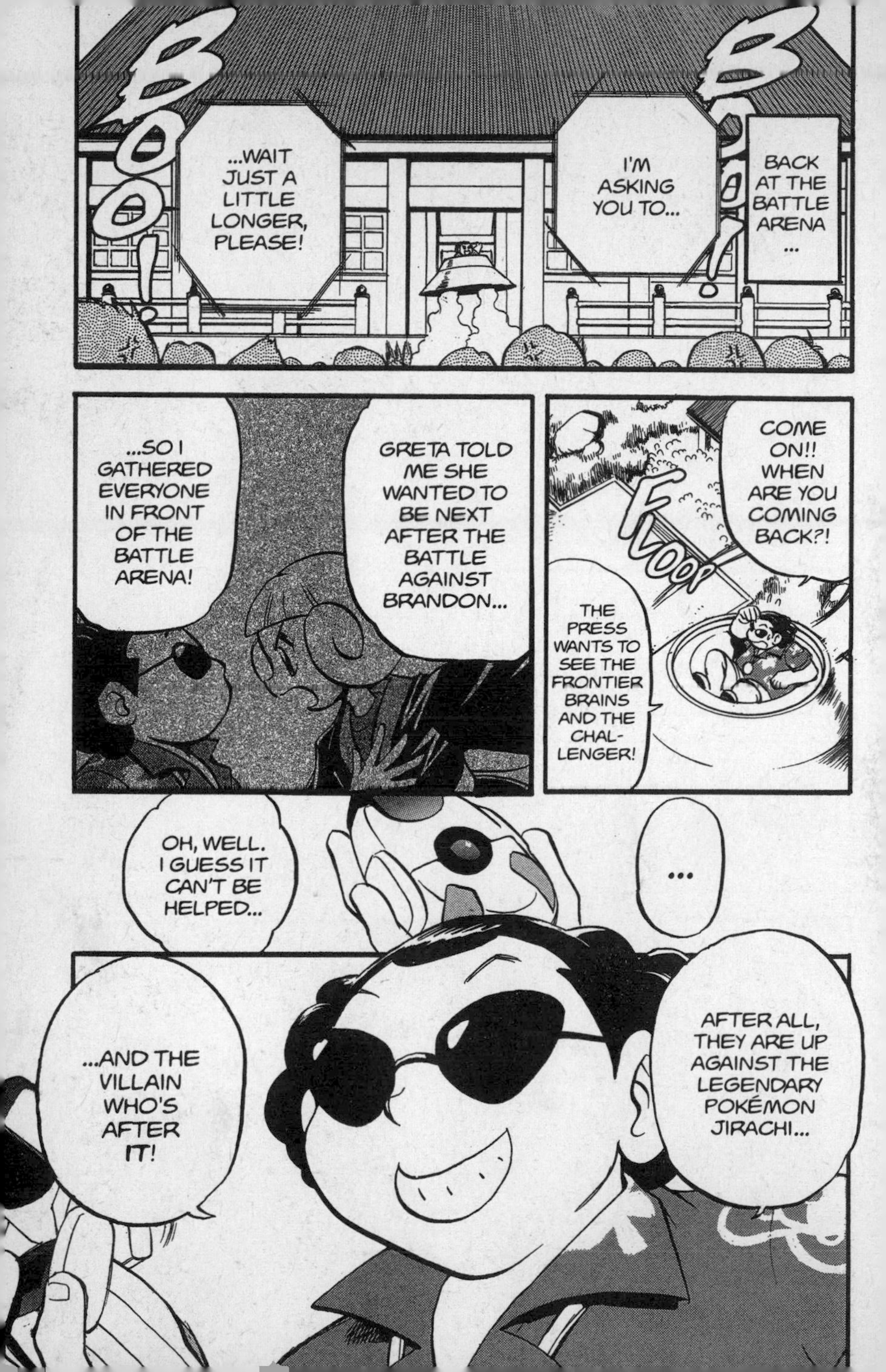
BACK AT THE BATTLE ARENA ...
BOO!
I'M ASKING YOU TO...
...WAIT JUST A LITTLE LONGER, PLEASE!
BOO!
COME ON!! WHEN ARE YOU COMING BACK?!
FLOOP
THE PRESS WANTS TO SEE THE FRONTIER BRAINS AND THE CHAL-LENGER!
GRETA TOLD ME SHE WANTED TO BE NEXT AFTER THE BATTLE AGAINST BRANDON...
...SO I GATHERED EVERYONE IN FRONT OF THE BATTLE ARENA!
...
OH, WELL. I GUESS IT CAN'T BE HELPED...
AFTER ALL, THEY ARE UP AGAINST THE LEGENDARY POKÉMON JIRACHI...
...AND THE VILLAIN WHO'S AFTER IT!

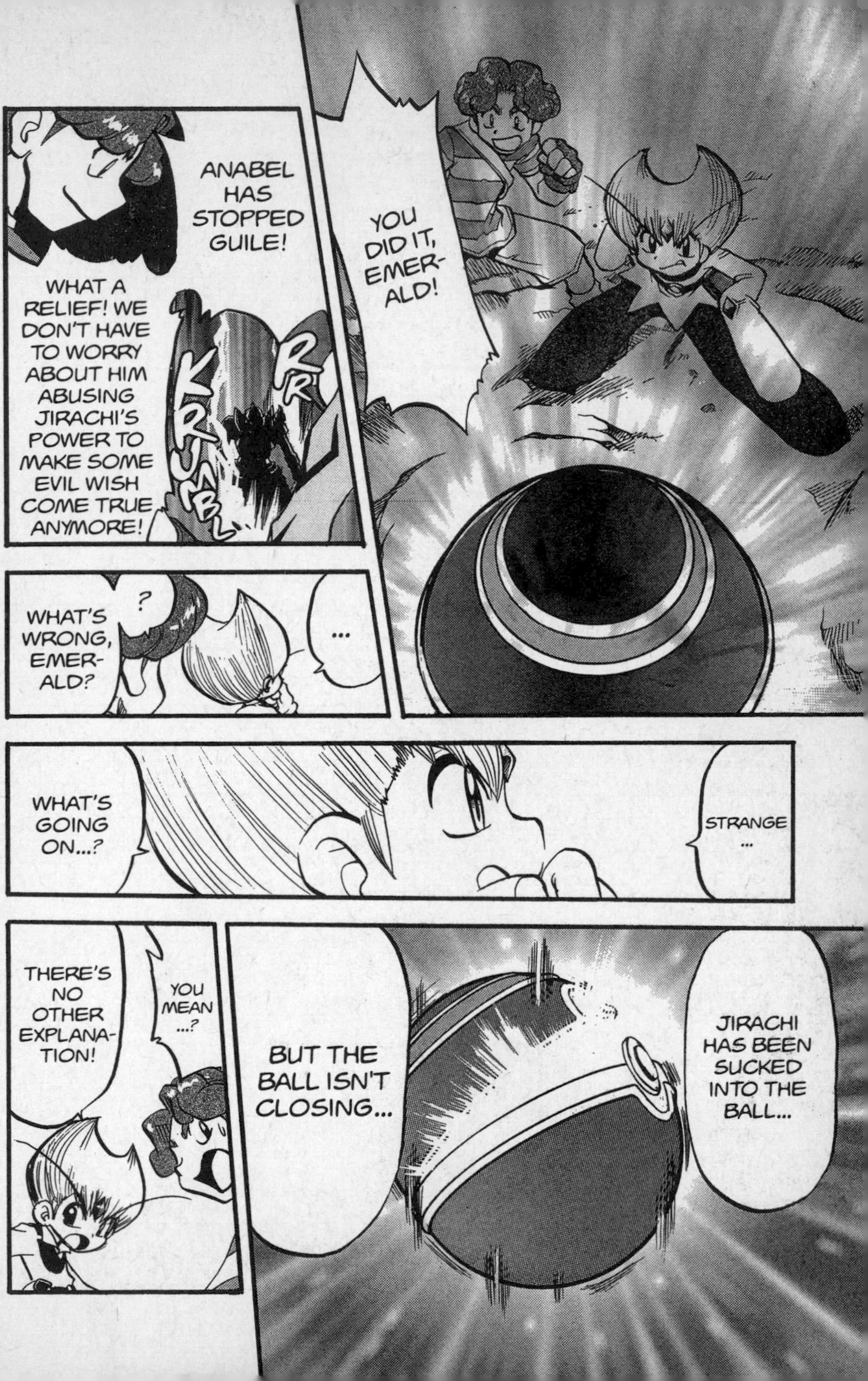

YOU DID IT, EMERALD!
ANABEL HAS STOPPED GUILE!
WHAT A RELIEF! WE DON'T HAVE TO WORRY ABOUT HIM ABUSING JIRACHI'S POWER TO MAKE SOME EVIL WISH COME TRUE ANYMORE!
KRRRUMBL
...
?
WHAT'S WRONG, EMERALD?
STRANGE...
WHAT'S GOING ON...?
JIRACHI HAS BEEN SUCKED INTO THE BALL...
BUT THE BALL ISN'T CLOSING...
YOU MEAN...?
THERE'S NO OTHER EXPLANATION!

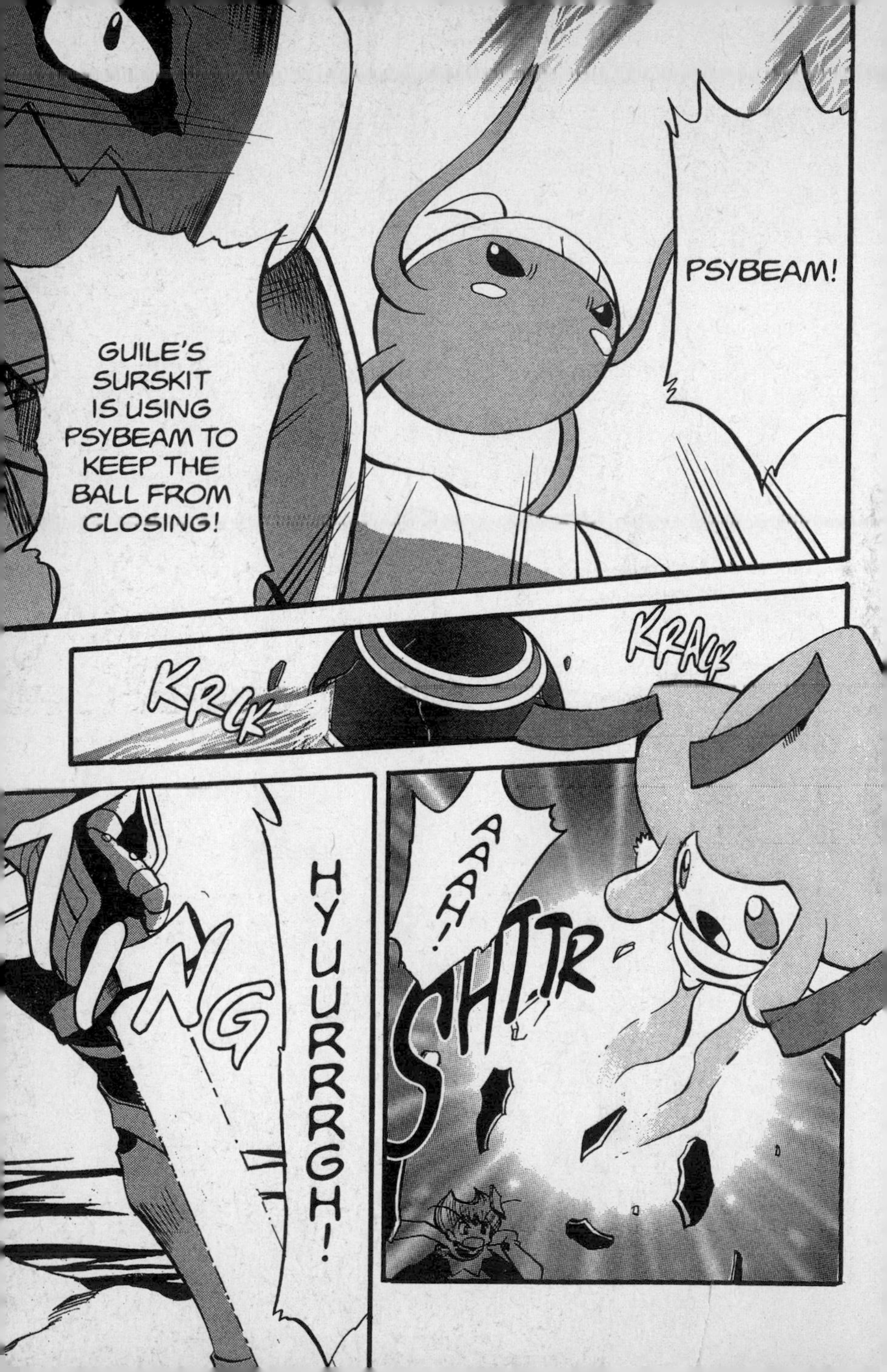
PSYBEAM!
GUILE'S SURSKIT IS USING PSYBEAM TO KEEP THE BALL FROM CLOSING!
KRACK
KRCK
AAAH!
SHTTR
HYUURRRGH!
NG

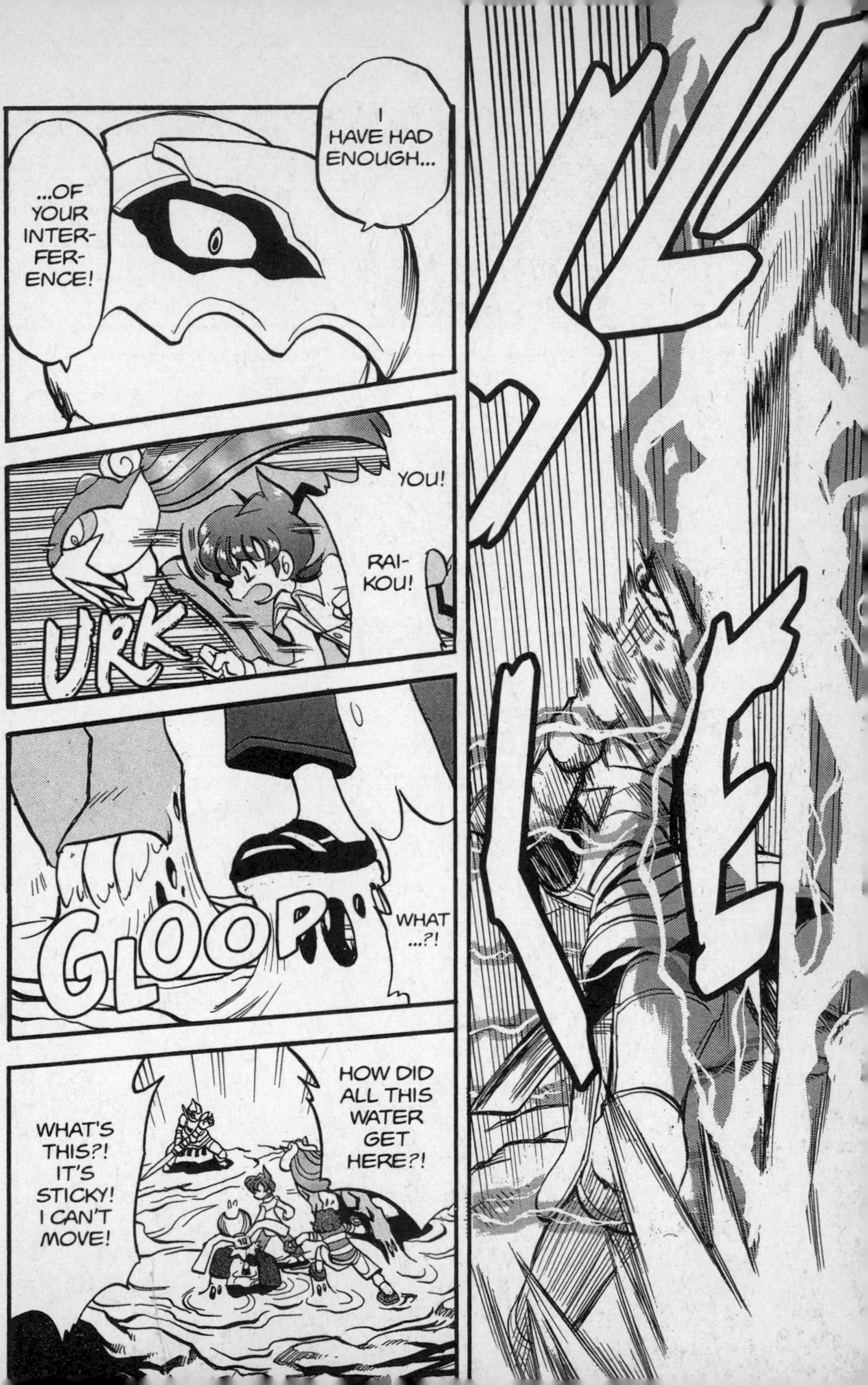
I HAVE HAD ENOUGH...
...OF YOUR INTERFERENCE!
YOU!
RAIKOU!
URK
GLOOP
WHAT ...?!
HOW DID ALL THIS WATER GET HERE?!
WHAT'S THIS?! IT'S STICKY! I CAN'T MOVE!

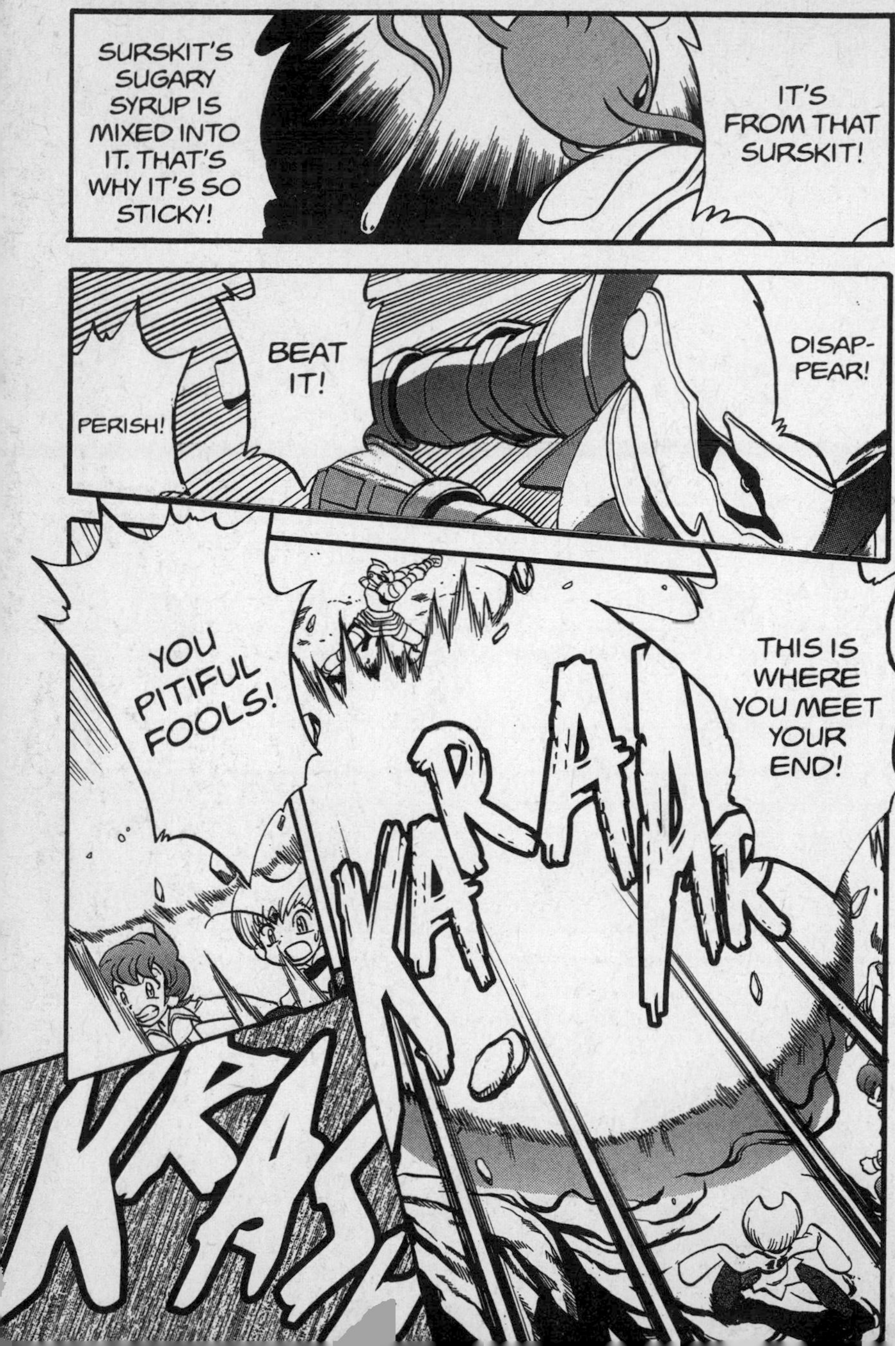
IT'S FROM THAT SURSKIT!
SURSKIT'S SUGARY SYRUP IS MIXED INTO IT. THAT'S WHY IT'S SO STICKY!
DISAP-PEAR!
BEAT IT!
PERISH!
THIS IS WHERE YOU MEET YOUR END!
YOU PITIFUL FOOLS!

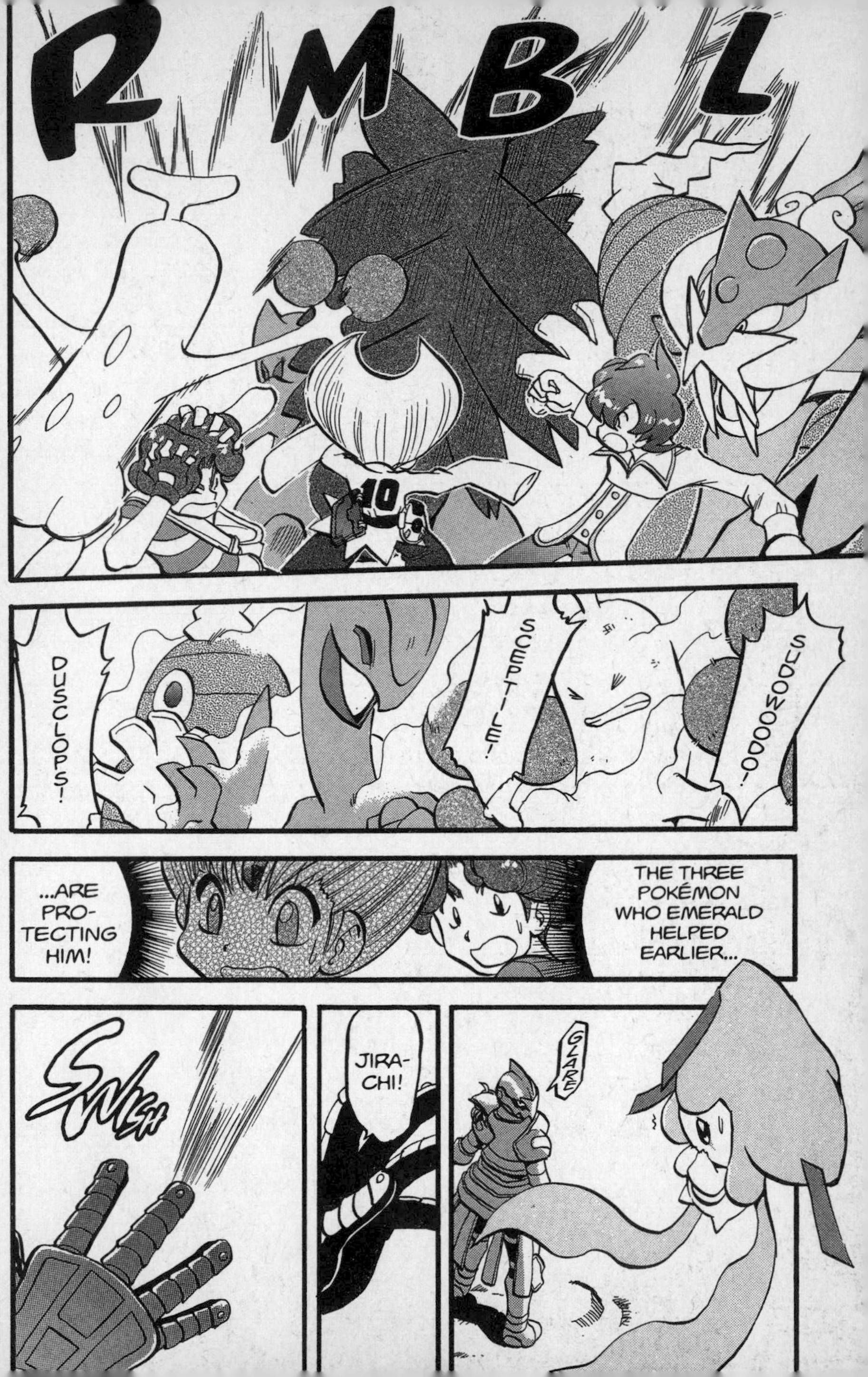
RMBL
SUDOWOODO!
SCEPTILE!
DUSCLOPS!
THE THREE POKÉMON WHO EMERALD HELPED EARLIER...
...ARE PRO-TECTING HIM!
GLARE
JIRA-CHI!

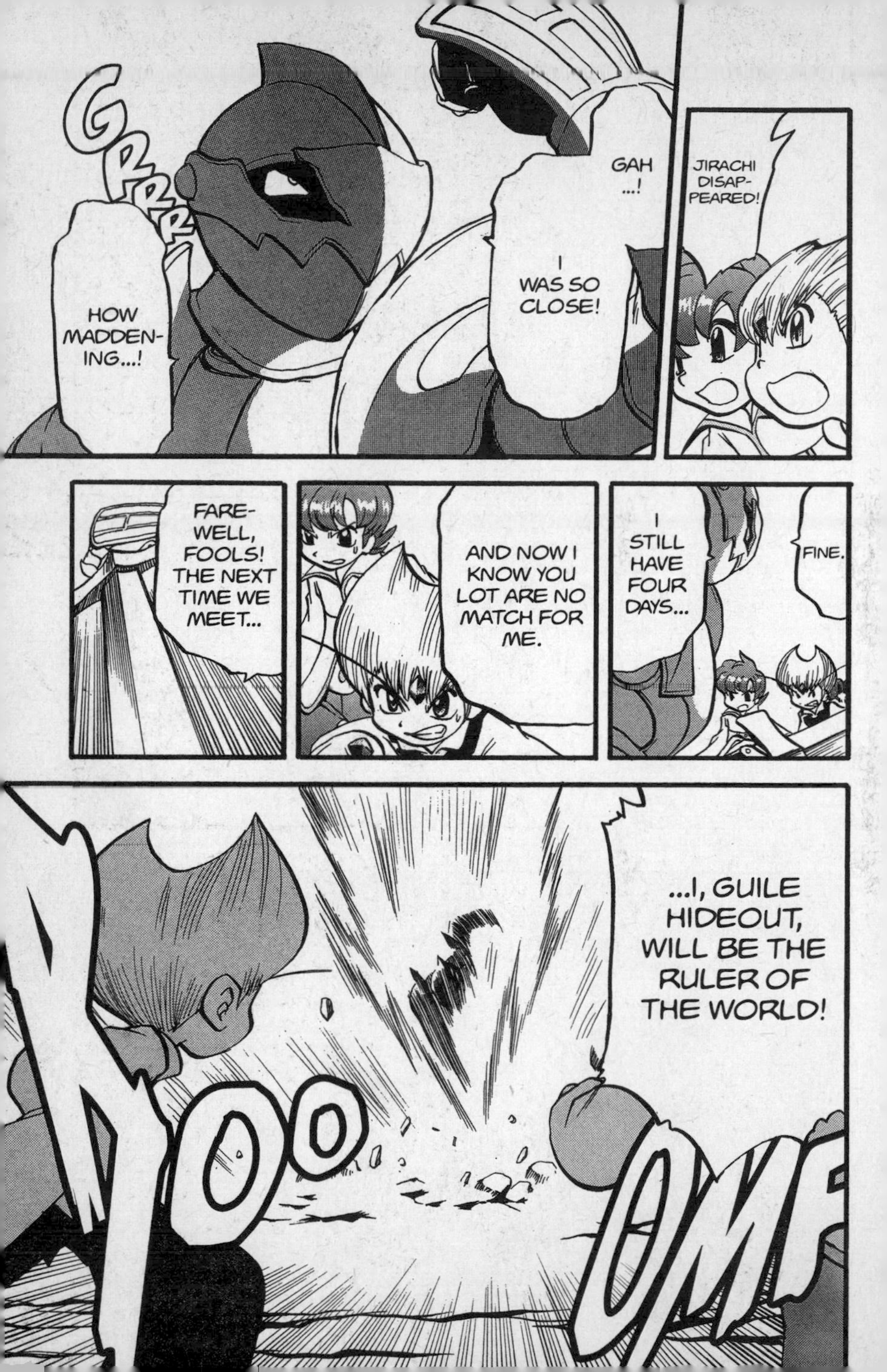
JIRACHI DISAPPEARED!
GAH ...!
I WAS SO CLOSE!
GRRR
HOW MADDENING...!
FINE.
I STILL HAVE FOUR DAYS...
AND NOW I KNOW YOU LOT ARE NO MATCH FOR ME.
FAREWELL, FOOLS! THE NEXT TIME WE MEET...
...I, GUILE HIDEOUT, WILL BE THE RULER OF THE WORLD!
WOOOMF

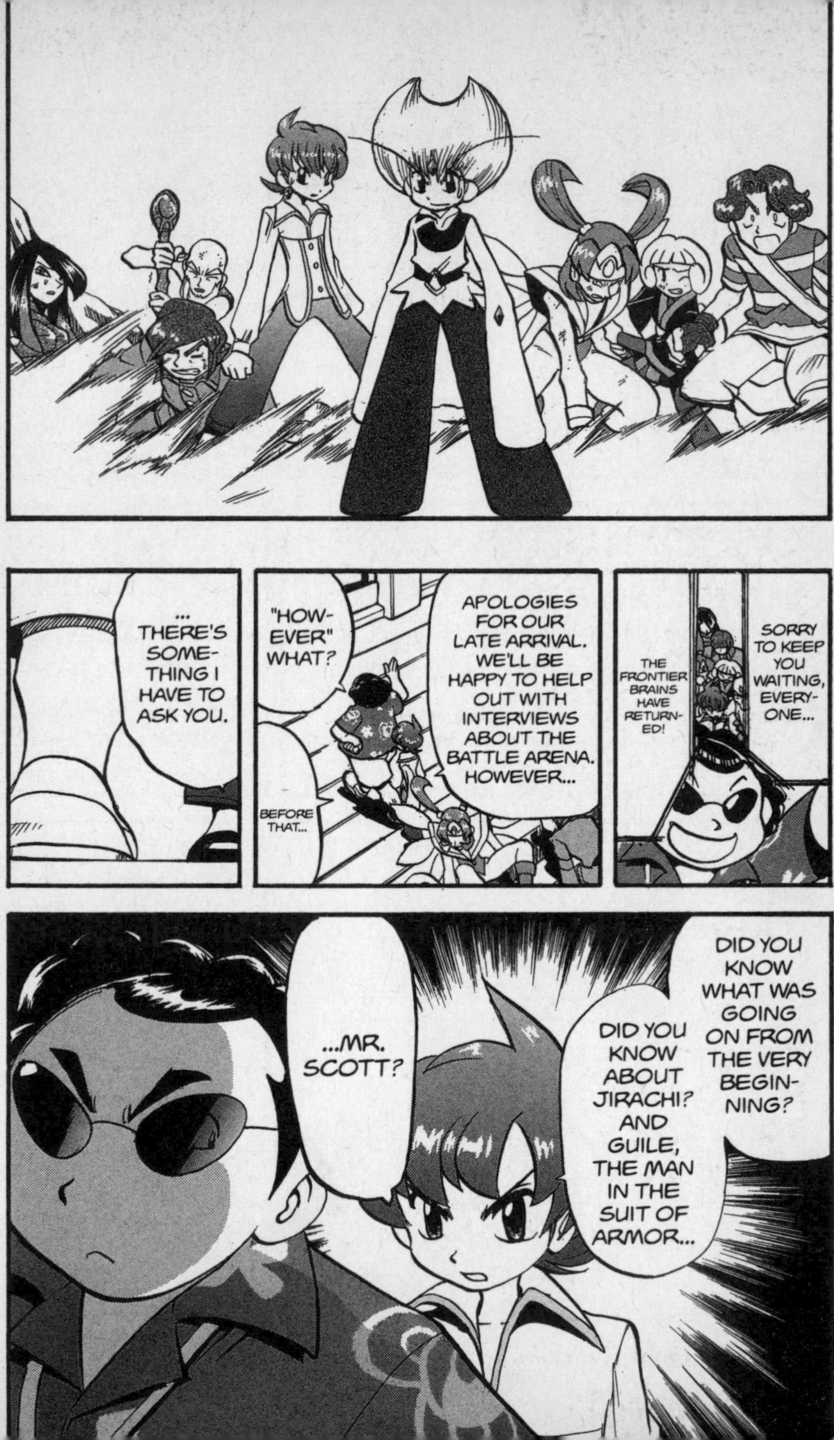
SORRY TO KEEP YOU WAITING, EVERYONE...
THE FRONTIER BRAINS HAVE RETURNED!
APOLOGIES FOR OUR LATE ARRIVAL. WE'LL BE HAPPY TO HELP OUT WITH INTERVIEWS ABOUT THE BATTLE ARENA. HOWEVER...
"HOWEVER" WHAT?
BEFORE THAT...
...THERE'S SOMETHING I HAVE TO ASK YOU.
DID YOU KNOW WHAT WAS GOING ON FROM THE VERY BEGINNING?
DID YOU KNOW ABOUT JIRACHI? AND GUILE, THE MAN IN THE SUIT OF ARMOR...
...MR. SCOTT?

DEAR MEMBERS OF THE PRESS...

Thank you for visiting the Battle Frontier today. Permit me to continue explaining the rules of this facility...

OWNER SCOTT

FACILITY RULES	Battle-type	Number of Pokémon	Type of Symbol	Wins needed to attain the Symbol
BATTLE DOME	• Single • Double	3 Pokémon	Tactics	Championships × 10 Rounds = 40 Consecutive Wins

At the Battle Dome, the challenger participates in a tournament between 16 Trainers. The Trainers must choose two of three Pokémon. Before the battle, the challenger receives an opportunity to view their opponent's data using a Battle Card with the following information...

① The Trainer's Pokémon
② The Trainer's rank amongst the tournament participants
③ The type of battle style the Trainer excels in
④ The emphasized status of the Pokémon

One must win four battles in a row in each round from the first to the last round to become the champion.

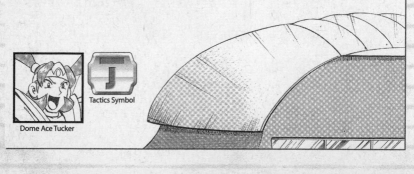

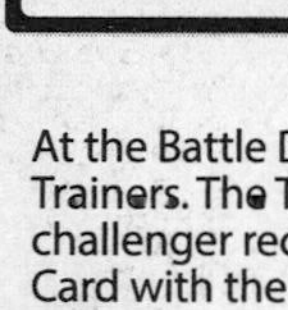

Dome Ace Tucker

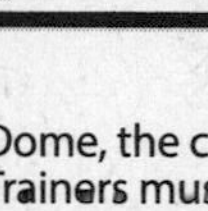

Tactics Symbol

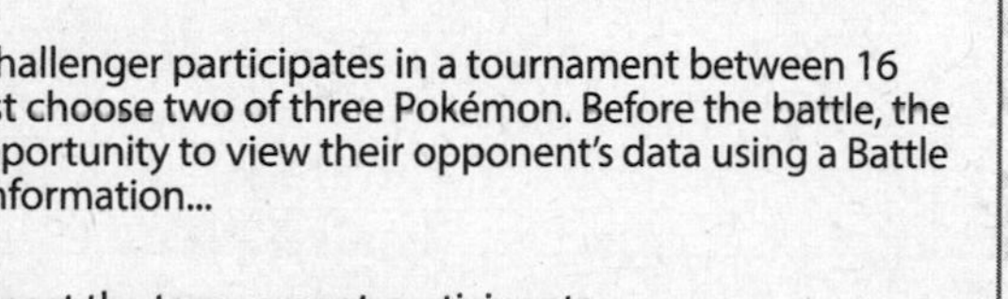

Sneaky Like Shedinja

OKÉMON ADVENTURES·THE SIXTH CHAPTER·EMERALD

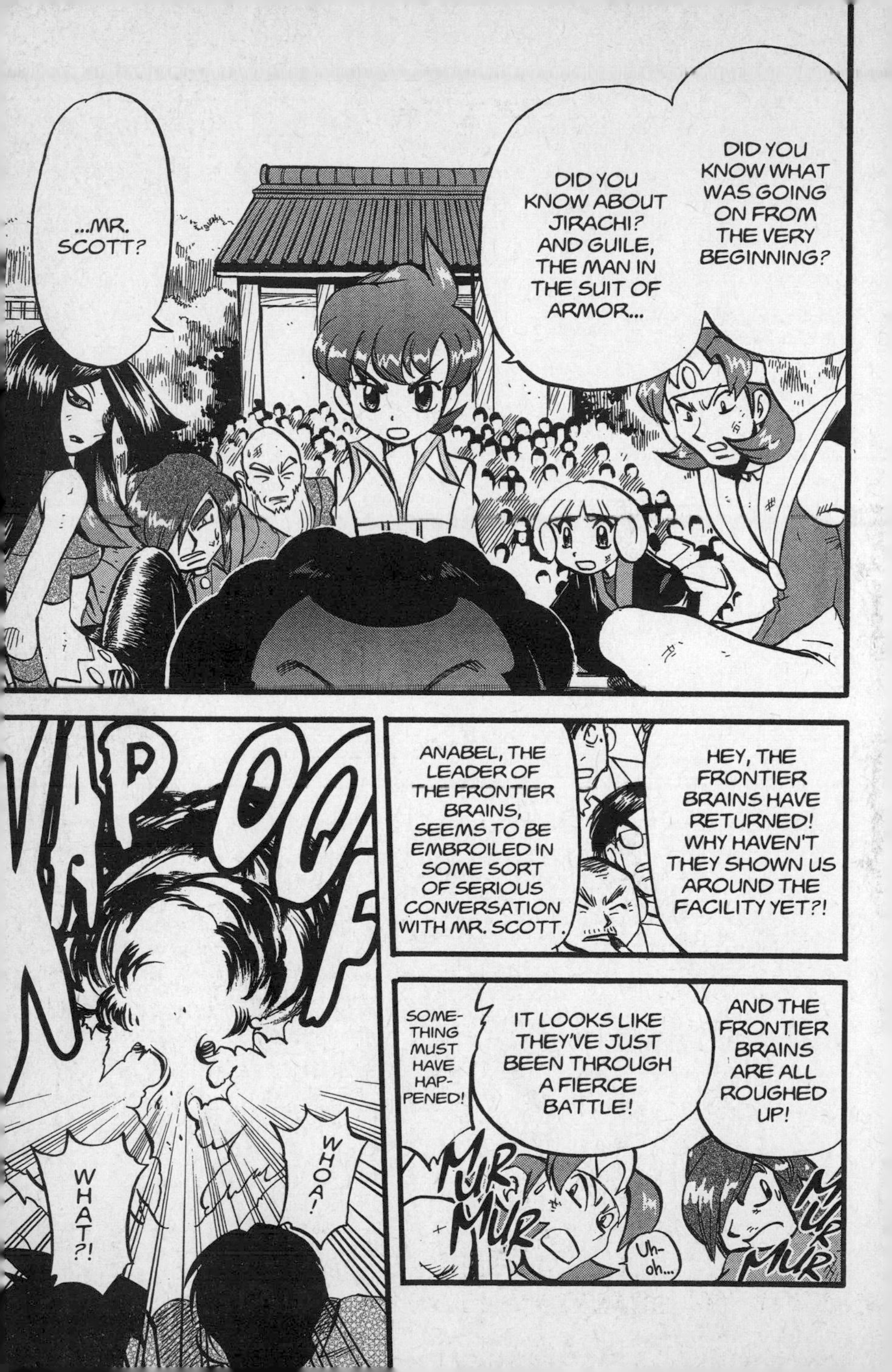
DID YOU KNOW WHAT WAS GOING ON FROM THE VERY BEGINNING?
DID YOU KNOW ABOUT JIRACHI? AND GUILE, THE MAN IN THE SUIT OF ARMOR...
...MR. SCOTT?
HEY, THE FRONTIER BRAINS HAVE RETURNED! WHY HAVEN'T THEY SHOWN US AROUND THE FACILITY YET?!
ANABEL, THE LEADER OF THE FRONTIER BRAINS, SEEMS TO BE EMBROILED IN SOME SORT OF SERIOUS CONVERSATION WITH MR. SCOTT.
AND THE FRONTIER BRAINS ARE ALL ROUGHED UP!
IT LOOKS LIKE THEY'VE JUST BEEN THROUGH A FIERCE BATTLE!
SOMETHING MUST HAVE HAPPENED!
MUR MUR
Uh-oh...
MUR MUR
OOF
WHOA!
WHAT?!

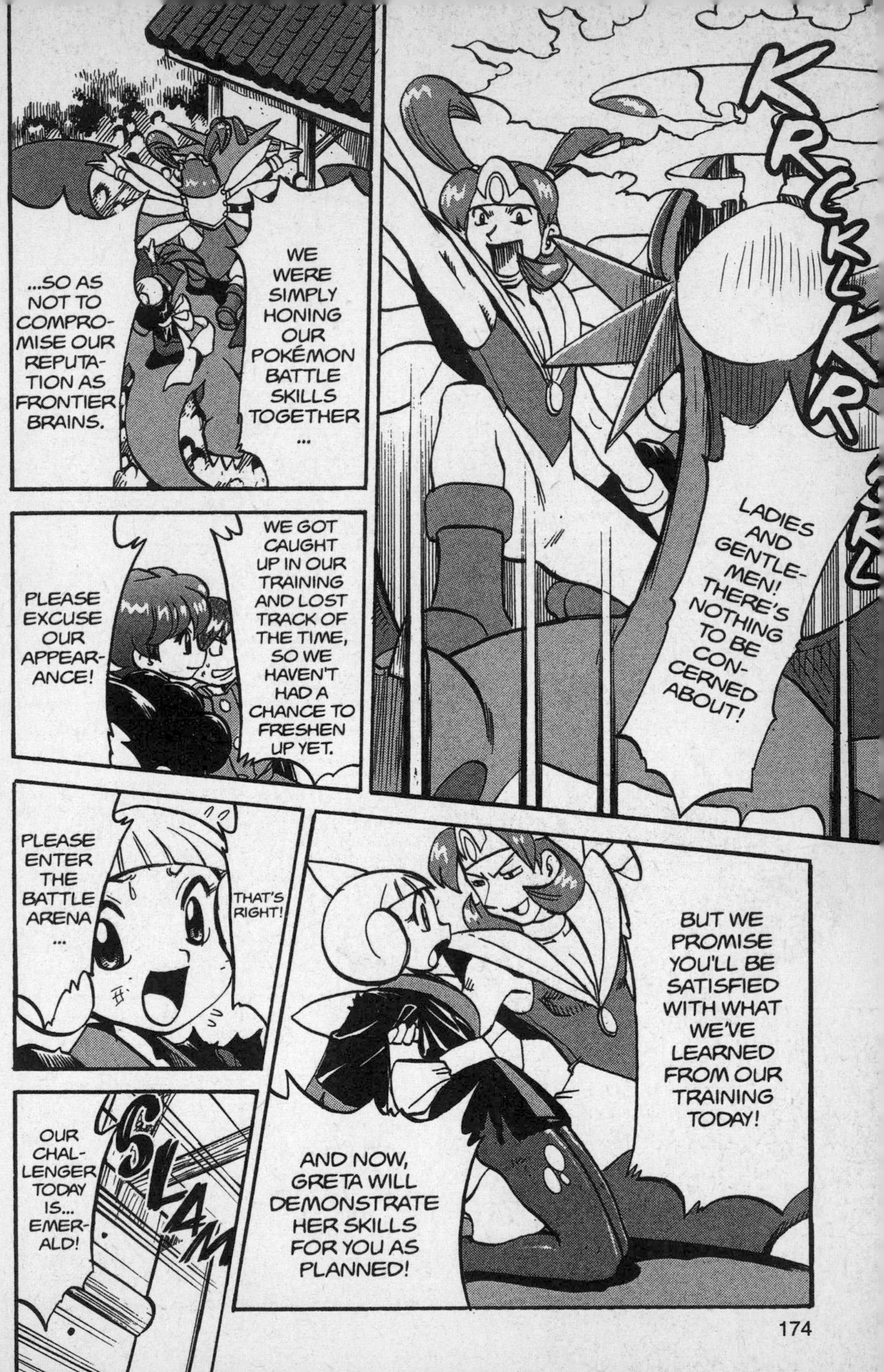
KRKLKRKL
LADIES AND GENTLEMEN! THERE'S NOTHING TO BE CONCERNED ABOUT!
WE WERE SIMPLY HONING OUR POKÉMON BATTLE SKILLS TOGETHER...
...SO AS NOT TO COMPROMISE OUR REPUTATION AS FRONTIER BRAINS.
WE GOT CAUGHT UP IN OUR TRAINING AND LOST TRACK OF THE TIME, SO WE HAVEN'T HAD A CHANCE TO FRESHEN UP YET.
PLEASE EXCUSE OUR APPEARANCE!
BUT WE PROMISE YOU'LL BE SATISFIED WITH WHAT WE'VE LEARNED FROM OUR TRAINING TODAY!
AND NOW, GRETA WILL DEMONSTRATE HER SKILLS FOR YOU AS PLANNED!
THAT'S RIGHT!
PLEASE ENTER THE BATTLE ARENA...
SLAM
OUR CHALLENGER TODAY IS... EMERALD!

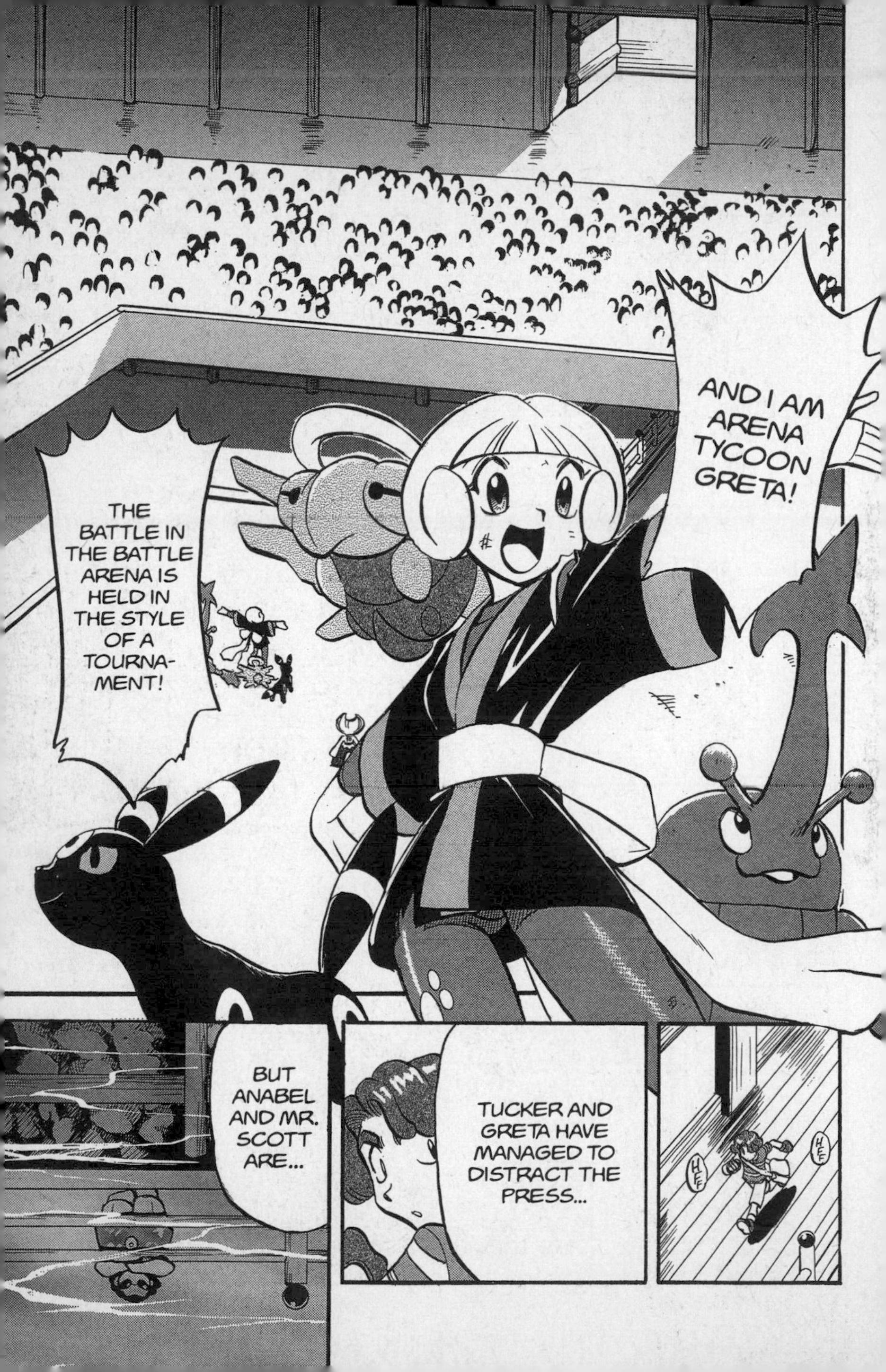
AND I AM ARENA TYCOON GRETA!
THE BATTLE IN THE BATTLE ARENA IS HELD IN THE STYLE OF A TOURNAMENT!
HFF
HFF
TUCKER AND GRETA HAVE MANAGED TO DISTRACT THE PRESS...
BUT ANABEL AND MR. SCOTT ARE...

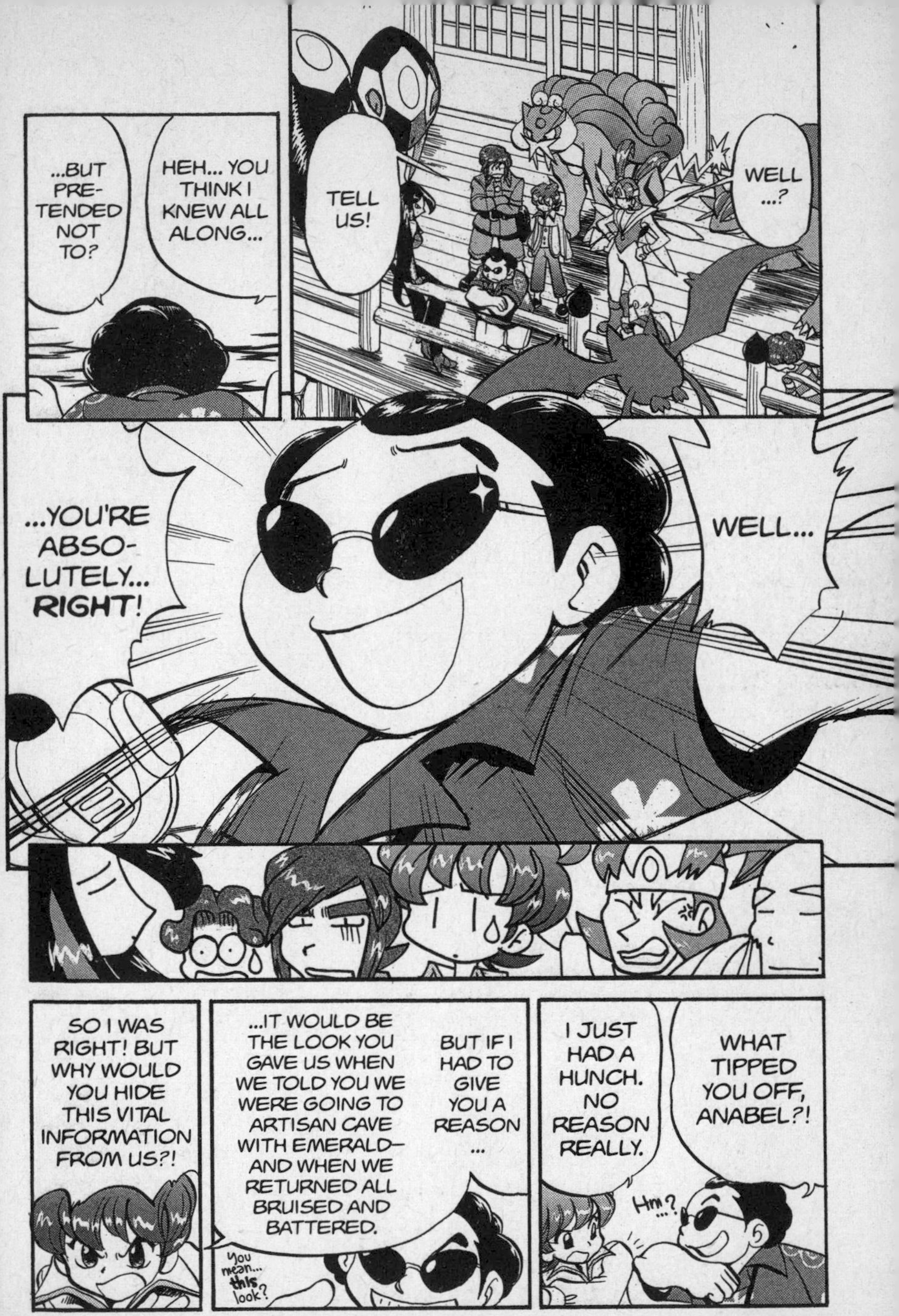
WELL ...?
TELL US!
HEH... YOU THINK I KNEW ALL ALONG...
...BUT PRE-TENDED NOT TO?
WELL...
...YOU'RE ABSO-LUTELY... **RIGHT**!
WHAT TIPPED YOU OFF, ANABEL?!
I JUST HAD A HUNCH. NO REASON REALLY.
Hm? ...?
BUT IF I HAD TO GIVE YOU A REASON ...
...IT WOULD BE THE LOOK YOU GAVE US WHEN WE TOLD YOU WE WERE GOING TO ARTISAN CAVE WITH EMERALD— AND WHEN WE RETURNED ALL BRUISED AND BATTERED.
You mean... this look?
SO I WAS RIGHT! BUT WHY WOULD YOU HIDE THIS VITAL INFORMATION FROM US?!

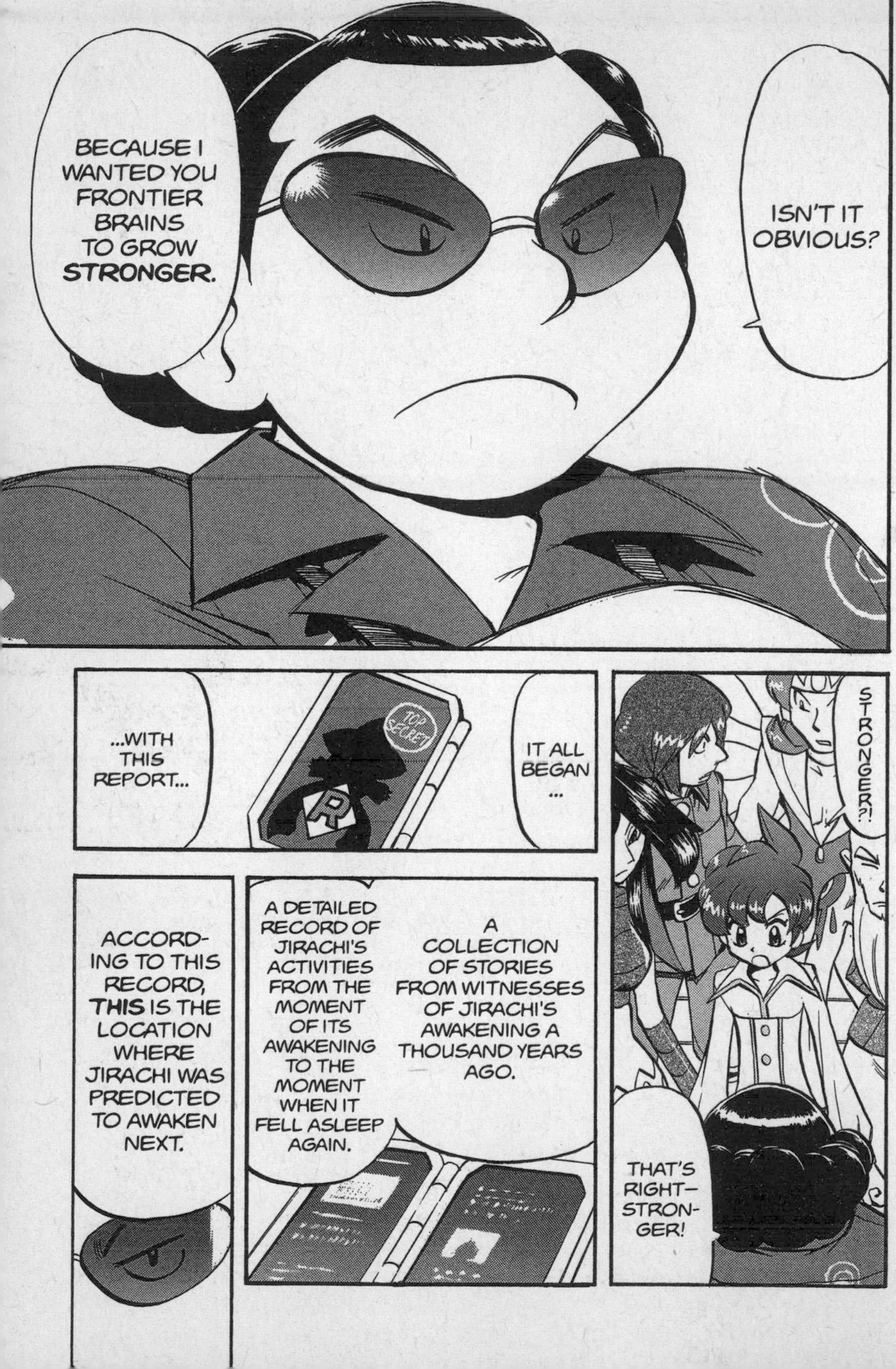
ISN'T IT OBVIOUS?
BECAUSE I WANTED YOU FRONTIER BRAINS TO GROW **STRONGER.**
STRONGER?!
THAT'S RIGHT—STRONGER!
IT ALL BEGAN...
...WITH THIS REPORT...
TOP SECRET
A COLLECTION OF STORIES FROM WITNESSES OF JIRACHI'S AWAKENING A THOUSAND YEARS AGO.
A DETAILED RECORD OF JIRACHI'S ACTIVITIES FROM THE MOMENT OF ITS AWAKENING TO THE MOMENT WHEN IT FELL ASLEEP AGAIN.
ACCORDING TO THIS RECORD, **THIS** IS THE LOCATION WHERE JIRACHI WAS PREDICTED TO AWAKEN NEXT.

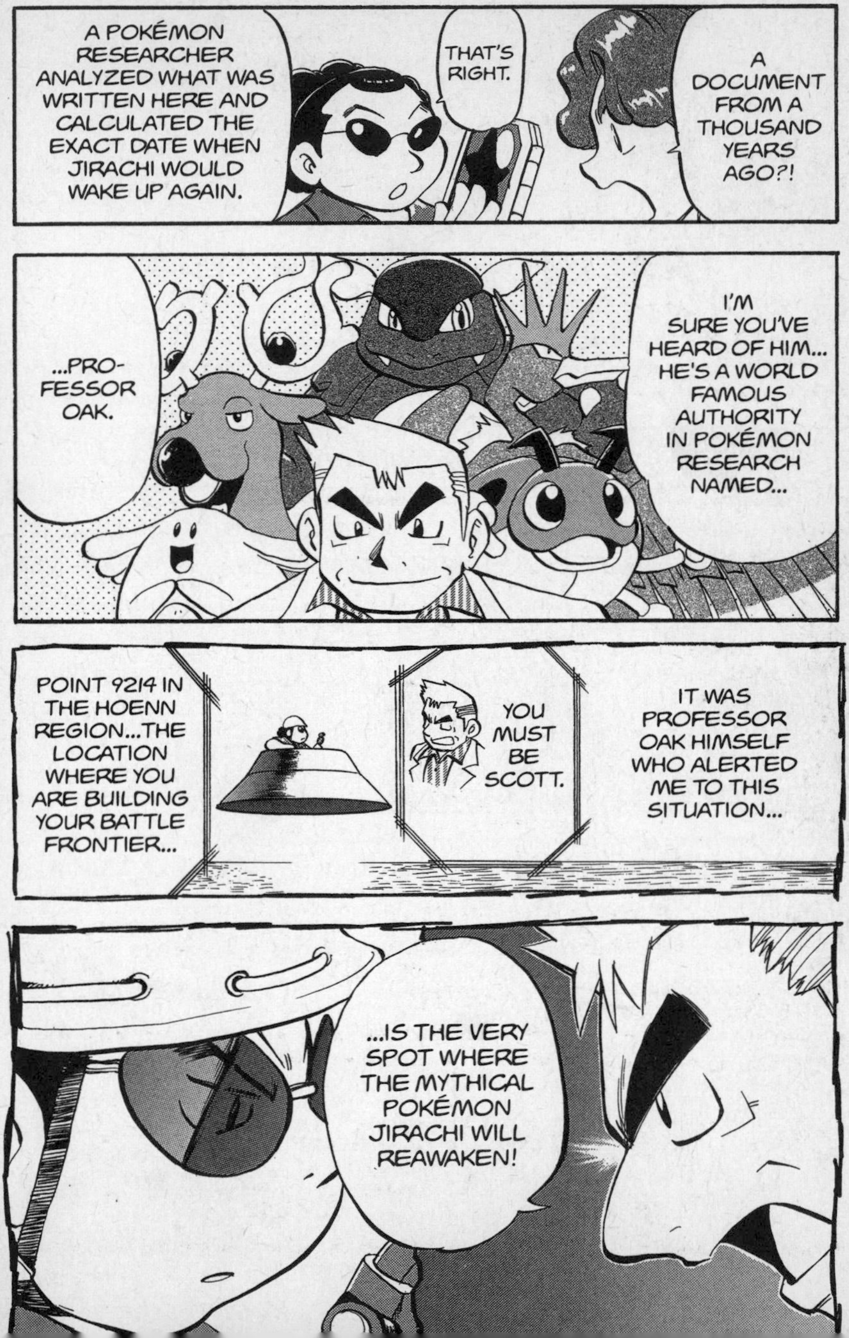
A DOCUMENT FROM A THOUSAND YEARS AGO?!
THAT'S RIGHT.
A POKÉMON RESEARCHER ANALYZED WHAT WAS WRITTEN HERE AND CALCULATED THE EXACT DATE WHEN JIRACHI WOULD WAKE UP AGAIN.
I'M SURE YOU'VE HEARD OF HIM... HE'S A WORLD FAMOUS AUTHORITY IN POKÉMON RESEARCH NAMED...
...PRO-FESSOR OAK.
IT WAS PROFESSOR OAK HIMSELF WHO ALERTED ME TO THIS SITUATION...
YOU MUST BE SCOTT.
POINT 9214 IN THE HOENN REGION...THE LOCATION WHERE YOU ARE BUILDING YOUR BATTLE FRONTIER...
...IS THE VERY SPOT WHERE THE MYTHICAL POKÉMON JIRACHI WILL REAWAKEN!

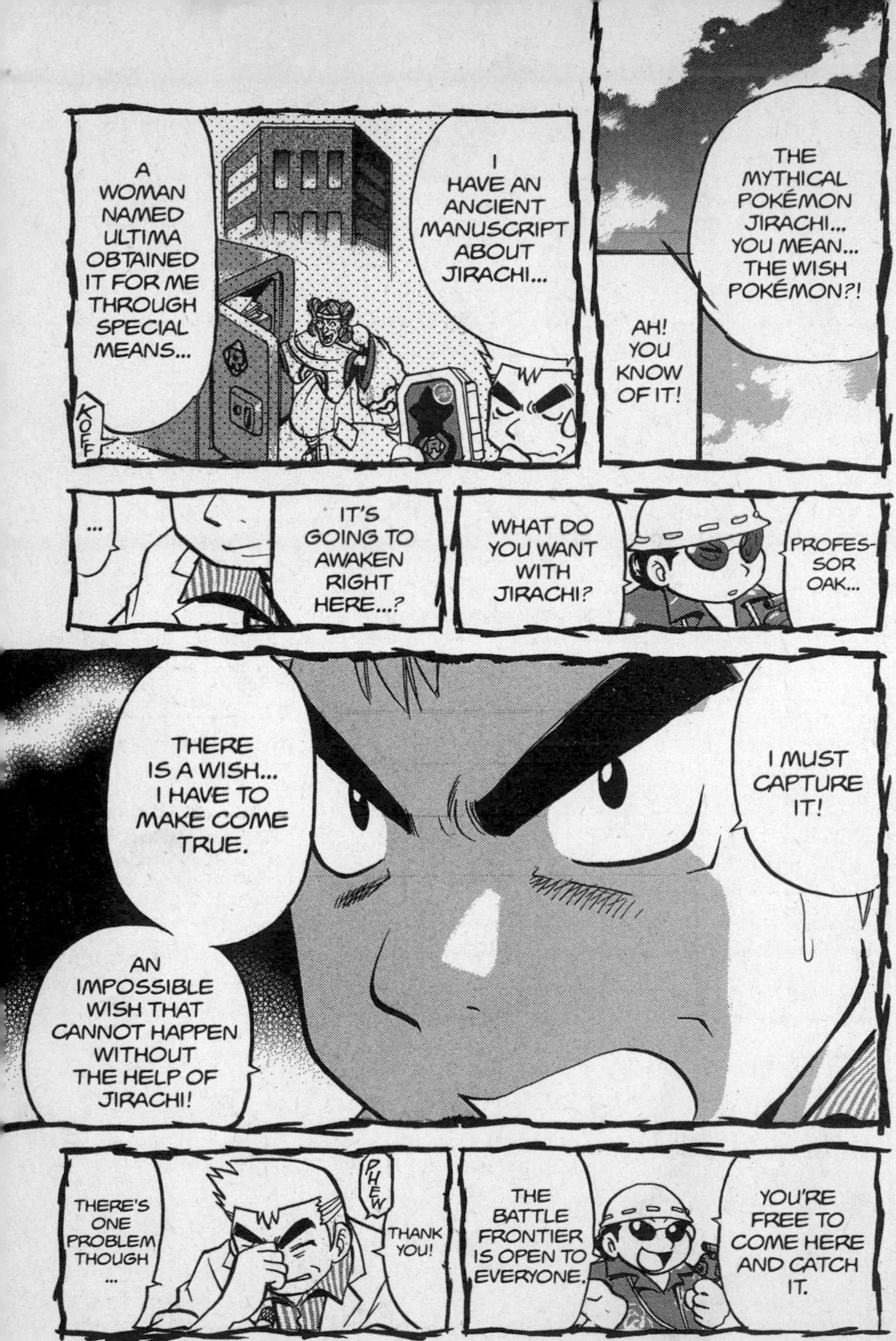
THE MYTHICAL POKÉMON JIRACHI... YOU MEAN... THE WISH POKÉMON?!
AH! YOU KNOW OF IT!
I HAVE AN ANCIENT MANUSCRIPT ABOUT JIRACHI...
A WOMAN NAMED ULTIMA OBTAINED IT FOR ME THROUGH SPECIAL MEANS...
KOFF
PROFES-SOR OAK...
WHAT DO YOU WANT WITH JIRACHI?
IT'S GOING TO AWAKEN RIGHT HERE...?
...
I MUST CAPTURE IT!
THERE IS A WISH... I HAVE TO MAKE COME TRUE.
AN IMPOSSIBLE WISH THAT CANNOT HAPPEN WITHOUT THE HELP OF JIRACHI!
YOU'RE FREE TO COME HERE AND CATCH IT.
THE BATTLE FRONTIER IS OPEN TO EVERYONE.
PHEW
THANK YOU!
THERE'S ONE PROBLEM THOUGH ...

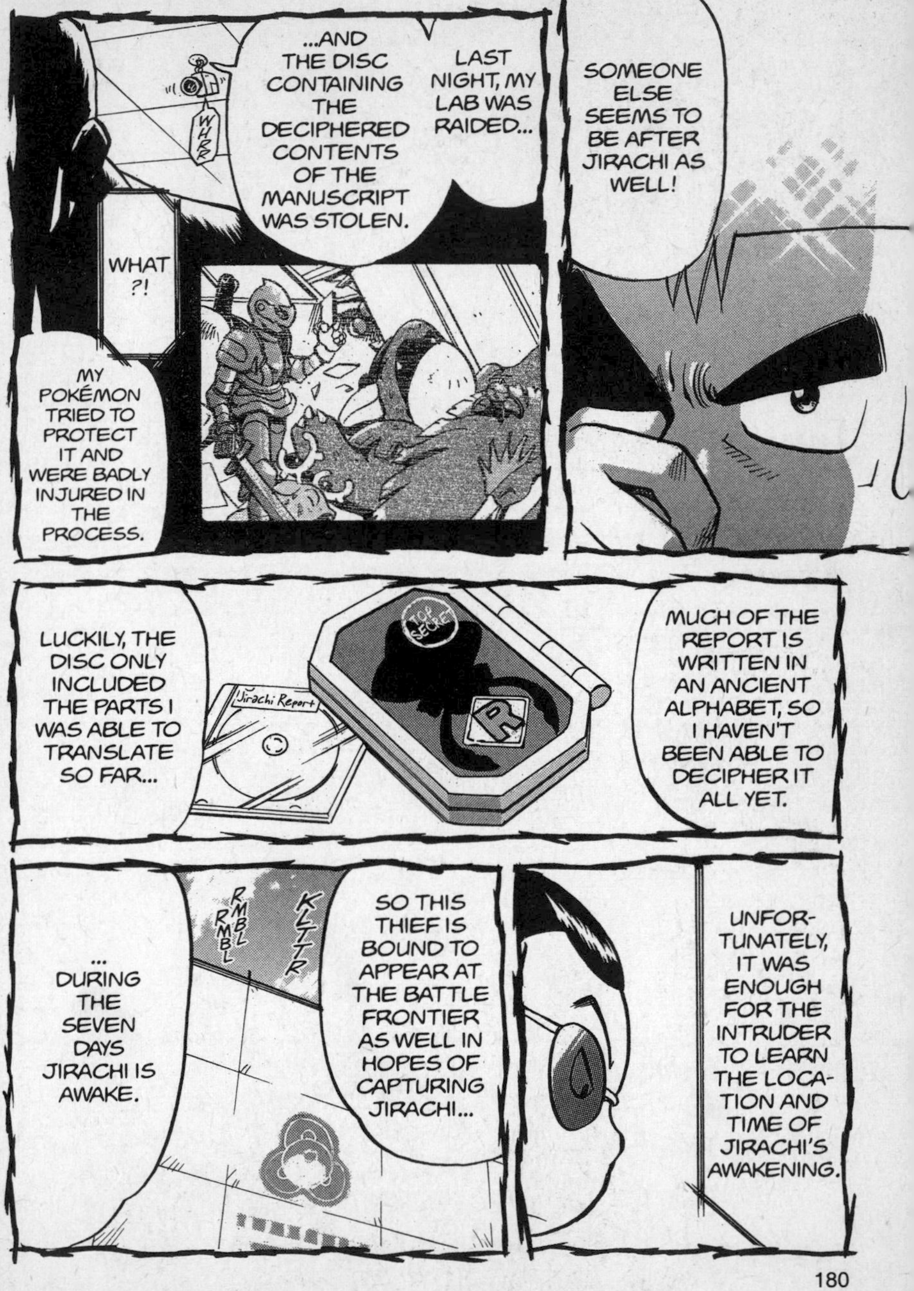
SOMEONE ELSE SEEMS TO BE AFTER JIRACHI AS WELL!
LAST NIGHT, MY LAB WAS RAIDED...
...AND THE DISC CONTAINING THE DECIPHERED CONTENTS OF THE MANUSCRIPT WAS STOLEN.
WHRR
WHAT?!
MY POKÉMON TRIED TO PROTECT IT AND WERE BADLY INJURED IN THE PROCESS.
MUCH OF THE REPORT IS WRITTEN IN AN ANCIENT ALPHABET, SO I HAVEN'T BEEN ABLE TO DECIPHER IT ALL YET.
TOP SECRET
Jirachi Report
LUCKILY, THE DISC ONLY INCLUDED THE PARTS I WAS ABLE TO TRANSLATE SO FAR...
UNFORTUNATELY, IT WAS ENOUGH FOR THE INTRUDER TO LEARN THE LOCATION AND TIME OF JIRACHI'S AWAKENING.
SO THIS THIEF IS BOUND TO APPEAR AT THE BATTLE FRONTIER AS WELL IN HOPES OF CAPTURING JIRACHI...
KLTTR
RMBL RMBL
... DURING THE SEVEN DAYS JIRACHI IS AWAKE.

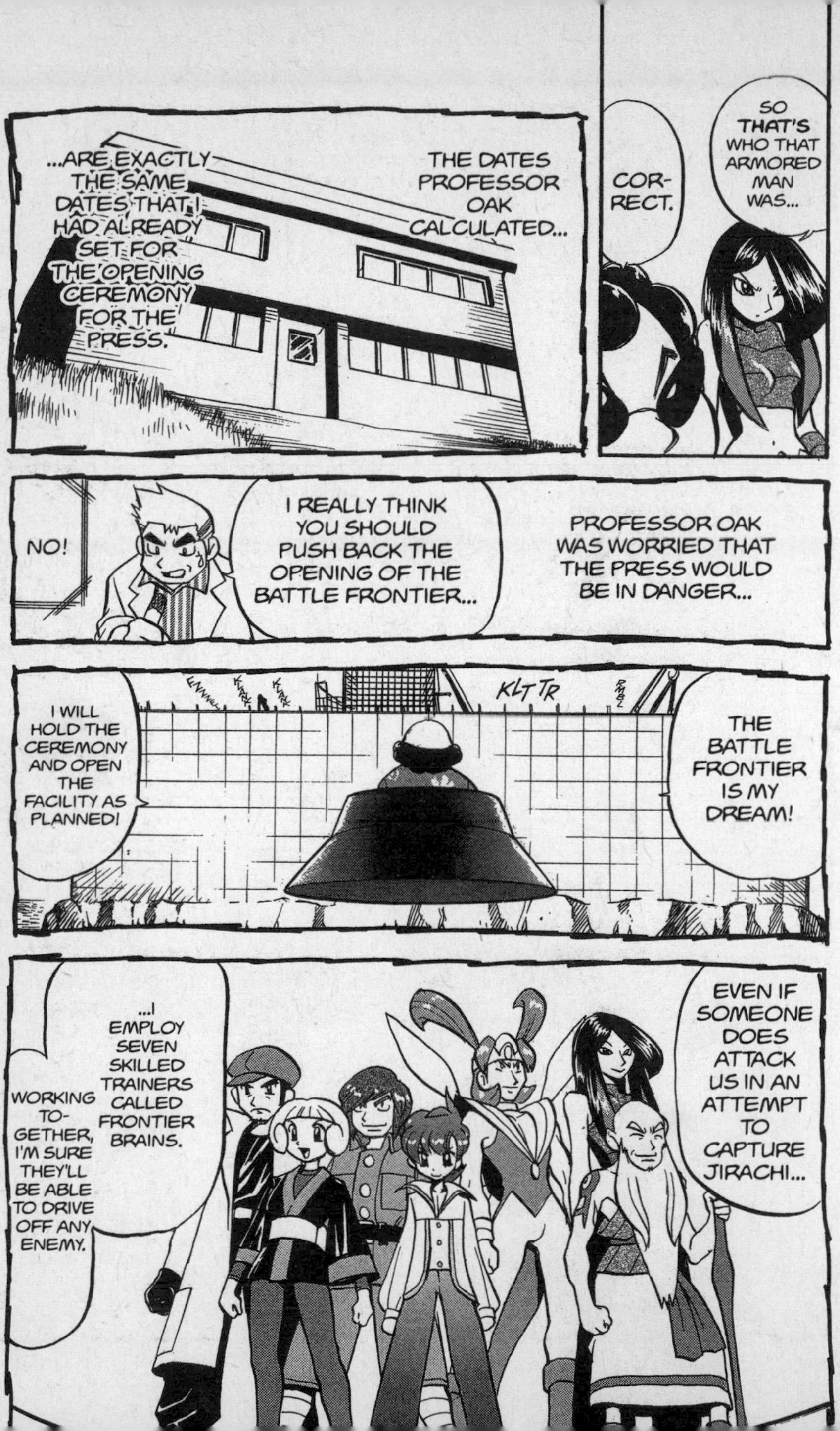
SO THAT'S WHO THAT ARMORED MAN WAS...
COR-RECT.
THE DATES PROFESSOR OAK CALCULATED...
...ARE EXACTLY THE SAME DATES THAT I HAD ALREADY SET FOR THE OPENING CEREMONY FOR THE PRESS.
PROFESSOR OAK WAS WORRIED THAT THE PRESS WOULD BE IN DANGER...
I REALLY THINK YOU SHOULD PUSH BACK THE OPENING OF THE BATTLE FRONTIER...
NO!
THE BATTLE FRONTIER IS MY DREAM!
KLTTR
I WILL HOLD THE CEREMONY AND OPEN THE FACILITY AS PLANNED!
EVEN IF SOMEONE DOES ATTACK US IN AN ATTEMPT TO CAPTURE JIRACHI...
...I EMPLOY SEVEN SKILLED TRAINERS CALLED FRONTIER BRAINS.
WORKING TO-GETHER, I'M SURE THEY'LL BE ABLE TO DRIVE OFF ANY ENEMY.

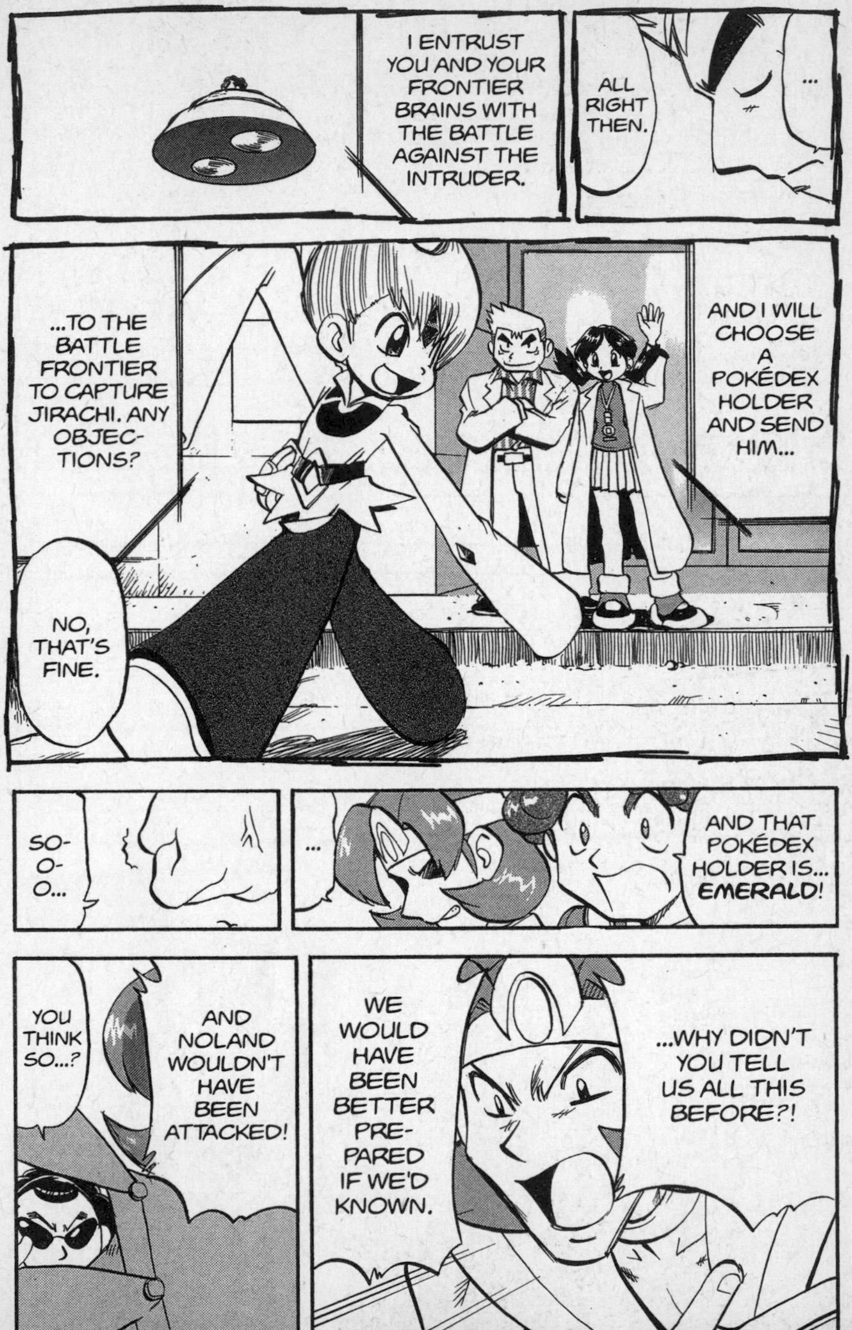
...
ALL RIGHT THEN.
I ENTRUST YOU AND YOUR FRONTIER BRAINS WITH THE BATTLE AGAINST THE INTRUDER.
AND I WILL CHOOSE A POKÉDEX HOLDER AND SEND HIM...
...TO THE BATTLE FRONTIER TO CAPTURE JIRACHI. ANY OBJECTIONS?
NO, THAT'S FINE.
AND THAT POKÉDEX HOLDER IS... EMERALD!
...
SO-O-O...
...WHY DIDN'T YOU TELL US ALL THIS BEFORE?!
WE WOULD HAVE BEEN BETTER PRE-PARED IF WE'D KNOWN.
AND NOLAND WOULDN'T HAVE BEEN ATTACKED!
YOU THINK SO...?

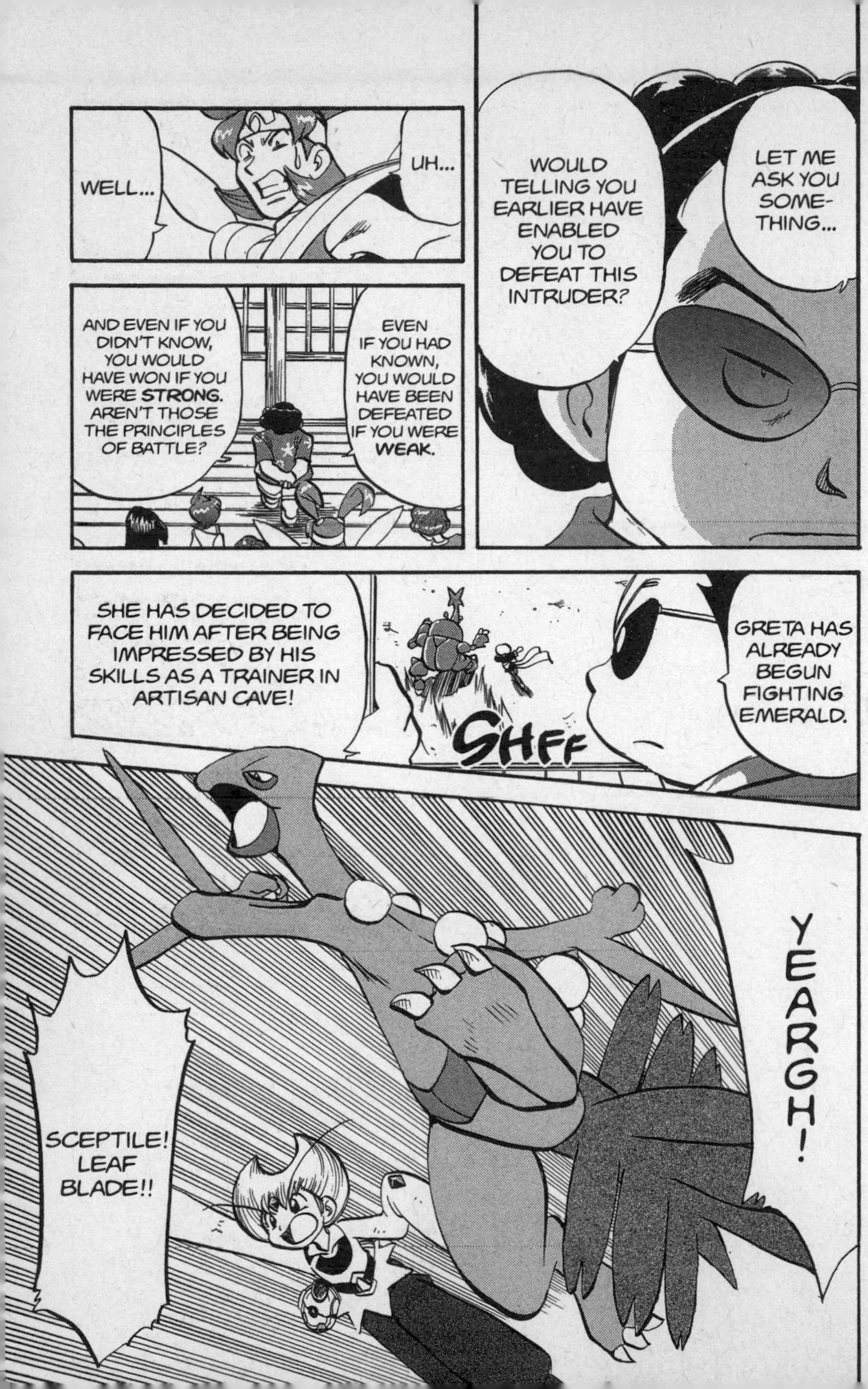
LET ME ASK YOU SOMETHING...
WOULD TELLING YOU EARLIER HAVE ENABLED YOU TO DEFEAT THIS INTRUDER?
UH...
WELL...
EVEN IF YOU HAD KNOWN, YOU WOULD HAVE BEEN DEFEATED IF YOU WERE WEAK.
AND EVEN IF YOU DIDN'T KNOW, YOU WOULD HAVE WON IF YOU WERE STRONG. AREN'T THOSE THE PRINCIPLES OF BATTLE?
GRETA HAS ALREADY BEGUN FIGHTING EMERALD.
SHFF
SHE HAS DECIDED TO FACE HIM AFTER BEING IMPRESSED BY HIS SKILLS AS A TRAINER IN ARTISAN CAVE!
YEARGH!
SCEPTILE! LEAF BLADE!!

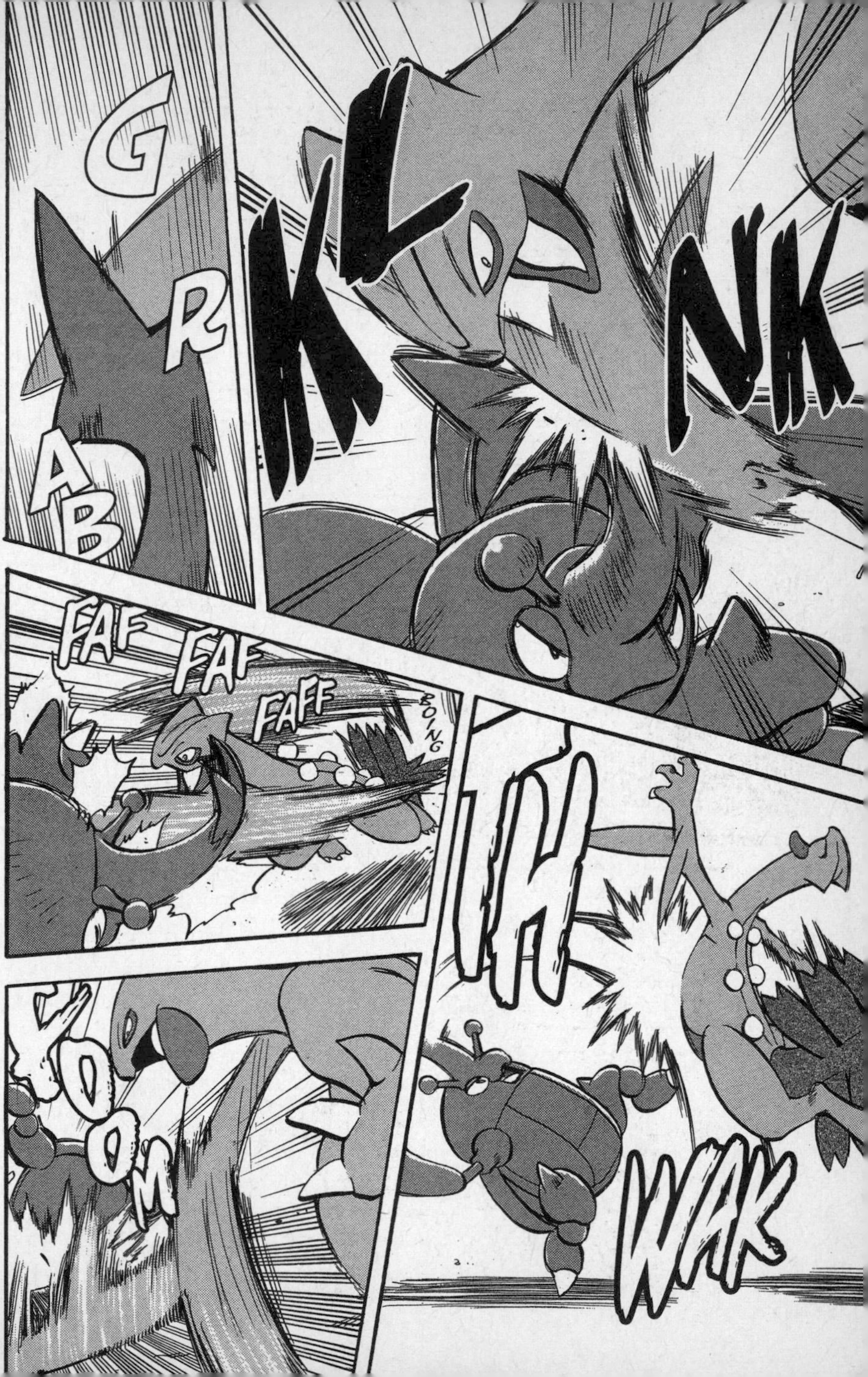
KL
NK
GRAB
WAK
FAF
FAF
FAFF
BOING
OOOM

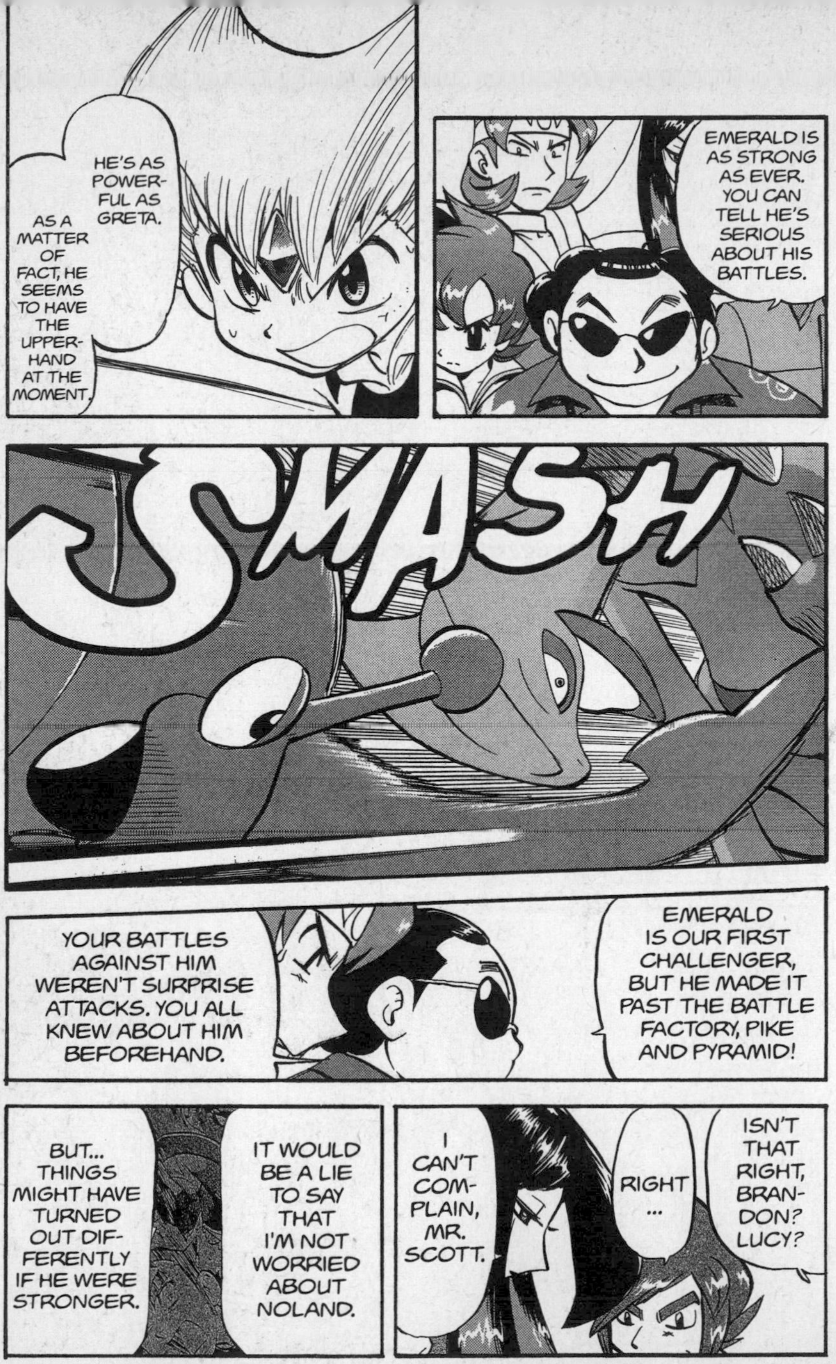
EMERALD IS AS STRONG AS EVER. YOU CAN TELL HE'S SERIOUS ABOUT HIS BATTLES.
HE'S AS POWERFUL AS GRETA.
AS A MATTER OF FACT, HE SEEMS TO HAVE THE UPPERHAND AT THE MOMENT.
SMASH
EMERALD IS OUR FIRST CHALLENGER, BUT HE MADE IT PAST THE BATTLE FACTORY, PIKE AND PYRAMID!
YOUR BATTLES AGAINST HIM WEREN'T SURPRISE ATTACKS. YOU ALL KNEW ABOUT HIM BEFOREHAND.
ISN'T THAT RIGHT, BRANDON? LUCY?
RIGHT...
I CAN'T COMPLAIN, MR. SCOTT.
IT WOULD BE A LIE TO SAY THAT I'M NOT WORRIED ABOUT NOLAND.
BUT... THINGS MIGHT HAVE TURNED OUT DIFFERENTLY IF HE WERE STRONGER.

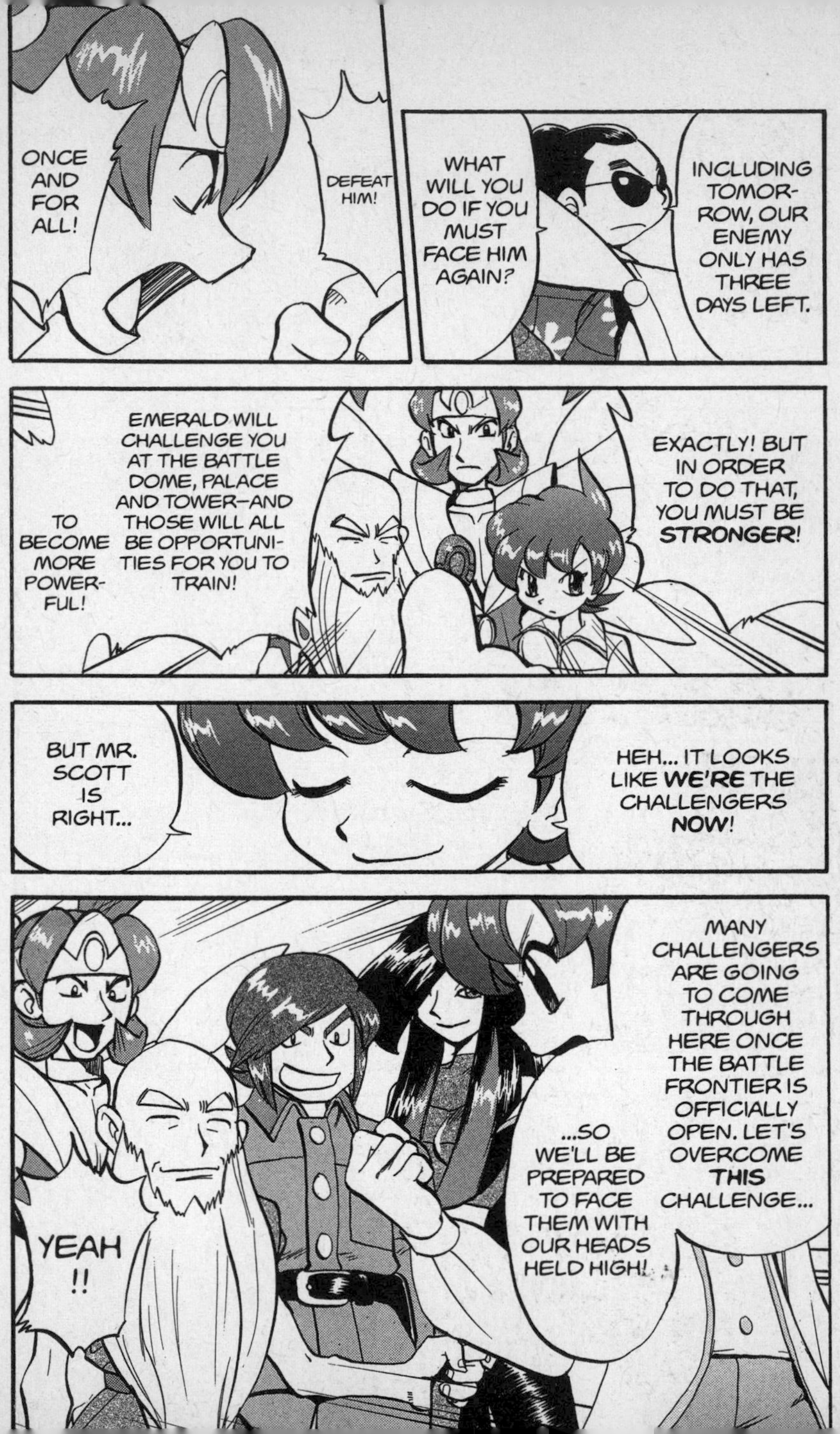
INCLUDING TOMOR-ROW, OUR ENEMY ONLY HAS THREE DAYS LEFT.
WHAT WILL YOU DO IF YOU MUST FACE HIM AGAIN?
DEFEAT HIM!
ONCE AND FOR ALL!
EXACTLY! BUT IN ORDER TO DO THAT, YOU MUST BE **STRONGER**!
EMERALD WILL CHALLENGE YOU AT THE BATTLE DOME, PALACE AND TOWER—AND THOSE WILL ALL BE OPPORTUNI-TIES FOR YOU TO TRAIN!
TO BECOME MORE POWER-FUL!
HEH... IT LOOKS LIKE **WE'RE** THE CHALLENGERS **NOW**!
BUT MR. SCOTT IS RIGHT...
MANY CHALLENGERS ARE GOING TO COME THROUGH HERE ONCE THE BATTLE FRONTIER IS OFFICIALLY OPEN. LET'S OVERCOME **THIS** CHALLENGE...
...SO WE'LL BE PREPARED TO FACE THEM WITH OUR HEADS HELD HIGH!
YEAH!!

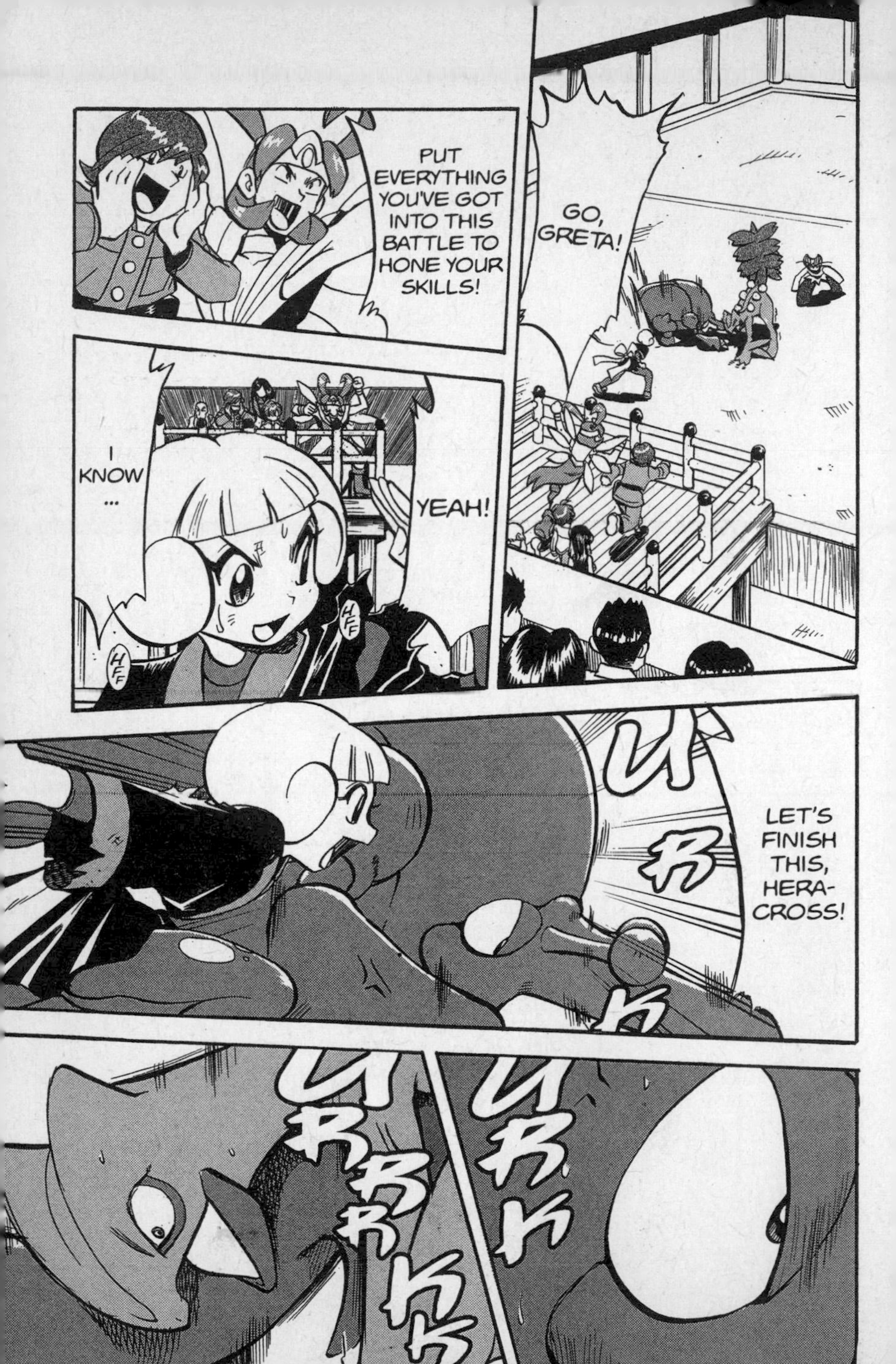
GO, GRETA!
PUT EVERYTHING YOU'VE GOT INTO THIS BATTLE TO HONE YOUR SKILLS!
YEAH!
I KNOW ...
HFF
HFF
LET'S FINISH THIS, HERA-CROSS!
URK
URRKK
URRRKK

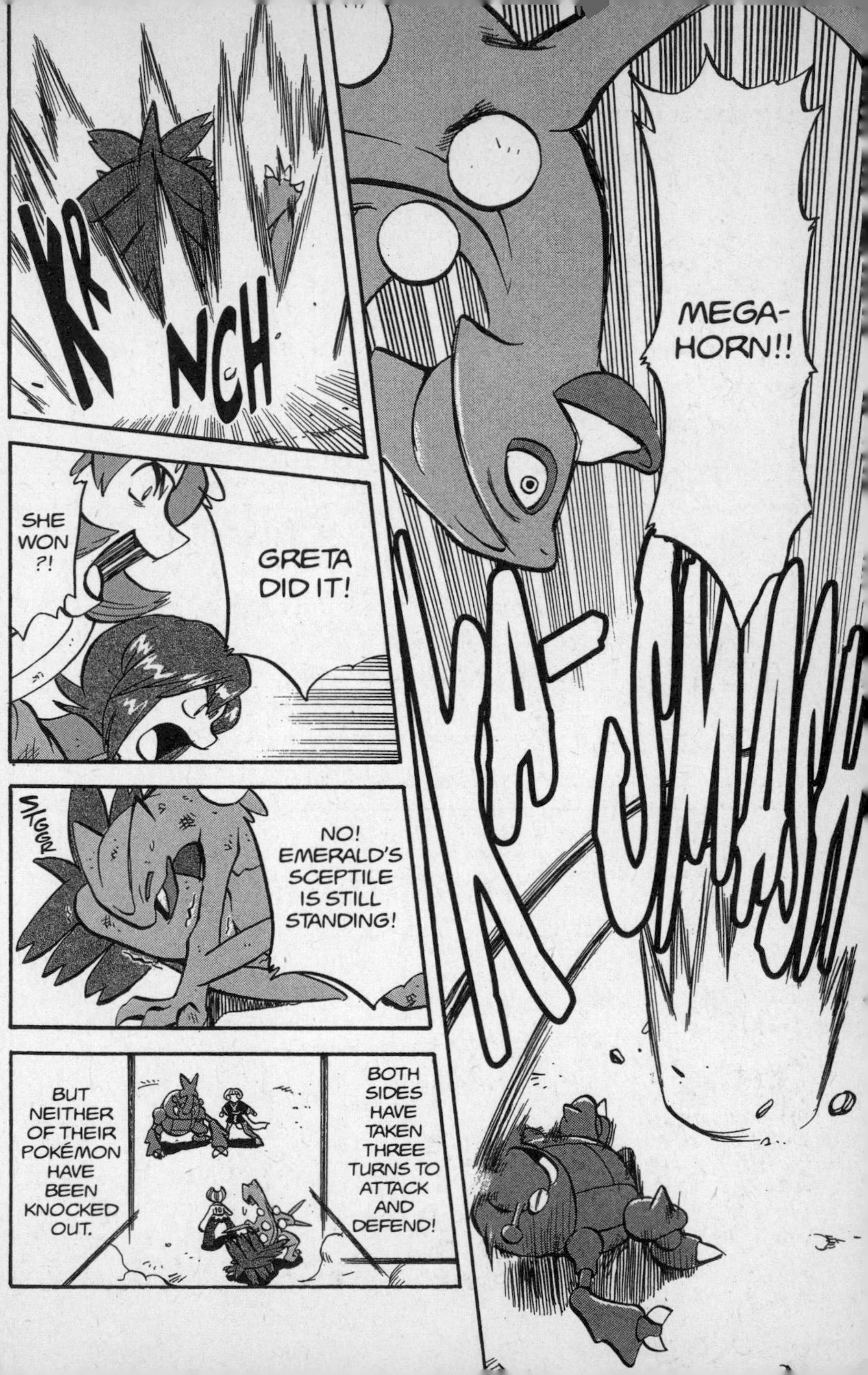
MEGA-HORN!!
GRETA DID IT!
SHE WON ?!
NO! EMERALD'S SCEPTILE IS STILL STANDING!
BOTH SIDES HAVE TAKEN THREE TURNS TO ATTACK AND DEFEND!
BUT NEITHER OF THEIR POKÉMON HAVE BEEN KNOCKED OUT.

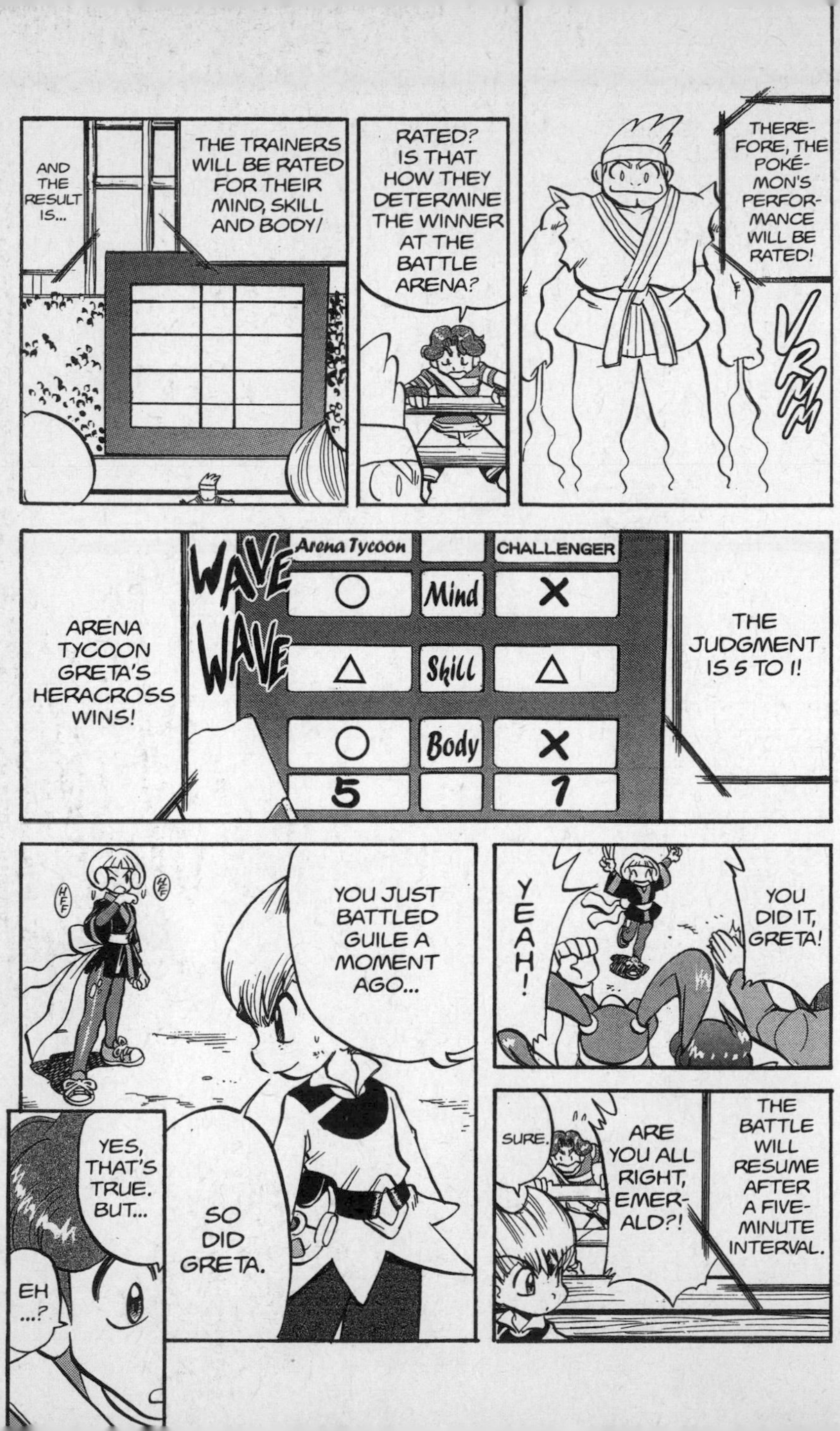
THEREFORE, THE POKÉMON'S PERFORMANCE WILL BE RATED!
VRMM
RATED? IS THAT HOW THEY DETERMINE THE WINNER AT THE BATTLE ARENA?
THE TRAINERS WILL BE RATED FOR THEIR MIND, SKILL AND BODY!
AND THE RESULT IS...
THE JUDGMENT IS 5 TO 1!
CHALLENGER
Arena Tycoon
Mind
Skill
Body
5
1
WAVE
WAVE
ARENA TYCOON GRETA'S HERACROSS WINS!
YOU DID IT, GRETA!
YEAH!
THE BATTLE WILL RESUME AFTER A FIVE-MINUTE INTERVAL.
ARE YOU ALL RIGHT, EMERALD?!
SURE.
HFF
HFF
YOU JUST BATTLED GUILE A MOMENT AGO...
SO DID GRETA.
YES, THAT'S TRUE. BUT...
EH...?

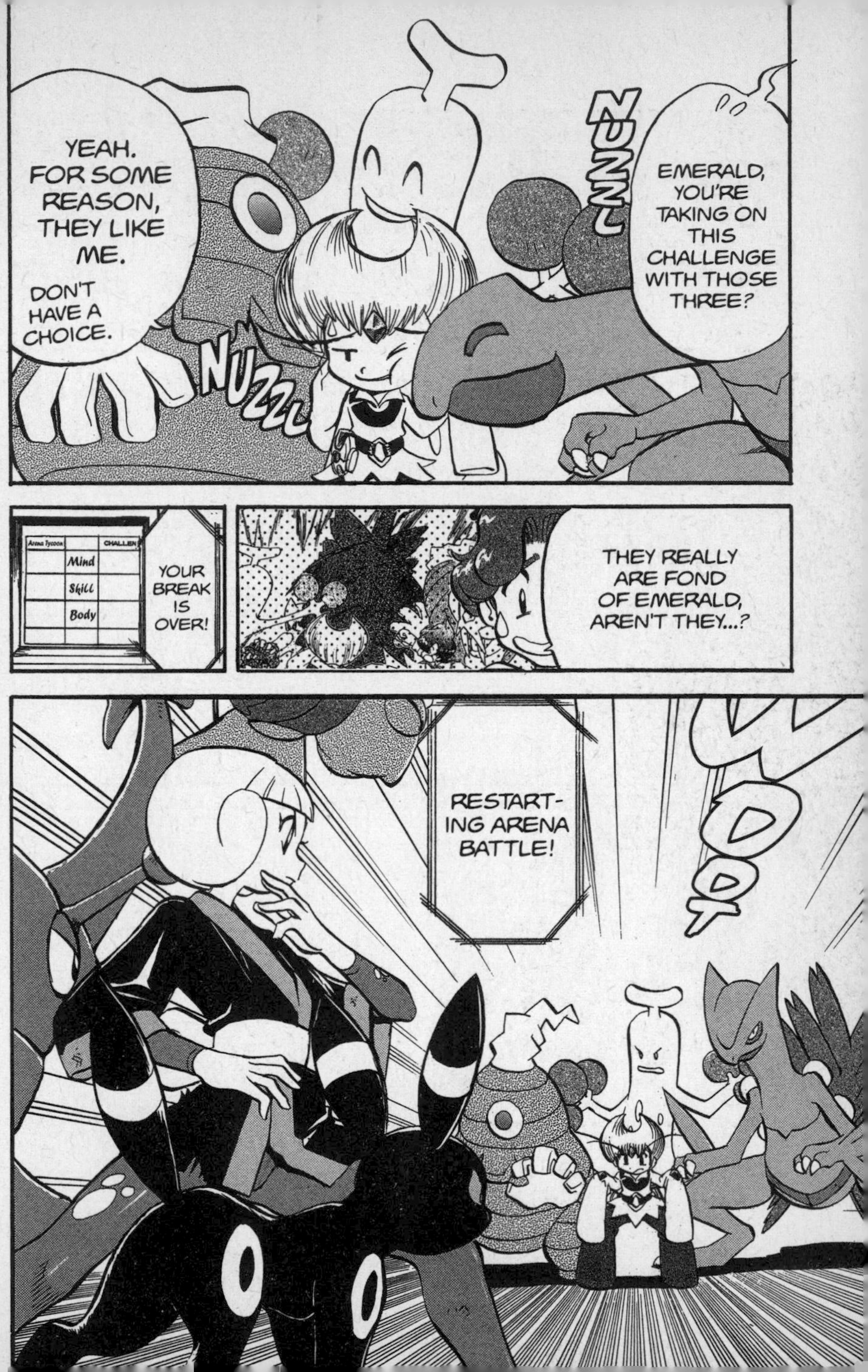
NUZZL
EMERALD, YOU'RE TAKING ON THIS CHALLENGE WITH THOSE THREE?
YEAH. FOR SOME REASON, THEY LIKE ME.
DON'T HAVE A CHOICE.
NUZZL
THEY REALLY ARE FOND OF EMERALD, AREN'T THEY...?
Arena Tycoon
CHALLEN
Mind
Skill
Body
YOUR BREAK IS OVER!
RESTART-ING ARENA BATTLE!

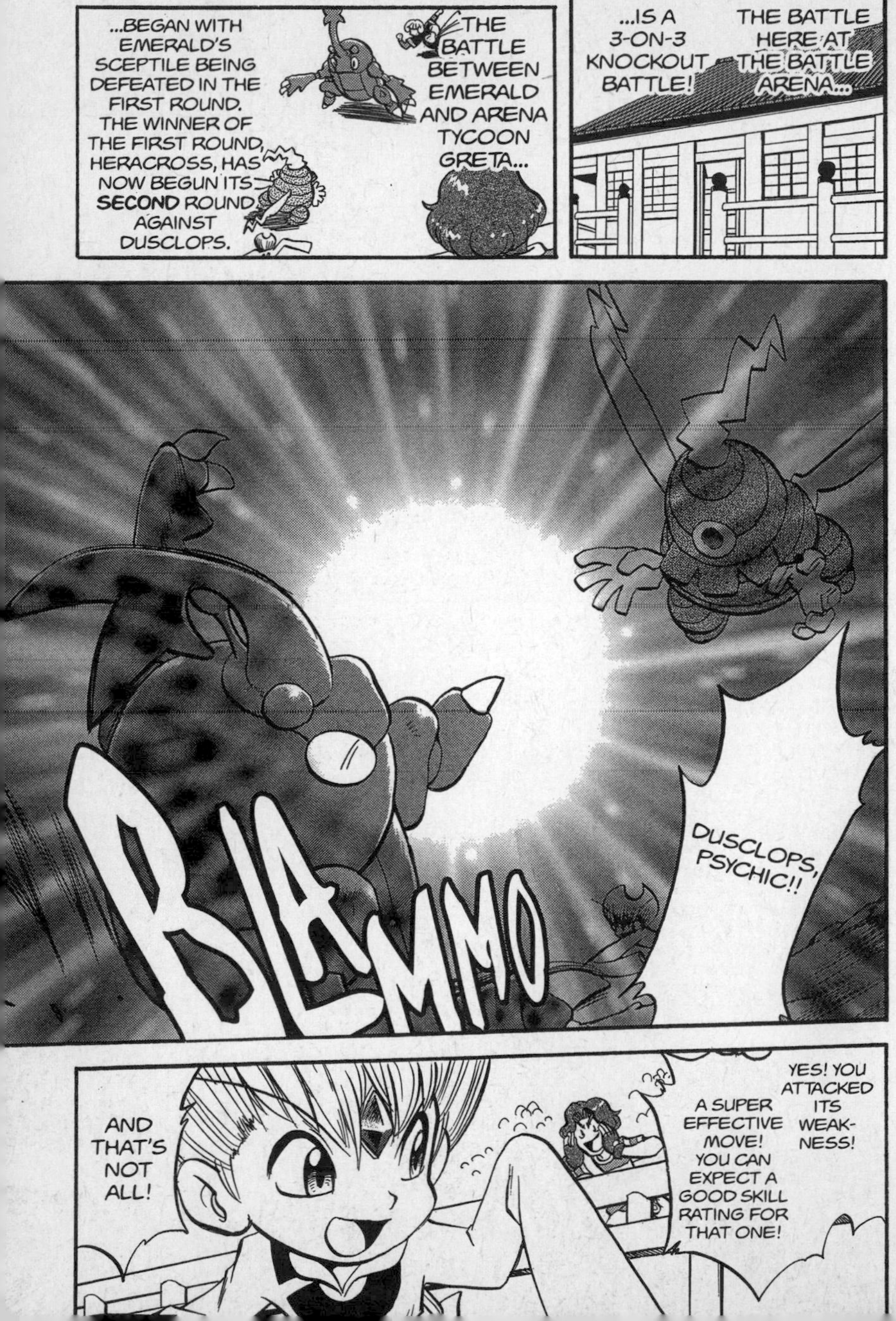
THE BATTLE HERE AT THE BATTLE ARENA...
...IS A 3-ON-3 KNOCKOUT BATTLE!
THE BATTLE BETWEEN EMERALD AND ARENA TYCOON GRETA...
...BEGAN WITH EMERALD'S SCEPTILE BEING DEFEATED IN THE FIRST ROUND. THE WINNER OF THE FIRST ROUND, HERACROSS, HAS NOW BEGUN ITS **SECOND** ROUND AGAINST DUSCLOPS.
DUSCLOPS, PSYCHIC!!
BLAMMO
YES! YOU ATTACKED ITS WEAKNESS!
A SUPER EFFECTIVE MOVE! YOU CAN EXPECT A GOOD SKILL RATING FOR THAT ONE!
AND THAT'S NOT ALL!

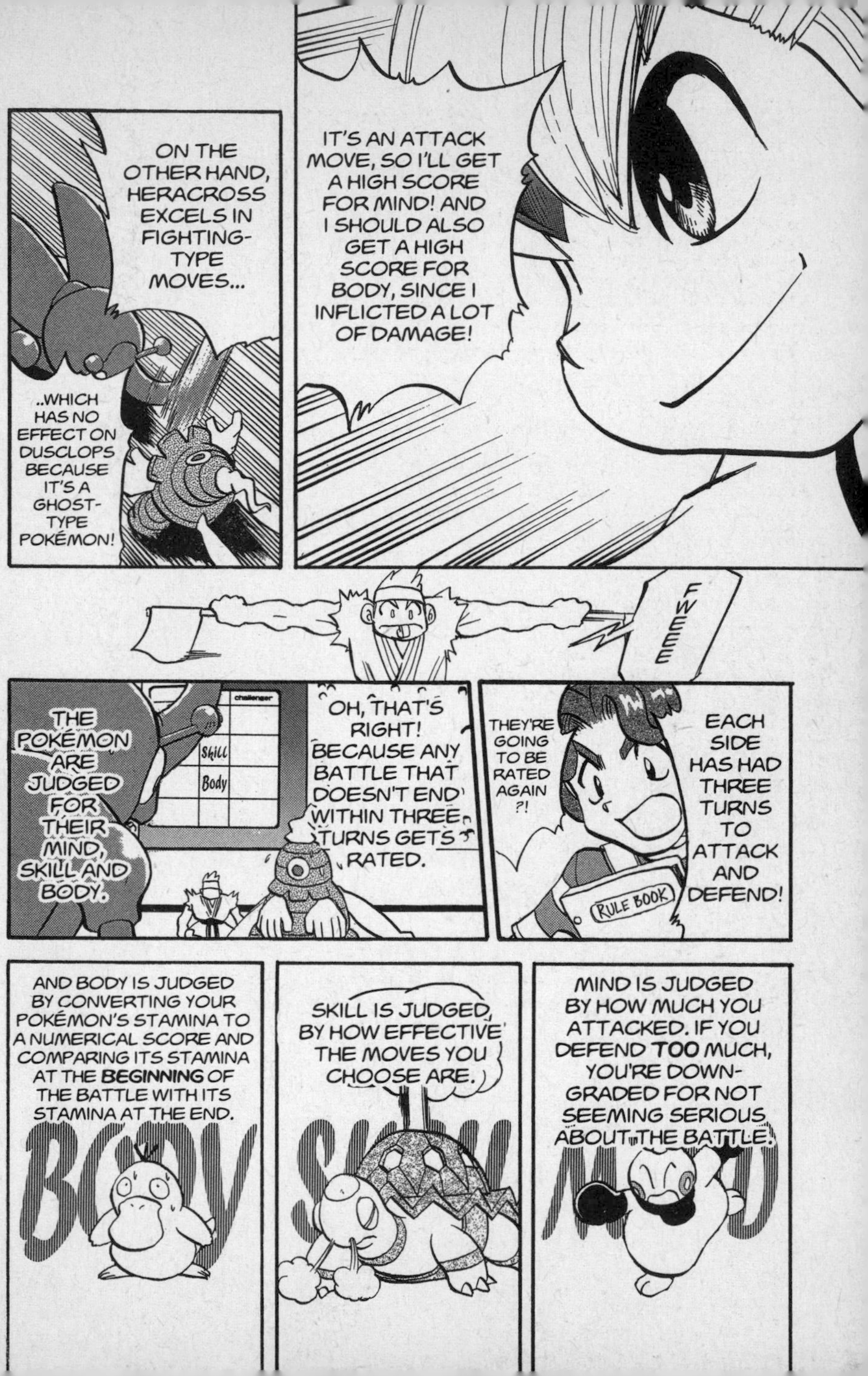

IT'S AN ATTACK MOVE, SO I'LL GET A HIGH SCORE FOR MIND! AND I SHOULD ALSO GET A HIGH SCORE FOR BODY, SINCE I INFLICTED A LOT OF DAMAGE!
ON THE OTHER HAND, HERACROSS EXCELS IN FIGHTING-TYPE MOVES...
..WHICH HAS NO EFFECT ON DUSCLOPS BECAUSE IT'S A GHOST-TYPE POKÉMON!
FWEEE
EACH SIDE HAS HAD THREE TURNS TO ATTACK AND DEFEND!
THEY'RE GOING TO BE RATED AGAIN?!
RULE BOOK
OH, THAT'S RIGHT! BECAUSE ANY BATTLE THAT DOESN'T END WITHIN THREE TURNS GETS RATED.
challenger
Skill
Body
THE POKÉMON ARE JUDGED FOR THEIR MIND, SKILL AND BODY.
MIND IS JUDGED BY HOW MUCH YOU ATTACKED. IF YOU DEFEND **TOO** MUCH, YOU'RE DOWN-GRADED FOR NOT SEEMING SERIOUS ABOUT THE BATTLE.
SKILL IS JUDGED BY HOW EFFECTIVE THE MOVES YOU CHOOSE ARE.
AND BODY IS JUDGED BY CONVERTING YOUR POKÉMON'S STAMINA TO A NUMERICAL SCORE AND COMPARING ITS STAMINA AT THE **BEGINNING** OF THE BATTLE WITH ITS STAMINA AT THE END.

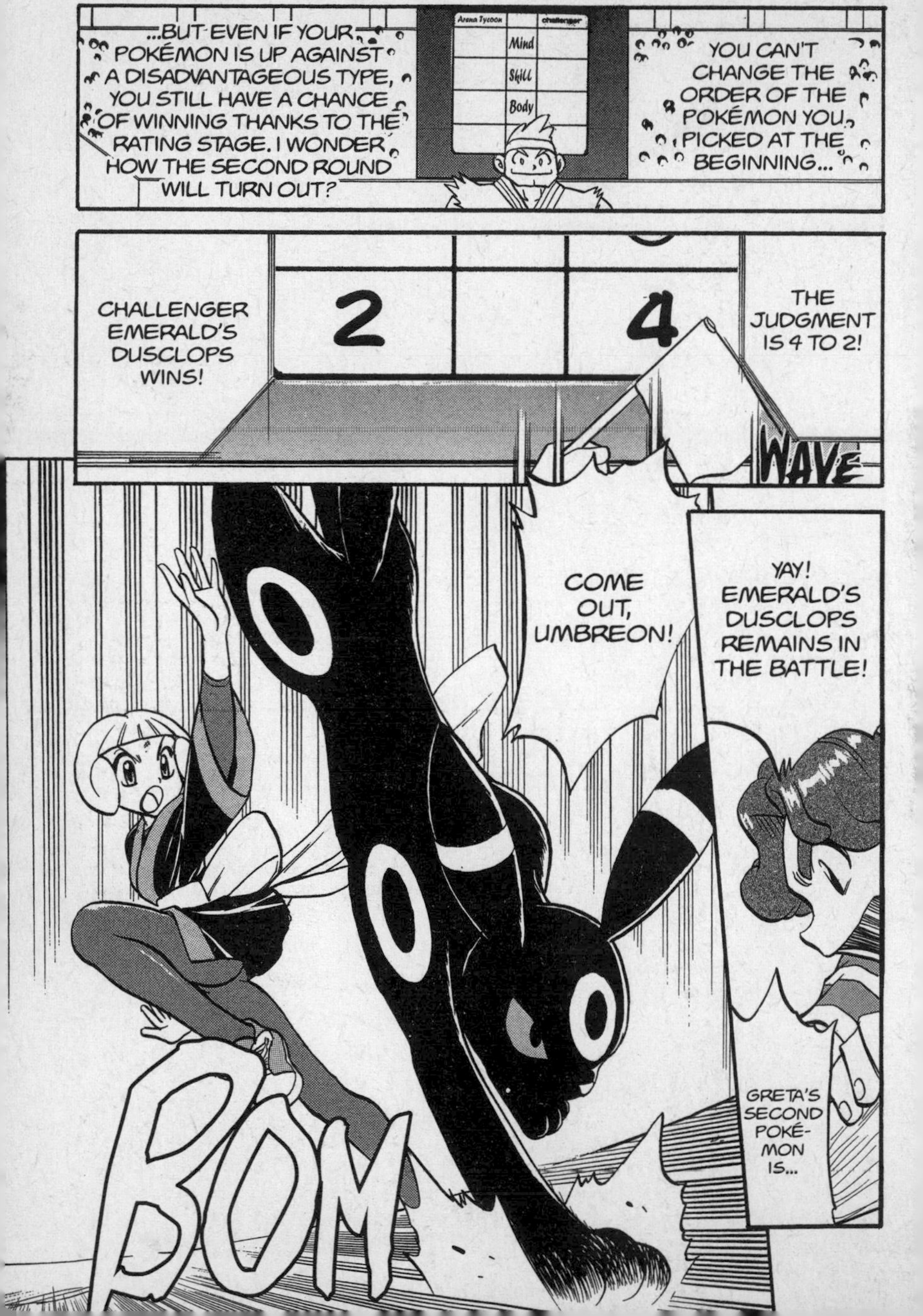
YOU CAN'T CHANGE THE ORDER OF THE POKÉMON YOU PICKED AT THE BEGINNING...
Arena Tycoon
challenger
Mind
Skill
Body
...BUT EVEN IF YOUR POKÉMON IS UP AGAINST A DISADVANTAGEOUS TYPE, YOU STILL HAVE A CHANCE OF WINNING THANKS TO THE RATING STAGE. I WONDER HOW THE SECOND ROUND WILL TURN OUT?
THE JUDGMENT IS 4 TO 2!
4
2
CHALLENGER EMERALD'S DUSCLOPS WINS!
WAVE
YAY! EMERALD'S DUSCLOPS REMAINS IN THE BATTLE!
GRETA'S SECOND POKÉ-MON IS...
COME OUT, UMBREON!
BOM

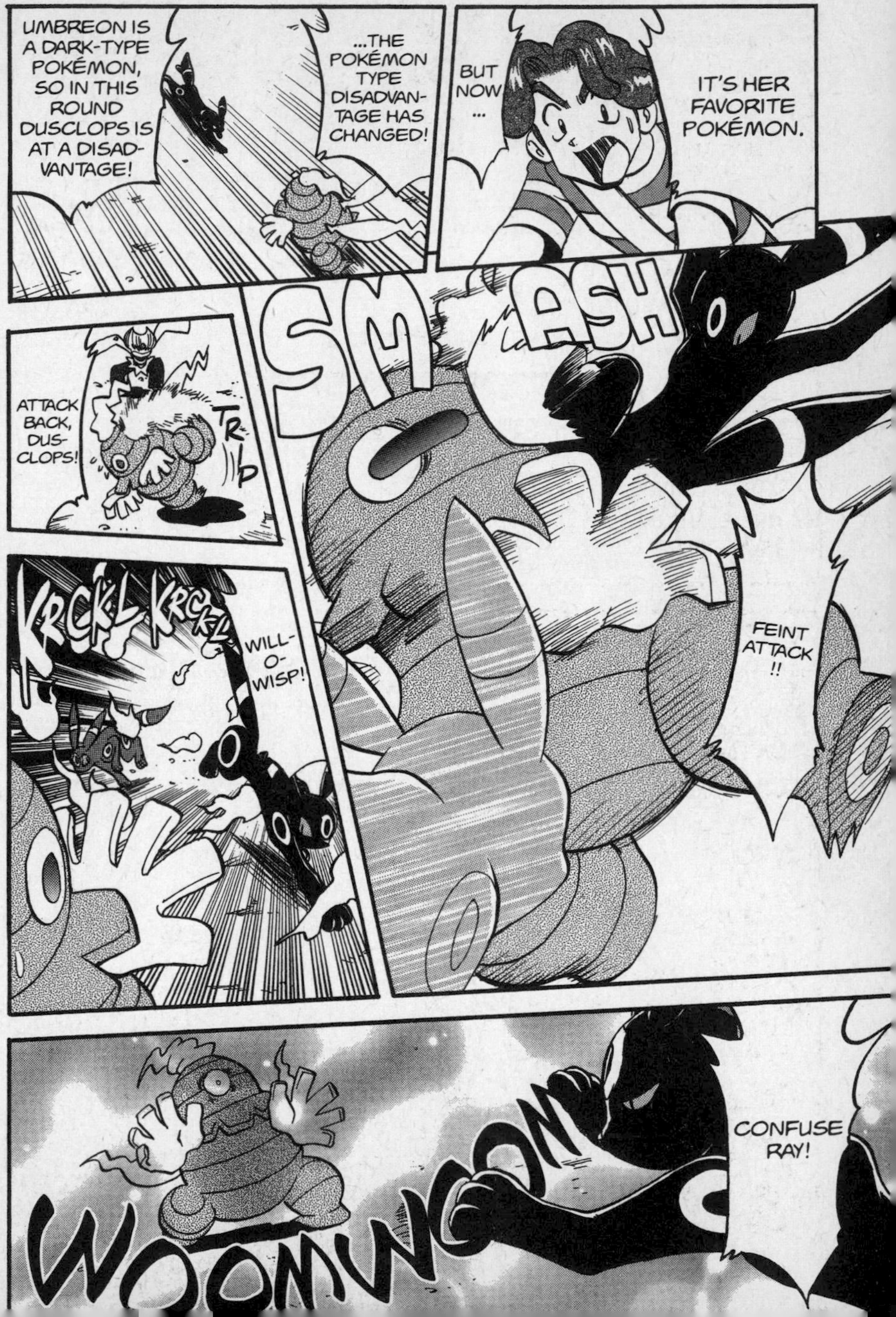
IT'S HER FAVORITE POKÉMON.
BUT NOW ...
...THE POKÉMON TYPE DISADVANTAGE HAS CHANGED!
UMBREON IS A DARK-TYPE POKÉMON, SO IN THIS ROUND DUSCLOPS IS AT A DISADVANTAGE!
SMASH
FEINT ATTACK !!
ATTACK BACK, DUSCLOPS!
TRIP
WILL-O-WISP!
KRCKL KRCKL
CONFUSE RAY!
WOOMWOOM

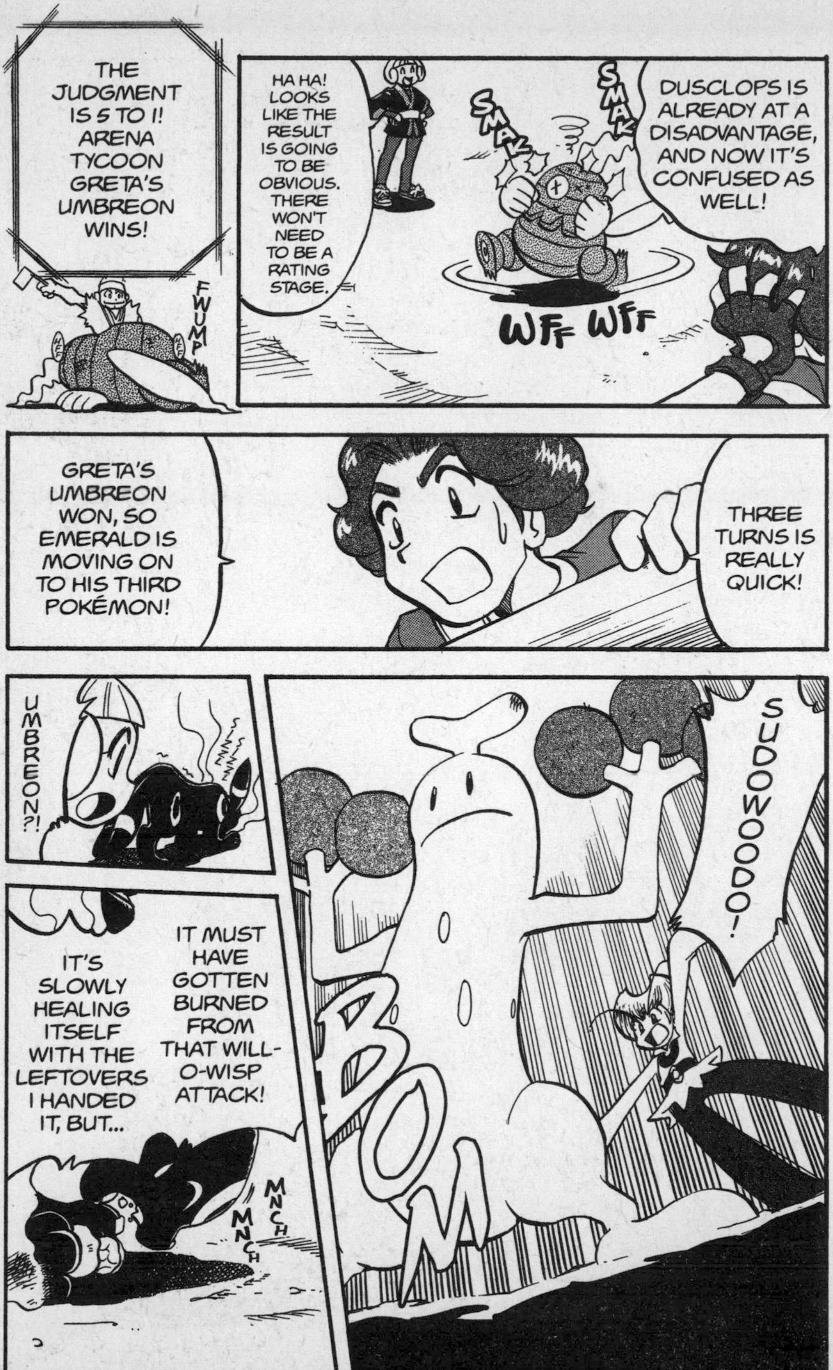
DUSCLOPS IS ALREADY AT A DISADVANTAGE, AND NOW IT'S CONFUSED AS WELL!
SMAK
SMAK
HA HA! LOOKS LIKE THE RESULT IS GOING TO BE OBVIOUS. THERE WON'T NEED TO BE A RATING STAGE.
WFF WFF
THE JUDGMENT IS 5 TO 1! ARENA TYCOON GRETA'S UMBREON WINS!
FWUMP
THREE TURNS IS REALLY QUICK!
GRETA'S UMBREON WON, SO EMERALD IS MOVING ON TO HIS THIRD POKÉMON!
SUDOWOODO!
BOOM
UMBREON?!
SIZZL SIZZL
IT MUST HAVE GOTTEN BURNED FROM THAT WILL-O-WISP ATTACK!
IT'S SLOWLY HEALING ITSELF WITH THE LEFTOVERS I HANDED IT, BUT...
MNCH
MNCH

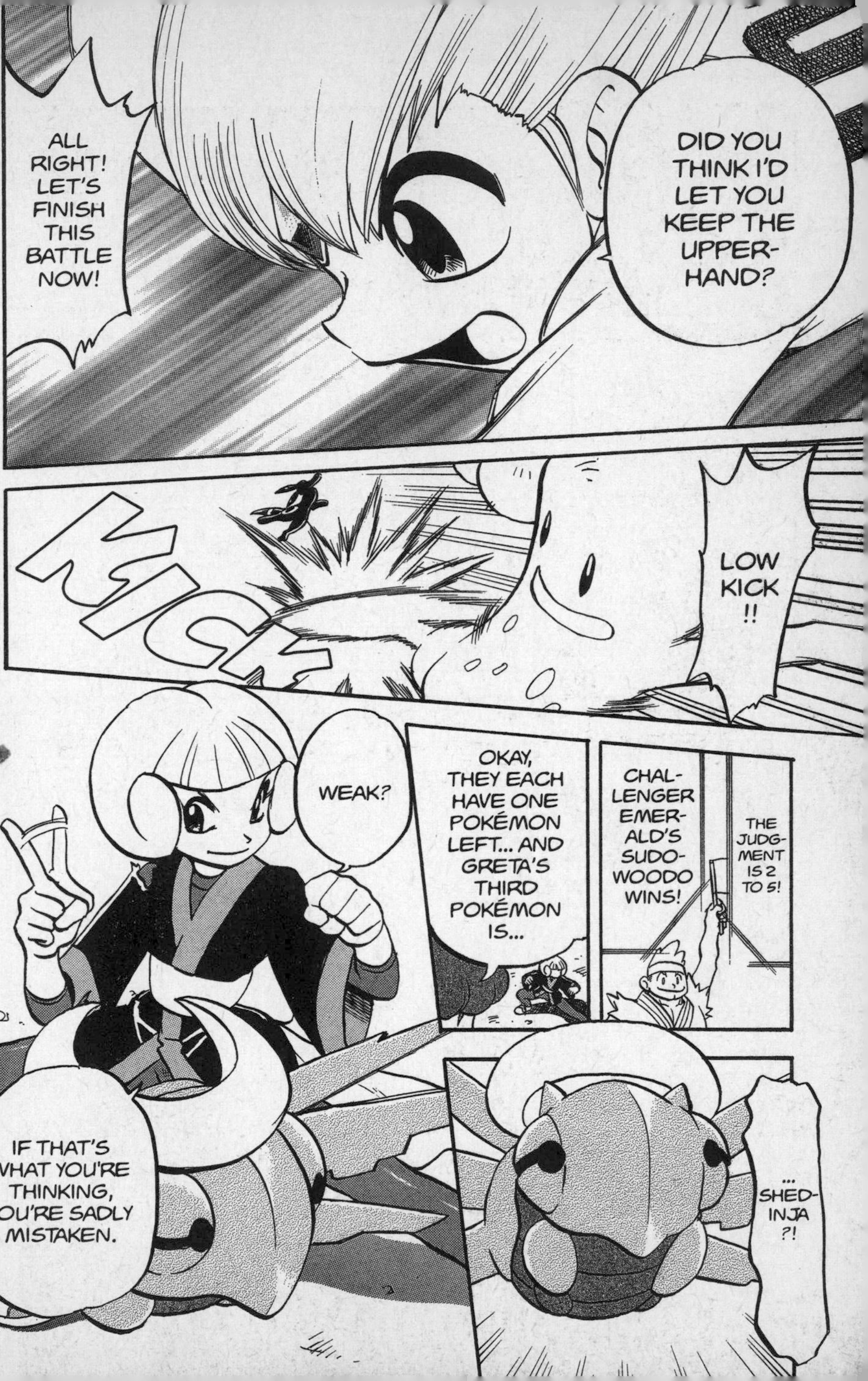
DID YOU THINK I'D LET YOU KEEP THE UPPER-HAND?
ALL RIGHT! LET'S FINISH THIS BATTLE NOW!
LOW KICK !!
KICK
CHAL-LENGER EMER-ALD'S SUDO-WOODO WINS!
THE JUDG-MENT IS 2 TO 5!
OKAY, THEY EACH HAVE ONE POKÉMON LEFT... AND GRETA'S THIRD POKÉMON IS...
WEAK?
...SHED-INJA ?!
IF THAT'S WHAT YOU'RE THINKING, YOU'RE SADLY MISTAKEN.

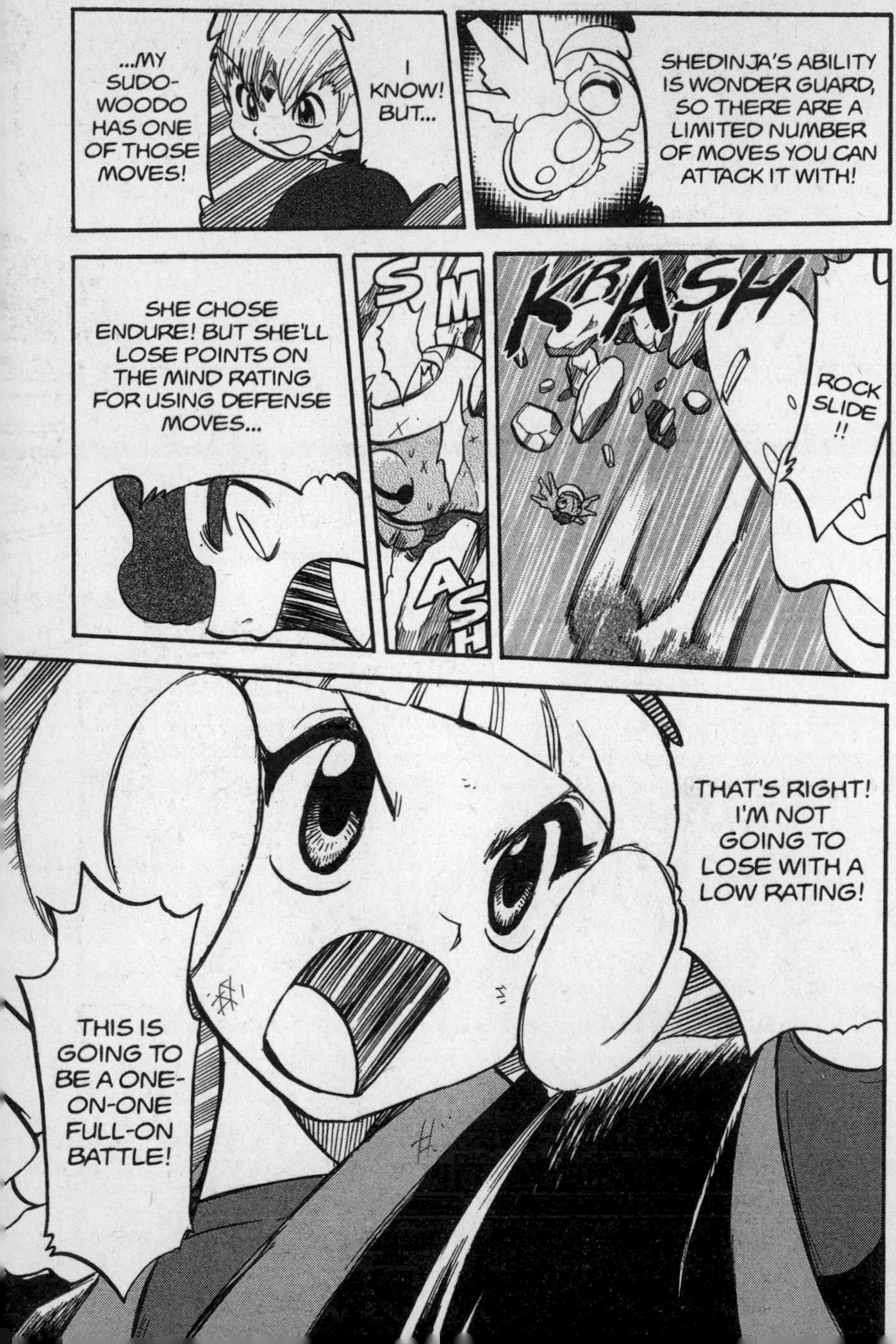
SHEDINJA'S ABILITY IS WONDER GUARD, SO THERE ARE A LIMITED NUMBER OF MOVES YOU CAN ATTACK IT WITH!
I KNOW! BUT...
...MY SUDO-WOODO HAS ONE OF THOSE MOVES!
KRASH
ROCK SLIDE !!
SMASH
SHE CHOSE ENDURE! BUT SHE'LL LOSE POINTS ON THE MIND RATING FOR USING DEFENSE MOVES...
THAT'S RIGHT! I'M NOT GOING TO LOSE WITH A LOW RATING!
THIS IS GOING TO BE A ONE-ON-ONE FULL-ON BATTLE!

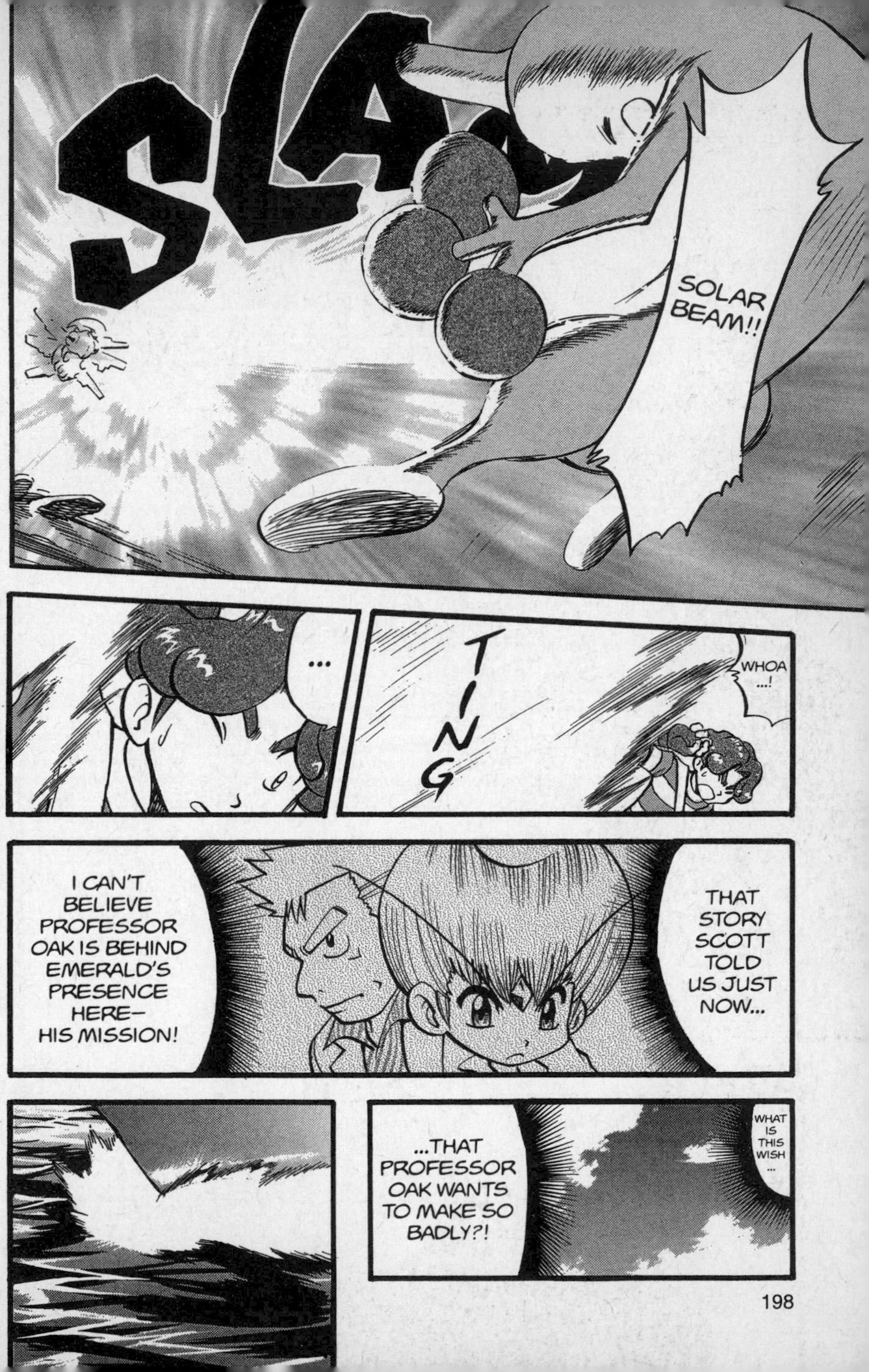
SOLAR BEAM!!
SLAM
WHOA ...!
TING
...
THAT STORY SCOTT TOLD US JUST NOW...
I CAN'T BELIEVE PROFESSOR OAK IS BEHIND EMERALD'S PRESENCE HERE— HIS MISSION!
WHAT IS THIS WISH ...
...THAT PROFESSOR OAK WANTS TO MAKE SO BADLY?!

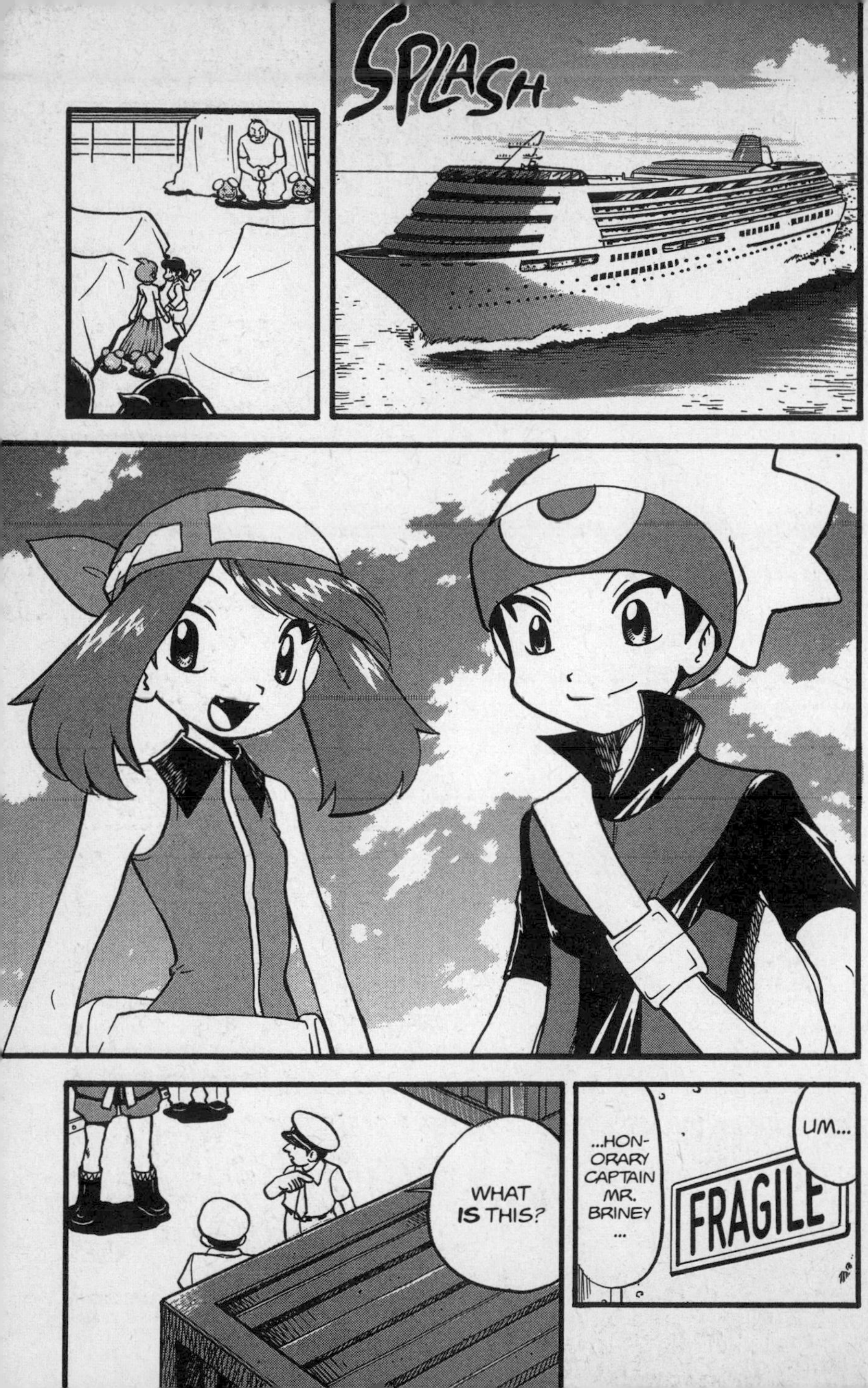
SPLASH
UM...
...HON-ORARY CAPTAIN MR. BRINEY ...
FRAGILE
WHAT IS THIS?

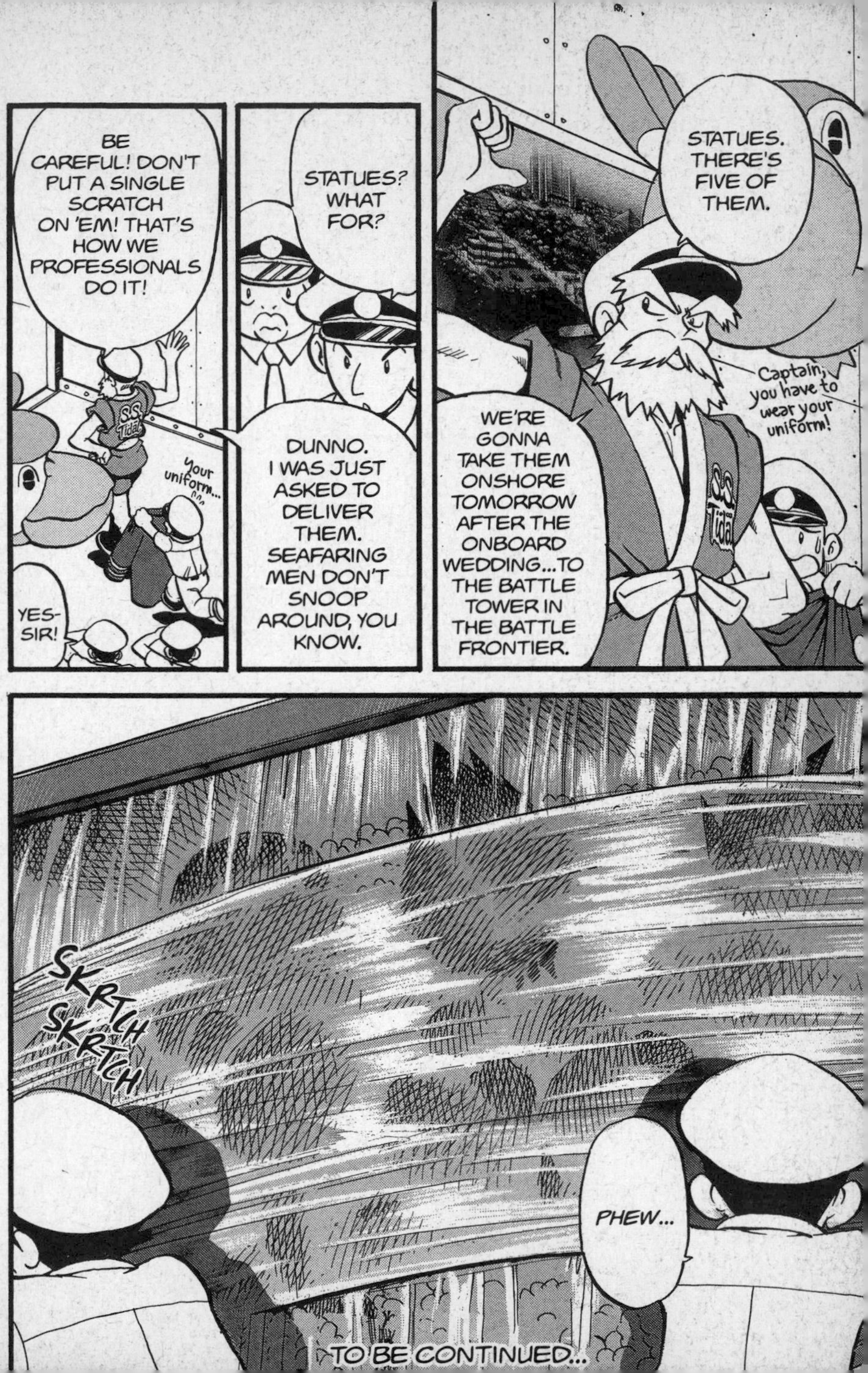
STATUES. THERE'S FIVE OF THEM.
Captain, you have to wear your uniform!
WE'RE GONNA TAKE THEM ONSHORE TOMORROW AFTER THE ONBOARD WEDDING...TO THE BATTLE TOWER IN THE BATTLE FRONTIER.
STATUES? WHAT FOR?
DUNNO. I WAS JUST ASKED TO DELIVER THEM. SEAFARING MEN DON'T SNOOP AROUND, YOU KNOW.
BE CAREFUL! DON'T PUT A SINGLE SCRATCH ON 'EM! THAT'S HOW WE PROFESSIONALS DO IT!
Your uniform...
YES-SIR!
SKRTCH SKRTCH
PHEW...
TO BE CONTINUED...

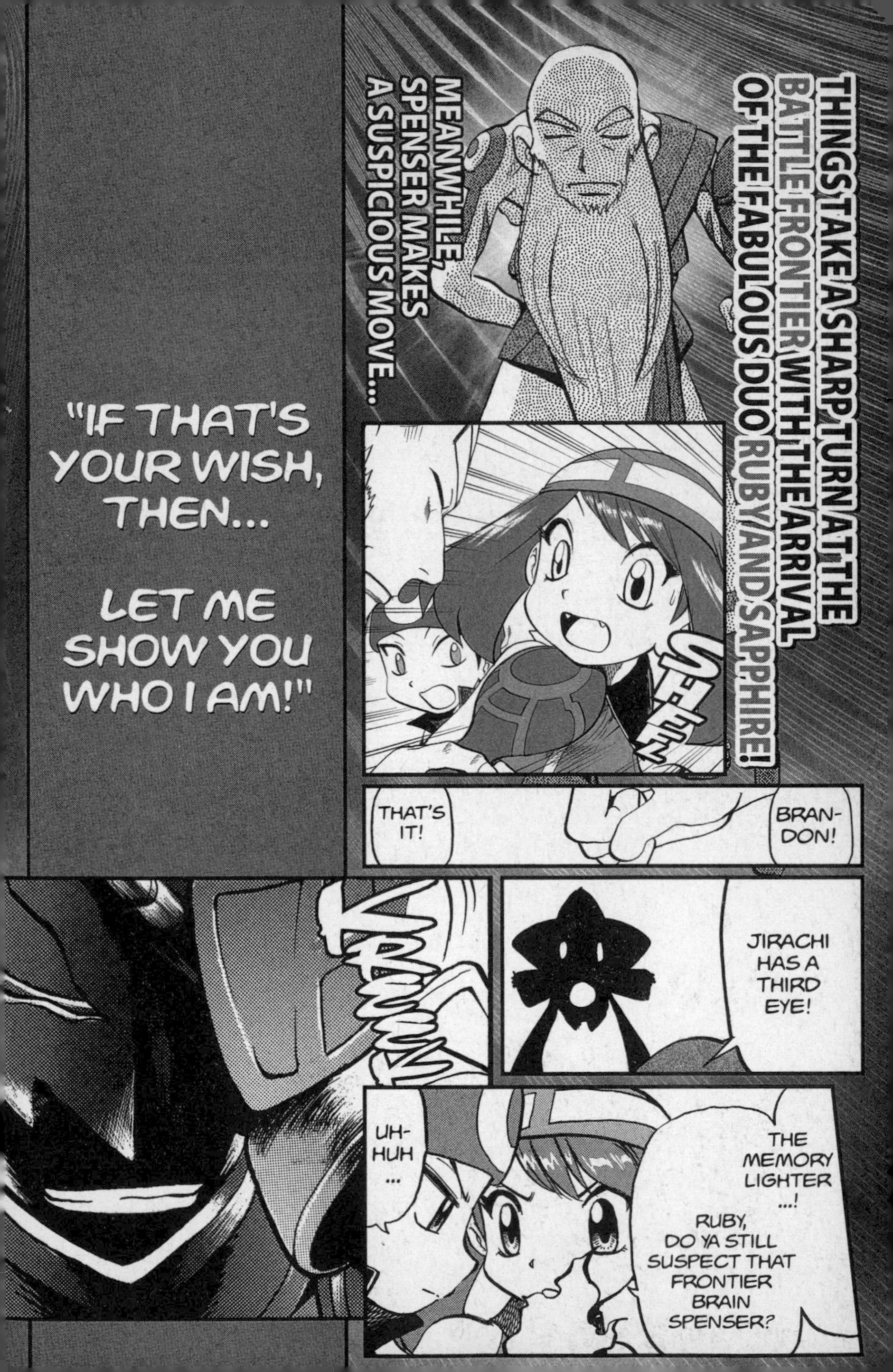

THINGS TAKE A SHARP TURN AT THE BATTLE FRONTIER WITH THE ARRIVAL OF THE FABULOUS DUO RUBY AND SAPPHIRE!
MEANWHILE, SPENSER MAKES A SUSPICIOUS MOVE...
BRAN-DON!
THAT'S IT!
"IF THAT'S YOUR WISH, THEN...
LET ME SHOW YOU WHO I AM!"
JIRACHI HAS A THIRD EYE!
THE MEMORY LIGHTER ...!
RUBY, DO YA STILL SUSPECT THAT FRONTIER BRAIN SPENSER?
UH-HUH ...

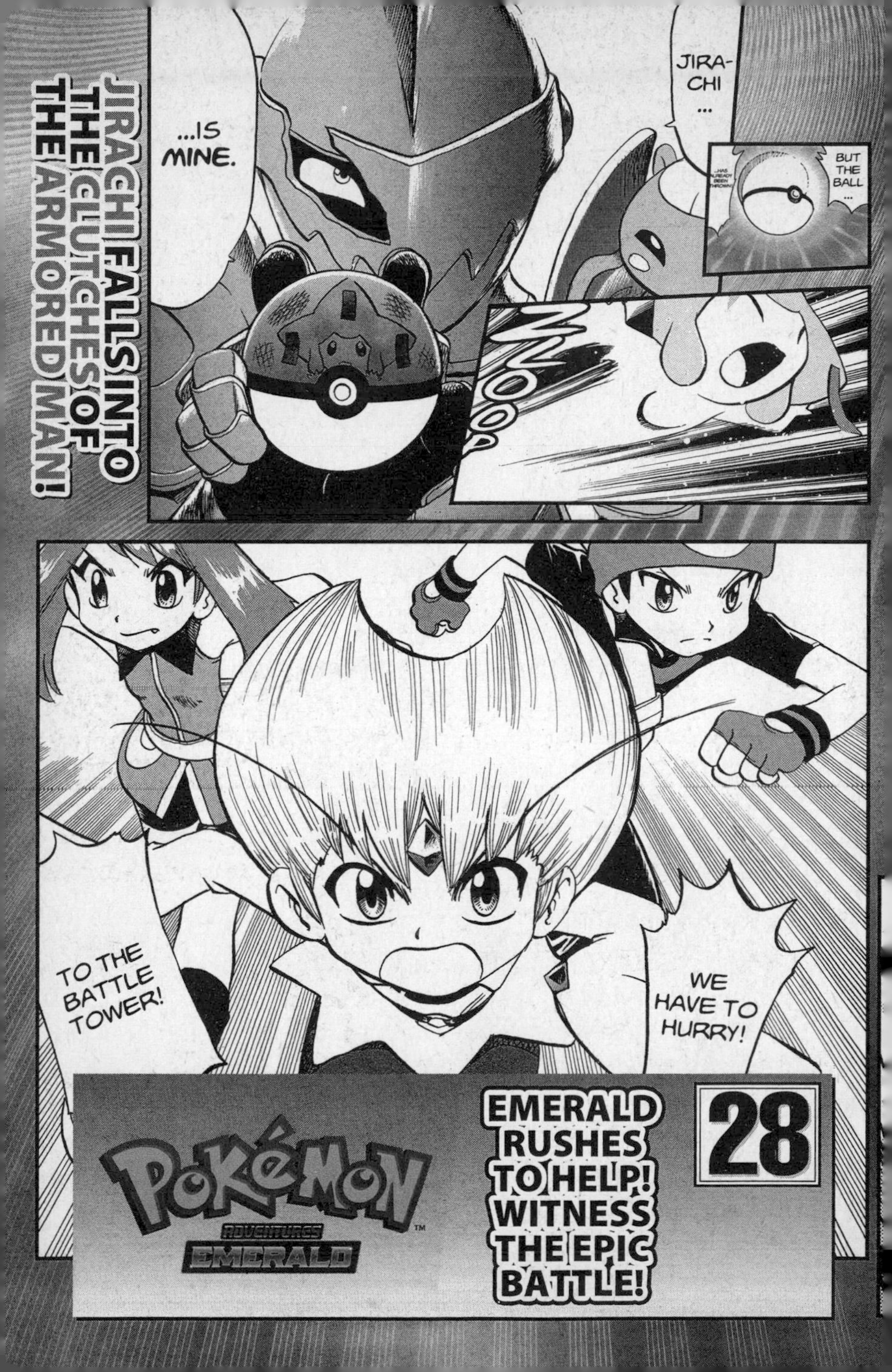
JIRA-CHI ...
BUT THE BALL ...
HAS ALREADY BEEN THROWN
...IS MINE.
JIRACHI FALLS INTO THE CLUTCHES OF THE ARMORED MAN!
WE HAVE TO HURRY!
TO THE BATTLE TOWER!
28
EMERALD RUSHES TO HELP! WITNESS THE EPIC BATTLE!
POKéMON™ ADVENTURES EMERALD

Message from
Hidenori Kusaka

This volume of *Pokémon Adventures* was originally published ten years after the first volume of the series came out in Japan! I've always had a passion for working on this series, and I've hardly ever thought back on it over the passing years, but...this realization really affected me. Fans seemed to have an even stronger desire to celebrate, and I received many letters saying "Congratulations on your tenth anniversary!" I was and continue to be so grateful...

Message from
Satoshi Yamamoto

The challenges of the Battle Pike and the Battle Pyramid, the slightly klutzy but skilled Frontier Brains, a mysterious stranger, Emerald's secret mission, the Pokémon Latias's support of Emerald... Vol. 27 is filled with all sorts of great adventures. I love all the adventures in this volume, and I've been reading them over and over again myself. I hope you enjoy them too!

More Adventures Coming Soon...

Ruby and Sapphire are back! Professor Birch sends the fabulous duo to help Emerald find the Wish Pokémon Jirachi. But first there are high-pitched Pokémon battles to fight in the Battle Dome Tournament... Then Ruby discovers something surprising about Emerald's Sceptile, and everyone learns the true identity of their arch nemesis, Guile Hideout.

Now, who will catch Jirachi...?

AVAILABLE MAY 2015!

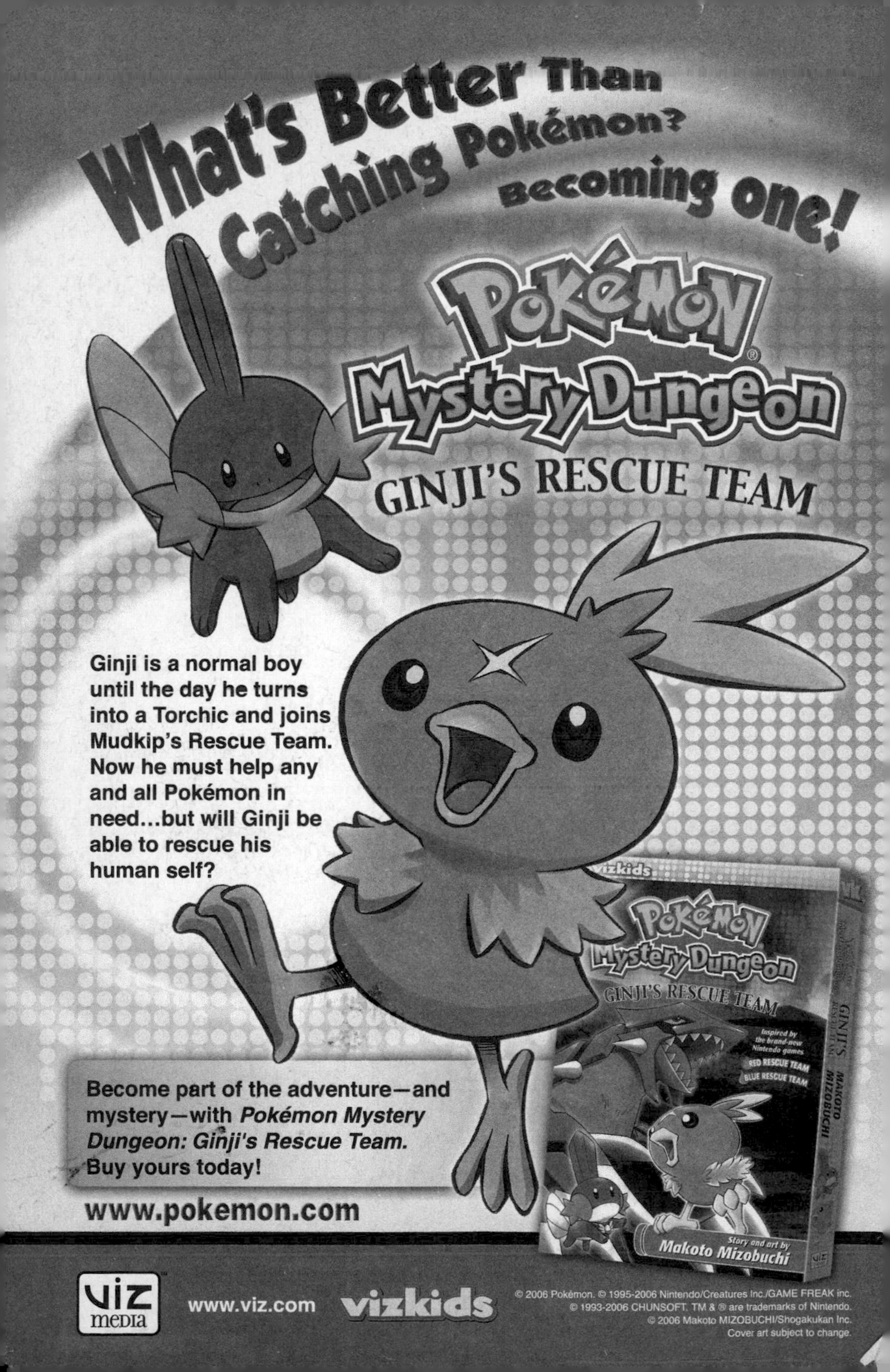
What's Better Than Catching Pokémon? Becoming one!
Pokémon Mystery Dungeon
GINJI'S RESCUE TEAM
Ginji is a normal boy until the day he turns into a Torchic and joins Mudkip's Rescue Team. Now he must help any and all Pokémon in need...but will Ginji be able to rescue his human self?
vizkids
Pokémon Mystery Dungeon
GINJI'S RESCUE TEAM
Inspired by the brand-new Nintendo games
RED RESCUE TEAM
BLUE RESCUE TEAM
Story and art by
Makoto Mizobuchi
Become part of the adventure—and mystery—with *Pokémon Mystery Dungeon: Ginji's Rescue Team.* Buy yours today!
www.pokemon.com
viz media
www.viz.com
vizkids
© 2006 Pokémon. © 1995-2006 Nintendo/Creatures Inc./GAME FREAK inc.
© 1993-2006 CHUNSOFT. TM & ® are trademarks of Nintendo.
© 2006 Makoto MIZOBUCHI/Shogakukan Inc.
Cover art subject to change.